She made a ~~small moan deep~~ in her throat, but she didn't pull away. Her lashes shivered; the color swept over her breasts, a dawning of desire.

He fingered one swelling rosebud—leaned to adore it with tongue and mouth, felt her heart thundering against his cradling palm. *Ah, marry me, Risa, and we'll do this every night of our lives!* He raised his head to replace his lips with his coaxing fingers. Perhaps it was male instinct that would brook no denial. He *would* have her surrender. "Say yes!" he demanded, his voice husky with emotion. "Only leap, Risa-Sonrisa, and I will catch you!"

"Truly?" She flattened a hand against his heart. "*¿De veras?* You really want me?"

More than all the oil in the world. He caught her slender waist and lifted her to kneel astride his lap. "You're all that I want!"

But that…that was a lie he'd pay for.

Dear Reader,

I still remember the first oil well my geologist father took me out on. It was some place in the Big Thicket country of East Texas.

What a circus of sights and sounds for a six-year-old! The towering rig, the massive machines bellowing and roaring—spinning and rising and falling. The muddy, greasy men performing their dangerous balletic feats up on the drilling platform. The rig lit up at night like a Christmas tree.

The trailer where my dad and others studied the wavering, intricate lines on long scrolls of paper as the drill bit gnawed its way down to black gold—or a dry hole that cost a fortune.

Big, drawling male voices, lots of laughter, the underlying tension and excitement. Back then in my preprinting days I never dreamed that someday I'd want to write about these men. I just knew that, looking up from buckle level, they all seemed like heroes to me.

So here I give you my latest hero, Miguel Heydt, a seeker, a searcher, who comes to Trueheart, Colorado—to Suntop Ranch—looking for treasure.

Thanks for coming along for his ride!

Peggy Nicholson

Books by Peggy Nicholson

HARLEQUIN SUPERROMANCE

The Wildcatter
Peggy Nicholson

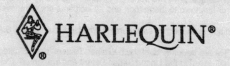

TORONTO • NEW YORK • LONDON
AMSTERDAM • PARIS • SYDNEY • HAMBURG
STOCKHOLM • ATHENS • TOKYO • MILAN • MADRID
PRAGUE • WARSAW • BUDAPEST • AUCKLAND

ISBN 0-373-71067-4

THE WILDCATTER

Copyright © 2002 by Peggy Nicholson.

Visit us at www.eHarlequin.com

Printed in U.S.A.

DEDICATION

This book is for the first and last wildcatter
in my life: Erwin Grimes, of Kerrville, Texas—
the man who taught me to dream big; to dare to back my
dreams with action; and to come back smiling...even when
a well comes up dry. Because there's always the next time,
the next dream, isn't there? And thanks so much,
Dad, for all your advice and background on this story—
couldn't have done it without you!

And in memory of Yaffa.
She came; she saw; she conquered. We wept when she left.

PROLOGUE

The Present

MIGUEL HEYDT TURNED the flattened wedding ring that rested on his palm. Not much thicker than a piece of tinfoil, the golden, metallic shape looked like a starburst. Or maybe a sunflower with the center shot out of it.

Shallow, crescent-shape gouges in the gold showed the imprint of whatever tool had been used to make this final statement. Flip it over, and the pebbled texture suggested that the object had rested on concrete at the time of its smashing.

Looking down at the ruined marriage band he'd carried in his wallet for eleven years, Miguel Heydt had to smile— even as all the other old emotions roiled within him.

Emotions like anger.

Disappointment.

Hot desire and biting humiliation.

Maybe even a touch of wistful sorrow?

But the first emotion this battered ring always evoked in him, on the rare occasions when he allowed himself a look, was reluctant admiration. *Aren't you something, though?*

For Risa Tankersly Heydt, without wasting a single word, had sent him her message, loud and clear: ''You can kiss my sweet ass goodbye!'' Miguel murmured ruefully.

That's what Risa was telling him when she mailed him his ring back from Las Vegas.

At the time she'd dropped it into an envelope and passed it to a postal clerk to postmark, he and Risa had been married for roughly eighteen hours.

Had to be one of the shortest marriages on record.

A marriage eleven years in the past, yet still he could close his eyes and taste her—taste that kiss he'd claimed at the altar, with Risa's father, her family and all her fine, fancy world to witness. She'd tasted like hot golden coins dipped in honey. Like a poor boy's dream of triumph.

"Ah, Risa." She'd annulled their marriage in Las Vegas—then married another man the day after. The happy couple lived far away from Trueheart, or so Miguel had been told.

Risa-Sonrisa. He didn't think about her often. A man couldn't look back and stay a man. A man walked forward into his life, with long strides in big boots.

But eleven years later he'd come full circle. His strides were taking him from Alaska back to where their story had begun. To Suntop Ranch, outside the small Colorado town of Trueheart.

Not that he was going back for Risa. Oh, no. That dream was over and done. Ashes. This time he'd keep his eye—and his heart—on the money, as he should have from the very start.

CHAPTER ONE

Eleven Years Earlier

IT WAS A RITUAL, some thirty summers old. Joe Wiggly would meet the boss up at the Big House half an hour past sunrise. He'd bring Tankersly his mount for the day— something half a hand too tall or a tad too rank for a man in his seventies, but then, that was the only sort of horse the boss would ride.

Seated astride his own sensible cow pony, the foreman of Suntop would smoke his first cigarette of the morning while he waited for the old man to walk out his front door.

When at last the door opened, always Ben Tankersly would stop short on his porch, as if stunned by first sight of this high-mountain valley. And to be sure, it was the finest view on Suntop Ranch—the biggest, richest cattle spread in all Southwest Colorado.

King of his own small kingdom, Tankersly would sweep his dark hooded eyes along the rolling meadows that sloped south, toward the distant main valley, invisible beyond the green flank of Suntop Mountain. Then he'd swing on his boot heel to inspect his eastern ramparts—a ten-mile-distant spur of the Trueheart Hills, which were low mountains, really, with big forested shoulders gashed by slabs of gray granite. The rising sun would be backlighting their craggy peaks with raw copper light.

From there Tankersly would draw a deep breath and swing north, toward the best view of all. The wild canyons and plateaus of the summer range, stair-stepping toward peaks high enough to scrape heaven—the San Juans, some fifty miles beyond. Already catching the sun, the lingering snow at their summits would be burning rose and gold in the clear mountain air.

On days when he had one of his pretty ladies in residence, Ben Tankersly would bounce out that front door to confront his view. As he stopped to survey his world, he'd be trying to rein in a dog-in-the-henhouse grin that kept breaking loose.

Days when there was no visitor to keep the family on its company manners, when one of Ben's three hellion daughters had been kicking the slats out of her stall and busting through fences, Tankersly would bang out the door, to stand with his big chest heaving and his gnarled hands clenched, glaring at his kingdom—but not seeing it. Then he'd stomp down the wide fieldstone steps to Joe and the waiting horses, looking ready to chew barbed wire or curdle the milk.

Today was one of those days. Ben swung up on his too-big gelding, gave a grunt that meant "Let's go" and shot away downhill toward the barns and pastures of the main valley.

Joe touched spurs to his mare and followed. Once they were loping along the dirt road, he stole a glance at his boss. After thirty years, neither of them would have presumed to call their relationship a friendship, but they understood each other.

"Risa," growled Tankersly by way of explanation.

His eldest, the one with hair like a sunset aflame and eyes like a fawn tangled in a fence. Sweet as wildflower honey till you rubbed her wrong, which Ben often did, then it was hang on to your hat, cowboy. Joe had always been mighty fond of Risa. He'd missed her this past year, when she'd been away in the East at college.

She hadn't hurried back home to them, either, come summer. Here it was mid-July and she'd arrived at Suntop only last evening. Joe had yet to see her himself, but word had got around. "I hear tell she has herself a beau," he observed mildly.

"Huh—fiancé, she calls him. She's wearing his ring. Diamond the size of a jackrabbit turd."

Ben had never taken kindly to men courting his daughters. Which was pretty laughable, considering he'd have given his left nut for a grandson. At seventy-two, the old man seemed to have finally outgrown the notion of siring his own son, but he sure wanted himself a boy to raise. A boy to be the next heir to Suntop.

No suitors, no boy. But a wise man didn't try to reason with Ben Tankersly. He might be as crafty as a lame coyote, but the owner of Suntop led with his heart, not his head. "Somebody she found back East?" Joe hazarded.

"Yep. A smooth-talking, limp-handed, self-satisfied snake of a Yalie lawyer." Tankersly reined his big buckskin to a sliding halt. Nodding bleak approval at the cloud of dust thus raised, he patted the gelding's glossy neck, then kneed him into a long walk. "Risa thinks the smilin' scumsucker hung the moon."

Joe fell in beside his boss again. "A lawyer." Cattlemen liked lawyers about as much as rattlesnakes, jimson weed or big government.

"Denver stock, though why any man'd send his son east to college…" Tankersly's growl died away to a mutter, probably as he remembered he'd sent Risa east.

Because she'd wanted to go west, Joe recalled. She'd wanted in the worst way to study film in Los Angeles, at

the University of California. But Ben didn't approve of
actors or acting, and considering the way Risa's mother had
met her end, maybe he had a point. So he'd sent Risa
against her will to Yale, and surprise, surprise, she'd paid
him back with a Yalie lawyer.

"Well, if he's a Denver boy, that's not so bad," Joe
soothed. "Likely they'll settle somewhere in state." Denver was only an eight-hour drive to the northeast of Trueheart. Keeping Risa close to home would be good.

"Huh! You know what his old man does for a living?
He's a developer! Chops up useful ranchland into five-acre
ranchettes. Has made himself two or three fortunes doin'
it."

They'd rounded the base of Suntop, and now they paused
on the crest of the ranch road to its south, overlooking the
lower valley. Lush and green, the pastures spread out below
them. The river rippled shallow and silver in the early light,
then darkened where it deepened, plunging into a lacy line
of cottonwoods that followed its meandering course down
the valley. Beyond the foreman's house, men and horses
were stirring, moving between the corrals and the barns and
the bunkhouse. A couple of dusty cars were climbing up
from the distant county road—the hay crews assembling.

"Used to be a man measured himself by what he built,"
Tankersly said softly, nodding at his world below. "Or if
he didn't build it himself—" Ben, after all, was the third
of his line to hold Suntop; since the early 1880s this had
been Tankersly land "—then he prided himself on holding
something precious together. On expanding his holdings,
improving his land, his stock. But nowadays seems a man
measures himself by what he can tear down—a corpora-
tion...a ranch...a way of life.

"Ranchettes!" Tankersly spat into the long grass and
rode on. "Risa's brought us home a wrecker. A limp-

wristed, stab-you-in-the-back-and-smile wrecker. I don't call that breeding stock.''

Joe sighed to himself. Not a cloud in all the clear blue sky, but it was gonna be a stormy summer. Two mule-headed Tankerslys with opposing notions...

''You find a replacement for that boy?'' Tankersly demanded, changing the subject abruptly. One of their haying crew had gashed his leg from knee to toe cutting hay yesterday. Joe had driven down into Trueheart last night, seeking a replacement.

''Nope.'' Haying was sweat-soaked, backbreaking drudgery. And hardly the safest of jobs, with all that whirling machinery. He'd tried the bars in town, the general store, Mo's Truckstop—and he'd come up dry. Only real prospect had been that young drifter in the Star, and he'd turned the job down flat. Which was probably just as well. A foreman got so he could smell trouble. Knew better than to invite it home.

''You tried the Lone Star?'' growled Tankersly.

A roadhouse out on the highway to the south of Trueheart, the Lone Star was dear to the thirsty hearts of local cowboys, passing truckers and in-town rowdies. Surest place to find a cold brew, a hot woman or a knuckle-busting debate. Or a bum broke enough to consider haying till he'd made the price of his next bottle. ''Did. There was one Tex-Mex kid...'' Big enough to buck bales and old enough to hold his own with a rough haying crew.

Watching him from across the smoky room, Joe had figured the kid was trolling for a job, the way he struck up casual conversations with this group of cowboys or that. He handled himself well among strangers, casual but confident, neither cocky nor shy. He'd do, Joe had decided after sizing him up for a while. So he'd approached and asked the drifter if he was looking for work.

"Might be," the kid had agreed pleasantly, with just the trace of a Texas drawl. "Where?"

Not *doing what,* but *where.* Now, that seemed sort of odd. "Ranch north of town," Joe allowed, playing his cards close to his vest. "We're one short on our haying crew. Just a summer job, but it pays pretty well. Plus bunk and board if you want it."

"Haying." The young man's excellent teeth flashed for a second; he knew about haying. His chin jerked in the start of a "No," then he paused. "On what ranch?"

"Suntop." Really no reason not to tell him. Still, something wasn't ringing true here.

"The biggest outfit in these parts."

So the stranger had made it his business to learn that much. "And the best."

"So I hear. But no, thank you."

Something just a little too polite and formal for a Texan in his manner, and he cut his o's short and soft. Mexican somewhere in his background? He was a big, rawboned, good-looking kid, maybe mid twenties, maybe older than Joe had first thought. But seen close up, this one had the eyes of a seasoned man and poise to match. He smiled now as Joe stood perplexed; tipping his head in the faintest of farewells, he swung away.

Joe covered his dismissal by ambling off to the men's. When he came back to the room, the kid was standing a round of drinks for some of the Kristopherson crew. Trolling for a date instead of a job? Somehow Joe didn't think so. The ledge of rock under the manners suggested far otherwise.

But then, what the Sam Hill's he after? Whatever, Joe was still one down on the haying crew. Settling his hat to a determined angle, he'd walked out the door, bound for Mo's.

"Didn't find a soul," the foreman repeated now glumly as they rode into the ranch yard and reined in to sit watching. Eyes shifted their way, then skated on by. A few hat brims dipped half an inch in laconic salute, but everyone went on about his business, as good hands should. Down at the horse barn a brawny young cowboy strode out of the tack room, toting a saddle toward a hipshot gray tied to the hitching rack. "So I reckon I'll tap Jake there for the hay fields 'fore he rides out." Joe shot a sly sideways glance at Tankersly. "'Less you want to loan me Risa's new sweetheart? Maybe he'd like to try his hand bucking bales."

Tankersly snorted. "The way a pig loves to tap-dance, he would!" He looked automatically back toward the Big House, then stiffened. "And speak of the devil, here he— they come. Didn't figure that one would roll out of bed before noon."

But Tankersly's eldest daughter would not have graced the lawyer's bed, Joe figured privately. Not by chance was Ben's master bedroom situated between the wing of the Big House that housed his family and the wing that held guests—welcome or otherwise. To tiptoe past the boss's door on the way to one of his cherished daughters would take balls of clanging brass. So, likely Risa and her man were up early, seeking a safer place for canoodling.

The little red sports convertible—Joe didn't bother with the names of cars—stopped as it reached the yard. Its top was down, but the foreman didn't waste a glance on the driver. With a wide grin, he sidestepped his mare over to the passenger side.

Risa threw off her seat belt and stood, hanging on to the top of the windshield. "*Joe!* Oh, Joe, you look *wonderful!*" She laid a smacking kiss on his leathery cheek as he swept off his straw hat and leaned in close to collect it. "Lord, I missed you!'' Her big golden eyes were starry with tears, though she was smiling to beat the band.

Joe blinked frantically and jammed his hat down over his nose to hide his own swimming eyes. "It's you that was missed," he said gruffly. And she'd come back prettier than ever, it seemed, though thinner than he cared to see. "Didn't even visit us for Christmas!"

"By December I was just getting over being homesick," she protested, laughing as she patted his wiry forearm. "I didn't *dare* risk stirring it up again. Another round would have killed me. That was before I met— Oh!''

She glanced around at her driver, then knelt on the edge of her seat so he could see past her. "Joe, this is Eric Foster, my..." The color rose in her heart-shaped face and she tipped up her chin as if she expected resistance—and likely she'd had a wagonload of that already. "My fiancé. We're engaged.'' She presented her left hand for Joe's inspection, slender fingers arching in one of those graceful girly gestures that a man couldn't have made in a thousand years.

The stone was not quite as big as Ben had described, but twice as gaudy. Still, Joe would leave disapproval to her daddy. "Very nice. And pleased t'meet you.'' He nodded graciously to Risa's young man.

"And you,'' agreed the blond, movie-star-handsome youngster—without a trace of real warmth. His hands were fixed firmly to the steering wheel; though with a bit of a reach, he could have shaken Joe's hand. "Risa, could you please sit down,'' he added coolly. "Unless you want everyone staring at you.''

"I...'' She slid abruptly into her seat, her smile fading for a moment before it rallied. "Sorry.''

She was taking that from this puffed-up young rooster? Their Risa of a year ago would have tweaked his long, haughty nose and bounded out of that fancy car without bothering to open the door. So this was what they taught a girl back East? Polished the grit right out of her? Joe's gaze met Ben's over the width of the convertible.

The boss man had ridden up close on the lawyer's side. "You've just arrived and you're off again already?" he demanded of Risa.

She had spunk enough to spare for her daddy, if not the fiancé. "We're driving down to Mesaverde. Just for the day."

"I'm fascinated by Anasazi ruins," added the boyfriend, putting the shine on for Ben that he hadn't for the hired man. "And with Risa to give me the tour, how could I resist?"

"I was thinking you might like to help us out 'round Suntop, today," Ben said, poker-faced, though his eyes were as intent as a coyote's at a gopher hole. "Seems we've lost one of our haying crew. Could sure use a hand. And it'd give you a taste of real ranch work." *That is, if you plan to be part of the family,* was the unspoken challenge.

The lawyer's wide, slick smile didn't waver. "Gee, I'd really enjoy that, Ben!" He shook his head regretfully. "But I'm a martyr to hay fever. Once I start sneezing... That's one of the reasons I thought it might be wise to spend the day off-ranch. Give my nose a break."

"Huh." Ben straightened in his saddle and fixed his shrewd eyes on his daughter. "Then you two be back by suppertime, princess, you hear me?"

Foster laid a hand on her knee as he cut in smoothly, "We'll certainly try."

Speaking for her, as if she had no mind of her own. Joe didn't like it a bit, as he tipped his brim to Risa and smiled her on her way. She brushed her blowing, sunset hair from her cheeks and waved back at him, then to her father. Then she turned forward to call a greeting to this hand or that as the convertible threaded through the bustling yard.

"Hay fever," Joe said quietly, looking after them.

"See what I mean?" Ben spat in the dirt again. "Can the girl pick 'em or what? You know what he asked me at dinner last night? How much land I have here!"

"He did?" That was the worst kind of manners. You knew how much land a man owned you knew his worth close to the penny. Might as well ask to see his bank book.

"Let a bad 'un like that into your breeding stock," Tankersly fumed, "and you'll be culling out his knock-kneed, greedy get for the next four generations!"

But try to tell a woman what to do. Joe had never had any luck at that, and neither, for all his land and wealth and sheer cussedness, had Ben Tankersly. Risa would follow her wistful heart, even if it led her straight on to heartbreak.

And ain't it a cryin' shame? Joe jammed his old straw down over his nose and rode off to spoil somebody else's day—Jake's, he decided. And if he heard one peep about hay fever...

CHAPTER TWO

HE'D HAVE TO EAT some crow, Miguel Heydt reflected as he turned his dusty old pickup off the county road. Serious crow. Driving under the arching name board, he glanced up. *Suntop Ranch* was emblazoned between two rising suns, both the letters and suns shining gold in the morning light—gilded to perfection. It was that kind of outfit.

With pride to match, he didn't doubt. The biggest, richest spreads always had the best jobs—and didn't they know it. He'd made a bad mistake rejecting that old man's offer last night.

Then to show up today, hat in hand and crow feathers all over his mouth? He'd be lucky if they didn't run him off the place.

But how was I to know? The one map he had, marking the Badwater Flats, was eighty years old. It located the plateau on Kristopherson land.

Last night at the Lone Star he'd learned that the Kristopherson Ranch was still in existence, still lying east-northeast of Trueheart. So he'd been looking for Kristopherson cowboys, not Suntop men. Buying them drinks when he found them, pumping them casually, discreetly. Making up stories, then seeing what stories he got in return.

He'd told his tale about a water hole that poisoned cattle back on a ranch in Texas where he used to work—and heard tales about locoweed poisoning in return.

He'd tried again, spinning that yarn about an old mud

pit on the home ranch—greasy thick mud, black as tar, that
would suck down deer, stock *ay, Dios!*, even unwary children.

His listeners came back with stories of quicksand, of bad
river crossings on trail drives. He laughed softly. That hilarious story the old-timer had spun about a pig wallow and
helping the boss's pretty daughter feed the sows, and his
punch line that even after that fiasco she'd forgiven him,
married him—and forty years later they were still happily
married...

Miguel rubbed the smile off his face. Wonderful stories,
but not the story he wanted to hear. Not one of those cow-
hands would admit to bad water on Kristopherson land.

By midnight he'd been ready to give up in frustration.
Badwater. The name could have come from most anything—a dog fell down somebody's well. Or some early
traveler had tapped a new keg on his wagon while passing
through here and found his drinking water had gone
scummy, so he named the flats to mark the occasion.
Maybe it was a corruption of an Indian word and had nothing to do with water at all.

Then another geezer had wandered over to the table
where Miguel had sat drinking and swapping yarns. Willy,
a Suntop man. Smiling insults had been traded—the Kristopherson crew had apparently bested the Suntop cowboys
in a local rodeo a few weeks back.

Fighting hard for his outfit's honor, Willy had dredged
up an ancient triumph. Let the Kristophersons sneer, but
Ben Tankersly's father had beaten old Will Kristopherson
decisively in the thirties, and they were *still* laughing about
it. Sam Tankersly had won the Badwater Flats in a game
of stud poker. He'd bluffed Kristopherson out of ten square
miles with a pair of threes and a pair of jacks, and what
do you think of that?

Miguel thought he'd better not kiss the old man, but he was tempted. Instead he'd bought him a round, then teased him, apparently defending his Kristopherson pals. Yes, Sam Tankersly had won the Badwater Flats, old man, but so what? Of what earthly use was a patch of range with bad water?

It was worth plenty, Willy had insisted. Since the creek made the cattle sick, Suntop had drilled wells. Put in windmills to pump up tanks of good, clear water. Nowadays that section was a treasure, with some of the best graze anywhere around Trueheart. It had been rechristened Sweetwater Flats, as the Kristopherson hands well knew. And weren't they sorry their boss's granddaddy had been such a blind fool at the card table back in '34?

Miguel was a lot sorrier than any of the Kristopherson crew, who shrugged amiably and ambled off into the starfilled night shortly thereafter. A bunch of hired hands, what did they care? It was Miguel who'd played his cards wrong, turning down the job at Suntop.

Because one look at the map told him the flats—Badwater, Sweetwater, by whatever name—were remote. Not to be inspected on foot from any public road. He'd need to ride in five miles through Suntop land to reach them. And from what he'd heard around the Lone Star, Suntop's owner didn't take kindly to trespassers.

He needed a job on the ranch as his cover.

But haying?

Only as a last—his very last—resort.

HE'D BEEN DRIVING as he replayed last night's happenings. Following what seemed to be the main private road, though smaller dirt roads branched off to left and right. He'd come more than three miles west across the wide, rolling valley. There was no sign of a house or barn yet; only the neat barbed-wire fences marching along either side of the road. A herd of twenty or so horses grazing on a distant hilltop, miles north. Two tiny cowboys riding a fence line, as far south. Hard to get a grasp on a place this big, and the mountains threw everything out of perspective. That big humped one up ahead might have been two miles distant— or twenty. The jagged peaks to the north, maybe fifty?

It wasn't just the scale of the place that was making him edgy. This land was too rich, too lush. Green as money. He was used to the red dusty plains of West Texas. Hard-scrabble land, where a man had to scratch for his luck— scratch hard and deep. Here luck seemed to be served up on a wide, green plate with a golden rim.

A plate set on some other man's table, not one where a poor boy from Dos Duraznos, Mexico, would be welcome.

But then, Miguel needed no invitation. No scraps from another's table. He'd been making his own luck for years.

Still, when he reached the river at last, it was a welcome change. The trees along it rose like a shaggy wall, cutting off the eastern valley from what lay beyond. His truck rumbled out onto a low concrete bridge that spanned dark pools, a yellow leaf drifting fast. With no car in sight, Miguel braked in the middle, to sit staring at the steep bank ahead.

He swung to study the one behind him. As he'd hoped, the valley floor was limestone and shale, not granite. Sedimentary rock. The blood tingled in his fingertips, his palms...the same way all his hunches started—as if he'd scooped up a double handful of luck. He nodded to himself and drove on.

On the west side of the river, the land rose abruptly in a series of wide benches, with the road winding to find the shallowest grade between them. His truck heaved over a rise and Miguel saw the ranch house on a hill ahead, with a clutter of barns and corrals intervening. Nearly there.

But again the road switched back on itself, entering a narrow pass cut in a ledge of rock. Miguel turned to glare at the cut as he drove by—granite, at this elevation—not so promising.

A horn blared out and he jumped violently. He whirled back toward his road, and stood on the brakes. Tires rumbled and skidded on the gravel. The pickup lurched to a halt. Its massive front bumper, with its greasy hydraulic winch, loomed only inches above the hood of the low, sleek convertible that faced it. A red Mercedes-Benz two-seater, top down. The dust his wheels had raised drifted over its glossy wax job, over its windshield, obscuring Miguel's view of the person or persons within. He blew out a soundless whistle. Now, *that* would have made a fine first impression—squashing this pretty toy.

His shoulders twitched as the Mercedes' horn blared again—too soon, too long, much too loud. On a particularly insolent note. *Out of my way, peón!* it yelled.

Miguel's back teeth came together with a click. Yes, he should have had his eyes on the road, but then the rich boy that he could now make out behind the Mercedes' wheel had been coming too fast. They both shared in the blame, but so what? No harm had been done.

Yet, he told himself as the horn blared for the third time. He drummed his fingertips on the wheel and schooled his frown to an expressionless mask. This cut was too narrow for the vehicles to pass each other. Somebody would have to back down.

Since Miguel was the one who needed a job—this scowling princeling with the golden hair clearly needed no job; that car had cost fifty thousand easily—it made sense that Miguel should humble himself and give way. This was

somebody of importance. Possibly the ranch owner himself,
or the rancher's son. To offend him...

The horn blared *yet* again. The driver leaned out his window. *"Hey!* Get that heap out of my way!" His voice
matched his horn—an arrogant tenor, bursting with pride.

Una lástima—a pity—to start out like this. But some
things a man could not do. Miguel sighed and reached for
the pack that sat on the seat beside him. After unzipping
the top compartment, he pulled out an apple. He fished his
knife from his jeans pocket, unclasped it and commenced
to leisurely peel the fragrant red globe. Turning to prop his
back against his door, he focused on his task. With care, it
could be done in one continuous spiral—much more satisfying that way.

The horn blared again—a series of impotent, outraged
squawks. Miguel pursed his lips and whistled "The Wichita
Lineman." Something his old friend Harry used to sing
when he was feeling soulful.

He caught a movement in the corner of his eye and
turned to look. The convertible's passenger door was opening. Someone—a girl—with windblown hair the color of
raw copper, of forest fires and wild honey, was getting out.
She touched one foot to the ground—but the driver lunged
her way, gesturing. He caught her arm, shook his head emphatically.

She hesitated, shrugged...closed her door again.

Her companion put his hand down on the horn and held
it there in an ear-splitting, nerve-grating protest. Miguel
sighed and cut a wedge of apple, ate it thoughtfully. Looked
as if he'd have to go over there and offer to flatten Mr.
Mercedes' nose for him. Not something he wanted to do
with a lady present.

On the other hand, maybe it was time she learned her
man was not only rude but gutless.

None of your business to teach her, he reminded himself. A rich *gringa* like that could buy all the lessons in life she needed—or buy her way out of them.

He was saved from choosing. The Mercedes jerked into reverse and roared backward at a reckless speed, its driver taking out his temper on his machine—and his startled passenger, who'd braced herself against the dashboard. *What some women put up with.* Smiling wryly to himself, Miguel put his truck in gear and followed.

After mounting a final rise, he turned into a wide, dusty barnyard. Several men on horse and afoot gazed off to where the red convertible had reversed all the way to a lone horseman, sitting a big buckskin horse at the far side of the yard. The rider leaned down from his saddle, listened as the driver of the Mercedes gestured wildly—then jabbed his finger at Miguel's truck.

So that was the man in charge. Not a good beginning, Miguel told himself as he parked alongside a corral and stepped out. *But play it as it lays.*

"NOPE," Ben Tankersly drawled, gazing across at the man who'd climbed out of the dusty old pickup. "He's not one of mine. 'Fraid I can't fire him for you." He swallowed his smile and glanced at his daughter. *You see what you've got here, princess? You want a man who can't settle his own fights?*

Risa's eyes touched his, then skated away. She stared off into the distance, arms tightly crossed, teeth buried in her lower lip, her cheeks the color of roses. Embarrassed, Tankersly hoped. She damn sure ought to be.

"Fine! Okay! Forget it, then!" Foster stomped on the gas and roared off the way he'd come, raising a cloud of dust.

Moving much too fast for the crowded yard. Ben's eyes

narrowed—*the damn fool*—then widened as he realized. The car was aimed straight for the stranger, who'd paused halfway across the open space. "You *idiot!*"

No doubt Foster meant to shame his target, forcing him to scramble for cover. Instead the young man stood, apparently paralyzed. Tankersly sucked in a harsh breath, bracing himself for the impact.

But the stranger took one long graceful stride to the side, whirled—and landed a thumping mule-kick on the driver's door as the Mercedes shot past.

One of the hands let out a blissful whoop. Tankersly's pent breath burst out in a guffaw. *Stove in his slats for him! Dented his door a good one!* The vanquished Mercedes roared out of the yard and off down the hill.

Tankersly's grin faded. That cowardly fool had his daughter aboard and there he was, trying to sprout wings, running away from his own humiliation. The rancher put the heel of his hand to his heart, rubbed it, then shrugged. Not a thing in the world he could do about it. If Foster didn't kill her in the next mile or so, maybe Risa would finally see. "That's not breeding stock," he muttered, then switched his attention to the oncoming stranger.

He blinked—and felt the dice teeter, then tip over, the way they sometimes did. One final roll and your life turned from empty pockets to can't lose. Foster was not breeding stock, but this one… Maybe…just maybe… Ben sat and let him come on, sizing him up as he would have any yearling colt, deciding whether to keep or sell him.

And this one looked like a keeper. On his mettle after he'd faced down that attack, his color was high, his eyes direct, fastened on Tankersly. He had that top-stallion strut—good spirits, good body and well-proven pride, combining to give a soft bounce to each stride, though you couldn't hear his feet hit the ground. With guts, good bone and reflexes. The young man halted beside Ben's stirrup. "They call me Heydt," he said, holding out a big brown hand. "Miguel Heydt."

Something south of the border in his deep voice—just a hint. And in his black Spanish eyes, though his hair was the same bronzy shade as the dark buckskin Ben rode. "Tankersly," Ben declared himself, squinting down as they shook. Maybe five years older than Risa's nineteen, he estimated, though Heydt's eyes made him seem twice her age. Eyes that had seen trouble and sorrow and come through it with just a trace of cool amusement at their corners. Eyes that said, *Come what may, I can handle it.*

Not like Risa's pretty boy, whose eyes said, *Come what may, I can buy my way free—or talk my way out of it.*

Heydt endured another minute of Ben's appraisal, then he spoke again. "I told him—" he tipped his head toward Joe Wiggly, who was riding up on them "—that I wasn't interested in haying. I'm looking to cowboy."

Standing there in a pair of old engineer's lace-up leather boots! Tankersly snorted. "Not what I need." If this one didn't answer to the rein, he wouldn't do in spite of his looks. Ben had enough trouble this summer without signing on an outlaw. "You'll buck bales or you can be on your way."

Heydt nodded impassively, but something was moving at the back of his dark eyes. "When I'm not haying, on my own time can I ride?"

To Ben's mind, any minute of life not spent in the saddle or in bed with a laughing woman was wasted. Still, his gaze sharpened. With those shoes, Heydt was no cowboy. But neither was he one of those wet-behind-the-ears dreamers who'd yet to find himself—though what kind of fool ever lost himself? Heydt was too old, too toughened, too savvy to be seeking a romantic new career the way some city slickers did every summer, to the locals' amusement.

So what's he want? Looking down at those steady eyes in the too-controlled face, Ben knew that asking would get him nowhere. He'd have to wait and see. "Why not," he agreed with a shrug, though he knew one good reason why not. After a day of haying, even the strongest man nodded asleep at the supper table.

He touched spurs to the buckskin and headed off toward the lower pastures. "Reckon he'll do," he told his foreman as he passed him. "Sign him up. And Joe," he called back over his shoulder, "come evening, if he still wants it, Heydt gets a horse."

CHAPTER THREE

WHENEVER FEAR or sorrow or confusion nibbled at her courage, Risa Tankersly reached for her camera. Through the lens of her ancient Nikon, somehow the harshness of the world was softened, or at least pushed back to a manageable distance. Framed in the viewfinder, half-perceived patterns became clear. Pain or chaos or uncontrollable events could be frozen into a sixteenth-second snapshot—frozen, reduced to a palm-size glossy rectangle, then tucked away out of sight and mind in one of the manila envelopes where she stored her photos until she felt strong enough to deal with them.

The Nikon had been Risa's escape hatch from the world since the summer she'd turned thirteen. One of her mother's last boyfriends, a cameraman with a minor studio, had left it behind when he stormed drunkenly out of their lives one night after a raging exchange with Eva about who should pay the pizza deliveryman. The next morning Risa's red-eyed and stumbling mother had dumped his camera bag in the trash can along with the rest of his possessions.

When her mother wandered back to bed, Risa had stealthily retrieved it, then hidden it under the T-shirts in her bureau drawer for a month—until Eva's next lover had come along to erase the last one from mind. Only then had Risa dared to bring out the camera and start—at first timidly, then with growing fascination—to explore the Nikon's possibilities.

The lovely old Japanese camera, with its scratched case, silken action and merciless, all-seeing lens, had been her best friend and confidant ever since. Had served her faithfully in the wrenching year that followed its coming, when her mother died and a tall, acid-tongued cowboy old enough to be her grandfather stalked into her life, claiming to be her daddy. Whisking her out of the helter-skelter gay and sorrowful world she'd always known, back to his enchanted kingdom called Suntop.

A world where fourteen-year-old Risa didn't know the players, the rules or even how to mount the standard means of transportation. A world where she'd come too late to ever quite belong.

Five years later, the Nikon was still a comfort and a consolation.

An hour before dawn Risa finally gave up the struggle for sleep. She slipped into her jeans and a green, pearl-snap western shirt, brushed her tousled, flyaway hair, grabbed her camera bag and set out to greet the first rays of the new day on Suntop Mountain.

Better, she told herself, pausing on the terrace to breathe deep the chill pine-scented air. Out from under her father's roof, she felt better already.

She took the stone steps in two long-legged bounds and strode off down the track. She'd have to hurry to make it to the summit by sunrise.

Passing close under the windows of the guest wing, she glanced upward, half fearfully, half wistfully. If Eric had spent as restless a night as she had... If he now happened to be leaning out his window, contemplating the east, where the sky was already fading from Prussian blue toward a heart-catching turquoise...

But his window was closed against the dawn. Eric wasn't

a lark as she was. Likely he'd sleep till she knocked on his door and coaxed him down to breakfast.

A faint frown drew her dark eyebrows together. He hadn't been very happy with her when he'd rejoined her on the landing last night. Whatever Ben had said to him after he'd summoned Eric into the library must have stung. Ben had a tongue like a rawhide lash and he didn't hesitate to use it.

But what was I to do? Ben was a tyrant, used to having his way around Suntop. Certain the rest of the world beyond the ranch's boundaries would also bend to his rock-bound will. No wonder Eric and her father were clashing—two strong men, from such different worlds...

And Risa caught in the middle, loving them both. She'd spent the night worrying how to do this. How to smooth the way between them. How to make Ben see how wonderful her man really was. Yesterday had been quite a setback.

She blinked, surprised to find that her brooding had carried her as far as the west shoulder of Suntop. *And now for the hard part.* She gulped in a breath and started up the horse trail that climbed the slope in switchbacks. Hurry! It could only be minutes before sunrise. No point to this exercise if she wasn't there to greet it.

Robbed of her mountain endurance by nine months at sea level, Risa arrived panting and light-headed on the grassy, rounded summit of Suntop.

Slowly she rotated, glorying in the three-hundred-sixty-degree view, greeting each landmark below in turn, saving the east as she always did for last. Oh, she did love Suntop, and she'd missed it terribly, for all the eagerness with which she'd fled the ranch last September. Someday soon she'd have to bring Eric up here to show him all this.

With that thought she swung east, and she'd timed it

perfectly. The first rays of the rising sun swept through the
notch in the far-off Trueheart Hills, to strike this enchanted
summit, this spot and this alone, with the first light of day—
a stroke of gold like a private benediction, a sizzling splash
of fairy dust, while all around it the world lay sleeping in
purple shadows. *Suntop.*

"Yes!" Laughing delightedly, Risa spread her arms
wide to welcome the sunshine and turned in the light. She
should take a picture, but for once she needed no layer of
glass between her and the world. it was simply enough to
be and be *here.*

Dizzy with her twirling, laughing softly to herself, Risa
stopped, opened her eyes—and found herself staring
straight into the eyes of a stranger. The fine hairs shot up
along her nape and her breath whooshed out in a startled
gasp. She'd spent too many recent months in New Haven,
where suddenly encountered strangers could be muggers or
worse.

But this is Suntop, she reminded herself, where her father
called her and her sisters "Princess." Here of all places
she was safe, if not always happy. She unfisted her hands.

"*Cielo,*" the man said quietly, and nodded—an oddly
courtly gesture.

Spanish. "Yes, it is," she agreed. "It's heaven, or 'bout
as close as you can get."

In the light now sifting down the mountaintop, his smile
was a slash of white against his tawny skin. Even as she
watched, the sun touched his straight, shaggy hair to
bronze, his face to ruddy gold.

There was enough light to see his dark eyes, and the
amusement in their depths. "That *is* what it means, isn't
it?"

"Yes, heaven—that's exactly what it means." Big hands

casually hooked in his back pockets of his jeans, he sauntered uphill to join her.

Risa had an impulse—born from who knows where—to
turn and run...run bounding and panting down the far side
of Suntop toward the safety of her father's house.

She stood, eyes narrowed, blood thrumming through her
veins, and leaned slightly back on her heels, but still held
her ground. Pinned in place by her pride. Then it hit her.
"You're—!"

The cause of all her misery yesterday! The outing to
Mesaverde had been utterly spoiled. "You're the man in
the truck!"

"Ah. I thought that might have been you. How many
women around here could have hair like a tequila sunrise?"
With one last stride he stood before her. "And how's the
car?"

That blasted car. It was Eric's shiny new toy, a gift from
his father on his graduation from Yale Law School last
month. After he'd seen the damage, Eric had been in a
black rage for most of the morning. "It has a dent in its
door. Quite a large one."

She'd tried at first to hint to Eric that it had been his
own fault for driving so close to the man—this man. He'd
been outraged that she'd think so, called her disloyal.
Whose side was she on?

"But I don't see it as sides," she'd protested, retreating
immediately from his anger. "I just didn't think it was
worth anyone's being hurt." She still didn't. How silly to
argue over right-of-way, like two Rocky Mountain bighorn
rams butting heads on a one-goat trail.

"Good. Perhaps that will teach your friend to watch his
temper."

Hardly. After she'd realized how furious Eric was, she'd
done her best to back away from their disagreement. In the

six months they'd been courting, they'd never had a real
lovers' quarrel. This had seemed such a stupid subject for
their first fight—a one-time event caused by a stranger
who'd blundered into their charmed circle for a few un-
pleasant minutes, but now was gone for good.

Or so she'd thought.

"Well, Eric said the whole thing was your fault, actually.
He says the uphill car always has right-of-way." She'd
never heard that rule before, but then, Eric knew so many
things that she did not. It was one of the reasons he'd first
attracted her. He seemed so assured, so at home in the wide,
daunting world into which she'd been thrust when she'd
gone East to college.

"Oh, well, if *Errrric* says so..." The corners of the
stranger's mouth curled wickedly as he rolled his *r*'s. He
had a very...arresting mouth for a man, with a beautifully
carved, full bottom lip and a certain mobility of expression
that was unlike the typical cowboy's poker face. Or an Ivy
Leaguer's stiff upper lip. And once noticed, that mouth
could not be ignored. It drew her eyes like a magnet. She
frowned to break its spell.

"And when he tried to run me down?" the stranger continued too politely. "I suppose there, also, it was my
fault?"

"He didn't try to run you down." Eric had insisted on
that, loudly and at length, till finally she gave in and admitted that perhaps only her viewing angle had made the
encounter appear so horribly close. "He was headed for the
gate—we were on a straight-line course for it—and
he...naturally he assumed you'd step aside." As much as
Eric had insisted on that, too, she'd had in the end to believe him. If you loved somebody, you had to believe in
him. Trust him.

"That's what he...assumed?"

He was giving her the lie, just by the tone of his low mocking voice. She hooked her own thumbs in her jeans pockets and tipped her chin up a haughty half inch. "Yes."

"I have—had—a friend who used to say, 'Never assume. It makes an ass out of "u" and me.'"

Arguing with an arrogant stranger was no way to spend a gorgeous dawn. She drew herself up—an action that put her on a level with most men's eyes. But not this one. "Oh? Well, *while* we're assuming, may I assume you have some very good reason for being here on Suntop? My father said you weren't one of his hands."

"When your *Errric* was complaining, I wasn't, *señorita*. But after that…your father hired me."

How like Ben to hire the man who'd offended her fiancé! Damaged his car! Her nails dug into her palms as it hit her. *So Ben really doesn't like him.*

And I have you to thank for that, she realized, glaring up at her companion. Her father hadn't formed an opinion about Eric, she didn't think, before yesterday morning. He'd still been weighing him in the balance. But once Ben made up his mind, it was carved in stone. She'd never be able to change it back to approval. *You've spoiled everything. Everything!* She would have gladly flattened her hands on this stranger's broad chest and sent him tumbling down the mountain if she could have.

Barring that, she had only words to pay him back for the harm he'd done. "Why would he hire you? You're no cowboy." Not with those work boots he wasn't.

Far from being wounded, he laughed. "So they keep telling me. Why is everyone so sure?"

No way would she give him a clue. "That's for me to know, and you to find out." A childish, spiteful taunt.

His dark eyebrows twitched as his mouth quirked in that

odd, irresistible way again. "Finding out things, I'm very good at that. For instance, how do they call you?"

"*Miss* Tankersly." A lie. All the men called her Risa. But not this one, if she had a say in it. This one she'd never forgive. "And you?" Might as well know her enemy.

"Miguel. Miguel Heydt del Rey." Giving her a formal Spanish name, first his father's surname, then his mother's. He didn't click the heels of his big, work-roughened boots together as he dropped his head half an inch in the faintest of mocking salutes, but still, she felt as if he had. She glanced warily down at his right hand, half expecting him to reach for hers and raise it to his lips. And if he'd done so, it would have been another kind of taunt, not so childish as hers. She shivered suddenly; the sun had yet to warm the mountain air.

"Oh." All at once she was at a loss for words, though not questions: *Who are you? Where do you come from, with a name like that, half German, half Spanish? And why are you here, so sure of yourself, though you were hired only yesterday?* And for what? Suntop took on no wannabe cowboys, only employed the best.

Whoever and whatever he was, he was trouble. She could feel that, the way sometimes, up in the high country, she could feel the hairs stir along her arms when a storm was coming. Something in the air... A charge building up. Some vast, awful polarity that would have to be bridged in a bolt of fusing fire.

"So..." Heydt turned away from her to look, for the first time, out over the world below, now turning from hazy lilac to green and tawny gold. He nodded at the eastern horizon. "Those mountains over there—those are the Trueheart Hills?"

"Yes." Why would he care about that?

"How long would it take to ride a horse from here to there?"

If he had to ask, then he wasn't a rider. "Depends on how many times you fall off," she said, straight-faced.

He glanced down at her sharply. "I wasn't planning to fall."

She gave him a wide, wicked smile. "No one ever does." And that was as good an exit line as she was likely to get. She turned on her heel and walked.

"*¡Luego, rubia!*" he called softly after her.

Later, blondie—though her hair was more strawberry than blond. And there'd be no later, not if she could help it. Risa hunched her shoulders and didn't glance back.

Not till she'd reached the trail that led down the west side of Suntop to safety.

But already Heydt had forgotten her. He stood staring out over the valley, or perhaps toward the distant hills he'd asked about.

The hairs tingled along her arms. Lifting her Nikon, Risa trapped him in the viewfinder. Reduced to half an inch in height, Heydt wasn't so threatening.

Kk-chick! Not by choice, but sheerly by reflex, her finger had pressed the shutter button.

CHAPTER FOUR

TODAY HE'D STACKED and shifted some eight tons of hay—seventy-five pounds at a throw. Miguel ached from his back teeth to his big toes and all points in between.

Worse than strained muscles was the exhaustion. All he wanted was to lie down on a soft bed—*ay, Dios!,* even the ground would do—and sleep for a week.

Instead here he sat, sore legs clamped in a death grip around this surly oat guzzler, miles from his goal. With the sun going down.

Pain he could always handle. And fatigue; his hands and his back would soon harden to the work. But at the end of this second day of haying, Miguel was beginning to realize that time was against him.

Yesterday, except for that dawn scouting trip he'd made to get the lay of the land, he'd not had a minute to spare. Cutting and raking in the fields till sunset, then a short stop for food, then the mower's blades had needed replacing and that job stole the evening.

Then this morning, again they'd started work just after breakfast—and his crew had stacked the final bale in the hay barn only an hour ago. He'd grabbed a shower at the bunkhouse, skipped supper in spite of his groaning stomach, then spent the past forty minutes wrestling a bridle and saddle onto this *diablo,* and strapping them in place.

Luckily no one had been around to see the show when he tried to mount! The beast could kick *forward* with his hind leg—Miguel had thought horses only kicked backward—and he'd done so with vicious glee, every time his would-be rider tried to step into the stirrup.

When Miguel had faced toward the back hooves and tried to mount that way, damn if the beast hadn't twisted his shaggy head around and bitten him in the butt! He'd lost fifteen precious minutes while they'd spun in a swearing, kicking, snapping circle, till finally he'd shoved the brute against the side of a corral and used the rails to scramble aboard.

Now, bruised, battered and bitten, he was taking the first ride of his life—with the sun going down. No way would he make it to the Badwater Flats tonight. But perhaps as far as the river? A man had to start somewhere. Clenching the reins, he clucked to his mount. "*Vaya, cabrón.* Move it."

The beast swiveled back his brown pointed devil's ears and left them that way, reminding Miguel of a cop's portable radar gun—two guns—aimed at approaching cars. He was being "watched" and measured. "Go on."

The horse snorted, shook his head and stepped out at a finicky walk.

Not daring to kick him, Miguel shook the reins. "Faster, you!" From the barnyard to the nearest border of the flats was nine miles, he'd calculated on his map. At this rate, he could not reach it before midnight.

Pulling on one leather, he hauled the horse's head toward the trail he'd seen riders take this morning, which must lead to the valley floor. "To the river," he told his conveyance. "You know the way."

The well-trodden trail sloped gently downward toward the outcrop of sandstone that formed the edge of this bench. Halfway there, Miguel felt his mount's ribs expanding beneath him—then he burst out with a shrill, shuddering whinny. "Whuh!" Miguel grabbed the saddle horn with one hand, while he jerked on the reins with the other. *"¿Qué tienes?"*

"He speaks Spanish?" A horse emerged from the narrow cut that led down through the caprock. Mounted astride it was Tankersly's daughter—she of the mountaintop and the Mercedes, though he'd heard there were two more about the ranch. But with her wicked smile and her golden eyes that seemed to take in his awkwardness all in a glance, this one was quite enough.

"No, and maybe that's the problem," Miguel admitted. "I tell him to go *a la derecha,* and he goes to the left. *Izquierda* gets me right. Tomorrow I buy the big mutt a dictionary."

She had a low, musical laugh—a fine thing in a woman. "The problem might be that you're holding your reins too tight. And then—there—you cluck at him, telling him to move on? He doesn't know if you want him to stop or go."

"So we're both confused." Miguel let his reins out a grudging inch. "Like so?"

"More. See the curve mine make?" Her horse, a golden palomino, sidled around to face the way it had come.

"Ah." Though what had caused her mount to turn like that? She'd made no movement he could see. "Weren't you headed to the barn?" he added as her horse leaned back on its haunches and started down the steep cut. He grabbed the saddle horn as his own horse snorted—and plunged after.

"Was, but this is more entertaining," she called over her shoulder.

Just what he needed—a witness to his incompetence. *"Sí,* entertainment must be hard to come by out here. Owning a ranch the size of Louisiana must be very boring."

"Not quite so big," she said, refusing to take offense. "And I don't own it. My father does."

"Ah, yes, a big difference." The only difference being that Tankersly worked, after his fashion, and she was a lily of the field, buying her right to existence by beauty alone.

Still, why quarrel with flowers? She wore a cream-colored Stetson this evening, which had slipped off her fiery head. A dark rawhide cord across her slender throat now held it in place on her shoulders. He could imagine hooking a fingertip under that cord, his knuckle brushing petal-soft skin as he drew her closer...

"Very different," she said under her breath, then added with an edge, "if the guys see you holding your saddle horn, you'll never live it down, you know."

Miguel let go the horn, stole a glance at her, then transferred his reins to the left hand the way she held hers. He rested his right hand on his thigh, fingers clenched in spite of himself. "Aren't you missing your supper?"

His own stomach growled at the taunt and she laughed. "Yes, but I'm waiting for my fiancé." Reining in, she gazed out over the twilit valley. "That might just be him there, coming back from Durango." She nodded toward the county road, some five miles to the east, and a tiny pair of moving headlights.

But they passed the ranch entrance and crawled on to the north. Her fiancé. "You mean Señor Mercedes?" A pity. He would make a poor husband, ill-tempered and overbearing. And a man who was full of himself would be selfish in bed.

"I mean Eric Foster, who does happen to own a Mercedes, and it's a nice one, too."

"Except for that dent in the door. Must be a careless driver?"

"Ha!" She touched her spurs to her palomino's ribs and the horse surged toward the river.

Without signal from his rider, Miguel's own horse followed. Miguel grabbed the horn—grimaced and let it go—yelped and clutched it again, half standing in his stirrups. *Dios,* a mile of this and he could forget having sons!

She glanced back at him around the brim of her hat and called mockingly, "Let go of that horn, cowboy!"

"*¡Brujita!*" he swore under his breath. She *was* a little witch, with her hair of burning embers blowing back over her face as she laughed and tortured him. Impossibly slim in the saddle. And graceful, her hips barely bouncing against the polished leather, while he slipped and jolted like a clown.

Abruptly she took pity on him and reined in, letting him catch up to her at the next cut down to a lower level. "Why haven't you sold these worthless brutes for dog food and bought yourselves something useful? All-terrain vehicles or dirt bikes?"

She smiled as she rubbed her horse's glossy neck. "Oh, they sort of grow on you. No bike's going to blow down your collar or rest his head on your shoulder."

"*Gracias a Dios.*"

"Of course, it's partly your choice of ride," she added with a twinkle. "Did they tell you his name?"

"Jack is what Wiggly called him."

Her smile broadened. "That's short for Jackhammer."

"And thank you, Wiggly!" He dared to touch Jackhammer with his heels, and miraculously the beast didn't resent it but moved on. His tormentor pursued, drawing even with him again. Their knees brushed for a moment and he glanced at her sharply. "I suppose you've been riding since you could walk."

"Oh, no. I started late myself. Fourteen."

He cocked an eyebrow; how could that be? But she'd swung away from him, was gazing off in the direction her fiancé would come. The pale line of her profile against the gathering dusk was a thing of beauty, like Venus rising in her veils of light, there in the east. Someday, once he'd made his fortune, he'd find himself a woman like this one, all grace and spirit and fire.

But first, but first, he reminded himself. First came the means to win, then keep her. Because a man without money—

"There he is!" she cried on a note of satisfaction. A pair of headlights slowed for the turn into the ranch, then seemed to glare at them across the intervening miles as the car topped a low rise.

She reached over and laid two fingers on Miguel's wrist. Her touch shot up his arm like a spark leaping to tinder and he sucked in his breath. "Pull back on your reins and hold them," she commanded.

"Like so? But why?"

"Because I've got to run and you don't want to follow."

Or do I? But already her horse had spun in its length, snorting and dancing.

She gave him an absent smile, her mind filled with another already. "Have a good ride." The palomino thundered away uphill.

Jackhammer threw up his head, fighting the reins, eager to race for the barn. "Whoa, you *cabro! ¡Cabrón!* Who's the boss here?"

A good question. By the time they'd settled it, she was long gone.

THIS WASN'T THE SUMMER Risa had pictured when she'd invited Eric to Suntop. She'd imagined them riding out daily. She'd show him all her favorite, secret spots—the canyons, the swimming holes, the high country. They'd pack picnics along every day, and somewhere outside, sometime this summer, sometime *just...right,* they'd make love. She wanted her first time to be outdoors, under the stars. Or in a high-mountain meadow, in the lush grass and flowers, with the sun blazing down, only eagles for witness.

Wanted some way that distinguished the act from the casual rolls in an unmade bed, in a small shabby room with cobwebs in the corners and cigarette smoke hanging heavy in the air. Half-empty beer cans on the bedside table. That was her earliest impression of love, the way her mother had gone about it.

For herself, Risa wanted something different, so different. But how was she to get it when Eric wasn't welcome at Suntop? Ben had looked her fiancé in the eye at the supper table for three nights running and asked how long he planned to hang around Suntop.

And Eric was sensitive. Eric had his pride. Eric could take a hint. He'd come back last night from Durango to tell her he'd found a job for the rest of the summer. He'd be working pro bono for the biggest law firm in that city. The senior partner was a friend of his father's. He'd sublet an apartment there, and they'd see each other weekends and evenings. "I'd like to be closer, sweetheart, but what with your father..." He'd shrugged and smiled bravely.

She'd flown to lock her arms around his waist. "Oh, Eric, that's just his way. He gives all our dates a hard time."

"He's going to have to get used to the fact that I'm not just some pimply-faced *date.* I'm here to stay, Risa. There's no way he's stopping me. Stopping us."

What had she done to deserve such devotion? she'd wondered as he kissed her. It seemed *such* a miracle. That a man like this could love someone like her. Too tall, too shy, too awkward. Neither brilliant nor beautiful. Never quite belonging anywhere.

A castoff, a stray. Her younger sisters were both legitimate, but she was not.

Ben had never bothered marrying her mother. Never troubled himself once in fourteen years to visit his daughter, not till Eva's death. Then he'd brought Risa back to the ranch like an afterthought. When he'd adopted her and given her his name, well, that must have been for no more reason than that all Suntop stock wore his brand.

Compared with Ben's brusque and offhand affection, Eric's unswerving attention was cool water in the desert. In his arms she'd found her home at last.

But, oh, she was missing him already, and this was only the second day he'd been working. So to pass the hours till sundown, she'd ridden out with her youngest sister.

"Who cares if we didn't bring our swimsuits? I'm positively, absolutely *melting!* Come *on,* Risa. Race you there!" Twelve-year-old Tess Tankersly wheeled her paint pony midbridge and spurred south down the river trail.

"Tess!" Risa had wanted to return to the Big House, in the hope of finding a message from Eric waiting there. But she couldn't let her youngest sister swim alone. "*Darn* it. Wait up, you silly goose!"

No answer but a wavering war whoop. Tess ducked her dark head alongside her pony's neck and vanished under the green-fringed curtain of a willow tree.

Risa growled something wordless and urged her lathered mare into a lope. Exasperating as her little sister was, she was right. It was hot today. They should have ridden into the heights instead of the valley, but Tess had wanted to show her the latest crop of yearlings. She had her eye on a black, half Arab, half quarter horse filly that she was determined to make her own. Her first grown-up mount.

So far, Ben, in his usual fashion, had made Tess no promises. There was so much more power in *maybe*, than *sure*.

That's why he doesn't like Eric, Risa told herself. *Because he can't control him.* And once they married, Ben would lose control over her. She smiled as she crouched along her mare's shoulder, willow leaves stroking her back.

Two more twists along the narrow trail and she came to the swimming hole. Here the river made a wide bend around the cliffs on the opposite shore. The current slowed, the bottom was sand, the water deep and dark.

Tess had shucked the saddle off her paint and was leading him into the river. She'd left her T-shirt on, thank heavens, but she'd wriggled out of her jeans. Her skinny little butt gleamed bright red with her cotton bikinis, then vanished beneath the olive-gold water. Beside her, her pony snorted and launched himself into the depths, paddling like a dog.

"You twerp!" Risa called. Now they'd have to wait for Oscar to dry off before Tess could saddle up again.

"He was as hot as I was." Swimming alongside, Tess grasped the pony's black mane and squirmed up onto his withers, then threw a leg over his surging rump. "Wheee, we're flying!"

"What do you think—want to swim?" Risa asked Sunrise as she folded her jeans on top of her boots. Sunny dipped her head and actually seemed to nod. Risa laughed and reached for the cinch knot. "Just like old times."

They swam the horses downstream as far as the next bend in the river, then back against the current, to come ashore on the opposite bank, where a narrow sandbar edged the cliffs. Sitting shoulder to shoulder, legs outstretched, digging their bare heels into the damp, sugary grit, they talked aimlessly, while Sunny and Oscar prowled the bank behind them, seeking mouthfuls of grass growing from the cracks in the rocks.

"You're really not going back to Yale in September?" Tess lay back on her elbows. "Dad will be sooo *mad* at you!"

"He'll get over it." Or he wouldn't. "Eric and I are marrying in October and that's that, Tessums. Just as soon as he starts his job—his real job—in Denver, as a public prosecutor." The job had been promised to him—the Denver attorney general was another friend of Eric's family—and the coveted position would open up when one of the staff left on pregnancy leave.

Once Eric started drawing a salary, they could marry. After that, Ben would have to make up his mind: he could smile on her decision and help her. Though this time—and from now on—he'd have to let Risa define what was help and what was interference. She hoped to transfer to the University of Colorado at Boulder; that should be a feasible commute from wherever she and Eric set up housekeeping.

But if Ben refused to help her, refused to give them his blessing... Risa's lips tightened as her fingertip traced a line in the sand. Well, she was marrying Eric anyhow. She'd have to work for a few years, then she'd put herself through college. This was her life and she'd live it her way. Ben had had his chance to shape her future back when it would have really counted for something, and he'd passed it by. So how could he complain now?

"But Eric's not a cowboy," Tess pointed out with a child's irrefutable logic.

Risa smiled to herself. Her youngest sister had been raised all her life at Suntop. She could imagine no world beyond its borders, conceive of no better life than one that circled around cattle and horses. "No, he isn't. Not every...interesting man rides." From out of nowhere the image of Miguel Heydt flashed across her mind, his big hand clutching the saddle horn for dear life, his dark eyebrows drawn together in a mock scowl while he swore at the horses. He'd been laughing at himself, as well as teasing her, the other night. Strange, that a man who could make fun of himself seemed not weaker for it, but stronger.

"Interesting." Tess smirked. "You mean sexy?"

Tess's fiercely tomboy years seemed to be drawing at long last to a close. Sometime in the ten months Risa had been gone, Tess had discovered boys. "What would you know about sexy?" Risa teased. "You mean like Robbie Kristopherson?"

"*Robbie?*" Tess made a gagging sound. "Robbie can't even walk straight! He fell over the wastebasket in Ms. Ever's class the last day of school! No, I mean *sexy*. Hot— like that new guy on the haying crew."

Risa's heels stopped their rhythmic sliding. "What new guy?" Tess knew every foal that dropped, every barn-swallow that nested at Suntop, but still, surely she was much too young to have noticed...

"The one with buns to die for! And when he takes his *shirt* off...!" Tess collapsed with a blissful moan and hugged herself.

"How did you see him without a— Ben will *shoot* you, you goose, if you've been hanging around the haying crew. It's dangerous." And Risa didn't mean just the machinery. The haying crew weren't regular Suntop men but temporary workers, hired only till the fields were cut. Unknown factors, unlike the cowboys, who were all dependable, hand-picked men, who knew their boss too well to flirt with the boss's daughters.

"I *haven't* been hanging around. But this new guy, Risa, you've gotta *see* him. He has a chest and arms like a—like a comic-book hero!"

"You haven't been peeking through the bunkhouse windows! Tess?" Risa prodded her in the ribs till the girl giggled and shook her head. "Hiding in the hayloft, you little lech?"

"Uh-uh! No, *stop,* don't *do* that! I w-watched him through my binocs yesterday, okay? When I rode out to look for b-bluebirds. He was stacking bales, then they took a break and he took off his s-shirt and dumped water over his head!"

"Oh, well, binoculars, of course," Risa said dryly. Add one Hunk, genus American Male, to the Life List in the back of her little sister's *Peterson's Field Guide.* And just because Miguel Heydt sprang to her own mind, his muscles shining with sweat and water, didn't mean that he was the object of Tess's admiration. Half the men on the haying crew were probably in their twenties.

"Anyway, if you won't marry a cowboy, why don't you marry somebody like that?" Tess muttered as she scrambled to her feet.

"Eric's got a nice chest. A perfectly wonderful chest."

"Ooooh, and how do you know *that?*"

CHAPTER FIVE

BY LATE AFTERNOON the crew had cut, raked, then turned as much grass as could be baled on the morrow. Since the weather promised to hold hot and dry, they'd be working straight through the weekend. So the hay boss had given them the rest of this day off.

Half the men were taking siestas in the bunkhouse. The rest had crammed themselves into two pickups and set off, whooping and jostling, for the Lone Star. They wouldn't come staggering back until closing time.

Miguel put all thoughts of blissful naps and ice-cold bottles of *cerveza* firmly from mind. Today, at last, he'd make it to the Badwater—no, the Sweetwater—Flats.

Well, he'd thought he would. But when he and Jackhammer came to the bridge over the river, he noticed the trace of a path heading south along the base of the cliffs. Any cut in the earth was a siren song and this one had been singing to him for days, each time he rode the hay wagon past this point. "We'll go only as far as that first bend," he assured Jackhammer.

What a lie. Once a man reached a bend, there was always an obligation to peer around it. Who knew that heaven didn't lie just beyond?

Miguel didn't find heaven, but he found enough to lure him on. The sedimentary strata through which the ancient river had carved its winding course lay level where the bridge made its crossing. But as he rode south, gradually it began to dip. Good, that was very good; he lived for folds in the earth. He glanced wistfully over his shoulder, since the sediments apparently were rising to the north, but still he continued south. It was just as important to find a marker bed, an identifiable stratum, so he could orient himself. In Texas it would have taken only a glance or two to know where he was, but this was virgin territory.

And he the eager bridegroom. His eyes roved lovingly over the striated cliffs—a layer of dark gray shale lensed out between two layers of limestone—Mancos shale, possibly? He twisted around and dug his rock hammer out of the saddlebag, then sidled his horse in next to the wall of stone. "Be still, you. This will take only a minute."

The steel spike chopped into the chunk he wanted—a chip ricocheted—Jackhammer's ears flattened to his head.

"Whoa!" The gelding spun on a dime, took two stiff-legged, jolting hops as his head swung down to his hooves. "So I'm sorry, I didn't—*hey!*"

The next thing Miguel knew, he was flying in a magnificent arc, hammer firmly grasped in one hand, mouth rounding to an outraged "Oh." Off to his left, Jackhammer kicked up his back heels—who knew the brown bastard could move like that?—then shot off toward the—

Miguel hit the water headfirst and forgot about horses. There was a moment of cold confusion, frantic splashing—air, where was the damn air?—then he surfaced, cursing and coughing. "*¡Hijo de—!*" He burst out laughing.

So a horse wasn't an unfeeling machine. The sooner he learned that, the better. He glanced around and grimaced. Jack hadn't waited for an apology. By now he'd be halfway to the barn, blasted brute.

Miguel swiped a forearm across his brow, wiping the hair from his eyes, shrugged and turned back to the cliff. From this low angle he could see details he'd missed look-

ing down from a saddle. And there in the shale, not a foot
above ground level—he narrowed his eyes and waded
closer—yes, *por Dios*, there where it had been waiting patiently for millions of years for a man to be thrown from
his horse... "You were right, Harry." Whatever the misfortune, there was always a balancing compensation.
Hadn't he held on to his hammer?

Miguel scrambled out, knelt, commenced delicately to
chip stone.

Once he'd pocketed his prize he wandered on, his boots
squelching softly. The beds continued to dip southward,
layers of shale, limestone and sandstone striping the cliffs
in diagonal alternations of gray and cream and gritty pink.
He took samples, loading his jeans pockets with rocks, regretting that he couldn't make notes and sketches of what
he found. But Jackhammer had run off with his notebook.
Miguel frowned. Wouldn't want anybody at the barn to
look into his saddlebags. He ought to go back.

But there was another bend up ahead. "Just this last
one," he promised himself, and, turning his face to the
cliff—the trail had become only a narrow ledge some four
feet above the river—he edged sideways along it. As he
rounded a bulge of water-smoothed limestone, as luscious
to the hands as a woman's hips, he heard laughter and
stopped short. Glanced ahead.

To where two mermaids, astride two sea horses, cavorted
and wrestled in the river. *Cielo,* indeed! Giggling breathlessly, each was trying to shove the other off her swimming
steed. Long arms flashing, pale legs twisting, the small,
dark one toppled with a hapless screech and a resounding
splash. The other mermaid raised her beautiful arms, arching her back as she shook her fists at the sky. *"Yes!"*

Miguel turned around on his ledge, leaned against the
rock and devoured her with his eyes. Tankersly's daughter.

For an instant he hadn't recognized her. Her hair was so much darker, wet, curling in coppery ribbons over her high, apple-sized breasts. *Manzanitas deliciosas.* She wore a drenched white T-shirt, which clung to her slender curves like a mermaid's pearly scales. And below that—he swallowed audibly—only a scrap of turquoise, above legs so long she might have wrapped them twice around his waist with inches to spare.

The little one scrambled up the side of her mount, then froze, propped on her locked arms, her eyes rounding as they met Miguel's across the pool. "It's *him!* Risa, it's—" She dropped from view behind her pony.

"What?" She—Miguel was beginning to think of her simply as she—spun so fast her hair whirled out around her, chains of copper dripping diamonds.

He laughed softly—how could anything be this perfect?

Her dark eyebrows—surprisingly dark, given her hair—drew together; her golden eyes speared him. She'd taken offense.

He couldn't blame her. Clearly he'd stumbled into Women's Magic here. But there was no going back. No way he could unsee what he'd seen. And whatever penalty he must pay in exchange for this vision, he'd pay it gladly. A man was the sum of what he'd witnessed, and he was richer for this sight.

Her far leg arched over the rump of her palomino and she dropped down into the water—spun again to glare at him, chest-deep in the river.

Ah, so that wasn't a bathing-suit bottom she was wearing. Odd how that realization heated the blood.

"What are you doing here?"

The little one appeared beyond the palomino, swimming toward the far bank, tugging her pony behind her by its bridle. She stopped when she reached waist-deep water, and swung to stare at him, much the way a doe will run, then turn to see if you pursue.

But her elder sister—Risa, was that what the little one had called her?—waded toward Miguel, eyes gold and fierce as a mama wildcat's. "I *said*—"

"I'm collecting rocks," he said easily, before she could scold him. "And better things." He dropped to his heels with care and fished in his shirt pocket. "Such as this." He held his find out and waggled it invitingly.

Ah, he had her. Her eyebrows went up. She was dying to see what he had.

"Cretaceous period," he told her, helpless to stop himself from showing off, any more than a stallion can stop himself from arching his neck and prancing around a ready mare. "Sixty-five million years old, give or take a couple of million."

"What is it?" shrilled the little one from the shallows.

He closed his fingers, hiding it from view. "An inoceramus." To fix his gaze on Risa's face as she waded warily closer took an effort of will. As the creek bottom shelved upward, she was rising like a nymph from the waves. His eyes yearned to melt down over her, praising every swaying curve and hollow.

"And what's that?" She stopped with the water lapping her slender waist.

"You tell me." He offered it, cocked his head in challenge. Her bottom lip pushed out a delectable quarter inch in annoyance, but still she reached. He laid it delicately on her palm. *Para tú.*

"Risa, what *is* it?" shrilled her younger sister, bouncing with impatience.

"A fossil." Intent on its ribbed and fluted shape, Risa turned it slowly. "Some sort of clam."

She hadn't said "only a clam." Abruptly it struck him

that liking a woman would be more dangerous than lusting after her.

"It's really that old?" she added.

He nodded. "Waiting here for us all that time."

"Let *me* see!" The little one had waded ashore, tied both the horses, and now launched herself across the stream. Heads almost touching, the mermaids studied the inoceramus while Miguel studied them. Such different coloring, sunset and midnight—*rubia y oscura.* When you looked for it there was not much resemblance, either to Tankersly or each other, but still, they were unmistakably sisters.

La oscura glanced up at him. "You found it underwater?"

"No. Embedded in the cliff. One finds such in shale."

"But you're all wet."

Miguel had to admit he was. "My horse threw me in the creek."

His wry look earned him a bubbling laugh from the *niña,* and a twitch of those luscious lips from her elder sister.

"Then you'll have to ride back with us," decided the little one. "Risa's Sunny can carry two."

"Thank you," he said quickly as Risa frowned and her lips parted to counter this offer. No way would he pass it up!

He waited on his ledge while the sisters crossed to the far bank. Turning his face gallantly to the cliff, still he could picture Risa shimmying into her jeans.

"What's your name?" the little one called, her shyness forgotten.

"Miguel. And you?"

"Tess. Tess Tankersly. And this is Risa."

Señorita Tankersly to him, till she herself made him free of her name. Still... Risa, whatever it might signify in *in-*

glés, in *español* it meant "laughter." *And if you were to laugh with me?*

But such a notion was madness. If all went as he hoped, someday soon he'd have to deal with Tankersly. Negotiations would hardly go well if he'd been sniffing about the rancher's daughter! Business might be one thing, but the old man would have a better match in mind for his crown jewel, his fire opal, than a flirtation with a Mexican halfbreed.

While the girls saddled their horses, Miguel let himself down into the river and waded across. On his dignity, he walked instead of swam. At the lowest point, for five yards or so, only his eyes showed above water. He waggled his eyebrows at Tess and earned another outburst of giggles. He smiled underwater. *Ay, chiquitas.* She was as easy to entertain as his own little sister had been last time he'd seen her, too long ago.

But Risa was not so easily amused and she stiffened when he mounted clumsily behind her. "I've never done this before," he confessed softly in her ear. What delights he'd been missing! Pale as a gibbous moon, her nape with its waving tendrils of reddish-gold was only inches below his lips.

She jammed her hat into place and its rim established a "don't trespass" perimeter.

"May I hold on?" he asked as they set off at a trot. His hands would almost span her supple waist; his palms itched with anticipation.

"To the cantle—the back of my saddle—please do," she snapped.

Tess rode before them, chattering over her shoulder. "So you collect fossils, Miguel?"

"*Sí.* Also stones. I'm a rock hound." It was close to the truth.

"I found a piece of fool's gold last year. On roundup. Would you like to see it?"

"Pyrite? With much pleasure."

"And I have a chunk of something that I used to think was a diamond when I was little. It's big as an egg! But I reckon maybe it's just quartz."

"More likely," he agreed. And there were compensations to hanging on to the cantle, he was finding. At this pace, over the rougher patches of trail Risa couldn't help but bounce a little. Her taut, smooth hips brushed his thumbs more than once. Tipping his head to one side to peer under her hat, he grinned. Her nape was now rosier than pale. Were he to brush his lips, rough with his afternoon beard, right...*there*, he bet she'd go off like a bottle rocket, all sparks and fizz and a firecracker pop! *Ah,* rubia, *you bring out the bad in me!*

"What were you doing back there?" she asked coolly in an undertone. "Aren't you supposed to be haying?"

His smile faded. "Even a *peón* gets a day off now and then."

"I didn't mean to—"

"No?" While he spun his fantasies, he should remember not to forget: she was a *ranchera rica* and he was a wetback. He had more hope of collecting fossils on the moon than taking such a one as this in his arms. At least, not while he had hay in his hair.

But someday... He glanced over his shoulder. Tess had chosen the easier grade of the road leading to the ranch yard, instead of the cowboys' trail. From this height, he could see the tops of the Trueheart Hills jutting east of the valley. He'd lost a precious day, flirting with mermaids.

The growl of an engine mounting the grade behind caused him to swing farther around. Uh-oh! Here came that ancient, caramel-colored Lincoln Town Car that Tankersly flogged around the ranch when he wasn't riding. He'd driven it down to the hay fields yesterday, gunning it ruthlessly through the muddy irrigation ditches.

"Daddy!" Tess cried, reining in as the car braked alongside them. "Look what Miguel gave me!" She waved the fossil that he'd intended for Risa. *Ah, hermanitas.*

Little sisters could get a man in all kinds of trouble. Tankersly was bound to resent any and all contact between a summer laborer and his daughters. Miguel met the old man's stony gaze, his own face expressionless.

"See, Daddy?"

"Huh." Tankersly hardly glanced at Tess's prize. His shrewd old eyes were measuring the distance between Miguel's chest and his beautiful daughter's shoulder blades to the very last quarter inch.

Or so it seemed to his hired hand, who was braced for the worst. *What a fool I've been*—¡qué tonto! To give this merciless geezer an excuse for firing him before he'd barely started... No woman was worth this!

"You're wearing your stirrups a notch too short," he growled at his eldest. "You learn that back East?"

"What if I did?" Risa leaned back in her stirrups till her hat brim brushed Miguel's mouth.

"Should have sent you west." The massive old sedan rumbled on past and vanished up the hill.

Not once had Tankersly cracked a smile. So why did Miguel have the strangest feeling that the old man had been pleased?

CHAPTER SIX

MORNING. Joe Wiggly and the Old Man sat their horses in their usual corner of the yard, watching the hands saddle up and ride out. Two cars rolled up the hill, parked by the tool shed and disgorged those men of the hay crew who slept down in Trueheart. The rest of the crew shambled out of the bunkhouse, stretching and yawning, to clamber aboard the two empty hay wagons that waited by the barn.

"Been keeping an eye on him for me?" Tankersly nodded toward Heydt as the young man vaulted onto a wagon's flatbed. He sat down immediately, then flopped backward on a broken bale, pulling his hat over his face.

Joe smiled wryly at that. He knew just how the fella felt. He meant to catch a few winks himself, soon as he and Tankersly had planned the day's work. "Yep, I've been watchin' him. Didn't get really interesting till last night." He'd hoped Ben would ask. He reached into his shirt pocket, pulled a cigarette out of his pack, and stuck it between his lips. Proceeded leisurely to light it.

The tractors fired up and hauled the wagons down the road, off to the fields for a day of baling. Tons of hay to be stacked and moved and stacked again. Heydt's tail would be dragging by the end of this day for sure.

"He's been ridin' most evenings, going a little farther every night, mostly upriver and down. But last night, danged if he didn't set off like a dog smelling a bitch over the mountain. Straight line. Along the road to the main gate, then north, then through our gate on the other side. On and on east till he comes to the gate to the Sweetwater Flats. I'm hanging way back, you understand, but 'bout then we lost the last of the light.'' The foreman drew on his cigarette, squinting through the smoke as he exhaled.

"You know how ragged that section is. Reckon I'd've broken my neck a dozen times if there hadn't been a half-moon.'' Maybe, come to think of it, that was what Heydt had been waiting for—enough moon to see by?

"Anyways, I move up a bit closer. I'm starting to wonder if maybe he's scouting cows to rustle.'' He'd begun to regret that he'd not thought to pack his .22 along. Heydt was unfailingly pleasant, but something told a man that he'd be a rough one to cross.

"Ya think?'' Tankersly scowled. Rustling was no longer a hanging offense, and that was a pity, because it was a growing problem in the West. A thief could fill a cattle truck with twenty head, drive 'em to hell and gone, earn himself a year's pay in a single night.

"Not now I don't. Eventually he comes to where we've fenced off the creek bed, and he ties his horse and climbs through the wire. I'm figuring he's forgotten his canteen and he's meaning to drink from the stream, and I'm grinnin' to myself, picturing his face when he tastes that water. So I wait, expecting him to come scrambling back up the bank, spitting and wiping his mouth. But he doesn't show.''

He leaned over to tap his ash off on his boot heel, then straightened again. "After a bit, I get kinda curious and I ride up t'where I can see over the fence and down into the cut. It's about twenty feet deep along there…'' He dragged in a lungful of nicotine, smiling inside at the look on the boss's face. Oh, he had him, all right. "'Bout a quarter mile on, I see a light–bright light, one of them halogen lanterns. Kid's walking real slow, playing his beam over the banks, first one side, then t'other. Stops every so often, looks real close at something, then moves on.''

''Huh.'' Tankersly spat thoughtfully into the dirt.

''I follow along the top of the flats, find another place to peek over the side. But he's just moseying on, flashing his light.''

''He ever find anything t'speak of?''

Joe shrugged. ''Not's so as I could tell. I hung around till two or so, till I was yawnin' so hard I feared he'd hear m'jaw crack. He was still hard at it when I headed on home.'' He'd flopped onto his couch at the foreman's house not long before sunrise. Had slept for an hour, then saddled Tankersly's mount for the day and set off to fetch him. ''If Heydt made it back to the bunkhouse in time to snatch the last biscuit, I'd be surprised.'' And served him right for keeping an old man out all night.

Tankersly rubbed his craggy jaw. ''Now, what the devil's he up to?''

RISA RODE her outrage all the way down to the ranch yard. How *dared* he? Did Ben imagine she was still a rebellious fourteen, to be sent to her room without supper when she disobeyed? Or fifteen, forbidden to drive with her girl-friends to Durango to see a movie?

But to have intercepted Eric's messages…this was a new low in high-handedness even for her father!

And worse, he'd almost succeeded in driving a wedge of misunderstanding between her and her fiancé. After three days of echoing silence, she'd begun to fear that Eric had stopped returning her calls. That perhaps he'd found some-one at the law firm where he was working. That he'd finally come to his senses and realized he could do much better than Risa Tankersly.

To call him one last time at work had taken all her courage. She'd gotten past the secretary who'd recorded her previous messages and reached Eric himself.

And learned that over the past three days, he'd called Suntop *four times!* Once her father had answered the phone, and the other times Socorro, their cook and housekeeper, had taken Eric's calls.

Neither of them had passed his message on.

Furious as she was, Risa couldn't blame Socorro; the woman had worked for Ben for thirty years and she knew who signed her paychecks. She only would have been following orders. But Ben? "You manipulative heartless bastard!" she swore, swinging down from Sunrise by the barn. Pity her father wasn't here so she could say that to his face! He was off in his Town Car, at one end of the ranch or another.

She knew because she'd checked the garage, up at the Big House. Had she found his car, she would have taken it and paid the consequences later.

But no such luck.

Which brought her here. She would *not* sit meekly at home, letting Ben think he'd won again. After tying Sunny's reins to the hitching rack, she loosened the mare's cinch, then stalked off toward the bunkhouse.

Her steps shortened as she neared it. The bunkhouse was off limits to her and her sisters. Ben insisted that the men liked their privacy, and no doubt that was true. But over the years, the forbidden had bred fascination. To the Tankersly women, the shabby old one-story barracks had an aura of masculine mystery, much like the sacred ritual house of Hopi men. A kiva for cowboys.

Don't be silly, she scoffed at herself. *It'll just be a bunch of hands, wandering around without their shirts on.* Bad enough. She should have brought Tess along for support.

Go on. All you have to do is rap on the screen door and ask for him.

Then endure the knowing smile on the face of whichever man answered her knock! She came to a halt, one foot on the bottom step of the stairs leading up to the sagging porch.

"You look lost, *señorita!*" called a low mocking voice from across the yard.

She jumped, then glanced over her shoulder. Miguel Heydt sat astride the tow hitch of a horse trailer that had been uncoupled and left parked alongside the tool shed. Leaning back against the trailer's streamlined front, he held a beer balanced on one blue jeans–clad knee. He tipped his head back in inquiry, but he didn't rise as she approached.

At least he still has his shirt on, she told herself. Actually, it was a T-shirt, clinging damply to his broad chest. She stopped close enough to smell an aroma of hay and hot male that did funny things to her pulse. "You're not inside," she said, suddenly at a loss over how to begin.

"Waiting for my turn in the shower." He rubbed the hard angle of his jaw and she heard the tiny rasp of bristles. He hadn't bothered with shaving this morning; the blue shadow gave a rakish air to his weary smile. He looked like a *bandido* one jump ahead of the posse.

But not worried about the outcome—far from it. "Looking for someone?" he inquired politely.

"You." There was no way she could think to hide that fact. "I was wondering if you'd—" She ran out of air, had to stop for a breath. "If you might loan me your truck—that is, if you don't mean to use it yourself. Tonight. I'd be happy to fill it with gas for you. Pay you something, if you like."

His dark eyes narrowed behind thick black lashes. "Ah." Absently he raised the bottle of beer to his lips, then seemed to focus on it. "Could I offer you *una cerveza?* Or maybe you're not of age. Perhaps a cold drink. We have lemonade."

He, also, saw her as a child? She felt her temper kick up a notch. "I'm *quite* old enough to drink, thank you, but no, thank you. But your truck...?" She couldn't manage an ingratiating smile—bit her bottom lip anxiously, instead; this was even harder than she'd imagined.

"Your own car is not working?"

"I don't own a car." She'd asked—begged—Ben for one, for her graduation from high school. She was so cut off from the world, here at Suntop. Most of her friends lived in Trueheart, some twenty miles away. She'd have been happy to take a job in town to earn the price of a car, but there was no way she could *reach* the job without wheels in the first place.

All that last month before graduation, she'd circled ads in the Durango newspaper for used compact cars at reasonable prices. Left the classifieds on Ben's desk where he couldn't fail to see them.

On graduation night, he'd given her a pair of two-carat emerald ear studs, which she'd yet to wear. Because she'd read his gift's message loud and clear. He'd treat her like a princess—as long as she remained under his thumb.

"You own all *this*..." Heydt's eyes swept the horizon beyond her. "But you own no car?"

Her problems were not his business. She shrugged. "I have the use of the ranch car when I need it." As long as Ben approved of her needs. It was a battered old Range Rover that rattled your teeth out. But there was a constant tug-of-war between her and Lara for its use, and since she'd been gone from home, Risa had lost this round. "My middle sister, Lara, has taken it to Albuquerque. She's visiting friends, so..." She looked at him pleadingly.

"Then, *perdoname* for wondering, but why not ask your father for his car?"

She almost stamped her foot with frustration. "He's out somewhere driving and I'm in a hurry!" Eric had to work overtime on a case tonight. But he'd promised her that if she could come to him, he'd take her out for a late supper, then show her his new apartment. Damn it, it had been nearly *five days* since last they'd kissed!

"Ah." Miguel sighed and rose stiffly to his feet. He swayed as he reached his full height, bouncing lightly off the trailer behind him. "In that case, *señorita*, I will drive you to Durango with pleasure. Let me grab a shower, then we can—" He paused as she shook her head emphatically.

That was the very last thing she needed—Miguel Heydt tagging along. Oh, Eric would love that, all right! "No, *please*—I mean—thank you very much. But I have to go alone. Look, I really will pay you. Whatever you want for a night's rental."

The corners of his mouth took on a whimsical tilt as his gaze seemed to drop a few inches.

She licked her lips nervously and felt a wave of heat rush through her. He was thinking of kissing her? Surely not! "Please?" she repeated, hating to beg. "Say...fifty dollars?" She reached into her pocket.

"No." He cut the syllable shorter than usual. A Spanish *no,* not an anglo one. A Latin-*male no,* she realized as his lips tightened and his eyebrows drew together. She blew out a breath and looked away. He'd offered her a favor; she'd spurned it, trying to *buy* his help, instead. But she was too frustrated to apologize.

"Tell me," he said after a moment. He patted the trailer behind him, drawing her eyes back his way. "Who owns this thing?"

"The trailer?" Lara's mother had owned it originally,

Risa remembered. So she supposed it had become her daughter's when she died. But Lara had written her elder sister in March, in desperate need of money—for what she would not explain. Some scrape that she'd had to conceal from Ben.

Risa had sold a classmate her favorite Zuñi bracelet, a corn blossom sterling-and-turquoise bracelet, and sent three hundred dollars on to her sister. Which meant that Lara owed her. Which meant that now, if Heydt's inquiry was more than idle curiosity... Her shrug was elaborately casual. "I do." At least, you could say she had a three-hundred-dollar interest in Lara's trailer. "I and my sister own it. Why?"

"Because I would like the use of it. I have so little time to ride after work. With this I could go farther."

"Oh? But I was talking about borrowing your truck *once*," Risa pointed out, fighting an urge to clap her hands in excitement. "If you mean to use this trailer often, then I'd want to..." She met his gaze squarely. "Then how about a one-for-one trade? For each time I get to use your truck, you get a night's worth of my trailer?"

His eyes gleamed like shards of obsidian. "*Bueno,* a woman who knows how to bargain! But there's *una problemita.* I'll need my truck to tow this thing."

Risa gave him a wide, close-lipped smile. "Oh, that's no *problema* at all."

IN SPITE OF his exhaustion, Miguel didn't fall asleep until nearly ten. The poker game in the bunkhouse kitchen was particularly raucous tonight; somebody was drawing good hands. Each time he laid his cards on the table, the shouts of disbelief and groans of indignation carried through the thin walls.

Lying on his top bunk in the darkened room he shared

with three other men, hands clasped behind his head, Miguel stared at the ceiling only a few feet above. It was too dark to make out the crack in the plaster, but he knew it already by heart; a line like a ragged river, cutting its patient way through limestone.

He wiggled his toes under the sheet with pure pleasure. The creek bed at the Sweetwater Flats! His hunch had been right. From the instant he'd stumbled across that old map of Trueheart in a flea market in Abilene, he'd known it in his bones. Somewhere along the course of that creek was an oil seep—maybe several seeps. He hadn't been able to find the upwelling in the dark. Every crack in the bank, every shadow cast by a rock, looked like a gush of black gold by the light of his lantern.

But though he'd yet to find it, he'd tasted the water and that told him enough. Bad water? This was water to make a man's fortune! *Agua bendito!*

An image of Risa's heart-shaped, haughty face flashed through his mind. *Would you look down your adorable nose at me, gringa, if I were as rich as your papá? Richer than your Mr. Mercedes?*

He could picture her standing in the midst of his miraculous stream. She was wearing only her white T-shirt and that scrap of turquoise silk. He stood before her, cupping the precious water in his hands and pouring it over and over her fiery curls, black gold for his *rubia.* And when she was drenched, her T-shirt clinging to her delectable body, water hanging in crystal from her long lashes...when she stared up at him, her big eyes full of wonder and admiration, he'd hook an arm around her slender waist and draw her slowly, *so* slowly... Miguel smiled, sighed luxuriously...and slept.

"HEY, HEYDT, you're wanted." A hand jostled his shoulder.

"Uh?" It could *not* be morning! He felt as if they'd

buried him under blankets—under the earth—then parked a hay wagon on his chest. "No," he grunted, rolling onto his stomach.

The knuckles returned to jab him harder. "I mean it. Get up! Wiggly wants you."

That pierced his stupor. "Uh." Wiggly?

Jake, one of the cowboys, nodded grimly, his square, freckled face level with the top bunk. "Yeah. What the heck'd you do?"

Reached for the stars? Miguel didn't know, but a summons in the middle of the night—because it was still dark outside the window—this could not be good. Would be anything but. "Where...is he?"

"Out on the porch. And if I was you, I wouldn't keep him waiting."

Miguel didn't. Tucking a clean shirt into his jeans, he zipped, buckled his belt, stepped out the screen door.

The foreman looked him up and down, not smiling. "The boss wants t'see you."

CHAPTER SEVEN

TANKERSLY WANTED to see him? Perhaps Miguel wasn't even awake; this was a nightmare to punish his dream of the old man's daughter!

But the packed dirt of the ranch yard felt solid and real under his boot heels as he walked toward the foreman's house, where Wiggly had sent him. He glanced overhead. And the stars were all in their proper places. It wasn't as late as it felt; by the moon it must be only eleven or so.

It hit him suddenly, bursting on his befuddled brain. *Risa had taken his truck.*

Ay, Dios, she'd wrecked it! He stopped short with a groan snagged in his throat. *Oh, please, no!* Over the years he'd lost friends to car wrecks. The men of the Texas Oil Patch were hard drinkers, hard drivers. When they raced back to the rig after a night of carousing, accidents weren't uncommon. But to take that golden girl? God could not be so cruel!

Oh, but he could. He could.

What was I thinking, loaning her my truck?

He hadn't been thinking, at least not with his head. He groaned again and trudged on toward the lit windows of the foreman's house.

A thump on the back door brought an answering shout from within. Miguel swallowed hard and stepped into the light. "Mr. Tankersly."

No answer. He drew a deep breath and moved on into

the house. Passed through the kitchen doorway and found himself on the threshold of the living room. Ben Tankersly slouched in a leather easy chair, with a drink at his elbow. A bottle of whiskey sat on the table beside him, along with a bag of chips.

The old man lifted his drink and sipped deliberately, his dark, hooded eyes measuring Miguel over the rim of his glass.

No offer of a seat. Miguel unfisted his hands and waited, determined not to speak first.

The rancher set his glass aside. "Got a question for you, Heydt. Do you know where my daughter might be? Risa's missing."

Relief surged through Miguel like a river breaching a dam. *¡Gracias a Dios!* He let out a long slow silent breath, fighting the smile within.

Which faded immediately. Because if Risa was alive and well, still he was in danger. *And thank you,* rubia! Lack of sleep must have made him stupid this evening. Any idiot would have realized that she was coming to a stranger for a car because her father did not approve or even know. Somehow he'd thought she came to him because...because... Just because.

Because she knows a sucker when she sees one! He shook his head. "Your daughter? No, sir. I have no idea where she might be." She could be off most anywhere, breaking men's hearts. She'd told him Durango, but maybe she'd lied. Clearly, Risa hadn't troubled herself about a hired hand's skin.

Or his job. *Dios,* if Tankersly fired him at this point, what would he do? He hadn't evidence yet to prove his find. Besides, if Tankersly blamed him for aiding his daughter in her mischief, why should he do business with the man who'd helped her?

"Huh." Tankersly took a long, considering sip of whiskey. "All right. Second question. What were you looking to find, prowlin' around my land at night?"

"Sir?" Damn, damn, how did he know?

"If it's gold or silver you're after, then you can pack your bags. No man will mine Suntop while I'm alive. Miners are rapists—greedy swine—tearing down God's mountains for a handful of shiny. Pah! Spoiling the land with their piles of tailings and the creeks with arsenic. Is that what you are, boy?"

Miguel pulled himself erect. "No, sir. I'm a wildcatter." The elite of the oil business. The men who dared much and risked all. Those who sought oil far from the known fields, in places where it had never been found before.

"An oilman, huh, that's no better! Rigs lit up like Christmas trees, trucks roaring in and out scaring the cattle, wastewater and oil spills. Well..." Tankersly stared broodingly off into the distance. "Well, that's a pity. Tell Wiggly to cut you a check, and be gone by morning."

He'd laid his fingertips on treasure, only to have it wrenched from his grasp!

But not without a fight. "Sir, it doesn't have to be that way. It's true that in the past oilmen have been careless, despoiling the land they drilled. But a man who cares can drill carefully, cleanly, taking the riches below without hurting the land above. The rig stays only till the pipe is set, then it goes away. The waste can be trucked out, the pits covered and resodded." He flipped his hands palms up and shrugged. "The cows will get over their fright."

"Huh." Tankersly swirled the ice in his glass till it tinkled. "That so?"

"That *is* so. And if a well is made, the money can flow like a river."

The rancher laughed a dusty, soundless laugh. "You think I don't have a cash flow already?"

"Can a man ever have enough money? With more money you could buy more land, if that is what matters to you. Or better cows."

Wry amusement froze to black ice. "There's none better in the West than my herd!"

"Oh. Then more range for your cattle." *Perhaps a car for your daughter.* But something was working behind the old man's eyes and Miguel held his tongue.

Tankersly nodded toward the kitchen. "Go get yourself a glass."

His palms were itching as if he'd scooped a double handful of luck. Still, he hardly dared to breathe; one wrong word and it could trickle through his fingers. And any minute Risa might drive into the yard in his pickup—its headlights would sweep these windows! Let that happen and her father would probably shoot him. But still, but still, he could feel his palms itch. This was a night to bet and bet big.

Returning, he held out his glass while the old man poured him a generous measure. Tankersly nodded at the sack of chips. "Some pork rinds?"

"Um, no, thank you." He dared to sit on the couch opposite. Took a wary sip, while Tankersly crunched a pork rind and considered him, much as a butcher might size up a side of beef, planning his first cut.

"So you found the oil seeps," Tankersly growled finally.

Miguel inhaled a gulp of liquid fire and choked. "Y-you know about—?"

Tankersly sighed. "It'll save us both a truckload of manure if you don't figure me for a fool, Heydt. Of course I know what's spoilin' my groundwater over on the flats."

"Yes, sir." But where was his leverage if the old man

already knew? Miguel had hoped to trade news of his discovery for the right to drill. Usually a landowner was surprised and delighted to be told that there might be oil below his property. But in this case...

"So that's where you'd figure to drill—on the flats?"

No, he shouldn't panic. He still had a bargaining chip. "Perhaps, perhaps not, sir. You see..." He sipped, gathering his thoughts. "After oil is formed deep underground, it is pushed toward the surface by the pressure, enormous pressure, of the rocks and mountains above. But it can only travel if it finds a highway, a layer of porous rock such as sandstone, along which to move.

"So what I seek is a place where the beds of sediments have *folded* over millions of years into an arch—an *anticline,* they call it. The oil travels along its permeable highway to the top of this arch, this dome, buried deep in the earth.

"Then, if by the greatest good luck there is a cap of impermeable, nonporous rock—say, a layer of tight limestone—above the dome, then the oil becomes trapped there, at the top of the arch. It can rise no farther. Geologists call this a *trap.* At this place there may form a pool of oil, perhaps an enormous pool. If we tap into this..."

"Then we're all driving gold-plated Cadillacs filled with dancing girls—I got that. But isn't this dome below the oil seeps?"

"I don't know yet. There is some sort of fracture in the rock, *sí,* there where the oil seeps out. But the oil may simply be rising in the sediments *past* that point, on its way to the trap, which might be three miles to the east or five to the south. What I must do is try to map the beds, see where they rise and fall, till I can discover where I think the top of the dome is located."

"Huh." Tankersly munched another pork rind. "Why

didn't you come to me in the first place and tell me you wanted to scout my land for oil?''

Because I'm a nobody again, now that Harry's dead. Sí, perhaps I could have shown you my map and persuaded you that oil might be present—but then you might have turned around and called in one of the big-name outfits to find it for you. No, Miguel had wanted his discovery firmly in hand before he came to the bargaining table. But now..."I'd heard the way you feel about miners," he lied tactfully. "If I'd come to you and asked permission to scout, would you have given it?''

"Nope.''

"So I thought it would be best to know there was a good chance of oil before we talked.''

The rancher's old eyes glinted with amusement. He wasn't quite buying it, but perhaps the whiskey was mellowing him. "Huh.'' For a while he ate pork rinds and Miguel prayed. "Here's how I see it,'' he drawled finally. "You've got a problem, Heydt. You're hungry for a crack at my oil. You don't even know yet, for sure, if you've got something here or not. And even if you find it—well, think you've found it—still, I'm not hungry. Maybe I'll decide I'm leaving that oil in the ground for my grandchildren. It's like money in the bank.''

It was—if it was truly down there in its vault of stone. In the end, Miguel could only say that to the best of his knowledge the oil *should* be down there. But the very best of the wildcatters drilled five dry holes for every well they brought home. It was a break-heart career, but still, gambler that he was, he'd choose no other.

"So you've got a problem,'' repeated the rancher. "And I've got a problem.'' He stopped for a swallow of whiskey, then sat, turning the glass in his big gnarled hands. "You met my daughter's fiancé the day you came to Suntop...''

Miguel nodded warily. *Where are we going here?*

"Well, I don't want that smilin' snake in my bloodline. And I damn sure don't want him calling the shots around Suntop once I'm gone." Tankersly brooded over his glass. "He'd chop this ranch up into ranchettes before the grass had grown on my grave. I don't know how much he could make wrecking Suntop—forty million? Fifty? *Huh*—that Ivy League scumsucker would sell his own grandmother for a membership in the right country club. Risa thinks he loves her, but that kind only loves the almighty dollar and the power it brings."

"So why don't you tell her this?" Miguel ventured to ask.

Tankersly grunted. "Because she doesn't listen to me. Never did. She's a little mule. Pull on her halter and she'll sit every time. Try and herd her north and she'll stampede south."

Miguel had to smile. He could well believe it.

"I could disinherit her and that would solve the problem. That greedy bastard would snatch back his ring before she blinked twice. But Risa's..." The old man sighed. "She's not the tough cookie she thinks she is. I cut her out of my will and she'll figure I don't love her. Then Foster learns she's no longer an heiress, and *he* dumps her—proving he never did love her. Her heart stomped twice, her pride kicked in the teeth—she doesn't need that. I'd as soon not hurt her if I can find another way."

Miguel stirred restlessly. *But what do you want of me? That I should shoot him for you? ¡Olvídalo! Forget it.* He might have punched Foster for the pleasure of rearranging his arrogant face, but he'd hurt no man for money. "And so?"

"So that's where you come in. If you want to scout my land for oil, here's the deal. I need a crowbar to pry that scrub right out of Risa's stubborn heart, and I need it pronto. I want you to take her away from Foster. Marry her.''

Miguel dropped his glass. ''¿Qué?'' So this was a dream, from first to last, and he still lay in his bunk!

Except that icy liquor was dribbling between his boot strings.

''You heard me. I want her married to somebody who'll do, and I want her bred—the sooner the better. Least I ought t'get out of all this nonsense is a grandson. Boys run in your family?''

Miguel laughed in spite of himself. Could this be happening? ''There's one of each, my younger sister and me. But Señor Tankersly—''

''Stuff your buts, boy. Refuse me on this, and you can hit the road.''

Miguel's smile faded. Slowly he got to his feet. Stood there, swaying slightly. ''No man talks to me así.''

For a moment they glared at each other, then Tankersly showed his yellowing teeth. ''Fair enough. But I'm offering you the deal of a lifetime, son—a chance to drill at Suntop and a beautiful woman who comes with a mighty fine dowry.''

It was like one of those tales his mother used to read him from the Brothers Grimm. The king offers his princess-daughter and a third of his kingdom, and all the beggar must do to win her— Miguel shook his head, more in wonder than refusal.

''That's a no?'' Tankersly inquired, frost creeping back into his voice.

''That means I'll have to think.'' Long and carefully. If this was a fairy tale, then there'd be dragons on every side. Only a fool would lunge at this bargain blindly.

From out of nowhere the image of Risa standing in the

oily creek as he'd dreamed her intruded on his mind—long pale limbs, drenched T-shirt, haughty mouth, yearning eyes. A princess of ice and fire. And all he had to do was reach out his hands for her? "I'll have to think," he repeated carefully. "And now, *señor...*"

"You'd better get t'bed before you fall on your face," Tankersly agreed. "But I'll want a yes or no on this by tomorrow."

ALL MORNING they'd been working like *demonios*—there was a chance of thunderstorms this afternoon, which would spoil the drying hay. Miguel hadn't had much time to think. Thought only in ragged snatches, between bales.

Stacking another one on the back end of the moving hay wagon, he paused for an instant, panting. *How can I possibly conspire with her father to wreck her engagement?*

But engagement to what? To whom? Foster would never make her happy. It would never enter that selfish bastard's head to even try to make her happy.

Even so. None of my business. Her life is her own to shape as she chooses. "I want no part of this," he swore, his voice drowned out by the clank and chuff of the baler and the roar of the tractor that was pulling its train of implements down the windrow of mown hay.

Liar! jeered the other half of his mind. *You want her and all that comes with her. Only a fool would not.*

Ned, his partner on the wagon, caught the next bale that was shaped, wired, then extruded from the baler's chute. Miguel hooked the one after that, swinging seventy-five pounds of fragrant grass in one deft arc, muscles quivering in his arms and back—to land it chin-high atop the final row of bales. The wagon held almost its full, eight-ton load, and still there was not a cloud on the horizon.

The last bale was arranged on the pile, then Miguel

glanced aside—and saw the big caramel-colored sedan, bouncing toward them across the field. *¡El diablo!* Here came Tankersly, wanting his answer.

The tractor headed up-valley, bound for the ranch yard and the sheds where the hay would be stacked and stored for the coming snows. Sitting on the edge of the wagon, feet dangling, Miguel met Tankersly's gaze defiantly as the tractor drove past the rancher's car.

As he'd feared, Tankersly gave a "get over here" jerk of his Stetson. Miguel dropped off the wagon, ignoring Ned's shout of surprise behind him, and strolled to the waiting sedan.

"I'm sweaty," he warned the rancher as he opened the passenger-side door.

"Huh. You see this spot here?" The rancher patted a dark splash across the seat's lustrous leather. "Blood of a newborn calf. This is a working car. Get in."

They sat side by side, each with an elbow out his window, and watched the tractor and wagon lumber up the road, its roar dying away to a distant mutter. "Well?" the old man said finally.

"Well, first, it's not necessarily doable," Miguel warned him. "If Risa loves this man…"

"Then you'll have to change her mind. The one thing I do know about women is they're changeable as windmills. Blow on her hard enough, she'll swing t'face you." The rancher rubbed his chin. "If I could figure some way to throw you two together…"

"Oh, no, if she thinks you're matchmaking it's *terminado*. Done for. If she's as contrary as you say, then much better you disapprove of me. Forbid her to speak to such a *malo* as me."

Tankersly gave a grunt of amusement. "Point taken. Okay, what else?"

And just like that, Miguel realized, he'd passed from toying with the rancher's ridiculous proposition, to figuring how to make it happen. "I need more time. Time to court your daughter. Time to seek my oil. Haying eats up the day."

"I'd thought of that. On the other hand, if you're just mooching around the place, she'll know something smells. We don't have idlers here at Suntop." Tankersly tapped his scarred old fingertips on his steering wheel. "The hay boss tells me you're pretty damn good with the machinery...."

"I've been working as drilling boss for a discovery oil firm these past five years, and as roughneck for years before that," Miguel told him. "If a thing's made of metal and gears and grease, I can fix it."

"Good. Then I want five hours a day out of you, same rate of pay as haying," Tankersly decided. "You figure when and where you want to work. I'll tell Wiggly to keep the projects coming. There's always something breaking around a ranch."

"*Bueno*. Then..." And on this he was determined he would not budge. "I'll need a written agreement. There is always a contract between the landowner and the driller, setting out each man's share of the profits, the lease of the mineral rights and the period for which they're granted."

"Yep." Tankersly pulled a smudged envelope off the dashboard, held it at arm's length to study the scribbles on its back. "Made some notes myself. 'Condition one,'" he read aloud. "'You marry my daughter and that gives you the right to drill *one* well on Suntop land.'" He turned to lift his grizzled eyebrows at his seatmate. "You find your own financing for the drilling, of course. And I, as land-owner, get the usual eighth share of all profits, with no drilling costs to me."

The old man had done his homework, indeed. This

would have been the split Miguel would have suggested had no marriage entered into the picture.

But it was less than he'd hoped for. Because financing was the sore point. Harry had been wildcatting for forty years. He'd been a legend in the Permian Basin of West Texas; it was said that he could smell the oil two miles down. With his contacts and his reputation, they'd never lacked for backers to drill exploration wells. But now that his mentor was gone, how many investors would be willing to gamble a few hundred thousand on Harry's right-hand man? A man with no formal degree in geology? Miguel had yet to put this question to the test.

And there was another problem. "Only one well? But if I discover a productive field, I might want to drill a dozen or more." Or sometimes the first well was dry, but the core samples you took as you drilled it gave you the additional information you needed to locate the jackpot on the second attempt.

"'Condition two,'" Tankersly continued, consulting his envelope. "'If you get my daughter pregnant within the first year, then you have twelve years from the date of marriage to drill as many wells as you want and can find the money for.'"

Miguel blew out a breath. That was better. But at the back of his mind, he didn't see a forest of rigs plumbing the earth. He saw himself standing behind Risa, his palms cradling her burgeoning belly. *Risa with my child...* Muscles jerked taut in his groin. "Any more conditions?" he said evenly.

"You bet. Third one is that if you get her pregnant the first year and she delivers a healthy boy—I finance your wells."

Miguel gasped. All his difficulties solved in an instant!

"Long as you hit oil and keep hitting oil, I'll back you,"

Tankersly clarified. "And as your moneyman, I take half of net profits...you get the other half."

At best, usually the wildcatter earned only a sixteenth share of profits, while his financiers took the rest. Such a deal as this could make him richer than he'd ever dared to dream. It was generosity beyond belief.

All he had to do... Schooling his face to no expression, he glanced at the old man. "All this for a grandson?"

"Yeah." The rancher's eyes were fixed on the far-off mountains. There were vast herds of Suntop cattle up there in their foothills, on the summer range, Miguel had been told. The ranch stretched miles to the north, then held grazing leases in the public lands beyond its own borders. "Time's running short. And that brings me to another point. The boy'll be my heir. You'll have to let me teach him to ride and rope. To know one end of a cow from t'other—to teach him everything he'll need to know, to run this spread someday."

Here was a hunger as deep and fierce as his own resolve to make good in the world. And Tankersly's need spoke to Miguel's heart; they were two like men, standing at the opposite poles of their lives.

Miguel had only begun to build his own kingdom, to stretch himself. To learn how much he could wrest from this world on his own terms, his only tools his wits and his energy and his passion.

Tankersly had earned and held his kingdom—and soon he must find someone to cherish and champion it for him through the coming years.

Miguel's eyes swept the wide, green, jagged horizon. The old man was right. Suntop was too fine a world to be torn apart. "I would be honored that you teach my son," he said quietly as he offered his hand. "These terms I can accept."

But he wasn't the only one who must accept them.

CHAPTER EIGHT

RISA UNSADDLED Sunny and turned her into the home pasture, then went looking for Heydt. They'd agreed to meet at five forty-five on the dot—and there he was now, bounding down the steps of the bunkhouse.

Freshly showered, she noted. His thick, tawny-bronze hair was still damply combed, though already it was going its own way, falling into his raven-dark eyebrows. As he stopped before her and looked down with a faint smile, she could smell soap and a tantalizing hint of spicy aftershave. The bristles of yesterday had vanished. "Ready to go?" she asked briskly. He was standing half a foot too close for comfort. An odd tickle of awareness moved across her skin—as if he pressed on the air around her.

"*Claro,* I've hitched up the trailer, and as you see, Jackhammer is waiting. But he tells me he has no intention of climbing inside."

She smiled in spite of herself. Heydt and his horse—a love-hate relationship was plainly developing. "I bet you looked at him."

"But of course I did. How else could one lead the surly jackass?"

"I'll show you." Risa untied the chestnut gelding, then grasped his reins near the bit. Leading him at her right side, barely sparing him a glance, she walked up the ramp and he followed, hooves clomping on the padded metal.

"*¡Bruja!*" Miguel called indignantly from outside the

stall as she tied off the horse, then rewarded him with a scratch behind his ears.

"If I'm a witch, then that's the simplest spell. You never face a horse and pull on his halter. You couldn't drag Jack out of a burning barn pulling on him face-to-face."

"No? Then he's as foolish as he looks."

Arriving at the rear of the trailer, she found Miguel waiting. He offered his hand, and though she didn't need it, she could see no polite way to refuse. She took it and stepped off the side of the ramp, landing neatly at his feet.

She let go instantly, but the feel of his big fingers, so warm and hard, stayed imprinted on her palm as she walked around to the passenger side, leaving him to fold up the ramp.

"Where to?" she asked when he climbed in beside her.

"The east end of the ranch. I'll show you." He steered the pickup carefully out of the yard, glancing back every few seconds in the mirror. "He won't fall? He's a clumsy brute, always tripping over his own big feet."

Heydt was a fine one to talk. She glanced down at his boots on the pedals—size 12 at least. Eric's feet were 9½, not so much larger than her own size 8's. "No, if you take your corners gently, Jack'll be fine." She looked out the window to hide a smile. Heydt's insults masked a grudging affection. So he cared for animals; that was rather sweet.

"How was Durango last night?" he asked as they rumbled over the bridge.

"Ohhh…" She followed the course of a branch floating down the current. "Very nice." And it had been, though somehow not as perfect as she'd anticipated. Probably she'd still been on edge from finding that Ben was intercepting her messages.

Eric hadn't been as angry as she was. In fact, he'd almost seemed to take Ben's side. "You've got to understand, darling," he'd soothed her, standing in the lobby of his law firm, his hands locked behind her waist. "You're his treasure and I'm the man who's going to steal you away from him. It may take him a while to come to terms with that."

"Eric, you don't know him. He's trying to split us apart!"

"Not gonna happen, honey." He kissed the tip of her nose. "No way, no how. But I'd never forgive myself if I caused any friction between you and your father."

"Friction? We've rubbed each other wrong from the very start!"

"Oh, I'll never believe that. He adores you as much as I do. He's just too crusty to show it easily."

"Ben's as hard as a cast-iron skillet and about that flexible. Once he's made up his mind..."

"Risa, Risa honey, don't worry so much. What he wants in the end is what all fathers want—for you to be happy. Once he realizes that I'm the man for that job, then he'll stop fighting this. We just need to be patient. Now, why don't you come up and see my office?"

So she'd admired Eric's office, then he'd taken her out to a sophisticated restaurant, where she'd felt underdressed. The cuisine had been an odd sort of fusion of Hispanic and Caribbean and Thai, big-city food. Eric had fed her tidbits of shrimp and steamed dumplings across the table, while he whispered words of love and admiration. Under cover of the tablecloth, he'd slipped off his polished cordovans and caressed her ankles and calves with his toes till she'd been grateful that the candlelight would hide her blushes.

Afterward he'd taken her back to his sublet apartment for a tour that had gone no farther than his big leather couch. He'd settled her there, poured her a brandy and made sure she drank it, then kissed her dizzy for hours on end.

"Come to my bed," he'd pleaded. Not for the first time, but always before he'd been patient. This time she'd sensed the tiniest edge under his passion.

And no doubt he was right. It was high time they sealed their love, time she proved how much she loved him—they were engaged, after all. But somehow...for some reason...probably because of the tension she was under... Maybe because this wasn't the outdoor setting she'd always imagined for her first time... Or possibly the smell of liquor on his breath reminded her too sharply of her mother's boozy romances?

Whatever the reason, she couldn't respond as he wanted. Finally she'd framed his face in her hands, kissed him and drawn away. "I can't tonight, Eric. It's so late already..."

"It is. You should stay the night."

She smiled regretfully. "And straggle back to Suntop in the morning to face Ben over the scrambled eggs? I don't think so. He's got one standard for men and sex, quite another for his daughters. If you really want his approval..."

"Sometimes you have to do an end run around approval, honey." Eric pulled her into another embrace. "If he knew we were lovers, he'd realize how serious we are. He'd *have* to give us his blessing."

He was grossly underestimating her father! You crossed Ben at your peril; forced him into nothing. In the end, Eric was going to have to give up on his quaint and charming notion that they must win Ben's blessing. Plenty of couples married without parental approval or aid; so could they.

But it was too late tonight to try to explain this. She shook her head emphatically as he refilled her glass. "No, really, I can't. I've got miles to drive."

"Ah, baby, you don't have to leave yet."

But she did. Finally he'd sighed, shrugged, walked her

down to Heydt's pickup. "Where'd you find this junker?" he'd wondered scornfully.

Luckily from the angle they'd approached the truck, he couldn't see the distinctive winch on its front bumper. "Borrowed it from one of the hands," she said, and kissed him to distract him.

"Not too late to change your mind?" he coaxed when they could breathe again.

"Soon, soon, soon. I promise."

"Then I'll hold you to that," he said huskily, closing her door with a tender smile.

Last sight of him she'd had had been in her rearview mirror as she drove away. Standing under a streetlight, he'd stopped waving, simply stared after her. Even at the distance of half a block, his posture didn't match his last smile. Something told her he'd been angry.

Maybe I'm just a tease, she wondered miserably now. It wasn't fair to ask Eric to wait forever.

"You went to see your *novio?*" Heydt inquired now, eyes on the road.

"*Novio?* I don't know that word."

"Fiancé—Mr. Mercedes? Does he live in Durango?"

"He took a job there for the summer so he could be near me," she told him coolly. "And it's really none of your business."

Heydt's sexy lips quirked in a half smile. "*Sí,* but don't tell him you're driving my truck. He looks like an eye-for-an-eye and a door-for-a-door *tipo.*"

"That's just your guilty conscience talking."

He laughed. "It's true. I feel guilty about many things, but only the deeds I regret, *señorita.*"

There was always just the tiniest taunt in his voice whenever he gave her that title. Like a work-roughened fingertip plucking at her nerves. "If I'm going to be driving your wheels, you might as well call me Risa."

"Risa-Sonrisa," he said softly, making almost a chant of it.

"Risa means laughter," she agreed. "But *sonrisa?*" She didn't remember it from her high-school Spanish classes.

"Smile," he translated, turning to give her his own, full-blast.

Lord, Tess was right! He was comic-book-hero attractive—and she'd yet to see him shirtless. If she hadn't given her heart already— Risa caught the movement ahead in the corner of her eye, swung to look—

As Heydt stomped on the brakes. *"¡Cuidado!"* He flung out his right arm as she lurched toward the windshield.

A second whitetail deer soared after the first, then a half-grown fawn. One flying leap carried it over the left-hand fence and onto the road, only feet ahead of the skidding pickup. Risa gasped and flinched away, pressing her face to Heydt's shoulder.

The truck shuddered to a halt.

No impact, Risa realized as, beside her, Heydt blew out a breath. She opened her eyes.

"I'm sorry. I should have watched where I was going."

His arm was still a warm, protective bar across her breasts, branding her. She leaned back in her seat and it fell away. "My fault. I distracted you."

"But by now I should take that into account."

Did he mean— She ducked his whimsical gaze, turning back to the empty road. "You missed her?"

"By a heartbeat. Now, if you'd excuse me *un momentito?*"

She looked back as he walked around to the rear of the trailer and disappeared. How odd; she could still feel the shape of his arm on her body. A shiver moved up her thighs and she frowned. *This is ridiculous!*

He returned in the little moment he'd promised. "Is Jack okay?" she asked him.

"He's on his feet, but he says I'll pay for scaring him that way. And he's a horse who remembers his grudges."

"Then I hope you'll be careful riding after sundown." Even experienced horsemen came to grief in the dark. *Why is he doing this?* she asked herself, not for the first time.

They proceeded more slowly, Heydt keeping his eyes on the road. "And tonight? Are you going to your lover again?" he asked quietly.

"My—" She stopped, cheeks warming as she realized: she'd been about to explain that actually Eric and she weren't yet—*quite*— But there was no reason on earth she should clarify that point to this man. "Um, no. Actually, I'm driving to Trueheart tonight to see my best friend, Jules Hansen. We went to high school together."

She smiled, thinking of Jules, then transferred the warmth to her companion. "I can't tell you how grateful I am, Miguel, to have the use of your truck. I've never been able to come and go when I pleased before. This is marvelous." There, she'd used his name for the first time. She liked the sound of it on her tongue; a name to be murmured, all resonant, rounded syllables, not spiky and hard like Eric.

His dark eyes flicked her way, saying that he'd not missed this first occasion, but his only answer was a smile.

They unhitched the trailer at the gate to the Sweetwater Flats pasture. Not the prettiest ride on the ranch, to Risa's mind. But then, he was a rock hound, she reminded herself. If that was what he was after, he'd find plenty in this section. "So I'll be back here at midnight," she reminded him.

"We'll be waiting." He shut the driver's door for her and stood, fingers curled on the window frame, head cocked slightly in thought. "And Risa, if it happens that you are late, visiting with your friend, please don't worry or hurry. It's most important to drive safely, okay?"

"All right." *And you be careful, too.* But somehow it felt wrong to say that.

Or maybe to feel it. So she simply nodded, waved and drove off into the gold-and-purple twilight.

AT MIDNIGHT, they rendezvoused as planned. "A good visit?" Miguel asked, opening her door and seeing her smile.

"An excellent one! Lots of food—we cooked supper instead of going out. Lots of girl talk—oh, and look what Jules made me." She pulled her hair up and back to show him a dangling earring constructed of silver and turquoise beads and parrot feathers.

"Muy bonita," he agreed, his gaze caressing her ear and cheek and neck. "The jewelry also is very nice. She is an artist?"

"She is." And unless Risa had misheard, that had been a compliment. She looked away and bit her lip, realizing she ought to snub him. Just imagine what Ben would say if he caught her flirting with one of his haying crew!

"And now, you'll pardon the hurry—" Big hands closed gently on her waist and he half lifted, half drew her off the high seat of the truck.

"Oh! You don't have to—" Whirling back to face him, she braced herself automatically on his broad shoulders as he lowered her feet to the ground.

"But it's past Jackhammer's bedtime," he continued easily.

They were standing *way* too close—so close his big boots straddled her feet. She could feel the warmth of his body as if she faced a blazing stove. For a second, his grasp seemed to tighten, and she stared up at him wide-eyed and dismayed. *What are you—*

"So if you'll excuse me?" Releasing her, Miguel pivoted slightly so that she was no longer trapped between him and the pickup.

"Of course." Snatching her hands from his shoulders, she squeezed past him, then stood to one side, perplexed and fuming, while he backed his truck neatly up to the trailer and proceeded to hitch it in place. What was going on here? Was she crazy? One moment she thought for sure he meant to kiss her—the next, he was ignoring her completely. She stood, eyes narrowed, arms tightly crossed, toe tapping, while he murmured Spanish curses and words of endearment to his stupid horse, then loaded him as if he'd done it a hundred times before.

Her skin had come alive where he'd touched her, as though his hands still gripped her. The sensation trickled downward; her stomach was swirling, like a kettle coming to a boil. This was ridiculous and...and totally inappropriate.

"Ready?" Miguel's glance was cool and even a little impatient, nothing romantic about it at all—as if she were a slow child, holding him up.

She stomped around the pickup and climbed in on the passenger side. Sat as close to her door as she could, knees clamped together, eyes straight ahead, chin tipped.

"We had a good night, too," he remarked after a mile or so. "I traced the course of the creek all the way up to the Trueheart Hills. Did you know that for the last quarter mile or so before the mountains, the water runs clean?"

"No, I didn't," she admitted, grudgingly interested. "But why do you care?"

"Who says I care? It's just...strange."

What was strange was that one touch could disturb her

so, and that she could misinterpret it so completely. She must have, because now Miguel was acting entirely himself—polite, amiable, intelligent, but slightly aloof. A hired hand who recognized the barrier between himself and his boss's daughter as well as she did.

Reflexively her hand went to her throat and she drew out the fine gold chain that hung there. Eric's ring. She'd taken to wearing it during the day as a pendant, since it didn't fit under her riding gloves. Tonight she'd shown it to Jules, who'd swooned over its size and brilliance. Jules had agreed to come to Denver in October for the wedding. And to be her bridesmaid, just as they'd fantasized way back in ninth grade. Risa slipped the ring over her little finger and turned it this way and that to catch the moonlight shining in her open window.

"Your engagement ring?" Miguel inquired as he slowed, then made the turn under the ranch's name board.

"Yes." She leaned closer and held it up for him to see. "Isn't it lovely?"

"*Sí*, but it's the wrong stone for you. The man lacks *imaginación*, doesn't he?"

Stung, she slid away. "What makes you say that?"

"Only that you should have fire opals, to match your hair and eyes."

She shrugged. "Speaks a rock hound." Tucking the ring back into the neck of her shirt, she frowned out the window, wondering in spite of herself what a fire opal looked like.

"I have a favor to ask," he said as they crossed the bridge.

And she was in no mood to grant him one! Which was silly; he'd done nothing wrong, really, even if he didn't like her ring. "So?"

"Tomorrow I change duties. No more hay, *gracias a Dios*. I'm the ranch mechanic from now on. Which means

I work when I choose. So I'd like to ride in the daylight tomorrow. May I have the use of this trailer?''

How did he get away with setting his own hours? No one else around Suntop did. ''You must be quite the mechanic,'' she said, amused in spite of herself.

''But of course. But about the trailer?''

''Sure—if I can have your truck tomorrow night.''

''To visit...Durango?''

''Sí.'' But not to visit poor Eric, who was finding, to his exasperation, that his boss expected more than forty hours a week from him—even if they offered his services pro bono to the community. But as long as Risa had use of a vehicle, she was going to revel in it. She meant to take Tess shopping tomorrow night, then out to a movie.

''Durango again—what a good and dutiful *esposita* you'll make,'' Miguel teased.

Esposa was wife; *esposita,* little wife. Risa clamped her teeth on a retort. Strange. Before, she'd thought him... appealing. But tonight she didn't like this man at all.

CHAPTER NINE

MORNING FOUND them both at the gate to the home pasture, calling their respective mounts by rattling oats in a can. Jackhammer gave Miguel a warmer welcome than Risa did, but then, perhaps she didn't like carrots, he reflected as he shared a second one with the chunky gelding.

Or perhaps—more likely—he'd pushed her too hard last night. But Miguel could think of no faster way to claim her attention than to put her off balance, then keep her that way.

And time was of the essence. Yesterday Tankersly had told him, among other things, that Foster might not have bedded her yet.

To Miguel, this seemed impossible. Preposterous. To see Risa was to bed her; already she ruled his dreams. And if he'd been engaged to her? *Katy, bar the door!* as Harry used to say.

Still, a man could hope—might even pray, he told himself, as he tied Jack alongside her palomino to the hitching rail outside the tack room. He ducked inside just in time to whisk her saddle out from under her hands.

"Hey!" she cried, but he was halfway out the door already.

He stood by her mare, placidly inspecting the sky, when she stomped out of the barn to glare at him.

"I can saddle my own horse," she growled, arranging the saddle pad on Sunny's back.

"*Sí*, but why should you when I'm around?" He set her saddle atop the mare, then pulled it up into position, just behind her withers.

"Wrong—take if off!"

Ah, rubia, *you've unsheathed your claws this morning.* He cocked his head quizzically, but complied. She fussed with the blanket again, then fixed him with a stern eye. "*Never* pull a saddle up your horse's back. You'll rub his hair the wrong way, maybe start a sore. Now, hold it *above* Sunny's withers, then drag it down into place."

"Like so?"

"Exactly so." She nudged him aside with a sharp little elbow in his ribs and tightened her own cinches.

Smiling to himself, he sauntered around to Jackhammer—examined his back when she wasn't looking, and was relieved to find no sores. "So where do you ride this morning?"

She gave him *nada* but the back of her head as she rearranged the contents of her daypack into her saddlebags. "Oh, here and there. I'm out for some photos."

"Ah, I'd forgotten your camera. Then there's something I should show you. It would be a great shot."

"What?"

"*Momentito.*" He saddled Jack as quickly as he could, threw a measure of oats in the trough next to the rail to keep him happy, then jerked his head toward the largest hay shed. "This way."

She followed him warily, not walking beside him as she would have yesterday, but still, snared by her curiosity. He'd have to remember that.

"Up there." He nodded at the ladder that led into the dim realms of the loft. "That is, if you're not afraid of heights," he added with wicked innocence.

"Ha."

He stood for a moment, turned to hot stone by the sight of her tight little rear undulating up the ladder—then he went after her in three tigerish strides, the blood pounding a jungle beat in his ears.

As he swung up onto the loft planks, he made himself stop—stood there until he'd regained his breath and his sanity. *This is not your woman yet,* he reminded himself. Tankersly might think she was a pawn to be traded at his pleasure, but Miguel was no such fool. But, *ay,* she did turn his head.

"So…" Risa revolved slowly in the warm fragrant dusk, surveying the bales stacked to the sloping tin roof. "What did you want to show me? The sunbeams and shadows?"

"You're right. It's very beautiful up here." Where the sun sifted through a crack or a nail hole, shafts and dots of sunlight spangled the dimness. Motes of dust gleamed like drifting fireflies. "But no, what I meant was up here. Be very quiet now." He climbed a rough stairway of sweet-scented bales to a high platform of hay. The horizontal vents in the rough-hewn triangular end wall let in light and good air. "*¿Mamacita?*" he called in a coaxing voice. "*No tienes miedo. ¿Meeeorrr?*"

"What are you—" Risa's shoulder brushed his as she knelt beside him to peer into the space between two bales. "*Ohhhh!*" All sharpness was gone from her voice as she crooned in delight. "Oh, you clever thing, you!"

"She is." Miguel smiled down at the nursing barn cat and her brood of five kittens, which squirmed and butted her belly. "She'd been waddling around all week like a little *fútbol,* but watching us, oh, so closely. The minute we finished stacking this loft, it was hers. I didn't see her for a day—I'd been feeding her table scraps—so I came looking."

And Risa was looking at him—really meeting his eyes—

for the first time this morning. He felt an easing of tension, something like laughter stirring around the heart. *Is this all it takes to get back in your graces, then—a scrawny tabby cat?*

He sat back on his heels while Risa introduced herself to the mama. It was good; she had a way with animals. He liked that she didn't presume. Once her finger had been gingerly sniffed and had passed inspection, she was graciously permitted to stroke the tabby's creamy throat and dark spine. When the cat resumed purring and licking her young, Risa pulled her camera from its case.

Miguel settled back against a bale. She was very serious about this. He had no idea if her photos would be any good, or only sweetly sentimental. But she took great pains to get the shot she wanted, framing it carefully, considering before she snapped. Moving high or low, nearer or farther away. He laughed softly to himself, even as the muscles tightened in his groin and thighs as she lay full-length on her stomach and wriggled to within inches of the mama cat—who looked up from the curled forepaw she was licking in mild astonishment.

Click!

"That one I'd like to see when you get your film back," he told her.

Risa leaned on one elbow and looked over her shoulder, tossing the silky hair from her eyes. "I develop my own film. And print it."

"You mean in a darkroom?"

"Where else?"

So she was more than a lily of the field. He was impressed. Would genuinely have liked to see her create images out of a bath of chemicals. But he could think of no way to ask that she invite him up to the Big House and show him. As far as she was concerned, he still had hay sticking out of his hair. *And how do I change that?*

Because a woman didn't consider a man if she thought he was beneath her. Oh, she might lie under him for a night, but she'd see him as her stud—then go home to her husband, who wore a suit and drove a Mercedes.

Restlessly he rolled to his feet. He should be seeking his own fortune, not sitting here wishing and wanting.

Lithe as a cat, Risa rolled over entirely onto her back and looked up at him through her camera. "Where are you going?"

Away from women who drive me loco! "Riding."

Click! Just like that she'd taken his picture.

"Don't do that." He rapped the sole of her boot with his toe. To be captured inside a camera...reduced to an image she could hold in her hand...

Click!

"Hey, I mean it!" He crouched to escape the lens, but the damn eye of the camera followed him. "*Brujita,* cut it out!"

"Why?" She laughed, bold behind her mechanical mask. *Click!*

"Because I don't like it." Catching her booted ankles, he flipped her neatly onto her stomach and grinned when she yelped in surprise. "Isn't that reason enough?" And now he'd really better go, before he found himself wrestling her in the hay. He spun away and was halfway down the ladder before she rolled over and sat up.

"Jerk!" she called after him—and shot him one last time before he could duck below the floor planks.

Tankersly was right. *Stubborn* didn't begin to describe the vixen!

She caught up to him outside a few minutes later as he

led Jackhammer toward the trailer. "I...shouldn't have done that. Truce?"

Those wide golden eyes could melt a man's anger. He twitched his shoulders. *"Supongo."*

"I suppose?"

"You suppose right." He led Jack into the trailer, tied his halter.

"Where are you off to?" she asked as he came down the ramp.

"Same place. Sweetwater Flats. When do you need my truck—this evening?"

She kicked the dust with her toe. "I was thinking five o'clock, if that's all right. But Miguel?" She scuffed the dirt again. "I haven't ridden the flats in ages. Mind if Sunny and I come along?"

He shrugged, elaborately casual. "If you like."

ONCE THEY'D LED their horses through the gate to the Sweetwater Flats, then mounted, Miguel expected her to ride off alone. She'd barely spoken to him throughout the drive—had simply stared out her window, nibbling on her lush bottom lip, making him wish he could do that for her.

"So we meet here at this gate at four?" he suggested, turning Jack toward the east.

"Ye-es." She sat her palomino and frowned after him, then called, "so where are you going?"

"A las montañas." He urged Jack into his bone-crushing jog.

"The Trueheart Hills? It'll take you all day at a trot. Can't you gallop yet?"

"Only when I hold the horn. And I'm not doing that till we get over that rise, where you can't see me."

"So macho!" she teased. "Come on, chicken. Let's run!" And her golden mare shot off from a standing start.

Horse and rider floated close by him, silver mane and coppery mane streaming in the wind of their passage. He sat transfixed by the sight—till Jack whinnied, threw up his head and plunged in pursuit.

"Whoa!" But Jack had the bit in his teeth. He braced his thick neck and hammered on; might as well try to stop a cement truck without brakes. So Miguel grabbed the horn, gritted his teeth and committed himself to the chase.

On she led them, over hill, down a long ragged slope, dodging brush and trees and outcrops of sandstone—and there, a dike stained with limonite.

Laughing, she looked back to see he still followed. "Let go of that *horn,* cowboy!" She came to a dry wash, plunged down its sandy bank and disappeared.

"*¡Brujita linda!*" But Jackhammer was undaunted. He slithered down on his haunches, then charged along the winding course of the arroyo, apparently more determined to catch their tormentors than his rider.

A sandy bluff reared out from one bank ahead, and Risa and Sunrise vanished beyond it. Jack pinned back his ears and stretched from a lope into a run—and just like that, his pace smoothed out. Miguel let out a whoop. Now they were flying!

They flew around the bend, to find Risa had reined in her mare and sat waiting—his chance to take the lead. Digging his heels into Jack's ribs, Miguel rushed down upon her. He dared to let go the horn and lift his hat in a mocking salute as they thundered past.

"Miguel—*no!*"

Jackhammer saw the problem first—a logjam of dried trees and tangled flotsam blocked the wash beyond from bank to bank. "*¡Mierda!*" Tossing his hat, Miguel hauled on the reins, but already Jack had sat down on his haunches and thrown out his forelegs in a desperate slide. Sand billowed chest-high. Risa shrieked. Not ten feet from the brutal wall, they plowed to a jolting halt—at least, Jack did.

Momentum carried Miguel on in a perfect somersault over his horse's lowered head. Still clutching the reins, he landed flat on his back in the sand. *"Oooff!"* No air available anywhere in the world. Gasping like a beached flounder, he stared blankly upward at blue sky—and a long, hairy, upside-down face—Jackhammer, giving him a deadpan horse smirk.

"Miguel! Oh, Lord, oh, gee—oh, I'm *sorry!"* Risa flew out of the blue, to kneel beside him, patting and tracing the shape of his bones. "Are you all *right?* Where do you hurt? Can't you *talk?"*

He sucked in his first blessed breath and blew it out in a laugh. *"¡Dios!* Am I still alive?" Or perhaps this was heaven, complete with remorseful angel. She was running her hands down his thigh. "Stop," he commanded. He'd embarrassed himself enough for one day. Any more of this touching...

But men on their backs are not taken seriously. She took hold of his other ankle and worked her way up. He sighed and decided to submit gracefully, then grimaced when she skipped over his crotch, moving on to examine his ribs, instead. Perhaps Tankersly was right and she was still a virgin.

But not for much longer if she didn't desist! As she reached his collarbone, he caught her wrists. "Stop. Bad enough that you break my neck. Then you tickle me to death?"

"Your *neck!* Is it—"

"It's fine." As was the rest of him, he thought, now that he could breathe again. Or if not fine, at least functional. Very functional. His thumbs fanned the velvety skin of her bare wrists. Her bones were as delicate as a fawn's; funny how big and strong that made him feel. Holding her, he could have spread his arms wide and drawn her down upon him like a starfish. Held her there at his pleasure while he plundered her lips of their honey. He sighed regretfully and let her go. "Truly, everything but my pride is fine."

After that, Risa refused to go her own way. She rode close beside him, watching him anxiously for belated damage. At last Miguel gave up trying to reassure her that he'd live, and he went about his business.

Which was to walk the creek bed from the foothills west, till he found where the water changed from clear to oily. She tagged along even there, wandering ahead of him down the cut, since he went too slowly for her taste. She'd take photos of this and that, then pause to look back with a tiny frown drawing her dark eyebrows together, as he scrutinized the banks, inch by inch.

Finally she settled on a high, water-smoothed boulder as he approached. "Are you looking for fossils?"

He tapped at a crack in the stone with his hammer, but it proved dry. "Well, they can be helpful for dating the sediments. For instance, you don't find trilobites after the Permian period."

She bit that delectable lower lip, met his eyes and frowned. Lifted her camera and aimed it at him.

Like a mask, he thought again. "Don't," he warned mildly.

"Why do you care how old the sediments are?" she demanded from behind her blockade.

"Did you know that this part of the world was once covered by ocean? No, more than once."

She lowered the camera. Narrowed her foxy eyes at him. "Vaguely. So?"

"So oceans deposit layers of mud and organic matter. Fish die, plankton fall to the bottom, algae and seaweed drift down. Coral and clams. Starfish and shark bones. Imagine years and years and millions of years of all that, building up on the bottom of the ocean.

"The mountains push up to the sky, then the wind and water grind them away again. Their sand is washed down the rivers to the sea and it covers this mud. The seas withdraw to the west and east and the land dries out. Volcanoes rise and rain down ash. Continents drift and bump one another and the land buckles and folds like a rumpled blanket. The seas rise again and lay down another fifty million years of mud and organic matter."

She tilted her heart-shaped face. "You're not just a rock hound."

"I'm not a 'just.'" He'd come to her boulder and stood looking up at her. *This I swear to you. Whatever I'll be— whatever I'll be to you—I'll never be a 'just.'*

"You're a...geologist?" she guessed.

"A geologist trained me, but I hadn't time or money for schooling. I earned my education in the field." Miguel had decided, he couldn't say when, that he'd have to tell her. A woman could not admire a man, could not desire him, if first she did not respect.

"So you have these marine beds covered by millions of years of rock and mud and sand. The weight of the world presses down on this organic matter, and pressure creates heat. And given millions and millions of years of pressure and heat, that murk and mud turns to..." He lifted his eyebrows. *Who am I?*

"Oil..." she said slowly. "You're an oilman?"

"A wildcatter." He inclined his head half an inch as if he'd been knighted. Maybe he had. "A wildcatter seeks oil where it has never been found before."

Her fingers rose to her delectable mouth. Sorrowfully she

shook her head. "If my father finds out, Miguel...you're history!"

"Oh?" It was hard not to smile. "We'll see about that." His eyes roved the cut ahead and found what he wanted. A narrow crescent of sandy beach, shadowed by an overhanging cliff. "But for now, what about lunch?"

Frowning faintly to herself, she followed him to his chosen site, where she drew an old poncho from her daypack and spread it on the sand.

He shrugged out of his own pack, then waited, unwilling to presume, till she glanced up at him, smiled and patted the spot beside her. She retreated to her troubling thoughts again as he sat.

Miguel unwrapped the generous ham and cheese and tomato sandwich he'd made himself back at the bunkhouse and set it between them. "I should have cut this in half. But will you share?"

"Um—sure. If you'll take some of mine." She unzipped a coldpack and brought out a blue cloth napkin, a container of yogurt, a spoon and a bunch of grapes—then looked up in surprise as he burst out laughing.

"You call that lunch?"

"What else would you call it?"

"Girl food."

"So I'm a girl."

"*Sí*, I might have noticed that." He was sorry she'd taken his words as an insult, sorrier still once she'd dipped her spoon into the yogurt and lifted it to her mouth. He wanted to *be* that spoon, caressed by her tongue! And if he didn't focus on something else at once... He ate his half of the sandwich, inwardly reciting the dusty geologic ages, from the present back into the past: Quaternary, Tertiary... He stopped with the Cambrian and set her share of the sandwich before her on its unfolded tinfoil.

She wrinkled her nose in disdain. "Guy food." Dipped her spoon in the yogurt.

"Most assuredly. But in the interests of foreign exchange?" He captured her wrist as she lifted the loaded utensil. "Sometimes strangers have more to teach one than do friends. At least, I've found it so." Holding her more with his eyes than his fingers, he gently conveyed the yogurt toward his mouth. "May I?"

Her golden eyes seemed to darken as the pupils expanded; her shoulders jerked in the tiniest of shudders. "If…you like."

I like. He could feel her pulse surging between his fingers—his own thudding in his ears like a wave breaking on a midnight shore. He closed his lips over coolness…sweetness…tartness…the silken slide of polished metal… With a small growl of satisfaction, he relinquished the spoon, then her wrist, but not her gaze. "The very finest of girl food."

Color dawning in her cheeks, Risa tore her eyes away. "You're just being polite." She set the container, still a third full, by his knee. "But if you want more…"

"Only if you'll have some sandwich." He lifted it and offered it to her lips. *Would you eat from my hand,* pasión?

She turned her head aside. "*No,* thank you."

The silence spoke more than words, and as it stretched, her hand crept toward the open collar of her shirt. She fumbled for, then found, the narrow gold chain that dangled there—and twined it twice around a fingertip.

CHAPTER TEN

HE'D PUSHED too far and now he must retreat. Miguel lay back and tipped his hat over his face. "A short siesta, I think." In truth, he was still hungry, but she'd share his sandwich or he'd leave it for the coyotes; her refusal had raised a point of honor. Smiling wryly as his stomach protested that decision, he wriggled his shoulder blades farther into the powdery sand beneath the poncho. Somewhere up in the hot, bright air, a crow was announcing their trespass, yelling *"¡Vaya! ¡Vaya!"*

Lulled by the sound, perhaps he'd drowsed off, or nearly so, when she spoke at last. "Heydt."

"Es como me llama," he agreed from beneath his hat.

"But…you're from Mexico, aren't you?"

"Originally, *sí.* But my father, Johann Heydt, came from Germany." He sighed and stretched luxuriously to his full length. "Came seeking gold, but found another treasure, instead. *Mi madre." At eighteen, she would have been as beautiful as you, lindissima, with eyes to drown a man.*

"He was a prospector?"

"Of a sort. A dreamer, an explorer, out for his fortune." *Truly his blood runs in my veins.* Miguel scrounged in a pocket of his jeans and drew out his lucky piece. "He was seeking more of these." Their fingertips touched as she took the gold coin. "A gold coin from the treasury of Maximilian, the Austrian duke Napoleon III made emperor of Mexico in 1864. My great-great—I forget how many greats—grandfather was one of his mercenaries." Lazily he spun her the story: the unwelcome, well-meaning ruler and his faithful wife, Carlota, naive outsiders whose reign was doomed from the start. The promises, the betrayals, the bloody downfall of their empire—the gaudy kingdom in ruins. Rich spoils for the taking in those final days of revolt and confusion and flight.

"This coin came down through the Heydt family, from father to son, along with a torn and scribbled map marking the place where a fortune, forty donkey loads of such coins and bullion and plate, supposedly lay buried. So my father at twenty-one, instead of sensibly teaching at the university as had his father and his father before him, came looking for treasure."

"And did he find it?" Risa's low voice sounded nearer. Perhaps she'd stretched out on the sand beside him.

Miguel shrugged. "We'll never know. If the map was not a joke, a fraud, it seemed to indicate that the gold lay buried in a cave somewhere in the mountains, above the valley where my mother's family owned a small peach farm. He would rent a room from her father, is how they first met, to use as his headquarters while he searched.

"After they married, once they'd started a baby—me— my father took a job in the town, at the school, teaching mathematics. But when he could, he continued his search, until one day in my seventh year..." As always, the shaft of pain surprised him. It had happened so very long ago. Another lifetime. He swallowed and went on lightly. "He went up into the mountains...and he never came home again."

"I'm sorry!" she whispered very close to his ear.

He fisted his hands so he wouldn't reach blindly for her. "The *murmuradors* of the town said that he'd tired of my mother and gone sneaking back to Germany. But I can still remember my parents' laughter in the kitchen…how he'd lift her up to the ceiling and spin her around, whenever he returned from the hills.''

"They loved each other."

"More than all the gold in all the world. He'd tell her that he'd come back from his searching someday to put a crown of gold and diamonds on her head. That he'd take her to see Paris, London, Berlin… So whatever happened up there…" In those high, wild mountains to a man alone. Bandidos, *a rock fall, the bite of a serpent*… Miguel opened his eyes to replace those images with blue sky and the fiery waterfall of Risa's hair as she leaned on one elbow beside him. "He did not desert her."

"No, of course he didn't." After a while, Risa touched the back of his hand gently with the coin.

He rotated his hand, drew one fingertip from her tender wrist, over her soft palm, out her graceful fingers to the coin, which she relinquished. "So…and now, back to work." He rolled easily to his feet and reached for his pack.

"Black gold being your treasure?"

"What can I say? I'm the son of my father." He shrugged into the shoulder straps, then held out a hand. She hesitated, then accepted it, and came up lightly before him. He wondered, if he lifted her up to the heavens and twirled her, would she laugh?

"SO, WHAT, precisely, are you looking for?" Risa asked as they started off downriver.

"A shining rainbow on the water? Perhaps a trickle of a dark liquid—oil—oozing from out of a crack. A black sand that looks like greasy tar and smells like hydrocarbons. Any of these would make me a happy man."

He seemed happy already. Perhaps that was the heart of Miguel's attractiveness, more than his looks, more than his self-confidence, more than his sexy vitality. He looked around the world and seemed to find it good, as if he expected to discover...treasure around the next corner. *And maybe he does*.

Pity that Ben would never let him drill for oil if he did find signs of it. She should tell him how her father despised miners and prospectors. It was a Tankersly tradition that went back to the 1880s; her ancestors had guarded their mineral rights jealously from the very start.

But that warning could wait for tomorrow. Somehow she didn't want to spoil this day. "That doesn't sound so hard. I'll take the other bank, okay?" She stepped from boulder to boulder to cross the narrow creek.

"*Bueno*." He'd dropped to his heels to dip a finger in the water and bring it to his tongue.

"Miguel, you shouldn't drink from the creeks anywhere in these mountains! It can make you sick."

He shrugged. "Occupational hazard. And I'm healthy as that excuse for a horse I ride. What makes me sick is that I can't find the *maldito* seep. It's got to be somewhere between here and that boulder." He nodded to a massive red rock the size of a Cadillac on end, which leaned out from the right bank, perhaps two hundred yards downstream.

They inched along, Risa finding it hard to go as slow as her companion, who combed every inch of bank and bed.

"So..." he said after a while, scanning the water's edge. "Once upon a time, you told me that you didn't learn to ride till you had fourteen years. But how could that be? Were you ill?"

"No...I lived with my mother in Los Angeles. There were no horses there."

"Your parents were divorced?" He glanced up at her, then quickly down at the rocks again.

"They…never married." Funny that she could tell him this. She'd told Jules, her best friend since the ninth grade. And Eric, of course, though only months after they'd begun dating.

Yet she'd given her secret to Heydt all in a day.

"They met in Las Vegas. She was a chorus girl at one of the casinos. He'd come to town to see the National Finals Rodeo. They…hit it off." She shrugged and smiled. "But I guess it wasn't anything lasting." *I was the only thing that came of it. Call me Oops!*

"But you ended up here." Heydt crossed the stream to her side in two lazy strides, eyes fixed on his stepping stones. Casually he bent to examine a rock she'd passed by. He rolled it over with his hammer, made a face, then straightened and drifted on alongside her.

"Yes…" She knelt, ran her fingers through wet sand, but it didn't feel oily. *Why tell him? It's none of his business. Hurts to say it, and yet…* "She d-died of an overdose when I was fourteen. Pills and alcohol. She'd…always run with a wild crowd. Film folk—directors, actors, cameramen. She wanted in the worst way to break into movies—she was really pretty, I think. And she loved to party."

He'd come to stand beside her, his knee almost brushing her shoulder. "I'm sorry."

She shrugged and tried to summon a smile, though she didn't look up. "It was long ago and far away."

"And still *te dueles*." His knuckles brushed her cheekbone in a butterfly stroke.

And still it hurts you. "*Sí.*" She shrugged again, blinked back the tears and said with determined cheerfulness, "But meantime, I don't see a rainbow on the water. I don't see an ooze of any kind. I think you're dreaming, Miguel. There's no oil at Suntop." *You should go. Should go quickly!* The touch of his fingers against her cheek stayed with her. Like a ray of sunlight, like a coin of antique gold.

"Ah, but there is. I can feel it in my hands." He turned his big, hard brown hands palms-up. "It tingles—itches—when my luck is in. We had a blowout once, on a well near the New Mexico border. I told Harry I must have been bit by fire ants or some such, that morning before it blew." He laughed softly to himself. "Last time I ever doubted these *manos*."

His hands were nicked and scarred and callused, but oddly beautiful, in the way all fine tools have grace and power. Hands of pride and competence, very clean. Altogether different from Eric's smooth unblemished fingers, with their buffed nails and his Yale class ring. Her thoughts swerved hurriedly aside to— "Harry?"

"Harry Kingman. The geologist who trained me. I apprenticed myself to him when I was fifteen. He taught me everything I know about oil—discovering it, putting the deal together and finding the money, drilling for it."

She'd stared at his hands too long. Breaking away, she moved on. "At fifteen? That's very young. How did you meet?"

He laughed again. "It's a long story. At fifteen I set out to make my fortune in the world. I'd left the town of my family, Dos Duraznos, hitchhiked north for three days to the border, hoping for work in one of the *maquiladoras,* the factories there. But there was no work and I didn't mean to go home empty-handed. So I hid myself in the trunk of Harry's car when he came across to eat at Piedras Negras. Harry always had a weakness for green enchiladas...."

TWO DAYS LATER, driving Miguel's truck to Durango to meet Eric, Risa still smiled at the story of a fifteen-year-old Heydt popping out of the trunk of Harry Kingman's old convertible.

"It was one of those wonderful old monsters from the sixties, with tail fins like a shark's—all chrome and two-tone colors, aqua and white. I was in love when I saw that car!" The Texan had given Miguel ten dollars to guard the car from thieves, while he and his loud, laughing friends—other men off the same oil well, as the boy later learned—went into a restaurant.

Miguel had watched the car faithfully, but he'd also jimmied the lock to its trunk. He slipped into this compartment at the last minute, tied its lid shut with a bit of wire. Covering himself with the greasy tarp he found there, he'd prayed the border guards would not search this special car, his chromed chariot to a new life.

What must it feel like, to throw yourself into an unknown world without a backward glance? Risa wondered. As intelligent as Heydt clearly was, surely he'd realized the risks—being caught by the customs agents at the border was the least of the dangers.

But apparently there'd been risks in staying, as well. Miguel had glossed over that part, but clearly things had not been well at home. His aging grandfather had fallen ill and lost his peach farm a few years after the disappearance of Johann Heydt. The family—his grandparents, his mother, his baby sister, Miguel—had had to depend on the charity of cousins—kindly people, but poor themselves.

Like so many before him, Heydt had looked north for salvation.

And he'd been lucky enough to find it. After miles and hours of dust and fumes and teeth-rattling unpaved roads, the car had come to a halt at last. Miguel had thought, once the vehicle stopped, that he'd wait till all was quiet, then slip away discreetly into the dark, none the wiser for his passing. But the convertible had been parked in a place where, seemingly, men did not sleep: before the doghouse of a drilling well.

He'd cracked the lid of the trunk to stare, appalled and awestruck, at the hellish scene—way past midnight the platform of the drilling rig was lit by glaring yellow lights. Men in hard hats labored and danced up there. Machines spun and rose and fell with an unearthly roar. The roughnecks were *tripping pipe*—hoisting a string of pipe two miles long out of the earth, unscrewing it every third muddy section, then stacking it in ninety-foot vertical lengths on the rig rack. Because somewhere two miles below the surface the drill bit lost its edge. Now it must be retrieved and replaced with a sharper one, then two miles of pipe lowered into the hole again, before drilling could continue.

"I was fascinated, watching them, but finally it came to me that this might go on forever and that the dawn was coming. I needed to go. They all looked so busy up there on the rig, I figured they'd never notice me. And that I was faster than any *gringo* in boots if they did happen to see me."

Slowly he'd raised the lid, unaware that Harry had been sitting on the doghouse steps off to one side for the past half hour, smoking a cigar and observing the lid of his trunk waver an inch up and down. Waiting, bemused, to see what creature would finally emerge.

Miguel had put one foot to the ground—and someone tall, swift and very strong had nabbed him by the collar. Had shaken him till he stopped struggling and yelping, then propelled him effortlessly up three steps and into the lit trailer. There his captor had leaned back against its only door, folded his arms and drawled in disgust, "Well, what d'ya know? If it ain't my dang car guard. Came back to my car and found you gone. I figured I'd thrown ten bucks to the wind."

"I was guarding it from the inside," Miguel told him defiantly, while he tucked in his shirttail and brushed himself off.

Harry tipped back his head and laughed, and that had been the beginning of their relationship. Which looked to be a short one, since the geologist swore he'd stuff the kid back in his trunk and drive him to where he'd found him, to Piedras Negras. "Might as well keep things simple." Harry had no more desire to deal with the immigration officers and their paperwork than his stowaway did.

But Miguel's expulsion would have to wait for the morning, since that night Harry had more important things on his mind. The drill bit had failed some twenty feet above the top of the Devonian reef where Harry fondly expected—prayed—he'd strike oil. He'd been two years putting this particular deal together, and he wasn't budging till they'd resumed drilling, then run the drill stem test on his prospective pay zone.

Meanwhile, he'd scrounged spare clothes from the smaller roughnecks for his charge, shown him the crew shower, then had a sandwich and soda waiting for him when Miguel shyly emerged, clean for the first time since he'd left home three weeks earlier.

And so it had gone from there. Harry had been outraged in the morning when he found that Miguel had damaged the lock on his trunk—even more outraged when the boy offered to pay for it with Harry's own ten-dollar bill. So Miguel had borrowed a file, found a few bits of metal and springs lying around the drilling site and rebuilt the lock from scratch.

And meantime, waiting for the results, there had been so many things to see around the rig. So many questions to

ask, so many things to learn. "There is a saying," Miguel
had told Risa, "that when you are ready, the teacher will
come. But I think, perhaps, it works both ways. When you
are willing to teach, the student comes. And *ay*, I wanted
to learn it all!"

Or perhaps, when a man is ready for a son, he comes?
Risa mused, driving through the outskirts of Durango. Miguel hadn't said if Harry had a family, but she suspected
not. Whatever the reason, the unlikely pair had clicked.
Miguel had realized that he'd found a fascinating, soul-
satisfying niche—if only he could cling to it. Not just a
job, but a calling. So he'd determined to make himself
indispensable to the geologist, and apparently he'd succeeded, rising through the years from a humble gofer and
car mechanic to Harry's cherished convertible, to a roust-
about on Harry's wildcat wells, to a roughneck, to a tool
pusher—whatever that was—to an informal geologist.

He'd have been working with the Texan yet, except that
six months ago, Harry had driven in from a well to a little
diner in Rocksprings, which he swore made the finest *enchiladas verdes* north of the Rio Grande. Driving back late
that night, bombing along in his big old convertible, with
the top down and a full moon high in the sky, he'd blown
out a left front tire and the car had spun—then rolled.

"Full of enchiladas and Dos Equis. No doubt smoking
a cigar. Figuring for sure he'd made a well," Miguel had
said, his wistful smile wavering for a second, then hard-
ening. "Harry would say there's worse ways to go."

But you miss him all the same, Risa told him silently as
she parked his truck and sat, looking up at the office building where Eric awaited her. For a moment its walls of steel
and stone seemed less real than the image in her mind...of
a young man standing up on the edge of a drilling platform,

searching the wide moonlit Texas plains for the headlights of a big old fin-tailed car...that would never come again.

THAT NIGHT the phone rang in the kitchen of the bunkhouse, where Miguel was playing poker. He held a hand fine enough to itch his palms—three aces, a pair of kings—and was calculating how much to raise the pot, when Willy answered, listened for half a minute, then turned with a sly grin. "For you, Heydt. A lady friend."

There was only one lady who knew to reach him at Suntop. Risa. She'd borrowed his truck and driven into Durango this evening to visit her *maldito* Mr. Mercedes. "Fold." He placed his cards facedown on the table and made himself walk casually to the phone, when he wanted to lunge for it. *¿Qué te pasa, Risa-Sonrisa?*

"*¿Bueno?*" he said cautiously, aware of the men around the table. Their eyes were fixed on their cards, their ears flapping.

"Miguel, this is *so* embarrassing!" Risa said, almost chattering. "But I can't start your truck. I was wondering if you had any ideas what might be—"

"Tell me where you are, and I'll be there."

"Oh, really, you don't have to—"

But she sounded relieved. "I'll be there quick as I can. Now *dígame*. How do I find you?"

CHAPTER ELEVEN

IT WAS NEARLY ELEVEN when Jake dropped him off on a street corner in Durango. "Sure this is the place?" The cowboy peered along a line of cars parked against the curb. "Where's your truck?"

"This'll do." It should be a block farther on, but Miguel saw no reason to expose Risa to the smirks and suppositions of the Suntop bunkhouse if he could avoid it.

"So go ahead. Play it close to your vest. Whoever she is, tell her she owes me a kiss!" Jake gave a good-natured wave and roared off, bound for the bar he'd been praising for the past twenty miles, where, he'd assured Miguel, there were more Buckle Bunnies on tap than Budweisers.

Down the road, Miguel found Risa sitting forlornly behind the wheel of his truck. "Risa, what are you doing out here? I told you I'd come to the door." With its sleek new condo buildings like the one before which his pickup was parked, it seemed a prosperous side of town. But still, she could have been molested.

"Oh, I…" Her voice trailed away and she shrugged. Her beautiful mouth drooped enchantingly. "I think maybe it's the battery. If you turn the key, it—"

"Move over." He stepped onto the dashboard and nudged her out of the way, then tried the key. *Nada,* not a wheeze, not a whirr. He swore to himself. A man who couldn't maintain his own wheels… But he would have sworn his old pickup ran like a Swiss pocketwatch. And he'd checked the oil, the fluids, the belts, the tires, before he left it for her this evening. *"Curioso."* He slid out from behind the wheel.

Peering under the hood, he stared for a moment, not believing, then straightened, came around to her open window. "Your Mr. Mercedes—"

"Eric!" she snapped, and crossed her arms tightly. She seemed harassed, flustered, looked more as if she'd spent an evening with her dentist than her *prometido.*

"Did your Errric try to fix my truck, by any chance, before you called me?"

"No. I mean he walked me out here when I was leaving, and when it wouldn't start, he offered suggestions, but—" She shook her head. "He didn't."

And did he leave you alone at some point this evening? Perhaps he told you he needed to fetch something from his own car. Just wait right there, querida. *I'll be back* en un momentito. *That's all it would have taken.* "Bueno, I need to…ask his advice, on this."

"If you mean about mechanics, he says there's no garage open anywhere in town this time of night."

"I'll check his phone book all the same," Miguel promised. "No, wait here, if you please, with the window rolled up and the door locked, okay? I'll be only a minute."

He rang the admittance bell in the foyer of the condo building until a slurred voice demanded, "Who is it? Risa?"

He held his silence and kept on jabbing.

"You're cute when you're mad, you know that, baby? But come on up. Glad you changed your mind." The buzzer sounded and the lock clicked on the inner door. Miguel took the stairs to the second floor two at a time.

He stood to one side of the peephole in the elegantly paneled mahogany door while he knocked. But it was unlocked without hesitation and Foster started speaking even as he opened it. "I told you it was too late to bother. Tomorrow I'll—" He stopped, gaping, nose to nose with Miguel. In one hand he clutched a bottle of champagne, in the other two crystal flutes.

"*Tonight* would be better." Miguel held out his hand, his fingertips nudging Foster's ribs. "My distributor cap, please." He watched the man blink too rapidly and a foolish grin come and go—ah, so his guess was correct.

The lawyer frowned, fumbled for a response, found one slowly; he smelled of whiskey. "W-what are you talking about? And what the devil are you doing here? I told Tankersly that if I ever met you again—"

"And now you have." Miguel caught his lapels with both hands and jerked him up on his toes—bounced him a couple of times. "And now it would be a shame if I had to mess up your pretty face, *rubio*. I don't like to hit drunks." Or dirty his hands on cowards. "But my distributor cap?"

Five minutes later he returned to his truck, his knuckles unscathed. Risa rolled down her window. "Did you find a garage that would send somebody?"

The day I need a "somebody" from some garage... He longed to cup her face with his palm but didn't. "No, but I had another idea. Give me a minute."

A minute under the hood was all it took. He screwed the cap back into place, connected its wires, shut the hood, then climbed in beside her. "Let's see if this works."

The engine purred and she let out a little crow of satisfaction that was reward enough for his trouble. "Home, then?" he said—and she smiled for the first time that night.

AS THE MILES PASSED in an oddly comforting silence, Risa felt her stretched nerves begin to loosen. Miguel drove with his window down, his elbow out, a faint smile curving his mobile mouth. He didn't bother her with questions she didn't care to answer.

She had questions enough of her own. Could Eric really have been plying her with booze tonight? It seemed that every time she'd taken a sip he'd refilled. And all those toasts he'd proposed: To the parking ticket case he'd succeeded in having the judge dismiss today. To their reunion after four days apart.

To their upcoming wedding. Her thoughts spun for a moment, trapped in an eddy of dismay and confusion, and Risa bit down hard on her lip. Everything that she'd been so sure of seemed to be shifting...fading... She'd found Eric rather irritating tonight, even before he'd drunk too much. He was *so* self-confident, almost to the point of arrogance, yet compared with the quiet, real-world competence of the man beside her—

She almost snatched at the radio knob. "How about some music?"

"Claro que sí." Miguel punched a tuning button and salsa filled the cab.

Suddenly her exasperation swerved his way. "You speak English as well as I do, Miguel. Why do you always—" *Bother me so?*

"But I don't want to—don't mean to—forget my own language, *cielito.* It's the language I think in, and I like to speak it with you. English is for practical purposes, for business and science. Drilling wells. But for poetry, for lovemaking—" A commercial had replaced the music. He twirled the knob till he came to an oldies station, playing "Ventura Highway." *"¿Mejor?"* Better?

"The salsa was fine," she had to admit. And she had no right to take out her worries on Miguel. "Thank you for coming for me tonight." Eric had tried so hard to persuade her to stay after the truck wouldn't start. But somehow, she just couldn't. The harder he'd pushed, the more she'd backed away. Tonight wouldn't have been the right night, the right way, for them to become lovers at last. She'd been so *relieved* to hear Miguel's voice over the phone.

"My pleasure," he said softly beside her. "And now I have a favor to ask. I seem to recall eating supper tonight, but my stomach swears this cannot be so. Could I perhaps buy you a burger?"

"Um, sure." She had no particular wish to return to Suntop. She was too restless to sleep and it seemed essential not to think tonight. A distraction would be very welcome. And after all, it wasn't even midnight yet, on a Friday night—a black velvety night glittering with stars.

Still, her lips parted for a second in a silent "Oh," when Miguel swung the pickup into the crowded parking lot of the Lone Star. She'd assumed he meant to go to Mo's, the truckstop on the far side of Trueheart. She'd still been underage last fall when she went off to college, and the Star was for a rougher, older crowd. She'd never set foot inside its door.

But now she was of age, and who better to make her feel safe in a roadhouse than Miguel Heydt? "Okay?" he asked quietly, searching her face as she took his extended hand and slipped down to the ground.

She didn't know if she liked that he could read her thoughts so easily or resented it. "Yes, it's just that I— Yes. It's fine."

The inside of the Lone Star was nothing like her and Jules's lurid imaginings back in high school. Booths with red vinyl cushions flanked two walls, each with a candle in a red glass cup, throwing flickering warmth and intimate shadows. A long, old-fashioned bar was lined mostly with men, most of them in Stetsons and boots. Among the bottles back of the bar loomed an enormous bull elk head, with a small Lone Star flag flying from each side of his magnificent rack. This gentle-eyed monster was flanked by a pair of stuffed jackalopes—those mythical amalgamated beasts with the heads of jackrabbits and the antlers of pronghorn antelopes.

Laughter and music rose to the rustic roof beams. The jukebox was playing Willie Nelson; a few couples leaned against each other as they swayed on a small dance floor at the dim back of the room. Jeers and cheerful catcalls came from the spectators gathered around a pool table at the other end of the bar.

And all the while, Miguel's hand at the back of her waist, warm, reassuring, guiding her through this cheerful bustle and confusion. They settled into a booth not far from the dance floor.

"What'll you have, honey?" A buxom waitress in jeans and checkered shirt bumped up against their table.

Miguel ordered burgers and fries for them both, in spite of Risa's protests. The waitress returned in minutes with draft beer in frosted mugs.

"So..." Miguel clinked his glass lightly against hers, filling the awkward silence. "You may congratulate me. Today I found the seep."

"Miguel, that's *wonderful!*" They hadn't talked since their day at Sweetwater Flats. Yesterday she'd ridden out with Tess, and this morning Miguel, truck and trailer were missing when she looked for him. But this evening his pickup was waiting for her, as promised, with its keys tucked under the seat and a note bidding her to drive carefully. "Where was it?"

"Oozing out behind that big red block of sandstone." They had turned back before searching that far. "And it's high-grade oil—very light. Paraffin-based, I'd say."

"That's good?"

"The best of news. The less refining it needs, the higher the price per barrel."

And now was the time she should warn him again about her father. That no matter the oil's value, Miguel's quest was in vain. But their waitress reappeared, plunking down their burgers, and he dug in with such gusto that Risa hated to spoil his pleasure. *I'll tell him tomorrow.*

Instead she found herself once again listening while he spoke of dips and rises in the sediments, and domes of rock holding pools of oil miles beneath the ground. He stopped eating frequently to gesture with his hands, or to construct a diagram of an anticline on the table—using knives and spare French fries—which showed her how the oil traveled, where it was trapped, how it typically floated on top of the ancient fossil water.

His eyes sparkled, his laughter rolled over her, his enthusiasm was contagious. He didn't just love the possibility of riches, Risa could see; he loved the rocks themselves—their colors and textures, the stories they told him, the mysteries they presented. "And you realize, of course, that at one time—oh, fifty million years ago—the Rocky Mountains were buried almost to their peaks with sand and dirt? Then, over the next ten million years, wind and water uncovered them again. Look up into the air, half a mile above your head—can you imagine it? There were rivers running up there, rushing along, where now there are only clouds."

"You're making this up!"

"I'm not, *corazón, te juro.* If there's one thing that geology teaches you, it's that everything changes. Wind will wear down mountains. Mud turns to rock. Oceans come and go, continents shift."

Corazón—didn't that mean "heart"? And if a continent could move half an inch a year, how long did it take the

human heart to shift? She swallowed painfully, groped for
the chain from which Eric's ring dangled inside her blouse,
but Miguel caught her wrist.

"You hear that song?" He inclined his head toward the
jukebox. "'Up on the Roof.' When I hear that song, I have
to dance. *Baila conmigo,* Risa."

"I'm a terrible dancer," she said, shaking her head.

But still holding her hand, he was already on his feet.
"To please me? I'll look like such a fool if I have to dance
by myself."

And he'd do it, too. She smiled and let him draw her out
onto the dusky floor, where most of the light was thrown
by the neon-lit jukebox. Stained-glass shadows... Other
couples drifting by in the dark. Deliciously hard, his forearm hooked around her waist, drawing her in till their legs
twined and their thighs brushed.

A wave of heat swept through her, then the tiniest of
shudders. *Oh, Miguel...*

His cheek caressed her hair; he'd drawn her right hand
to his heart. She rested her left on a shoulder like sun-
warmed rock. He was singing the words softly, in a husky,
happy baritone, about the stars, how they'd put on their
show for free, how two lovers could share them up on the
roof. The instruments took over from the singers in a lush
sweep of horns and violins, and he spun them both, his
strength and grace carrying them, floating them away someplace safe and exultant and starlit and utterly free.

Someplace where feelings replaced words, where a song
could mesh with the beat of your heart, and anything...anything at all was possible. Gradually the music
faded off into the stars, and still Miguel rocked her gently.
Eyes closed, she floated with her head tucked beneath his
chin, inhaling the stirring scent of his skin. *Do not wake
me. Don't break this spell!*

"Risa," he half whispered.

She sighed and lifted her face. "*¿Sí?*"

"Only this." He dipped his head and kissed her.

THE BOLT WAS FROZEN in place and there wasn't room between the truck's exhaust pipes to swing a breaker bar and free it the easy way. Which left only manpower. Bracing one foot on a tire and another on the chassis, Miguel got a two-handed grip on the wrench and threw heart and soul into the effort. "*Muevalo, hijo de—*" The bolt turned; the wrench slipped; his knuckles slammed into rusty metal and split. "*¡Ay, cabrón!*"

His head fell back against the barn floor, and he lay panting and wincing beneath the feed truck. As in the fairy tales, this beggar must suffer through all kinds of trials before at last he won the fair princess! And like some evil henchman to the king, Joe Wiggly seemed to be determined to try Miguel to his limits. The foreman had brought him this ancient, misbegotten four-wheel-drive truck, war surplus from some long-forgotten war, which the cowboys used to carry feed out to the cattle in winter. It needed everything from new shocks, to brakes, to a muffler, to an ignition, to a tune-up.

It needed junking, in Miguel's considered opinion. "Why a man with more money than God would keep *este aborto*…"

"First rule of money is when you have it, you don't throw it away. You squeeze it till it hollers," drawled Tankersly from somewhere out in the tool shed. "Take a break, Heydt."

"Gladly!" He grabbed the axle behind him and dragged the dolly he lay upon toward the light. Rolling out from under the truck's front bumper, he clasped his bleeding knuckles on his stomach. "Yes, sir?"

Tankersly grunted with amusement, then stiffly lowered himself to sit on the bumper and peer down at him sideways. "So…you're getting results, I hear."

"Do you?" He'd driven Risa up to the Big House at nearly two this morning. He'd helped her from his truck, then kissed her hand, since it was crystal clear that she was confused, in a turmoil, and would not have welcomed—no, would not have tolerated—a second kiss on the mouth.

But, oh, that first one! A man could be patient in the hope of more kisses like that one.

So either Tankersly had witnessed that brief, formal farewell or Risa had told him about their dance at the Lone Star. And somehow Miguel found that hard to believe. "How do you hear?" he asked bluntly.

The old man followed the swoop of a barn swallow up in the rafters. "Her snake of a knock-kneed lawyer phoned me 'bout an hour ago."

"No!" Foster seemed like a boy—like a petulant brat—to Miguel. Knowledgeable in terms of books and the law without a doubt, but in the ways of the real world? But even so, to run, wringing his hands, to his sweetheart's father? "Called you to complain?"

"Called t'ask me if I realized one of my hands was sniffing 'round my daughter. Loaning her his pickup." The rancher chuckled dryly. "I thanked him, but said I reckoned a smart boy from Yale could handle the competition."

"Or not."

"But then Foster said something else… Said, with your accent, he was wondering if you were in the States legal? Which happens to be a good question. Are you?"

Bright magical castles crumbling in the air. And it was Risa, more than his chance at Suntop oil, that he'd mourn. But what could he do? Miguel looked the old man straight in the eye. "No, sir, I'm not. The man I worked for in

Texas was sponsoring me, but we waited too late to start the process. Harry always hated the paperwork. And it takes years to complete. He died before I became a citizen.''

''Huh.'' Tankersly nodded to himself, bleak calculations moving behind his hooded dark eyes. ''Well, anyway, Foster tells me that he means to check you out. Says his friend, the attorney general in Denver, ought to be able to get a line on you. Maybe pass a tip to Immigration if it turns out you aren't a citizen.''

''Did he?'' A thread of ice wormed its way up Miguel's spine and his fingers clenched till they ached. Foster... If he did that, there would have to be a reckoning... Because it wasn't just his own life at stake here. He had a mother who depended on his earnings; a little sister who attended university only because he could pay...

''Yup, but I told him, 'fore he tried that, he'd better think again, and he'd better think lo-ong and hard. Foster told me, the first night Risa brought him home, that his long-term goal is politics. First state, then maybe someday national. The law's just the first step on that road.''

''Politics! I knew he was a black-hearted weasel.''

Tankersly laughed dryly. ''You see why I'm going to lengths to keep him out of the family tree, t'say nothing of the family bank accounts. But you can rest easy. I told Foster that before he asked his attorney general pal about you he better ask him about Ben Tankersly...how much I contributed to his last run for office. And to his boss's campaign. And his boss's boss's campaign. And about how much he reckons I'll give them next time, if he starts interfering in Suntop affairs.''

''Thank you,'' Miguel said quietly.

''Don't think I did it from the goodness of my heart. I expect help in return,'' the rancher growled. ''That going well?''

"It goes." No way would he reveal details of what passed between himself and Risa. The slow, shy dance they were dancing toward each other was theirs and theirs alone.

Tankersly laughed and pushed himself to his feet. "Stiff-necked son of a gun. I damn sure expect some results for my trouble."

"And when I have news for you, sir, I will tell you. But now, if I'm to earn my wages..." Miguel caught the edge of the bumper and rolled back beneath the truck.

CHAPTER TWELVE

IT WAS HIS DAY for interruptions. Not twenty minutes later, Miguel heard the chirp of a young girl's voice somewhere in the shed, followed by the lower, liquid notes of a woman. Risa-Sonrisa—a smile gathered around his own heart at the thought of her.

"I don't see him," Tess cried, her tennis shoes pattering into view, her voice dramatically disappointed. "He isn't *here*, Risa."

"Maybe he's...Miguel?"

"Vengo, cielito." He rolled out from beneath the truck. Tess yelped and shied like a startled colt, dropping an armload of books into the dust.

"Your pardon, Tess. I didn't mean to scare you." He sat up and his eyes met Risa's in a moment of laughter that was theirs alone, then he bent to help her little sister. Books on birds, on horses and... "Who is Nancy Drew?" There were three of these novels.

"A detective," Tess said solemnly, clasping the books to her narrow little chest. "I'm going to be a detective when I grow up. Catch cattle rustlers. Crack codes and solve mysteries."

"An excellent profession," he lauded as he rose, and now, how could he persuade her to go? Even a moment alone with Risa was unlooked-for treasure.

"We were wondering if we could perhaps borrow your pickup, for the afternoon," said Risa. "The library and some errands.'' Though she looked happy to see him, she seemed subdued, big eyed as a little owl, with shadows beneath her long lashes. As if the night had brought her no rest.

To see you all soft and tired like that in my bed—that morning cannot come soon enough! ''Of course,'' he said huskily. ''The keys are under the seat.''

''Hooray!'' Tess shot away, screeching, ''And *thank* you, Miguel!''

''She loves to read,'' Risa explained, glancing ruefully after her, then starting when she turned back—to find him standing as close to her as he dared. ''She's finished three books already this week.''

He could span her waist with his fingers, bend her to him like a young aspen. Taste the honey of her lips again. He'd dreamed of her all night—probably looked as hollow of eye as she did.

But she swallowed convulsively and took a step back and he clenched his hands. *Paciencia.* Risa was aware of him; that was sufficient for now.

''I have a favor to ask, as well,'' he said, instead. ''Tomorrow I need to scout other parts of the ranch. I hear there is a canyon—a very large canyon—to the north?''

''Blindman's Canyon, yes. It leads up into the foothills.''

''Would it be possible to draw me a map how to get there?'' He looked casually away, held his breath.

''Oh, yes, I suppose I could—'' Her own breath whispered out in a low, silky sigh. ''Well, actually…it's a little complicated, Miguel. Perhaps I should show you.''

His pulse shot away like a racehorse from the gate. ''If it's not too much trouble, I'd be grateful,'' he said with a fine show of indifference.

''I…no, it'd be no trouble at all.'' She licked her lips nervously and he nearly lost control. ''Early would be best.

It's a two-hour ride. Say, start at eight?'' When he nodded, she smiled. "Well, I... Then..." Her eyes were troubled, questioning, growing hurt as a child's when he didn't return her warmth.

His heart slammed in his chest, a beast trying to reach its mate. He held his ground. Broke away to look back at the truck, as if it was that which called him. "*Sí.* Then I'll see you tomorrow." *Mi pasión.*

"Right." Her soft footsteps traveled away from him, hesitantly at first, then faster and faster.

He blew out a slow breath, looked over his shoulder, found her gone. Missed her already. But *mañana...* He scratched a palm reflectively, glanced down at the spot where it tingled—and laughed. There in the warm dusk of the shed, he threw out his arms and spun on one foot—one slow, exultant turn—then lowered himself to the dolly. *¡Mañana!*

WHY HAD MIGUEL been so *cold?* Risa wondered all the way down into Trueheart, while Tess chattered on beside her. She couldn't think how she'd offended him, un-less...*because I didn't want to be kissed last night when we said goodbye?* Yet he'd kissed the back of her hand with such courtly tenderness...

She'd lain in bed for hours with that hand pressed to her lips, reliving that kiss when she should have been forgetting it. Trapped in such a sweet, sorrowful dilemma.

How could she feel like this about one man when she wore the ring of another? How in one...short...*week* could she have swung from certainty to utter confusion? And all the time, all the time, all the time while she tossed and turned and sought vainly for sleep, there was that moment when their lips had touched—and fused. Something like a bolt of lightning had slammed straight to her heart, cleaving

away all that had gone before. Leaving only that magical
moment when their mouths mated.

She had no idea what that kiss had meant to Miguel—
apparently not all that much, judging from his indifference
today. But though that stabbed her to the heart, still, that
wasn't really the point.

She'd risen from her bed this morning, admitting at last
what that kiss must mean to her.

If another man's kiss could shake her to her soul, then
she wasn't ready to commit herself to a lifetime of loving
Eric. At the very least, she must pause and reconsider.

Which meant in all fairness, Eric must be put on notice.
She'd wrapped and boxed his ring, intended to deliver it to
his law firm's receptionist to pass on to Eric. That was the
real purpose of this expedition to Durango, though Tess
didn't know it.

Along with his engagement ring, she'd enclosed a short,
humble note in which she'd done her utmost to convince
him that she in her indecision, was the one at fault. It had
nothing to do with his lovableness; Eric was entirely lov-
able. Any sane woman would want him—pounce on him.
No, this had to be some unsuspected flaw in Risa's own
character, which she must face and overcome before she
could return to Eric with a clear conscience, if indeed he'd
still want her.

A flaw… *Mother was fickle, a new boyfriend every
month. Could it be that I take after her?* Much as she'd
loved her mother, Risa had spent most of her teen years
trying her utmost to distinguish herself from her parent. Eva
had been the perfect lesson in how to lead an unhappy life.

"Are we going to see Jules on our way back?" Tess
demanded beside her.

"She'll still be at work, I'm afraid." Jules was enduring

long hours as an apprentice to a jewelry designer, in a studio down near Mesaverde. "Why?"

"I was thinking, since she works in metal, maybe she could make me some lock picks. Detectives use those all the time when they're investigating."

At least Tess wasn't asking for a cute little derringer with which to apprehend the bad guys—*yet,* Risa told herself. "There aren't a lot of locks that need picking at Suntop."

"Well, there's Daddy's desk. Or I could practice on the front door. And Lara's diary."

"Next time I see Jules I'll ask her," Risa promised gravely, laughter fluttering like hiccups behind her breastbone. Last year she could have laughed and tousled Tess's hair. But now that her little sister had turned a dignified twelve… "Or I suppose we could check Hansen's. If they don't carry lock picks, at least they'll have ice cream."

"Excellent!"

"So WHAT DOES that tell you?" Risa asked while Miguel aligned a metal instrument along the margin between a layer of dark-red sandstone and a straw-colored dolomite. They'd been riding along the west side of Blindman's Canyon, skirting the base of its high rosy vertical walls. He'd dismounted to wriggle into this cleft, like a tiny side canyon, then pulled out what seemed to be some sort of level, with a floating bubble.

"It tells me…" Miguel squinted at the numbers inscribed along the device, then set it down and drew out his notepad. Scribbled something. "It tells me, *cielito,* that the beds of sediments are rising roughly eight degrees above the horizontal, in that direction." He nodded off to the east.

Cielito. She'd looked that up in her high-school Spanish dictionary a few nights ago. It meant "little heaven—sweetheart." The coolness she'd sensed in him yesterday, which had wounded her so, had vanished today. Still, all morning as they rode and laughed and talked, she'd felt the weight of his dark eyes upon her.

It gave her the *oddest* feeling—reminded her of the beach back in L.A., the sensation she'd get after sunbathing for hours. As if she lay on a blanket spread on the baking sands, rumble of surf in her ears. She'd be stunned and sleepy with the day's warmth…sunlight pressing her down, sliding through her veins like hot honey.

Just as well that once they'd reached the canyon, she'd lost his attention before she melted like a bar of chocolate in the sun! Now Miguel was engrossed in the rocks and their stories, barely remembered she was with him.

But that was fine, too. Absorbed as he was, she could watch him with impunity. And he was so achingly beautiful, with his thick lashes and his sculpted mouth, and those elegant, eloquent, scarred hands. So deliciously sexy, with his broad shoulders and his long legs and his tight buns. "Eight degrees—that doesn't sound like much," she said, just to provoke him.

"You think so?" He made a straight line of his forearm and stiffened fingers. "You extend a line like so, rising at eight degrees, for a mile? That means a mile to the east of here, this bed will lie a thousand feet higher than it does here, as will the layers above and below it."

"And so?" she teased, looking down at him from the back of her palomino.

"*¡Ay!*" He caught her boot, his fingers pressing into her ankle through its supple leather—gave her an exasperated little shake. "As I've explained, Risa-Sonrisa, oil rises as it travels through permeable beds. So any oil around here is rising that way, and what lies in that direction?"

She squinted through the opposite canyon wall. "Sweetwater Flats, if you carry your line twelve miles or so."

"*¡Exactamente!* And if you look at the limestone beds along your home creek, where the bridge crosses, those formations are rising toward the north, making a line that would cross this east-west vector. I'm seeking the spot where the beds slope away from me on *all* sides—the top of the anticline. When I stand there, I'll know where to drill."

And then? She supposed then he meant to make some sort of proposal to her father. *And once Ben realizes what you are, he'll throw you off the ranch before you can say "Scat!"*

No more rides together. No more talking and teasing. No more time to try to understand why he disturbed her so. Why when his gaze lingered, her heart trembled. She'd never felt—*seen*—before—truly seen—before Miguel's dark eyes found her. And she didn't know who he was seeing, but she wanted to meet that woman.

To be her?

Oh, she was a fool to wonder if this could be more than a summer's flirtation! Touching spurs to Sunrise's ribs, she loped on ahead, leaving him to follow.

As she'd been a fool, no doubt, in returning Eric's ring. He'd phoned her yesterday evening, after she and Tess had come back from Durango. Risa winced at the memory.

Eric had alternately pleaded his case—swearing that she'd broken his heart—and harangued her, calling her a fickle, ungrateful little idiot who was thinking with her hormones not her head. He'd said such vicious things about Miguel that she'd sworn she'd hang up if he didn't stop.

Finally, hoarse with emotion, Eric had extracted a promise that she'd meet with him one last time—tomorrow. "Have the decency to break our engagement face-to-face, if you're stupid enough to break it at all!" he'd demanded.

Oh, she dreaded tomorrow's confrontation.

But as for returning his ring, funny, she didn't feel like a fool; she felt only...relief. A sense of a heavy weight rolling off her shoulders, so that now she soared high and free, up into the blue, above these red canyon walls.

On they rode, measuring, noting, observing. Wherever the canyon walls closed in, Miguel would send her across to the eastern face. Using a surveyor's laser, he'd shoot a beam of horizontal light from a formation on the west side to where she waited with a piece of chalk, ready to mark the spot, like a ruby trapped in the stone, where the laser touched her wall. Each time they performed this operation, the results were the same: the beds tilted up toward the east.

Each measurement seemed to add to Miguel's excitement. He worked with a passionate, silent intensity, stopping to tip back his head and study the striated, towering walls, then make a hasty sketch or a cryptic note on his pad.

They came at last to the box canyon in the eastern wall and Miguel let out a little crow of satisfaction.

"This is where they always pen the remuda, the horses, on the last night of roundup each year," she told him. Blindman's Canyon formed a miles-long corridor, leading up through the foothills toward the summer range. All the ranchers around Trueheart used it, combining their forces each spring and fall to bring the cattle back and forth in what was the biggest traditional roundup remaining, in this part of the West.

"¿Sí? But even better, it will show us if the formations continue their rise toward the east." Miguel swung Jackhammer right at the natural intersection, as if they turned a city street corner onto another block lined with skyscrapers.

Risa followed, thinking that this half-mile-deep alcove in

the stone contained one of the most beautiful spots on Suntop, a place she'd intended to bring— No, she would think no more of Eric today.

They watered the horses in the shallow stream that riffled out of the box canyon—hard to imagine that this was what had carved and hollowed these walls. They splashed through it and rode on, stopping every hundred yards or so along the north wall to measure the slope of the beds. The farther they traveled into this rift in the plateau, the higher its striated walls rose around them, yet still the sediments climbed. Miguel rode with a silent exultation, gazing keenly upward at the slanting bands of rose and brick and tan and gray.

Till at last they could ride no farther. In a twining swath of lace and crystal, a high, delicate waterfall poured down the sheer face of the end wall, to spatter into the green pool at its base. Overflowing this cup of hollowed stone, it formed the stream that ran off down the center of the narrow valley. "If only I could climb up there, sample those beds," Miguel murmured, peering upward. "Shale and sandstone mostly, I'd say, but there's no way to know its porosity, its permeability, without examining pieces under *magnificación.*"

"There's a way up—part of the way up." Till she spoke, Risa hadn't known that she'd tell him. This was one of the places she most cherished around Suntop, a secret and very special place.

"*¿De veras?* Then show me!"

"If I do, we'll have to take our lunch along." She'd been too nervous this morning to have more than juice and toast

"But of course." While Risa unbridled and staked out their mounts to graze, Miguel loaded the instruments he needed plus their sandwiches into his daypack. "Now, where? How?"

"There're a couple of routes. The first one is...here." She moved to their right along the cliff, till she came to the deep crack, whose ragged shadow concealed the hand-holds and footholds carved into the stone at perfect inter-vals. Risa kicked off her boots, peeled out of her socks. "It's Anasazi, I think." The ancient ones, those shy, mys-terious people who'd built their hidden dwellings at the top of remote cliffs in the far canyons of the Southwest a thou-sand years ago.

"Oh? But it's very steep. Why don't you wait here be-low?"

"Ha, I've been climbing this since I was fourteen." She swarmed upward, leaving him to follow. "It's easy as a ladder." So saying, Risa reached up to hook her left hand around the rim of a narrow ledge, hoisted herself higher.

As her head rose past her fingers, she heard the eerie buzz.

Instinct recognized the sound before conscious thought— the fine hairs on her nape, on her arms, electrified—stood on aching end. Her breath feathered out in a gasp. Not two feet from her rounding mouth, a rattlesnake glided neatly into its coil, the coil from which it would strike. The ugly triangular head lifted as it swung her way—

She stiff-armed the ledge and dropped—spun outward from the cliff as all her weight hit her right hand and, below her, Miguel yelled a wordless warning. Her feet kicked and scrabbled at the rock.

"Risa, *háblame—¿qué pasa?*"

"*S-s-snake!*" God, if it slithered over the edge, dropped on her face! Too panicked to find the footholds, she scrab-bled and kicked.

"Jump, *corazón!* I'll catch you!"

"*I ca-a-an't!*" Her grip was frozen to the stone, even as

it weakened. She glanced frantically downward; Miguel
stood perhaps eight feet below, arms uplifted.

"Risa, leap, and I'll catch you. *Do it!*"

No choice, really, as her wrist gave out. Closing her eyes
she dropped with a tiny wail.

"*Ooof!*" Arms cradled, then clamped around her, Mi
guel staggered backward, caught his balance, hugged her
tight to his body. He sucked in a savage breath. "*Ay*
Risa!" His eyes roved fiercely over her face, her breasts—
scanned her all the way to her bare toes and back again
"Did it bite you? Touch you?"

Speechless with relief, she shook her head.

"*¡Gracias a Dios!* You crazy woman! You would go
first." His scowl was softening; a smile twitched his lips
He swung her around in slow waltz time, marveling, his
smile growing to a grin. "Risa-Sonrisa, like an angel drop
ping out of the sky!"

The rush of adrenaline was making her giggly. "More
like a bomb from above!"

"Ba-*boom!*" He laughed, still twirling her. "Look up
and it's raining *rubias!* My lucky day."

"No, mine." Where her breast was pressed to his chest
she could feel his heart thundering; her own, running like
a river in snowmelt. "*Great* catch," she added softly.

"You leap…and always I'll catch you." It sounded like
a promise. A vow. He dipped his head; she lifted hers—
their mouths molded hungrily together as slowly, slowly he
turned…then came to a standstill, nothing moving but their
lips, their tongues, their racing hearts.

Gathering her closer with a groan, he tore his mouth from
hers—to kiss the tip of her nose, her lashes, her forehead
while her fingers twined through his silky hair. Again they
broke apart, to catch their breaths as they stared at each
other.

If she kept on looking, he'd have her soul out through her eyes and then what? She buried her face beneath his chin with a little moan of happiness and confusion.

"Sí." The strong brown column of his throat convulsed against her cheek. "And now, *cielito,*" he murmured huskily, "how shall I punish your friend up there? Would you like a belt? Perhaps a hatband?"

Laughing, she lifted her head. "It was his sunbath that I interrupted. Let's leave him be."

So they took the second route, some fifty feet down the cliff—this time Miguel insisted on taking the lead.

At the top of the climb, she accepted his waiting hand and he lifted her to her feet—hooked an arm around her waist and kissed her then and there at the edge of the cliff.

Standing on the brink. But then, hadn't she fallen already?

When their lips parted at last, he turned, still embracing her, to survey their private kingdom. *"Paraíso!"*

Paradise. *So you feel it, too, the magic of this place?* They stood at the edge of an emerald meadow no larger than a grass tennis court, enclosed on three sides by sheer canyon walls, on the fourth by the fifty-foot drop to the lower canyon. At some time, in time as Miguel counted it—geologic time—the stream had carved its way down through softer levels of stone till it came to the resistant layer that created this hanging shelf. Gracefully accepting defeat for a million years or so, the stream had shrugged and drawn its ribbon of rippling silk through the green grassy middle of the ledge—to spill over its rim, falling to the pool below.

"There's no way down from above?" Miguel's hushed voice reflected the peace and privacy of this place.

"Not even the deer can reach it." Which was why the grass was so lush, high as their knees. "I don't know why the Anasazi didn't build a permanent house up here. Maybe they used it as a temporary camp on hunting trips.''

''Or as a place of worship?''

It had always seemed so to her. While Miguel explored the perimeter walls, taking his inevitable measurements, Risa spread her poncho beside the stream and sat. Her knees were trembling—all of her trembled. Aftereffects of danger and kisses.

And the certain knowledge that no one could find them here. There might have been no one else in all the world but she and Miguel. Pressed down by the warm hands of the sun, Risa sank back onto her elbows, tipped her face to the sky and closed her eyes. Heard only the lyrical, liquid song of running water.

And the swish of long grass…the vibration of a man's feet coming her way, like an echo of the drumming in her ears.

''*¡Sirena!*'' He knelt beside her, the heat of his body washing against hers, warming her without…and within.

''Who *is* that?'' she murmured haughtily, eyes closed. Laughter quivered, barely contained. If she didn't look, then this couldn't be happening. It was all a dream, a delicious fantasy.

''A clever beggar out of a fairy tale, come seeking a princess.'' Soft as velvet, his lips brushed across her cheek, then feathered away—returned as she smiled a close-mouthed, mischievous smile. The hot tip of a tongue probed the corners of her lips, seeking entry.

She smiled wider but didn't grant it.

His tongue glazed the curve of her bottom lip with languid honey.

Heat—blossoming out from her center, spreading down to her toes, rising up her breasts. She let out a tremulous sigh. "No princess here, I'm afraid." *I'm afraid, I'm afraid, oh, Miguel, I'm—*

Hot and slow and tantalizing, his tongue traced the shape of her mouth. Sighing her surrender, she parted her lips— he groaned with triumph and entered her. His big hard fingers slid around her shoulders, spread across her spine, laced up through her hair and gathered a handful, as if to thwart any thought of escape. Of turning back.

She had no such thought—no thought at all now as he tugged on her hair, tipped back her head, the better to plunder her mouth. No thought, only a fierce and abiding joy.

Once he'd made her mouth his own, he laid a trail of tiny kisses from the underside of her jaw down the side of her arching neck, growling, "Risa-Sonrisa-Sonrisa-mi Risa," as he kissed his way down.

Abruptly he paused, at the angle where neck flowed into shoulder. "*Ay,* this I'd forgotten!"

Shuddering with the touch of his lips on that exquisitely sensitive spot, she opened her eyes—to find him scowling. "W-what?"

For answer, Miguel swung one knee over her thighs so that he knelt astride her. "*Éste…*" He hooked a finger under the fine golden chain at her neck. Grasping it two-handed, he snapped its delicate links. Held up the two glittering ends before her eyes. "This, *cielito.* I'd forgotten this. But now…what shall I do? Buy you a pretty chain to replace this one? Or…are you content that I set you free?" His expression was stern, measuring, showing not a trace of a smile as he studied her face. "*Dígame.* What shall I do?"

"Well, for starters, you might look at the rest of it." When he narrowed his eyes and tipped his head in question, she took the chain from his unresisting fingers, drew up the loop of gold from inside her shirt, on which dangled—

A simple Zuñi cornflower pendant of silver and turquoise, a piece of jewelry she'd treasured from childhood.

"No ring..." he noted carefully. "*¿Por qué?*"

Why? She could feel her face growing hot under his inquisition. *Certainly not because I planned this!* "I...didn't feel like wearing it," she muttered almost sulkily, lowering her lashes and half turning away. *And don't think you can make me say why!*

"Ah?" Now there was a smile in his voice. "Then—" Leaning forward, he paused, his mouth hovering not half an inch above hers. "Then let us see what *I* can make you feel!"

He halved that distance, then paused again, so tantalizingly near, so ruthlessly far. *But you must meet me in the middle,* his eyes insisted, and at last she must have leaned forward the last eighth of an inch—*enough.* Their lips brushed...brushed, clung and moved, speaking their own silent, yearning, liquid language. *So sweet, so soft, so right...*

Gradually he increased the pressure of his kiss, leaning into her. And as slowly she yielded, sinking back toward the earth.

Miguel followed her down, inevitable as a wave breaking over her head. His wonderful weight settled into the cradle of her parted thighs for the first time, rested warm against her belly; his hands cupped her breasts—and she and he laughed breathlessly with the perfection of the moment.

CHAPTER THIRTEEN

ALL THAT LONG, lovely afternoon, they rolled like a couple of young lions in the grass, mating, napping, cuddling, talking in lazy whispers, taking each other again. It was as if they both knew, somehow, that they had no time to waste, not a precious minute to spare.

"And this one?" Kneeling beside him, Risa traced the scar that wound up his left ankle, across his calf, ending near his knee.

Inch by inch, she was mapping his body with a tender boldness that both amused him and swelled him with pride. All in an afternoon, she'd gone from fawnlike shyness to the happy confidence of a swallow sailing down the wind. "That? It's nothing. A motorcycle accident years ago. I took a corner too fast."

"Oh, Miguel!" She swooped down upon him; warm lips traced the path of the scar. "You could have been killed!"

"Ah, no. *Nunca.* Never. I had an appointment with you to keep." Sitting up, he slid his fingers through her tousled hair to cup her nape—held her wet-velvet mouth pressed against his skin for a moment and sucked in his breath with the sensation.

When he freed her, she rolled over to lie with her cheek pillowed on his thigh. Smiling wickedly, she lifted an eyebrow. "*¿Otra vez?*"

Again and again and again till forever if he had his way, but— He glanced around. The canyon walls to the west had stolen their sunlight. "Only if we mean to spend the night."

She caught her teeth in her beautiful bottom lip. "Ben would send out search parties if we didn't come back. He doesn't care if I miss supper—we all do that—but once Joe tells him that Sunrise isn't back in the home pasture..."

"Then we'd better go. But first..." Suddenly, he didn't know how to even begin. Making love to her was one thing, as natural and necessary as breathing. But asking? He'd never cared to ask anyone for anything. He paid his way through life with his hands and his wits. But this...this could neither be purchased nor taken; there was nothing but the asking...

"Yes, what is it?" She was learning to read his face as he could read hers.

He wasn't sure he liked that. Naked in body was one thing; naked to the soul another.

She sat up and touched his cheek. "Why the frown?"

He drew a deep breath. "*Oígame, corazón.* Listen to me. You know that I'm not a rich man. It's plain to see. I have my truck, my tools, a few thousand in savings back in a bank in Texas. Not much, I admit. Most of the money I've earned has gone back to *mi familia.* But I have skills and knowledge and the will to use them. I'll always make my way."

"I don't doubt it," she murmured, playing with a curl of hair on his chest. "Not for a minute. But, Miguel—"

"But you, Risa, you're the daughter of *un ranchero rico.* Anything in the world that you want, your father can buy you."

She laughed painfully under her breath, shook her head, but he plunged on. "I cannot match that, but someday, *pasión,* someday soon, I will have money. There's oil here for the taking." He swept one arm toward the east. "I can

feel it in my hands, see the signs in the rocks. In one well—
or two, at most—I'll be able to—

"Hush!" She grabbed his upper arms. "*Whoa!* Miguel,
listen to me! If you talk to my father about drilling a well,
he'll send you away! You mustn't do this. *Please!*" Her
eyes sparkled with tears. "Please. He would, and I couldn't
bear it! We've only just started to… To…" She ducked
her head, resting the top of her silky head against his bare
shoulder.

To? *Love* was a word that women used. He thought more
in terms of need. It was becoming necessary to have her—
had been from the start, to complete the deal he and Tankersly had struck—but now…

No, even before this shining afternoon. For days, he'd
known he had a deeper, greater need. *And if you feel it,
too,* querida, *then*—

He kissed her ear, the only part of her he could find
through her storm cloud of hair. "I won't let him send me
away, *pasión.* Not if you don't want me to go." Someday
he would explain how he could promise that with such
confidence. But right now it wasn't important.

"I don't! *Please* don't go." Still braced against his chest,
she tipped her head so that he could find her mouth.

He kissed her through a veil of fiery silk—her lips sweet,
salty, softly trembling. "But that means you can't tell him
you're hunting for oil," she insisted when they broke apart.
"Not at Suntop. Believe me, Miguel, he'll—"

He kissed her again, harder, to silence her, then tipped
his knuckles beneath her chin and raised her face to his.
"There's another way. Better than sneaking around. If we
were *casado*…married…"

Her eyes went as round as the gold coin in his pocket.
Color swept her cheeks, the way a fire opal sends out waves
of radiance when it's shifted. "Y-you and me?"

He stifled a laugh. "Me and you." He'd as good as given her his vows already this day, but she was too inexperienced to realize.

"But...but...we've known each other less than a month..."

He smoothed the hair back from her winged eyebrows. She wasn't dismayed by his offer, only incredulous. "There is more to learn, *sí*, but I think already we know the things that matter." At least, he did. She was kind, quick, funny, beautiful. And his bed would be *paraíso* on earth if she shared it with him; after today, he had no more doubts about that!

"Oh, Miguel, I—" She swallowed and shook her head.

He brushed his knuckles across her velvety nipple, seducing when he should have waited and let her think it through.

But once he'd begun, one touch could never be enough; she was silk and fire against his fingers. An aching emptiness that must be filled.

She made a little moan deep in her throat, but she didn't pull away. "I..." Her lashes shivered; the color swept over her breasts, a dawning of desire.

He fingered one swelling rosebud—leaned to adore it with tongue and mouth, felt her heart thundering against his cradling palm. *Ah, marry me, Risa, and we'll do this every night of our lives!* He raised his head to replace his lips with his coaxing fingers. Perhaps it was male instinct that would brook no denial. He *would* have her surrender. "Say yes!" he demanded, his voice husky with emotion. "Only leap, Risa-Sonrisa, and I will catch you!"

"Truly?" She flattened a hand against his heart. "*¿De veras?* You really want me?"

More than all the oil in all the world. He caught her

slender waist and lifted her to kneel astride his lap. "You're all that I want!"

But that…that was a lie he'd pay for.

AFTER THEIR AFTERNOON in *paraíso*, events moved with the speed of a diamond-tipped drill bit cutting down through soft limestone. Their return to the real world was all too public.

It was nearly midnight by the time they neared the Big House. Miguel had insisted they ride slowly, since Risa was clearly uncomfortable. How he'd cursed himself for not thinking of that—to ride a virgin halfway to heaven, then expect her to bounce back home on a hard leather saddle? But there was no help for it, and his beautiful *rubia* bore the ordeal without a whimper, smiling bravely each time he leaned across to kiss her cheek and whisper words of encouragement.

A worse ordeal than this was in the offing. Half a mile north of the Big House, they sighted the search party—two unsmiling Suntop hands loped their way, with Ben Tankersly riding grimly at their head. Other parties had fanned out along the river and were scouring Sweetwater Flats, Miguel later learned.

Tankersly reined in and made them come to him.

"I will *not* let him fire you," Risa swore under her breath. "Don't worry, Miguel!"

"Risa, this is for your man to handle. Say nothing, do you hear me?"

"B-b-but—"

"Nada," he insisted.

On they rode, Risa with chin defiantly uplifted, Miguel's outward calm belying his inner wariness. Because here was the test. The old man might think that he wanted someone to court and win his daughter away from Foster, but once the deed was done, would he be able to step back and let another man take her? Kings didn't relinquish their playthings so easily.

They halted their horses before him, and even by moonlight the rancher's eyes missed nothing. They flicked over Risa's tousled hair and bee-stung lips, noted that indefinable air of pride that announces a woman has taken a man. "Huh," he grunted finally, his hooded old eyes giving nothing away. He turned to the cowboy on his left. "Robbins, you and Carter see Risa on back to the house, then go after Wiggly. Tell him we found her."

"Ben, I won't be sent home like a—" Risa sucked in her breath as Miguel caught her wrist. Claiming her there before them all.

"I said I'd handle this, *corazón*. Go on home. It's been a long day." *And a sweet one,* his smile reminded her.

She frowned, but she obeyed him, glancing anxiously back over her shoulder as she rode off under escort. Miguel watched her out of sight, feeling as if a cord of gold stretched from her heart to his, compelling him to gallop in pursuit. It took an effort to tear his gaze away and turn to her father.

Who'd been sitting there studying his face. "Well?" Tankersly growled.

No indication of what he felt, but no matter. There was no turning back now for Miguel. "Sir, I've come to ask for the hand of your daughter."

"Huh!" The old man's shoulders shook—in harsh, dusty laughter, Miguel finally realized. "Oh, you're a cool one, Heydt! Bring her home with grass in her hair and *then* you ask for her!"

He was too old to punch, but Miguel rode so close their opposite knees touched. "You will speak of her with respect, Tankersly, or I swear to you—"

That only set off another round of dry chuckles, which ended with Tankersly groping in the pocket of his jacket. He drew out a slim pack of cigars, flipped it open and offered it wordlessly.

So... After all, it was to be peace, not war. Miguel blew out a breath and selected one, stuck it in his teeth. Leaned out from his saddle to meet the match that Tankersly had struck with a thumbnail.

They sat for a few minutes in silence, allowing the tension between them to drift off with the smoke, then Tankersly said, "So...where d'you reckon to drill your well?"

My first well, Miguel corrected him silently. By their contract, there would be many wells—as many as he pleased—if Risa bore him a son within the year. *Mi hijo...* The words felt like a sunrise in his stomach. "I'm still deciding," he said coolly. "But first..." By the contract and by his own unshakable desire, "There must be a wedding."

"TWENTY MINUTES to show time, girls!" announced Belle Lowrey, bustling into Risa's bedroom. Catching sight of Risa, who stood with Jules before the pier glass, she stopped short and clasped her hands to her ample breasts. "Oh, mercy, look at you, darlin'! The both of you. Now, that was worth a trip to Denver!"

In giving his miraculous—his astonishing—consent to their marriage, Ben had made only one condition. He hated fusses at Suntop. Would have none of that drawn-out torture that women imposed on men—months of foolish dithering about colors and flowers and guests and music—when they planned their dream weddings. If Risa wanted to marry Heydt, that was fine by him. He'd foot all expenses and it went without saying that the ceremony would take place at the ranch—but she had one week, and one week alone, in which to do it.

The next morning he'd sent for Belle Lowrey, once upon a time his mistress, now his friend and adviser in all matters of surpassing femininity. Belle descended on them from Dallas like General MacArthur returning to the Philippines. Beachheads were established, marching orders issued, reinforcements arrived daily.

And the men vanished like guerrillas into the bush, appearing only when hunger drove them in from the range, then fleeing again. Ben must have put a thousand miles on his Lincoln Town Car, cruising the back roads of Suntop that week. Miguel discovered a burning need to map and measure the country northeast of Blindman's Canyon. Not even the cowboys rode within miles of the Big House if they could avoid it.

Which was just as well, given the frenzy at Wedding Headquarters. Socorro, the longtime Tankersly housekeeper, had determined that her domain must be polished and waxed from threshold to chimney cap, and she'd recruited a horde of family and friends to aid her in this mission. Risa's half sister Lara had been summoned back from her friends in Albuquerque and was now in charge of invitations, issued by fax and phone, and also hotel reservations for the guest overflow, who would be bedded down in Durango. Belle herself devised menus, bullied the caterer in Cortez, drove the florist to tears, found the classical guitarist Risa had requested, the string quartet she herself thought more appropriate and the country-and-western band for the postwedding barbecue bash on the lawn.

Risa and Jules had been dispatched to the boutiques of Denver by private plane, with orders not to come home without a wedding dress and gowns for two maids of honor plus a flower girl. "You look magnificent," Belle gloated, turning Risa around. "You'll knock that handsome devil's dark eyes right out of his head!"

"You think?" Risa asked shyly. She'd chosen a simple gown of heavy cream silk cut on the bias, with a low, halter-cut bodice and a clinging, softly swaying silhouette. No train or wide skirts, though the handkerchief hem grazed her ankles. The stylist Belle had imported from Dallas had pinned her hair up, but the effect was softened by the wisps of red-gold she'd left curling around her cheeks and nape and the spray of gardenias and baby's breath she'd tucked in at the back.

"I *know,*" Belle said warmly, then turned her attention to Jules. "And you, my dear, will set all the cowboys to swooning!"

Jules, with her artist's eye for color, had picked out the other gowns—simple spaghetti-strapped velvet cocktail dresses in coral for herself, pink for Tess, pale gold for Lara.

Belle glanced at the watch on her plump freckled wrist. "And now, where are those sisters of yours? We've only—"

The door opened again and Lara sailed into the room, to scan its corners with a frown. "You don't have the brat?"

Tess had been a pain all week, whirling like an overwound top, with all the excitement. Perhaps because she felt slighted with so much attention focused on her eldest sister, she'd regressed emotionally to her tomboy stage, insisting that she *had* to fly to Denver with Jules and Risa so that she could choose her own wedding outfit. She wanted a tuxedo just like Miguel and her father would be wearing.

When Belle had squashed that idea, Tess had packed up all her Nancy Drew books, taken her pony and vanished for an entire day and half a night—till Joe Wiggly found her camped along a creek four miles to the west, reading by firelight.

Hustled home again, she'd begged Jules to make her some lock picks—*absolutely* essential if she was to become a detective like Nancy Drew! Unwise in the ways of little sisters, Jules had indulged the plea, giving Tess a set of old broken dentist's tools that she carried in her jewelry kit for odd jobs and manipulations, suggesting that these might do the trick. And indeed they had. The junior detective had spent the rest of the week skulking around the house, picking the locks to Belle's luggage, the front and back door locks and—biggest triumph of all so far—the lock on Lara's diary.

Though Lara wasn't speaking to the trespasser, Belle had encharged her with cramming Tess into her gown, then delivering her to the stylist. "She's dressed, yes. She looks wonderful. But I turned my back for *one* second and—" Lara threaded her fingers up through her silver-blond locks and squeezed her temples. "*Blast* the little brute! She's probably out practicing hot-wiring, on Risa's Cadillac."

Belle caught her elbow and steered her toward the stylist. "Hon, you sit down and compose yourself while Mary-Lou combs you out, and *I'll* find the stinker."

Risa drifted over to the window to peer at the baby-blue convertible, parked behind the house with its top down. "She's not in the Caddie." Her and Miguel's car, their wedding gift from Ben. Gazing at its sumptuous, gleaming curves and its white leather upholstery, she bit her lip. It had caused the one real note of discord between them so far.

"I don't want it!" she'd tried to tell Miguel last night after their rehearsal dinner, at which Ben had presented his gift, to a round of applause from all the guests. "Can't you see what he's doing? He always has to control everything—

everyone—and he does it with money! This car, even this wedding..."

Which was spinning out of her control. It would no longer be the simple, deeply emotional ceremony for a few friends and family, which she'd envisioned, but a Matrimonial Production by Belle, for the greater glory of Suntop.

Miguel hadn't seen. "Risa-Sonrisa..." He'd laughed as he nuzzled her neck. "¡Calmate, cielito! I told you we should elope, but you would not listen. And now it's too late. We must make the best of this."

That he was right didn't make her feel any better. Did he hate this fuss as much as she did? Worse, was he regretting his impulse in proposing a week ago? The bond that had seemed so simple and right out there in their private paradise was still fragile as any newborn. Could it bear the weight of all this public scrutiny, these public expectations and rituals?

Every night this week she'd awakened in a panic, wondering if Miguel was still in her life, waiting patiently for her down there at the bunkhouse, where he'd insisted on staying—or if this would be the night that, tiring of this circus, he'd pack his bag and drive off in his old truck, to wherever the rocks might call him.

"Please," she'd begged him, catching his tie—he looked wonderful in a suit, with a tie on, but too elegant to be the man with whom she'd rolled in the grass of their secret valley. "Please, we don't need it! Let's give it back." A baby-blue Cadillac was no part of the life she imagined with Miguel, the two of them living humbly and happily, traveling the West in his old pickup, searching for oil.

"Risa, it's a gift from your *father*. To show that he loves you, and—*sí*—to show the world that he can afford to give you such gifts. But a man has his pride. We can't throw it back in his teeth. You *must* accept it."

"Then *you* drive it and I'll take your pickup!" she'd cried, her sorely tried temper fraying at last.

"*¡No seas ridícula!*" he'd snapped, shaking his forefinger under her nose. Then they'd both heard laughter and the sound of feet tromping out onto the terrace and they'd stepped guiltily apart.

They hadn't had a chance to make up, either. Their guests—most of them Ben's friends and neighbors, really—had swept them up and away, the men demanding to be introduced to the Cadillac, the women keen to pump Risa about her father's breezily mysterious hostess to the festivities. She and Miguel had exchanged one last burning, yearning, half-resentful look across the terrace and that was the last she'd seen of him.

Next time they met would be in ten minutes, down in the living room before some one hundred guests. *Oh, my God—oh, my God—oh, my God. Are we really doing this?* She wanted him, yes, she did—she'd ached for him all week. But she felt so rushed, so flustered. So turned around.

They should never have come back to Suntop after their day in the canyon. They should have grasped each other's hand and run for their love and their lives!

But where? How? And anyway, they hadn't. It was too late now for regrets. Too late for anything but plunging straight through this flaming hoop and out the other side.

Only leap, he'd told her.

To you, yes, I will, Miguel. She closed her eyes for a moment, there at the window, clasping her fingers below her chin. *As long as I'm leaping into your arms—as long as you want me—then everything will be fine in the end. Just let me live through this day. Once they leave us alone...*

"I can't find her!" Belle cried, rushing back into the room. "And we can't wait. We're late already. Risa, honey, let's roll!"

CHAPTER FOURTEEN

EVER AFTER in Risa's memory, her wedding would be a cascade of bright images and sounds and piercing emotions. A ceremony seen through the lens of a kaleidoscope, some gigantic hand rotating the flashing patterns:

Jules catching her by the waist at the top of the stairs and murmuring into her ear, "The next pretty thing you see will be a Jules Hansen original. Hope you love it, sweetie!"

"W—what?"

But already Jules and Lara were preceding her down the curving flight, stepping in time to the achingly beautiful strains of Pachelbel's Canon in D played by Belle's string quartet. The staircase gave directly onto the big room that stretched half the length of the house. The floor below was a sea of smiling faces as the guests swung in their rows of chairs to watch the procession.

Joe Wiggly and Jake Houseman flanked the newel posts—offered elbows in solemn gallantry to the maids of honor, then escorted them down the aisle toward the altar at the end of the room.

The altar! Risa dared not look that far; let her just make it down the stairs without tripping over her heels and making a total fool of herself and—*oh, God*—Miguel must be there already, watching her, and what could he be thinking? Was he happy? Regretful? Terrified as she was?

And what was Tess doing there at the bottom of the

steps, peering out from behind Ben? Gesturing at her frantically. Shaping words silently, then scowling in frustration when Risa didn't understand.

Whatever it was she wanted, Belle pounced on her from behind, whirled her around and gave her fanny an emphatic smack, sending her scampering down the aisle. As flower girl, Tess should have followed close behind the maids of honor.

But too late now. Resentment plain in every line of her skinny little body, she stomped down the path between the chairs. Remembering her basket of rose petals halfway to the altar, she hurled handfuls at the chuckling guests. She reached her goal, then let out an audible yelp as Lara snatched her and wheeled her into place.

But somehow Risa had reached the bottom of the stairs upright, and there was Ben, offering her his arm, his craggy face creased in what might have been the first uncritical smile he'd ever bestowed upon her. It stopped her cold for a moment, as she looked up at this beaming stranger. *Daddy?* If only he'd approved of her like that before today!

But it was too late to go back and fix the past; she was sweeping into her future, into a new and happier life. Ben's fingers were clamped over hers where they rested on his sleeve, as if she might be thinking about bolting if he didn't prevent her.

For the first time she'd dared to gaze to the end of the room, and there stood a man before the altar, a big, hard man in a black tuxedo, and from that moment on she had eyes for no one else. *Oh, Miguel. Do you really want me?*

You and no other! his dark eyes seemed to declare down the length of the room, drawing her to him as if he reeled in a thread of gold that was looped around her heart. Adrift on the lush music, she floated to meet him.

Then came the ritual question, ''Who gives this

woman?'' and Ben was handing her over as if she were his possession to be given, a bit of baggage passed from man to man. She felt a stab of resentment, but now was no time for protesting, and if she must be given to any man in the world...*I give myself,* her eyes told Miguel proudly as she moved to his side.

And it's I who take you! Heedless of the hundred guests at their backs, he bent to press his lips to her bare shoulder. Then they turned as one to the preacher.

Ritual, ringing vows... Lifelong promises... *To honor and cherish...in sickness and in health...*and *I will...*and he will, then a ring for her finger and one for Miguel's— shining, twisting, sensuous circles of heavy gold—pretty things! Had Jules made them? Oh, Risa hoped she had! Then *you may kiss the bride* and he did—a fiercely tender, lingering kiss as intoxicating as wine, flooding her body with raw heat, reminding her all over again just why she was doing this...that it was no mistake. No mistake at all.

Their lips parted, but their eyes held fast. *''Mi amada,''* he whispered.

My beloved. *And mine,* though he was vanishing behind a curtain of crystal. Risa laughed through her tears and he smiled and kissed her again.

Then laughter, hugs, a scratchy, tobacco-flavored kiss from Joe Wiggly and a smacking, hearty buss from Jake, the cowboy who was Miguel's best man. Tess tugging at her arm and hissing, ''Risa, I've gotta, gotta, *got* to talk to you!''

But Jules hugged her from the other side. ''Do you like it?''

''You made it, Jules? And Miguel's? They're lovely!''

''From an antique coin he brought me—a gorgeous bit of metal to work with.''

His lucky coin. His father's talisman, his family heir-loom. "Oh, Miguel, you shouldn't have!"

"My luck is yours, *corazón*, but aren't we supposed to be moving?"

They were. The musicians had already started the reces-sional. Lara peeled Tess off Risa's arm. Miguel caught his bride around the waist and whisked her down the aisle through a whirl of smiling, laughing, well-wishing faces, and so she was married.

And then at the foot of the stairs there were more kisses, more hugs, exclamations and congratulations, and Belle do-ing her best to shoo them all out onto the terrace for rice and pictures.

Tess wriggled through the crush and grabbed her. "Risa, *listen* to me!"

"Sweetie, can't it wait? I—"

She burst into frustrated tears. "*Nobody* listens to me! This is so-o-o important and—and— *Darn* it, you're so *stupid,* Risa! If you'd only—".

She'd been neglected and bullied and shunted aside all week, and now Risa was going away, leaving the family symbolically, if not actually. "Oh, Tess, Tessums, I'm sorry! Don't cry. Come on, sweetie. Let's go freshen up a second." The photographer could wait. Miguel had been swept from her side; he stood in the midst of a loud laugh-ing circle of Suntop hands and men from the haying crew. He could spare her a moment. After all, they had the rest of their lives together.

So she whisked Tess along to the top of the stairs, then down the corridor toward her room. "What is it, kiddo?"

Tess wiped the back of a hand across her pink nose, then reached into the bodice of her gown. "This!"

Risa stopped, smothering laughter. Belle had insisted that Tess be fitted with her first brassiere for this occasion, a strapless, but she'd already discovered its use as a hiding place. "Whatcha got, Nancy Drew?"

"Did you know about this? I found it in Daddy's desk." She thrust a folded paper into Risa's hands.

"You *didn't* pick the lock to his— Tess, he will *skin* you!"

"Did you know they want you to have a baby?" Tess demanded with a shudder. She was still at a stage to find babies and pregnant women disgusting; the means to achieve this status, mysterious and threatening.

"To have a—what are you talking about?" Risa unfolded the paper, which looked like a contract. Her eyes skimmed down the page, then she blinked as she came to Miguel's bold signature. To her father's spiky scribble. *What?* Her heartbeat seemed to be slowing; the blood freezing in her veins, pounding in her ears—one deliberate, rocking blow after another. The three terms of the contract falling like hammer blows on her unguarded heart:

If they married, then Miguel could drill an oil well. What nonsense was this?

If they married and she became pregnant within one year of that marriage, he could drill more wells.

And if she bore a son, then— Then— Her fingers clenched of their own accord, crumpling the paper to a wad.

"See what I mean?" seethed Tess. "Did you know about this?"

But when, but when, but when? That was most important of all! Because, *yes,* Ben loved to manipulate and control, but it was one thing if he'd done it after the fact and quite another if— Risa's fingers were shaking as she smoothed out the paper again and searched for the date.

A low grating cry escaped her lips as she found it. *They'd signed this contract three weeks ago!* She and Miguel hardly knew each other back then; they'd barely been speaking at that point. That must have been the first night he'd loaned her his truck or thereabouts.

Which meant…which meant…that his love was a sham. This wedding the most cynical of farces. And she the love-struck fool…tricked by her own hungry heart. "Tess…" she said calmly, her voice sounding faint and strange and cold in her ears. "Would you go find Jules for me?"

But she didn't wait for Jules. Hearing Belle's indignant tones at the bottom of the stairs, Risa bolted to her room. Found the keys on her bureau and tore out again, down the back stairs, on through a kitchen of startled caterers.

Three Suntop hands stood out back around the baby-blue convertible, admiring. They turned with embarrassed smiles, which faded as she yanked open the door, slid into place with a rustle of creamy satin, thrust the key into the ignition.

"Um, Risa?" One of them dared to tap her shoulder.

The Cadillac rumbled into life and she clashed the gears, finding first. Swiped her face with a forearm to brush away the streaming tears.

"Hey, Risa, do you think you should—"

"Yes," she said pleasantly—and stomped on the gas.

A THOUSAND HORSES under the hood couldn't carry her fast enough and far enough to wherever she was running. Away from her pain. Away from betrayal and deceit and utter humiliation. *And I thought he loved me!*

The Caddie roared around the base of Suntop. Rushed down the hill, raising a cloud of dust as they stormed through the empty ranch yard. She threaded the cedar gate-posts like a smoking needle, shot into the switchbacks down to the river, barely touching the brakes on the hairpin turns. Let Ben's gift kill her if it would; she *wanted* to die.

But her miserable life was charmed. The car took the

river bridge in a feline bound, lunged up the far bank, then she was on the straightaway to wherever, the speedometer needle climbing toward a hundred—past it—red dust rising like a whirlwind in her wake.

As the arc of the Suntop name board reared into view a mile ahead, for an instant Risa thought she wouldn't turn the wheel—just sail straight under it, across the county road, then slam through the barbed wire on its far side and into the rocky pasture.

But Miguel would be there to pick up his bride's pieces, and not even dead would she let him touch her again. *Damn you, damn you, damn you to hell, Miguel Heydt!* She stomped on the brakes as she swept under the gilded suns—spun the wheel. The Cadillac fishtailed out onto the empty highway, clawed at the concrete, then roared off to the south.

HALFWAY ACROSS Arizona, sometime after sunset, she blew out a back tire. Numbed by hours of grief and rushing wind, she didn't bother to hit the brakes, and that probably saved her life. The lopsided car coasted to a halt, then she steered off onto the shoulder. And stared blankly around.

Nothing but sand and stone and stars and empty road. A desert without, to match the desert within. Was this what she'd been seeking?

She'd been seeking distance. Needed it still. Wouldn't get enough of it just sitting here. With a desolate sigh, she trudged to the trunk and found the spare tire and the tools and a flashlight. Trust Ben to have made sure she had them.

Kneeling by the road in her wedding dress, she could barely see through her tears as she fumbled the jack into place. With that accomplished, she fingered the wheel lugs. These…had to come off.

But someone far stronger than she had tightened them.

Try as she might, she couldn't turn them. Weeping with frustration, she threw herself against the tire iron again and again and they wouldn't budge.

Miguel could have turned them for her easily. "Oh, *damn* you!" she cried, wrenching at the tool with all her might.

The socket slipped off its lug, and her hand smashed into the gravel. *"Ow! Oh… Ohhhh…oh, no-o-o…"* Risa sank to her knees, cupped her face in her hands. Sobbed her heart out.

When finally the spasm had passed, she sat up, sucked the blood off her knuckles.

Her lips grazed cold, unfamiliar smoothness, forgotten in all her grief. Miguel's wedding ring, promise of forever—which had lasted less than an hour.

"Ha!" She wrenched at it frantically, as if it scalded her skin. Tore it off and flung it down.

The ring didn't bounce. It lay there heavy and indifferent and as cold as a stone on the roadside, gleaming in the rays of her flashlight. Mocking her dreams. *"I'll* show you luck!" She brought the tire iron smashing down on top of it.

"I'll show you h-h-honor and cherish!" She slammed it again and again and again. "In sickness…in health…and all that lying *rot!"* The soft gold flattened to a wafer, conforming to the gritty pavement below it. If she could have beat it back into the center of the earth from which it had sprung, she would have, but it only spread with a glimmering, stubborn endurance.

Panting, she gave up at last and stared down at the splash of metal. Like a sunflower, with the center shot out. Like a starburst. "Boom," she whispered.

Ba-boom, it's raining rubias, his voice laughed, way back in her mind. *My lucky day!*

And maybe it had been, for a man seeking treasure. A rich rancher's daughter with a dowry of oil rights...

Drearily she turned back to the damaged tire. Discovered, after a while, that if she stood and balanced almost all her weight on the end of the tire iron, she could loosen the lugs. Finished at last, she rose with a groan, wiped her greasy hands down her satin-clad thighs. "There."

She heaved the blown-out tire into the trunk; no telling if she might need it again. Then the jack. She went back and stooped for the tire iron, then paused, staring down at the splash of Mexican gold.

Miguel's fortune.

Her misfortune. She blew out a long, slow breath, then peeled the ring off the roadside. Tossed it into the trunk with her filthy tools.

Sometime around midnight Risa coasted into Kingman on the last fumes in her gas tank. Rolled up to the pumps of an all-night station and sat there, staring into the distance, drumming her fingertips on the steering wheel. No money. She hadn't thought to grab a penny on her way out the door.

And Jules had moved in with a roommate last week, down in Mesaverde, and Risa could not remember the roomie's last name or number, though she'd racked her brains for the last ten miles. And Jules didn't have a credit card, anyway.

She could think of only one other person on which to call. *I can't.*

Her pride was in shreds already. Could it hurt any worse?

And she had to keep moving. If Ben had called the state troopers, told them to watch out for her... Though she held one advantage; he hadn't a clue where she might be headed. She hadn't known herself till the highway signs had begun to beckon.

But she'd never make it without gas. And some money to do what she had to do once she got there. So she swallowed her pride and called collect, then stood in the booth, listening to a heartless, digitized voice demanding if a collect call would be acceptable from Risa Tankersly.

No reason that it should be. Seven days ago, she'd called Eric to tell him of her upcoming marriage. She'd chickened out on her promise to meet him face-to-face. She'd been too blissfully happy loving Miguel to let Eric's anger intrude. Instead she'd begged his forgiveness at a safe distance. Told him goodbye and God bless, wished him all the happiness in the world.

He'd been almost speechless with bewildered rage and wounded pride.

"Risa?" Eric demanded now on a note of harsh incredulity. "What's going on? Where are you?"

"Um, Kingman. L-listen, Eric, I know this is asking a lot, but I...need a favor—an enormous favor. I was wondering if you could lend me some money."

"Huh! *Ha!* Oh-ho, that's *rich,* babe! Money from me? Why don't you ask your Mexican hayseed for a loan?"

"I've...left him." Her eyes filled. Tears clogged her throat. "I—I—I— Oh, Eric!" What a mess she'd made of things! She *was* her mother all over again, throwing happiness away with both hands, loving losers and users.

"I thought today was your wedding."

"It...was." Her voice squeaked on the admission. "That's...another thing I guess I should ask you. Do you know anything about getting a divorce in Las Vegas?"

"You married him and you've left him already?" His laughter was close to a bray of delight. "Honestly? I told you it'd never last, but even *I* didn't figure..." He paused and his voice softened. "Listen, baby, I'm sorry. It's just

I'm so glad you came to your senses. You say you're in Kingman?''

"And out of gas. But they take Visa here, if you could give the man your card number..."

"You need more than that, baby. You need a good lawyer. And I happen to know a crackerjack attorney who'd come running if you crooked your little finger. I'm thinking an annulment is the way to go. I can catch a plane in the morning, meet you there by breakfast."

"Um...I think...maybe I should handle this myself." Even if Eric didn't gloat, she felt raw. Abraded to the soul. She longed to crawl in a hole and pull it in after her. The last thing in the world she wanted was to tell him how she'd been fooled. Then suffer his sympathy...and his irony.

"Sorry, Risa, but no way can I let you do that. You need backup. A shoulder to cry on."

"Eric, really, I—"

"That's the price of the loan, babe. If you want my Visa number, you have to promise you'll let me meet you in Vegas."

CHAPTER FIFTEEN

The Present

"MO-OM, HOW SOON do we get to—" Morgan paused as Risa growled and aimed a warning forefinger his way without taking her eyes off the climbing road. "I know, I know—"

"Figure it out!" they chanted in laughing unison.

"Allll right," he added on a note of grudging patience, as if it were she'd who'd asked that question every twenty minutes for the past two days. He collected his pad and pencil from the dash of their old Toyota; the top page was covered with scribbled columns of numbers. "Well. When we left Denver it was four hundred thirty-six miles to Suntop. And now we've come—" He leaned over to consult the digital counter below the speedometer needle.

She dipped to brush her nose stealthily through his soft, silver-blond hair, careful that he didn't feel the caress. At ten, he had little tolerance for mushy moms.

"We've come—um—three hundred ninety-eight miles..."

Even with an overnight stop in Alamosa, the drive had been very long for restless Morgan, who twitched even in his sleep. As for Risa, ten thousand miles wouldn't have been too long a journey. Her dread had built with every mile that slipped away behind them. *Am I crazy, taking us back to Suntop after all these years?*

Ever since they passed Durango, emotions that she'd thought she'd locked away in her heart forever had been ambushing her, washing over her in cold, bitter waves like the swells of some distant, approaching hurricane. Feelings of rage and sorrow and utter betrayal. No wonder it had taken her eleven years to make this trip!

"Thirty-eight *miles!*" Morgan groaned, smacking his pad down on the dash. "Thirty-eight miles is forever! We're *never* gonna—"

"Suntop is nineteen miles north of town," she said quickly to distract him. "So how many miles is it to True-heart?" *Oh, light of my life.* Morgan was the reason she was braving the past, facing all her old demons and defeats. Suntop might mean nothing but humiliation to Morgan's mother, but to her small son she prayed it would prove a haven. A bolt-hole from an increasingly threatening world.

Because Suntop was a country unto itself. A kingdom with its own well-defended borders, its own laws and values. If she could gain Morgan a toehold in that world, help him expand that somehow to some right of citizenship there, then maybe she could protect him—Suntop could protect him—from his father.

From her ex-husband, Eric Foster.

Who was hurting his son more and more with each passing year.

Since their divorce three years ago, Eric had demanded shared custody. In spite of her protests, despite the fact that Eric was rarely home, he'd insisted that Morgan be shuttled between their households every other week. This was a terrible arrangement as far as Risa was concerned; it left her child bewildered, disoriented and increasingly resentful.

Torn between two households with entirely conflicting philosophies. With no sense of belonging anywhere.

As he approached his teen years, Morgan was starting to express his unhappiness through misbehavior—mild acts of impatience and rebellion.

But the more he acted out and acted up, the more Eric insisted that he needed harsher discipline, that Risa must be spoiling him. Now Eric was talking about sending him away to one of those military schools—where Morgan's high spirits would be ground to dust, Risa feared. His freewheeling, inquisitive mind imprisoned in endless drudgery and savage routine.

When all he needs is roots! Stability. And a real, loving, caring father to guide him safely into manhood.

Or failing that—and given Eric, that failure seemed a given—then Morgan needed a surrogate father.

Or perhaps a grandfather would serve, as well?

And that was why they were spending this summer at Suntop, in search of all of the above. And if Risa didn't like it, she would lump it, because Morgan came first. Always and forever.

"It's nineteen miles to Trueheart," Morgan announced, sitting up straighter and peering over the dash, as if the town might any second pop up out of the highway pavement.

"And we've traveled six miles since you started figuring, so it's even closer than that. Want to stop there and get an ice-cream cone?" Or they could, assuming Hansen's general store was still in existence, she reminded herself as he nodded emphatic agreement. But Trueheart must have changed—would have changed. Look how much she herself had changed, from tearful bride of nineteen, storming off to Las Vegas to cancel her mistake, to rueful, seasoned woman of thirty, divorcée and mom.

And how much will Suntop have changed?

Morgan propped his bare feet on the dash and slumped in his seat. "Will my grandfather be there when we get to Suntop?"

How many times had she explained this? "No, sweetie. Nowadays he lives in San Antonio, Texas, with your Aunt Lara. When he had his heart attack, it seemed best that he move someplace closer to good doctors. It can take hours to reach a hospital from Suntop, especially in winter with all the snow." And once Joe Wiggly had retired and her sisters moved away, it must have been lonely—Ben rattling around the Big House with no one but a housekeeper to boss or bully. Not that Ben would ever admit to needing anyone. "But he comes up to the ranch every August, for six weeks or so, and you'll meet him then."

It was mid-June now. Even if their encounter with Ben didn't work out as she prayed, still she would have bought Morgan a summer of stability, a few precious, happy months to explore his heritage.

Or what would have been his heritage if Ben hadn't disinherited his mother eight months before Morgan was born.

But maybe Ben will repent once he sees him. Risa didn't give a damn about making her own peace with her father. Until this spring, they hadn't communicated except for a brief, coldly formal exchange of announcements and ultimatums in the first month after she fled her wedding.

But if Ben fell for Morgan—and to see her child was to love him, as far as Risa was concerned; he was perfect, even in his imperfections. *If Ben falls for Morgan, he'll protect him.* Ben had the power to stand up to Eric, where his ex-wife did not.

At least, she prayed he still had. That, too, could have changed.

LESS HAD CHANGED in Trueheart than Risa feared. It had grown larger, but it was still a small, charming town, with nineteenth-century carpenter gothic cottages and abundantly treed streets and a fine view of the San Juan Mountains to the north. The high school might have doubled in size, but the Lone Star still survived in more than Risa's bittersweet memories.

Simpson's café had received a fresh coat of turquoise paint, window boxes filled with red geraniums and a sign that declared it to now be Michelle's Place. But the general store was still in business on Main Street, still selling everything from bridles and horse feed to aspirin and homemade ice cream. And apparently the Hansens still owned it, though they were out back in their house, eating lunch, the teenager who'd scooped their cones had explained. So Risa couldn't ask about Jules, with whom she'd lost touch years ago.

Just as well; too many memories were flooding back all at once, and suddenly she was too tired to deal with them. *Four hundred and thirty-six miles in two days,* she reminded herself wryly—or it would be in another mile, because up ahead on the left she could see the main entrance. She swallowed around the lump in her throat. "And there's the ranch name board. See the suns?" Still gilded to perfection; whoever had taken over from Joe Wiggly was doing his job.

"Are they setting or rising?" Morgan wanted to know, looking up as they drove beneath.

"You know, I never thought to ask Ben. I suppose one of each, because the sunlight strikes Suntop Mountain first of all places in the valley during June and July, then last of all places toward the fall. I'll have to show you. It's lovely." Last time she'd stood up there and turned in the light was the morning she'd met— *Stop!* she told herself

harshly. She'd have to face up to those old memories eventually, she supposed, but not yet. Let her see Suntop now
through her son's eager eyes. "And up ahead, that line of
cottonwoods marks the river."

As they rolled over the bridge, she hooked a thumb
south. "Down that way is the best swimming hole."

"Swimming! Can we go now, Mom? *Please?* Can we?"

"Not just yet, sweetie. I want to settle in. Unpack and
put the groceries away." They'd stopped to buy minimal
supplies at a store in Durango, and the meat should hit a
refrigerator soon.

Tell that to a ten-year-old wiggle-worm.

"Aw," he whined, kicking something under the dash.
"I'm *hot*. I wanna go *now*."

Though she was tempted to tell him they could swim
this evening, she'd learned not to promise till she was sure
she could deliver. "Up ahead is the ranch yard," she said,
instead. "The barns and the bunkhouse where the cowboys
live. And the foreman's house." The foreman—ranch manager was apparently the title these days—was a man by the
name of Rafe Montana, Ben had informed her in his letter,
when he'd agreed that they might stay at Suntop for the
summer. Montana would be expecting them, and he'd open
the Big House and see that it was ready for their use.

Morgan thumped the floorboards.

"And there'll be horses in the home pasture," she added
brightly. "I used to ride a palomino named Sunrise."
Sunny would be seventeen now, Risa calculated, if she was
still alive. But winters were tough on old horses, and Ben
had never believed in stabling; said it bred soft stock.

Morgan's sulk vanished in typical fashion—instanta-
neously. "Do I get my very own horse?"

"We'll see what the foreman—the ranch manager—says.
You'll certainly get to ride." Risa was looking forward to

teaching him. For a split second, her mind offered up a picture of Miguel feeding a carrot to Jackhammer. Sailing spectacularly over his head, that time in the arroyo at Sweetwater Flats. *Oh, stop!* "You can ride all you want. Maybe we'll even go overnight and camp out if you like."

"*Yeah!* Will we see a grizzly bear?"

"Lots of deer, at any rate. And elk and eagles. And he-e-ere's the yard." She turned carefully through the gates and winced in spite of herself, remembering her last exit. *How did I miss killing myself?* Reaching sideways, she brushed her son's cheek with her knuckles. *And if I had, I'd never have had you.*

"Errr," he growled absently, turning away from the caress, then let out a gasp. "Horses! Baby horses! Oh, *look*, Mommy!"

Risa laughed under her breath as she parked the car near the training corral. He must be excited. Morgan hadn't called her Mommy in almost a year. "A baby horse is a foal," she informed him. But he was already bolting from the car, scrambling up the fence rails beside a tall cowboy who'd been peering into the pen.

The man reached out and caught her son's arm as he swung a leg over the top rail and started down the inner side. "Whoa! Hold on there," Risa heard him say in a voice of quiet authority as she hurried to join them. "You don't want to spook 'em, son."

"Morgan, listen to the man," she added, hooking her fingers over the back of her son's belt.

"'Kay," he breathed on a note of rapture, his eyes locked on the animals. A lanky, sandy-haired young man and an older hand each walked a mare and foal around the circular corral.

"We're halter-breaking the colts," their companion told Morgan in a deep, easy voice with no hint of patronization.

"They'll follow their dams—their mothers—anywhere. So if you tug on their halters and ask them to come along, they're happy to cooperate. They'll be broken to lead before they know it." He leaned back from the rail to offer Risa his hand and a crinkle-eyed smile. "Rafe Montana, ma'am, and you must be Mrs. Foster?"

"Ms., if you don't mind. I'm divorced." She'd wanted no reminder of Eric after she left him, and if she hadn't had a child, she'd have reclaimed her maiden name in a heartbeat.

But no way would Eric have allowed her to change Morgan's last name. And she hadn't been able to separate herself from her son any more than those mares could bear parting from their foals. "But I go by Risa, please," she added, "and this is Morgan."

"Hmm." Montana studied her mesmerized offspring for a moment. "What do you reckon, Morgan? Want to help out? We could use another hand."

Without sparing him a glance, Morgan nodded so vigorously he almost fell off the fence.

"Good. Then you think you could walk over there *very* slowly and quietly to my son, Sean? No sudden movements now, okay?"

Risa felt her eyes sting as Morgan tiptoed in exaggerated slow motion across the corral toward the sandy-haired young man and his charges. Eric gave Morgan orders constantly, but had he ever in his life asked her son for help? She sincerely doubted it. This was what she'd brought him to find.

"Sean, you've got an assistant," called Montana.

Sean glanced up, grinned and pulled the mare and colt to a halt. Bent to talk quietly to her son, who nodded several times, then reached out his fingertips to the foal—timidly stroked his short, fuzzy neck.

"You've had quite a drive," Montana noted while they watched Morgan take the colt's halter and begin to walk sedately beside Sean and the mare.

"Yes," Risa agreed, eyes on her son. He shot her one glance of flashing joy, an expression that said, *Look at me. Oh, look, look! Can you believe this?* Then he forgot her entirely as they circled the ring.

"If you like, Risa, you could go on up to the Big House and settle in. See if you need anything else we can help you with before we leave for the day. I'll tell Sean to drop Morgan off soon as he tires of this."

"You may have him on your hands for quite a while!" But the offer was tempting. There were the thawing groceries, but more than that, she was exhausted.

And sorely in need of some solitude to confront her old ghosts.

Whereas Morgan had the exercise needs of a Great Dane puppy; after two days cooped up in a car he needed running. And after all, to find him the company of men was why she'd brought him to Suntop. "If you really mean it, then, yes, that sounds perfect."

THE ONLY JARRING NOTE came just as she left the ranch manager. Montana had informed her that the water and electricity were turned on, and that he'd sent up a cleaning woman to air out the rooms and see to the bed linens and laundry. Anything she needed, she had only to ask; nights, when Rafe was not in residence—he lived with his wife, Dana, who owned the Ribbon River Dude Ranch to the west of Trueheart—Risa could count on Anse Kirby, Rafe's right-hand man, who now lived in the old foreman's house above the yard.

"So that's about it," he concluded. "Your housemate arrived 'bout an hour ago, I understand. Didn't get a chance to speak with him, myself. He drove straight on through as if he knew the way. But if he wants anything, a horse, or fly-fishing advice or whatever, tell him to see me."

"Housemate?" Risa repeated, lifting her foot off the gas pedal.

"Ben didn't tell you? Some old friend of the family who's been given the use of the Big House for the rest of the summer. We get guests like that every so often, usually for the fishing or the hunting." Montana's blue eyes sharpened on her face. "He'll stay over in the guest wing, of course. As big as the place is…"

She rallied a smile. "Oh, it's fine. I just didn't know." Trust Ben to keep her in the dark; withholding information had always been one of his favorite ways of staying in control. *No changes there.* "And you're right. The place is plenty big enough."

Nevertheless, Risa was disappointed. All this day she'd been coming to realize that she'd returned to Suntop with a twofold quest. Primarily she'd returned for Morgan, but it seemed she had her own minor mission, as well.

Because clearly, the past hadn't been erased, as she'd told herself all these years. It had only been hiding out at Suntop, sharpening its claws.

So her task this summer would be to come to terms with the old hurts, the old memories. To forgive, forget, then to let them all go. Maybe that was what she needed to do— must do—before she could claim the happy future that so far had eluded her.

And anyone who intruded on that mission would be at best a distraction, and at worse, a nuisance.

CHAPTER SIXTEEN

COMING BACK to Suntop had been harder than Miguel had expected. The sight of that big sweeping staircase had stopped him cold as he walked in the front door. The last time he'd seen her...

A lifetime ago, though his eleven years in Alaska, working as a driller for the biggest outfit north of the Arctic Circle, had felt more like two lifetimes....

Still, neither time nor cold nor half a dozen wistful women had rubbed out the memories that lurked here at Suntop.

Miguel shook himself, shrugging that vision of a bride in white satin aside. Hoisted his duffel bag and case of instruments and strode across the hardwood floor, almost bounded up the stairs. He'd dump these in his room—Tankersly had told him to take anything in the guest wing that pleased him—then get out of here, back out into sunlight where he could breathe.

Maybe I should have asked for a room in the bunkhouse—my old bunk. Miguel smiled wryly and kept on climbing. At thirty-five, he was old enough to know that heartaches came and went, but a bad mattress could kill a man.

He turned right at the top of the staircase per Ben's directions—he'd never been up here before. Hadn't made it to the top floor once that last crazy week before the wedding. With that aging Texas vamp—how had they called her? Belle Lowrey?—playing moral watchdog, he hadn't had a snowball's hope in hell of sneaking into Risa's bedroom that last week.

And if I had? If I'd had a chance to tie the knots a little tighter?

Forget it, he told himself harshly. *It's over, done with.* But that was harder to remember here at Suntop, with all its ghosts of old dreams, than it had been back in Alaska.

So he'd stowed his gear in an enormous guest room with a fireplace and a fine view of the Trueheart Hills and a bowl of fresh flowers on the bureau, and set off to visit the only dream that mattered. He'd climbed Suntop and stood, staring off to the north.

Somewhere out there was the mother of all anticlines. He hadn't had time to locate it the last time, but this time… His hands tingled and he flipped them over and flexed his fingers, laughing softly. This time the luck was with him!

He swung to look down over the home valley. In the ranch yard, tiny figures plodded around a corral—two men, a child, two mares and their babies. Tomorrow he'd have to go down there. Ask for a mount. No hope that Jackhammer would still be around, he supposed. Some exasperated cowboy must have shot him by now.

A dusty gray car bumped up the road past the foreman's house, then climbed the hill to disappear below the shoulder of Suntop, headed for the upper valley and the Big House. Probably the housekeeper's car. Somebody had clearly been in to ready the place; the sheets had been turned down on the bed in the room he'd chosen and that vase of flowers…

More hospitality than he'd expected. He'd half figured Tankersly to refuse him, once he'd finally succeeded in contacting him this spring, told him that finally he was coming back to Suntop to drill his well.

Because by the first term of their contract, Miguel had
done *his* part. He'd married Ben's daughter, earning himself the right to drill one well. Nobody had thought to put
in a revocation clause in case the bride changed her mind
the following day.

Still, if the old man had wanted to block him, his lawyer
could have had a fine, lucrative time arguing just when a
wedding was truly a wedding. At the altar? The morning
after, when the bride demurely emerges from her bedroom,
all blushes and giggles?

Remembering Tankersly's towering fury after the wedding fiasco, Miguel had half expected he'd have to sue the
rancher for his right to drill. Certainly he hadn't expected
to find a bed waiting for him at Suntop, with sheets turned
down.

Time must have softened the old fox at last.

HE STAYED UP on Suntop for more than an hour, pacing
with excitement, planning his attack. He needed to move
fast if he hoped to bring in a rig before the snows. What a
pity that Tankersly wouldn't let him call in a seismic crew.
Their readings could have shortened his search; would have
given his theories a credibility that he'd need when he went
looking for investors. But on that point the old man had
dug in his heels. No seismograph trucks would be crawling
over *his* ranch, walloping the land with their hydraulic ham-
mers, sending sound waves through the earth to scare the
cattle, distract the hands... None of his objections had made
an ounce of sense in Miguel's book; his stand seemed to
be pure contrariness.

But there was no swaying him on this point, and Miguel
dared not lose his cooperation overall. So he'd just have to
do it the hard way. The same way he'd started the search
eleven years ago. He'd left off his mapping three miles east

of Blindman's Canyon. Tomorrow he'd continue from there.

Striding back to the Big House through the late slanting sunlight, he considered the problem of supper. After he'd picked up his rented Jeep at the airport in Cortez, he'd been too impatient for grocery shopping. So tonight he'd drive into Trueheart, find himself a good meal. Perhaps a burger at the Lone Star, if it still existed. He could sit there and stare out over the dance floor—and maybe watch a ghostly young couple sway and hold each other tight, as if there were no tomorrow beyond a kiss.

So thinking, he opened the front door, then paused as a movement caught his eye.

A woman in a white dress descended the staircase—saw him and stopped halfway down. Slowly her hand rose to her slender throat.

Hair the color of the sunset, of burning dreams and lost lucky coins of Mexican treasure. Big eyes bruised with shock; long lashes blinking, incredulous. She shook her head and with the movement she became real—tawny flesh, not wistful vision.

"Risa-Sonrisa." He'd forgotten how beautiful.

"No," she said softly, and wheeled on the stairs, graceful as a fawn.

He'd forgotten how angry he'd been. How humiliated—the spurned groom, facing their amused and bewildered guests alone. How he'd searched for her all that long night, when he should have known precisely where she was—in his bed, in his arms, in his heart. And all the while wondering—

And here she was, fleeing him all over again. She tripped, recovered, her sandals rattling on the stairs.

"¡Esperame!" Wait for me! "I want to talk to you!" *¡Por Dios,* I do!

"Ha!"

He charged up the stairs, taking them three at a bound, the blood humming in his ears, muscles burning in his thighs, instincts of the hunting male lunging out of the cave in the mind where they always lurked—a long-legged, willful woman running away, and by God he'd have an answer this time! *"Risa!"*

She skidded on the landing, sobbed and shot off to the left.

He hit the second floor running, panting—if she made it to a room and locked herself in? No way would he permit that. "No!" he called as she reached a door, grasped its knob.

He lunged past her and stiff-armed it shut again. "Wait. I've a question for you!" She spun as if to dart past him along the wall, and he slammed his other hand into the paneling, trapping her between his arms. "Be still!"

Not that she could. Her breasts were heaving under the soft white cotton of her sundress, only inches from his chest. She threw back her head to meet his eyes. Buried her teeth in that delectable bottom lip and gave him glare for glare.

"Calmate," he said, as much to himself as her. "I have a question for you." Eleven years he'd been wondering.

She shook her head, maybe incredulous or possibly refusing and defiant, but, oh, he'd have an answer! He drew in a deep breath—reaching for his temper—and inhaled the perfume of her hair, of her skin, still familiar after all these years. *Increíble* that it could have stayed with him.

"Dígame," he insisted, leaning closer, the heat of their bodies melding. Tell me.

"W-what?" she growled, sounding like a feral little cat, looking like one with those golden eyes, their pupils dilated with shock and resentment.

"After our wedding, why did you run?"

For a moment all motion ceased—her breath stopped; her face froze; maybe even her heart paused—then her hand sailed out of nowhere to crack against his cheekbone. *"Why?"* She burst into tears. "You *bastard!"*

She swung at him again and he caught her wrist. "Stop that!" She struggled and he pressed her hand back against the wall, pinned it there. Her knee rose toward his groin. He cursed and crowded closer, sliding one leg between her thighs, leaning in to flatten her against the plaster. "Stop it. ¡Bruja! Be still!" Before she drove him to madness— this was madness, to hold her so, in this travesty of everything he'd ever wanted from her. "Calm...down!" He pressed his cheek to hers, trying to lend her some control, trying to find some.

For a moment they simply stood locked together, breathing as one, then he said huskily, "Risa-Sonrisa, why are you crying?" *When it's I who was insulted and abandoned?*

He felt her body jolt—her breasts bumping against him—then realized she was laughing—bitter laughter like gold coins showering down upon him. Hot tears flowing.

He brushed his lips along her wet cheek, tasting her saltiness—he couldn't help himself—then warily leaned back a few inches, so that he could peer down at her.

Whenever he'd dreamed of this moment, of confronting her at last, he'd imagined her fearful, shamefaced, maybe defiant. But never...wounded? How could this be? She was seriously confusing him, body and soul; from the waist up he was still furious, but from the waist down—*ay*—there were stirrings of forgiveness.

He should step back, but to do so would risk a gelding. There was no forgiveness in *her* smoldering eyes. "Why, *mi esposita?"* he demanded with a jeering tenderness.

She trembled against him. "You *know* I'm not your

wife! I sent you your ring back from Vegas—and the annulment papers.''

Ah, yes, his poor savaged ring. For a moment, to deny it pleased him. ''What makes you think I got such a package?''

''Ben must have given it to you. D-didn't he?''

''You think so? But how long did you think I'd wait for you here, kicking my heels? Wondering and worrying?'' In truth, he'd stayed until her express letter had arrived, the second day after the wedding. Along with a letter to her family, a cold announcement of her marriage to Eric Foster; directions to send her camera and clothes to his parents in Denver.

After that, publicly proclaimed a loser, he couldn't bear the sight of the place. Oil or no, he had to get away. And Ben had no use for him once he'd failed to serve his purpose. He'd driven back to Texas, stayed a few weeks, but a bitter restlessness had seized him, driving him on. He'd headed north and west again, stopping only when the roads ran out in Alaska.

''But somebody *must* have told you,'' she insisted. ''Even if you left, surely you stayed in touch till you heard—''

Ah, does it frighten you so much, cielito, *that I might still think you my wife?* He was tempted to push the joke at least as far as a husbandly kiss—his lips longed for the taste of her. ''No,'' he admitted reluctantly, ''I know you annulled our marriage—the next day. That then you married your rich lawyer—Mr. Mercedes.'' He gave her a wry bitter smile. ''Which makes you Mrs. Mercedes, doesn't it?''

And where, come to think of it—not once had it crossed his mind—was her damn husband? Miguel glanced warily left and right. Were he to come upon *his* wife held in such an embrace as this, there would be hell to pay and the payment would be prompt. But Foster, that sneaking coward... "Am I risking a lawsuit, here?"

"From Eric?" She tipped her head back to rest it against the wall, looking up at him with a strange, cool expression. "I doubt it. I divorced him three years ago."

"*¿De veras?*" A shaft of delight shot through him, like the sweep of a lighthouse beam through the dark—as quickly extinguished. *Such a waste.*

"*De veras,*" she agreed mockingly. "I seem to have terrible taste in men, don't I? Maybe there's a gene for that," she added under her breath.

"So..." He was suddenly at a loss. He still meant to have his answer, but now there were so many questions, more than he'd dreamed. And all the old feelings flooding back. Whatever had gone wrong between them, there had never been a lack of desire, not on his part. He reached to brush a strand of gleaming copper off her dark eyebrows. *Risa-Sonrisa.* How was it possible that she'd grown more beautiful through the years?

"Take your hands off me," she said with a deadly calm. "In fact, Miguel, why don't you back off? I promise I won't kick you."

"Ah," he said wryly, and stepped away. "Your pardon."

"Don't hold your breath for it." She swung toward the nearby door, then froze with her hand on the doorknob. "You're the—" She dropped her forehead against the door's paneling and let out a little sound, somewhere between a growl and a moan. "Of *course!* You're the houseguest. Which means—" She turned her head slightly, eyeing him through a veil of fiery silk. Blew out a resigned breath. "What is Ben up to?"

"Ben?"

"That he brought you here? Back to Suntop?"

She was adorable; he'd forgotten that, too. "Ben had

nothing to do with my return, beyond giving me a place to lay my head. This was my idea. I've come back to drill a well. You remember I was searching for—''

"Ohhh, yes. I *do* seem to recall that," she agreed in a dangerous singsong, turning entirely around to brace herself against her door. "I seem to recall a *contract*—" She almost spat the word, reminding him of a mama cat he knew in Fairbanks, a Siamese—in fact, she seemed almost to be arching and puffing herself up the way the cat did when dogs came around—

But wait a minute. The contract? Where did she… When did she—

"A contract giving you the right to drill a well—*if you married me!* How could you? Oh, you *despicable,* money-grubbing—" The tears glittered in her eyes; her lips trembled. "And now you've come back to claim your *payment?*"

"So you learned about the contract." He was still groping with that. Who could have told her? Ben never would have—

"Why the hell do you think I left you!"

For that? She might as well have slugged him again. He stood thunderstruck. She could have pushed him over with a fingertip. Never in his wildest dreams had it occurred to him that she might have— But then that meant—

"Mom?" called a child's voice from far away. Somewhere downstairs. "Mo-om!"

"Oh," Risa muttered on a soft note of consternation. Her hands flew to her hair, smoothing it, tucking it behind her ears. She licked her lips and tried on a wavering smile. Glanced up at him and winced in dismay.

"Mom?"

"Who is this?" he demanded. A child—her child. That she should have a child and it was not his? At some gut level, that made no sense.

"My son," she hissed, moving toward his voice, brushing one hand along the wall as if she needed its support. "Would you beat it? Please? I'd rather not try to explain—"

"Foster's son," he stated, catching her wrist, needing to hear her say it. "Mercedes Junior." A wave of bitterness washed over him. He should go to his room before the brat found them. He liked children—loved them—but this one? How would he be able to look upon him and smile?

"Mom! *Hey*, where are…" The voice trailed away on a note of uneasiness.

"I'm up here, sweetie! Hang on, I'm coming." She jerked herself free. "Would you go away? *Now*."

But it was too late. The kid came clattering up the stairs, making an astonishing racket. So he must be big, a child of the first years of her marriage, not a recent one.

A silver-blond head came into view, then the rest of him, rising up the last few steps, slowing as he spotted a stranger standing beside his mother.

"Morgan," Risa said faintly. "We have a visitor. This is Mr. Heydt, a friend of your grandfather's."

A man who stood speechless, while his world shifted on its axis…then commenced to spin slowly backward, everything changing at once and forever.

Because the boy who stood awkwardly before Miguel was the image—the precise image—of his little sister, Consuela, at the same age. And the boy's hair was the same shade of fine German silver-blond that Miguel's mother wore in a locket every day of her life.

"Morgan?" he said, testing the name on his tongue for the first time as he held out his hand, "*Mucho gusto*. A pleasure to meet you."

And if he didn't speak Spanish, it was time he was taught.

CHAPTER SEVENTEEN

AFTER HEYDT LEFT, Risa hadn't been able to eat a bite of the meal she'd cooked Morgan.

Not that her son had noticed. He'd been nearly bursting with excitement, determined to tell her everything about his colt—Mr. Montana had said he could train him for the summer! Could even name him if he liked! He was thinking Rocket, maybe, or maybe Comet, since he had a white star—the prettiest white star on his forehead—had she seen that?

Risa had smiled, murmured agreement to whatever he'd said and somehow survived the evening without Morgan ever realizing that she was shattered, flummoxed, her mind spinning a thousand miles beyond the kitchen table where she sat with him while he ate.

What in God's name am I going to do?

She'd spent months pleading and persuading before Eric had agreed that she could have full custody of Morgan for the summer, that she could bring him to Suntop. She still didn't know why he'd allowed it, since for the past three years Eric had steadfastly refused to let her take his son anywhere beyond the city limits. And if he realized she'd chosen Suntop for her own reasons, in the hope that Ben would help her pry Morgan away from a father who didn't love him, who only used him to hurt and spite her?

And so what now? She *couldn't* go back to Denver and give up this chance to save Morgan.

Yet how could she stay here—stay in the same house!—

with that despicable, treacherous... That Miguel should look the same as before—or even better—somehow it only made her angrier. The years should have treated him as he deserved—punished him—yet there he'd stood, bigger than life, bigger than she'd remembered, smiling that old irresistible smile. Looking her in the eye without a trace of shame.

Had he no shame?

No, she couldn't bear it. Suntop had become impossible, Risa told herself as she stood staring sightlessly into the refrigerator, hugging herself against the cold air flowing out around her. *Unless I can drive him away somehow.*

But how?

Or perhaps he'd gone already. Slunk off like the cad he was, more embarrassed than he could admit to her face. Miguel had disappeared only minutes after Morgan's appearance, and now it was midnight—no, nearly one—she realized, glancing at the clock over the ancient black six-burner stove.

Her stomach growled in the late-night silence, dolefully reminding her that her last meal had been an ice-cream cone some twelve hours earlier. Its complaints had finally driven her down to the kitchen; if she couldn't sleep, she might as well eat something while she dithered.

Oh, what am I going to do? She grabbed a carton of cottage cheese, a bowl of grapes that she'd set out hours earlier for Morgan, found a spoon, then sank down at the scrubbed pine worktable, old as the house itself. Dropped her aching head into her hands. *Think, Risa. How can I drive him away?*

Or maybe he'd gone. If God had an ounce of mercy, Miguel Heydt was gone.

"Can't sleep?"

"*Aggh!*" Her spoon clattered on the flagstone floor. Miguel stood in the doorway that led to the rest of the house. She closed her eyes for a moment. *And thank you, God!*

He stooped beside her, reaching for the utensil. She could have put out a hand and touched his soft, thick hair; he was that close.

"Couldn't you sleep?" he repeated, tossing her spoon in the sink, then opening drawers till he found the right one. He brought her another.

"I thought you'd gone." She drew the spoon through fingers that trembled.

"Wished it?" he suggested silkily, his dark eyes glinting.

"Oh, that too."

"No such luck, Risa-Sonrisa. I've been walking. It's better than punching holes in the wall, I've found." He pulled out a chair and sat with a precision that she suddenly realized was anger. Rage.

I've never seen him angry before, she marveled inwardly. Except for that one fight they'd had over Ben's Cadillac, and that had been a mere spat compared with the emotion she sensed now, rolling in subsonic waves across the table. *How could I have married someone I barely knew?*

Except that she'd done it twice. In two days. Hadn't she?

At least Eric, bad as he'd been, had given her Morgan. And much as she'd come to dislike the man, for that she'd always be grateful.

But this man...who'd betrayed her love, used her for his own shabby ends... And why, now that she thought of it—"*You're* angry? Whatever for? You got your well, didn't you? Though I suppose I did do you out of clause two and three of your despicable contract."

"Oh, you did me out of something I value much more than that, *pasión.*"

"Don't you call me that!"

"I'll call you whatever I please!" His voice cracked like a bullwhip. "Why didn't you tell me?"

"Tell you…w—what?" She felt the first flicker of real fear. There was no one for a mile or more whom she could call on. And here she sat with a man who seemed to be trembling on the verge of explosion. A man who'd never been what she thought he was. Never what she hoped or dreamed.

"That I had a son, *un hijo.*" He tipped his head toward the distant staircase.

No…Oh, no-o-o. The air was sucking out of her lungs, as if she'd been shot out into space with neither helmet nor suit. She shook her head. "W—what are you— He's Eric's son!" Of course he was! Born nine months to the day after their wedding in Vegas.

"*¡Mentirosa!*"

Liar, he was calling her. Risa gripped the edge of the table and shook her head. He was deluded—quite possibly insane. "Of *course* he's Eric's! He doesn't look in the least like you."

Didn't look like anybody on either side of the family. She'd always assumed Morgan's hair came from her mother, who'd been blond—so many shades of blond, in fact, her daughter had never been quite sure which was the real one. But what other explanation could fit? And his developing size must be a gift from Ben, since Eric stood two inches shy of six feet, though he'd never admit it.

"No, he doesn't look much like me, except that he'll be tall, as I am. As was my father." Miguel shifted, pulled a wallet from a back pocket. "But tell me who this resembles?" He flipped it open to a plastic window that held a photo of a teenage girl.

She could have been Morgan's older sister, with that same mischievous triangular smile, those same broad cheekbones. "They don't have the same hair," Risa protested. The girl's straight thick hair was the same bronzy shade as Miguel's. But, oh, the eyes were *precisely* Morgan's, the way they squinched merrily in laughter.

"His hair comes from his grandfather, Johann Heydt."

"I...think I'm—" She was. Risa shot up from the table, stumbled out the back door just in time, to lean, heaving, over the grass. *Oh, no, please, no!* Struggling to throw up the poisonous knowledge along with the acid in her roiling stomach.

The screen door shut softly; a warm hand came to rest on her shaking back. "Easy."

Oh, easy for you to say! She spat one last time, wiped the back of a hand across her mouth, straightened with a wretched groan.

He handed her a warm wet paper towel and stood silently while she used it. Then gave her a glass of water.

She rinsed out her mouth, spat, drank the rest. He took the glass and set it down on the steps. She hugged herself— she was shivering violently—and drifted away, staring upward. The stars, she'd forgotten how many, how bright, how beautiful, up here at Suntop... If she could only drift off along the Milky Way...wake in her own bed back in Denver in the morning to find this had all been a terrible dream.

Miguel loomed alongside, cutting off the sky toward the south. "Truly you didn't know?"

"No...I guess I...didn't want to know." His betrayal had hurt her so deeply. Not just his betrayal, but what it proved—that the love she'd thought they shared was a mirage. Nothing but a cynical, shabby seduction. To survive that loss she'd had to obliterate Miguel from her thoughts— from her heart. She'd annulled him along with their marriage. Then a few weeks later when she'd learned she was pregnant... *I had to deny.* Who knows what she might have done if she'd realized she carried a part of her seducer inside her? To love her baby, she'd *had* to believe he was Eric's. Anything else was unthinkable. "I never even thought...not once..."

"Ah." He walked beside her, the cool grass swishing against their calves. "But now...this changes everything, you know."

Fear scorched through her mind like a shooting star blazing across the dark. "No, I don't know that. It doesn't change anything!" She wouldn't let it.

He caught her arm, swung her to face him. "Risa, don't be ridiculous. He's my son."

"Not in any way that counts for anything!" She wrenched free, stepped back.

"And that's my fault? If you'd given me a chance—"

"Oh, you had a chance and you blew it—sold it for oil rights! So don't talk to *me* about your precious fatherhood."

"And Morgan? He'll feel the same?"

She closed the distance between them in one savage stride and jabbed him in the chest. "Don't even *think* about telling him," she cried. "You do that, Miguel, and I swear I'll—I'll—" He'd reached to gently grasp her forefinger, hold it pinned against his heart. Through her fingertip she could feel it swiftly beating, under the hot, hard flesh.

"And you'll what, *mamacita?*" A thread of laughter laced through the mockery.

Little mother? Oh, he'd *better* take her seriously! "I'll take him straight back to Denver and you'll never see him again. Eric's in politics now, you know, a state senator, and he trades favors with every judge and prosecutor in the city—in the state. I promise you he can block you at every turn." As he had her, for years.

"Ah." Still holding her finger, Miguel tipped back his head and consulted the stars. "I think..." he said finally, looking down again, "that you've had a long day. Too many surprises. Why don't we discuss this in the morning.''

She was weary, beaten, tears hovering behind her lids. If he'd only let her go... ''You promise you won't tell him?''

''Not before you and I speak again.''

It wasn't good enough, but maybe it was enough for now. ''All right, then.'' She tried to reclaim her hand—

''*Bueno*...'' He lifted it to his mouth, kissed her fingertip, let her go.

She spun and left him. And it didn't occur to her till sometime later, after she'd scrubbed his kiss from her finger, then fallen into bed: he'd promised not to speak to Morgan—and here she was, trusting that promise. Would she never learn?

WAKING CAME SLOWLY, sunlight sifting under her lashes, bringing a lazy smile to her face—which vanished abruptly. *Miguel!* A dream, a nightmare, she told herself, bolting upright in bed to stare around the bedroom.

Her old bedroom at the ranch. So it was no dream. She really had come to Suntop, met Miguel. ''Morgan?'' she called. Last night she'd left open the door that led to the bathroom, then on into Tess's old bedroom beyond, so that if her son awoke in the night, needed anything—

''Morgan?'' she cried again, suddenly frantic. She slung the covers off and glanced down at herself, then clutched them to her; she'd fallen asleep clothed, then apparently had squirmed out of her T-shirt and shorts during the night. ''Still asleep,'' she assured herself, bundling into her bathrobe. She hurried through the bathroom to lean in the doorway beyond—let out a slow sigh of relief as she saw his bed with its tangled heap of covers—and the long lump buried in the middle. Morgan was always as restless in dreams as he was awake.

Good, let him sleep. She'd grab first rights to the bathroom.

She showered and brushed her teeth, determinedly shoving all thoughts of Miguel aside. A cup of coffee first, then she'd decide what must be done, how to neutralize this threat.

"Hey, sleepyhead," she called teasingly, combing out her wet hair. "Rise and shine!" He didn't usually sleep this late. And just how late was it? Her internal clock told it must be nearly eight.

It was past nine, she realized, when she consulted the clock on her bedside table. Later than her son ever—

"Morgan!" She hurried into his room. "Sweetie?"

The lump in the bed was two pillows and a mound of comforter—not purposely arranged, she realized; she'd simply assumed. But still—

"Morgan?" Heart pounding, she tore down the stairs.

God, oh, God, Miguel had taken him—snatched him! If he'd run for the border, whisked him off into Mexico— Half-blinded by tears, she hit the first floor running, sobbing—

The sound of distant laughter brought her skidding to a halt. She sucked in a hiccuping breath, clutched her bathrobe to her throat. *Calm down,* she told herself. *Hysterical ninny.* She grimaced, wiped a forearm across her eyes as Morgan's bubbling laughter came again, with a baritone echo running beneath it.

Calm down. Morgan was all right. And she could shoot Miguel later for scaring her so. Her steps quickened as laughter turned to a hapless yelp, followed by the clatter and smash of crockery.

Bracing her hands on the kitchen doorway, she stopped short.

Morgan stood on a footstool by the massive stove, staring down at the sea of batter and broken bowl that surrounded his platform. Clutching a spatula, he looked ready to cry. "I...I d—didn't mean to—"

He turned anxiously to the man who'd swung around from the open refrigerator.

"And who thought you did?" Miguel asked easily. He glanced down at the mess, and a grin started curling. "It would take a master criminal to plan a disaster like this. This isn't an accident—it's an event. A tidal wave! Imagine if you were an ant down there and you looked up and saw that coming?" He laughed.

"Wham," Morgan said faintly, the color flowing back to his cheeks.

"Ba-boom! It's raining pancakes! Call out the ant life-guards! Call out the navy! Call the ant *presidente*. We've got a disaster here. Meltdown!"

"Splat!" Morgan giggled.

Laughing, Miguel stepped through the ant disaster to grab him about the waist. "Come here, master criminal!" He swung him to a dry bit of floor and set him down. "You grab some paper towels and I'll get the life preservers."

He turned and strolled toward Risa. "Good morning, *rubia*." With his big body shielding them from Morgan's view, he caught the lapels of her bathrobe, tugged them together. "You're coming undone," he murmured whimsically. "*I* like it, but—" He caught the two ends of her sash, snugged them tighter.

His hands on her, so sure, so casually possessive. A wave of heat washed over her, as overwhelming as the ants must have found their pancake deluge. He brushed a lock of loose hair behind her pinkening ear. "We were cooking you breakfast," he said ruefully, his eyes roving over her face and breasts with frank approval. "Come sit down and we'll try again."

She started to brush past him. "*Don't* bother. I can fix some—"

"No." He caught the back of her sash, which brought her to an instant halt. "This morning it's gentlemen's treat. *Sientate*. Which means sit down," he explained as Morgan looked up from where he knelt, dabbing at the puddle. "In the affectionate sense. When I speak to someone I know and care for. If your mother were a lady I'd never met before, I'd say *sientase*." So saying, he pulled out a chair for Risa, who gave up and sat. She'd shoot him after coffee, first private moment she got.

THAT MOMENT WAS a while in coming. Consigned to the sidelines, sipping her coffee at the kitchen table, Risa spent the next hour progressing through all the psychological stages that stem from disaster.

First came denial: *no, please don't tell me they're going to start pancakes from scratch again!*

Then rage: couldn't Miguel have simply minded his own business—driven into Trueheart if he wanted a hot breakfast, since clearly he hadn't cooked one for himself in years?

From whence she moved on to bargaining: *If you guys would let me take over from here, then we could all get on with our day, now, couldn't we? Why, Morgan, you and I could even go swimming, and I'm sure Mr. Heydt has his own matters to—no?*

And finally, resignation: Yes, the pancakes were raw in the middle, and the bacon charred, and the butter ice-cold, but all she had to do was clean her plate and the ordeal would be over. And after all, just look at that smile on Morgan's face!

As far as she knew, he and Eric had never cooked a meal together. Breakfasts at Eric's house were prepared by either his housekeeper or Morgan's nanny. Suppers and lunches Eric ate away from home.

No grown male had ever showered such extended attention upon her son. Not that Miguel was obvious about it. It was delivered in an offhand, casual way, with mild teasing and gentle insults, as if he and her son had known each other for years. Still, Morgan's every statement or opinion or timid joke was treated with grave attention, or mischievous attention, or skeptical attention. But always Miguel attended.

And Morgan bloomed like a little cactus spreading its rare flowers to a passing thunderstorm.

Passing—that was the reason she should be stopping this. Snatching up her son and fleeing, stuffing him into their car and driving off over the horizon as fast as she could. Because no matter how flattering to Morgan, Miguel's attention would be a passing one.

Because no way was Risa letting him into her son's life. This was a onetime event that she'd never have permitted, if only she'd wakened in time.

"*So,* go brush your teeth, *muchacho,* and grab a hat, while I throw these dishes in the sink," Miguel declared, pushing back from the table. "Then let's see this *caballito* of yours. Want to take my Jeep?"

Risa came out of her worried musings with a start. Frowned and shook her head as she put down her coffee cup. But it was too late.

Morgan had already yelled his agreement and torn out of the room.

"No. Oh, no, Miguel. Don't even think it!" She rose from the table.

"It's thought." A plate in each hand, he paused before her. "Besides, he's dying to show off his horse and I want to see it." He cocked his head. "*Cielito,* don't be mad. You can come, too, if you hurry."

She stamped her foot. "Miguel, he's not yours to show anything!"

"Oh? I seem to recall—" His eyes took on a dangerous

glint as he set down the plates and drifted closer. "In fact, I *know* I remember every last minute of how we got him." He brushed his knuckles across her bottom lip. "*¿Te acuerdas?* That was me, that was you, up there in Paradise."

"Stop it!" she whispered, turning her head aside. She wouldn't remember. *Would* not.

"And which time do you think it was?" His voice was a husky caress. "I'm thinking the second time, after you'd gotten over your shyness and surprise, the time you wouldn't stop laughing. Even inside my mouth you laughed while we kissed, you remember? And now, *mira*—look at him. We have a child of laughter."

"*Hush,*" she said desperately, hearing Morgan yelling something from the top of the stairs. "If you don't stop, I'll take him away!"

"You think I wouldn't follow? Risa, you can't run from this—not this time. This you will have to face. He's my son and nothing will change that."

Prove it! She opened her mouth to cry the words, but Morgan was clattering down the stairs. She flattened a hand to her hammering heart. She mustn't panic. Must consider calmly and coldly and logically how to beat him. He'd stolen the first march on her, but he wasn't going to win. No way would she let him.

"So…" He studied her face with a wary smile as Morgan charged into the kitchen. "We'll wait for you outside. Don't be long."

"She's coming? *Hooray!* Wait till you pet him, Mom! He's so…so fuzzy!" Morgan banged out the back door.

Risa clenched her hands till they ached. "I'll only be a minute."

CHAPTER EIGHTEEN

ASIDE FROM HIS OWN desires, he was glad they'd brought Risa along, Miguel reflected, watching her corner the mare and colt in the home pasture. He'd forgotten most of the horse skills he'd learned at Suntop so long ago, and never had he dealt with a young one such as this.

Pinning him gently against his dam's side, Risa spoke softly as she buckled the halter straps, her words soothing the skittish baby at the same time as they instructed her child. "See? He isn't too worried so long as he's touching his mama. Oh, yes, sweetie, he's gorgeous with that star. And sorrel is what you call his color. Bright red with a red mane and tail."

She'd ignored Miguel entirely on their drive down to the main valley. Now she was using her words and her superior knowledge to shut him out. Drawing an intimate circle around herself, her son and the two horses, with him left on the outside, the rueful spectator.

Not for long, he promised her.

She told Morgan to let the foal out to the end of his ten-foot lead and let him wander for a minute, reaccustoming himself to the feel of the tack. "Okay, now reel him in nice and slow as I move off with Mom. He'll be happy to follow."

The colt wheeled and broke into a tiny explosion of bucking, kicking his teacup hooves at the sky, then prancing after his dam, with Morgan trotting alongside.

Miguel laughed. "Bravo! What a performance!"

Morgan was pink with pride. "Bravo? Does that mean he's brave?"

"Brave and fearless. And it also means 'Well done! Very good!'"

"Then that's what I'm going to call him!" Morgan crowed. "Bravo! It's perfect! He isn't afraid of anything."

Miguel gave him a grin and a thumb's-up. "An excellent choice. I like it."

Risa sniffed and kept on moving toward the gate. *You'd better worry,* he told her silently. He had things to offer his son that she wouldn't be able to match. *Gracias a Dios,* he added, admiring the sway of her slender hips as she walked in her tight jeans and high-heeled western boots.

But a half hour later he was less optimistic. She'd closed herself and Morgan in the circular pen, where they walked mare and colt around and around. Miguel was shut out again, left to smile foolishly each time they passed him. Standing there trying to think of something witty to say at each round.

Enough of this. He reached to catch Risa's elbow the next time she walked by. "I need to talk to you, *cielito.*"

Morgan stood on tiptoe to look over the mare's low-hanging neck. "See-lito? What's that mean?"

"Ci-eh-lee-toh. It means—"

"Never you mind," Risa cut in with brittle cheeriness. "Let go," she added under her breath.

"Nunca. Come talk to me. It's urgent. And besides—" he raised his voice "—Morgan can handle both *caballos,* can't you, son?" His hand clenched on her with the power of that word. The first time he'd used it aloud. *Mi hijo.*

"Uh, yeah." Morgan nodded, dubiously at first, then with growing conviction. "Sure. 'Course I can."

"I'll be right here, sweetie," Risa assured him, handing

him the mare's lead with obvious reluctance. "If you need
me, just holler."

Miguel grinned over her shoulder and Morgan rolled his
eyes. *Moms. Women.* It was a moment of pure masculine
bonding.

"What?" Risa growled, climbing up on the top rail to
sit next to where he stood. She cast down one wintry
glance, then fixed her eyes on her son.

"He's doing okay, you see? You don't want to coddle
him too much."

"I've done *just* fine with him for ten years without your
advice, thanks all the same." She wriggled forward, pre-
paring to jump back into the arena. "And if that's all you
had to say—"

"Wait a minute." He grabbed the back of her belt—
sucked in his breath as he realized his fingers had slid past
the waistband, as well, so that now his knuckles nudged a
soft swelling curve—the top of her hip. "That's not all. I
wanted to ask you—" He frowned up at her, meeting her
stare for stare. "In the kitchen, when he dropped the batter,
the way he looked... Who's been yelling at him? Making
him feel the fool?"

Her anger faded gradually to dismay, even guilt. She sat
looking down at him, her teeth buried in her lush bottom
lip. "Eric," she said finally. "He's *so* critical, Miguel—so
hard on him—and there's nothing I can do. He has him
every other week. I've gone back to the judge three times,
asking for a better custody arrangement, begging for one—
but Eric...Eric has pull."

*Pull? If he tries that again, I'll pull his head off like a
chicken for the pot!* "I see," Miguel said, mastering his
outrage. "Well, that changes from here."

"That's why I brought Morgan to Suntop," she added

hurriedly as he and the horses approached. "You're doing wonderfully, kiddo," she called in a brighter tone.

"*Bravissimo*," Miguel agreed. "But aren't you getting bored? What else can you do?"

Morgan chewed on his lip and Miguel had to smile. He knew where his son had learned that trick. The boy let out a little grunt of inspiration, and steered his pair across the corral, cutting from one side to the other.

"Ah, good thinking. That shows 'em who's boss," Miguel called as Morgan glanced back at him with a roguish grin. Another thing he could teach his son: that a man set his own path, his own agenda; he didn't just follow the rail.

"I've brought him to Suntop so he'll meet other men," Risa murmured once he'd turned away. "Men who don't criticize or yell. The cowboys here were always so wonderful and patient with me and my sisters. I thought he needed some of that, before it was too late."

He'll have that and more from now on. Miguel's hand flexed of its own accord, pressing his knuckles gently into her softness. The cheek and delicate ear he could see in profile had flushed rosy pink. She growled something wordless and reached behind—caught his wrist, gave a tug.

He let her hold him for a moment, savoring the imprint of each slender finger on his skin, then he relinquished his grasp. "*Perdoname.*" *But don't think it will be the last time!* He didn't know what he wanted from her yet in the larger sense but, oh, in the smaller—in the *minuto.* His blood was racing; his jeans, too tight.

"Hey, what about this?" Morgan yelled from where he was weaving Bravo and his dam in a tight figure eight, mid corral.

"*¡Excelente!*" he approved with a broad grin. "I could get seriously bored with horses," he added under his breath.

She gave a haughty shrug. "So beat it. Nobody's asking you to stick around. Go play with your oil wells."

Ah, yes, they would have to talk about that—the contract, his intentions back then—and now. She'd hardly forgiven him and he'd still questions of his own. But he'd save them for later, when he got her alone. "Not today. But why don't we all go for a ride," he suggested. "Maybe down to the river?"

"He doesn't know how to ride yet. I'll probably start him here in the pen."

"Doesn't know how to ride? But don't you two come back here often—every summer?" He frowned as she tipped back her head in a bitter, laughing yelp—

Then spoke, gazing off toward the mountains, each word like a shard of ice chipped from those far-off summits. "This is the first time I—we—have been back to Suntop since— Since that *glorious* day when I vowed to love and honor—" she jumped down into the corral and spun to face him, eyes blazing as she backed away "—a lying creep!"

If words could flay a man... But they couldn't, not if he wouldn't permit it. "Perhaps I was...perhaps not. This we need to discuss."

"Oh, no, we don't. It's nothing but history. And the rest of the sorry history, the reason we haven't returned before this, is that Ben disinherited me a month after I married Eric Foster. He gave me a choice of leaving my husband and coming back to Suntop—or be forever cut out of his will."

Miguel winced. Such a hard old man. And such a tough young *rubia*, his stubborn little mule, who would not be led. "You should have taken him up on it."

Instead she'd thrown herself away on a man like Foster. Why, the dumbest hay cutter at Suntop could have told her what she was letting herself in for. Ben had known it. He himself had seen it within a minute of meeting the arrogant, self-satisfied bastard. That she'd let that man touch her, disrespect and hurt her, when he—Miguel—would have worked himself to the bone to keep her happy and safe... "More fool you, Risa-Sonrisa!"

"And *that's* where you've got it wrong," she retorted, shooting him with a finger, though her aim was none too steady. "No fool ever again, Miguel Heydt, not this woman! I've learned my lesson well. Now...if you'll excuse me?" Head high, she stalked off to join her son.

Their son.

And who is the fool?

FOR THE NEXT HALF HOUR Miguel stood there pondering that, while Risa schooled his son and the colt. By turns she directed Morgan to lead Bravo behind the mare, on her right flank instead of left, then back on the original side but at a gradually increasing distance. Accustoming the foal to the day when he must forsake his dam to follow a human.

Bravo wasn't weaned yet, of course; in fact, Risa stopped once mid arena to allow the baby a break—five minutes of greedy nursing. Weaning... Miguel shifted restlessly. There came a time when every boy must leave if he was to be a man, but Morgan was only ten. Too young yet to step away. *But if she won't permit me my place?* What then?

He glanced up as a black pickup rolled into the yard from the river road. Its driver nosed into the fence alongside him, then stepped out with big hand extended. "Rafe Montana. I'm ranch manager here, and I take it you're Ben's house-guest?"

"Yes. They call me Heydt. Miguel Heydt." Miguel thought he caught a flicker of surprise in the man's keen blue eyes as they measured each other. They were much of a size, though the cattleman looked to be a few years older than his own thirty-six.

"Welcome to Suntop." They drifted over to the fence, to cross their forearms on the top rail and watch the training session. "I see you've met Risa and Morgan already," Montana observed.

"Oh, Risa and I are old friends." *And hombre, don't even think of coming between us.* The flash of sheer possessiveness startled Miguel. He glanced sharply at his companion's hand and relaxed somewhat. The man wore a simple gold wedding band, and now that he looked for it, a certain air of...contentment. This one was not on the prowl. *Bueno.* As well for him.

Besides, Miguel was beginning to realize he had worse competition than anything walking on two legs, at least for his son's affections.

"He sure likes that colt." Montana chuckled as Morgan stopped to stroke the foal, then gave him a fervent hug.

Miguel nodded gloomily. He needed to get on with his survey. Time was precious if he was to drill before the winter. But Morgan—coming to know him, to win his affections—that was even more important. *Except now I need money more than ever!* Which meant he needed to make a well and a good one. Which meant he shouldn't be standing here losing a day, and yet...

And Risa? What was he to do about Risa?

"What about you?" Montana drawled beside him. "D'you need a mount? Ben said I was to help you any way I can."

Did he? Truly the old man had gone soft. "I do need a horse," Miguel admitted. "Last time I was here, I rode one named Jack—Jackhammer—an exceedingly ugly brown gelding. You wouldn't know if by any chance—" He grimaced as Montana shook his head. "It was a long time ago."

"Yeah. We lost him. Reckon it was four years back—a hard winter. But we've got some nice stock. You ride much these days?"

A tactful way of asking how much horse he could handle. But Miguel laughed as inspiration struck, the way to have his cake and maybe eat it, too. "What about the mare? That one?"

Montana tipped back his Stetson. "Columbine? She's a broodmare, not one of the working remuda. We retired her years ago."

"But she was trained to ride?"

The rancher shrugged. "Of course, and she's gentle. But she's with that foal. You'd have him tagging along every step of the way."

"And that's why I want her," Miguel admitted. "You see…" He paused, but there was something about Montana that invited trust, and maybe he wanted to brag. "That's my son there, and I want most urgently to make his acquaintance. Much more than that. But time is…short. So…"

"Morgan's yours?" Montana's gaze swung to the boy, then back to Miguel's face with a frown. "But his last name is Foster. I thought—"

A picture was worth all the words in the world. Miguel pulled out his wallet and showed the photo. "My little sister, Consuela. The last time I was here at Suntop was eleven years ago, for a wedding."

Montana studied the photo, then slowly he nodded. "Heydt. I thought the name sounded familiar. You're that Heydt?"

"You've heard the story?"

"Of that wedding?" Montana grinned. "I hired on here

the year after, and they were still talking about it down at the bunkhouse. They still do today. That's become one of the Suntop legends." He glanced back at the corral, where Risa stood speaking to her son, brushing his silvery hair back from his upturned eyes. "And yeah, you can have Columbine," he added almost to himself. "Might not be a half-bad idea at that."

THE PROBLEM with Suntop, aside from Miguel, Risa mused that evening while she constructed a salad, was that there wasn't a take-out Chinese restaurant within fifty miles or more. To say nothing of pizza. She was utterly beat, yet supper still had to be made.

And tempting as peanut butter and crackers sounded, they wouldn't do. She'd set herself standards once she'd left Eric and Eric's housekeeper behind. She and Morgan might not have much money to splash around, but they'd eat nutritionally well-rounded meals. A sit-down family dinner each night, with conversation, not TV.

Morgan wandered into the kitchen, hair wet from his shower, face drooping with disappointment when he saw only her. "He's still not back?"

"Mr. Heydt? No, sweetie, and he probably won't be for hours. I imagine he's eating in town."

She'd been delighted this afternoon when Miguel finally grew bored with watching them and had wandered away, saying he had errands to run in Durango. She'd prolonged the halter lesson, hoping for just that reaction, praying that Morgan's attention span would outlast his father's.

His father. A shiver of some unnameable emotion skittered across her heart. How could nothing—and everything—change with one little fact? One photo?

Morgan kicked a chair. "Why...why didn't he take us?"

"Because he didn't want to. He's got his own life to

lead, kiddo. He didn't come to Suntop to be with us, you know." *Don't get attached to him, sweetie. Oh, please, please, don't.* She knew Morgan was starved for male companionship, but— *Not that one. Never that one.* He needed somebody who'd stay. Somebody who could be trusted, not that…that rolling rock hound. Why, look how long his interest had lasted on this their first day! Miguel hadn't even bothered to stick around to see Morgan take his first ride.

Suddenly she could have quite cheerfully shot him. *If he hurts Morgan…* Hurting her was one thing; painful—yes, oh, yes—but she'd endured it, gotten over it. But hurting her child? *Try that and you're buzzard meat, bub!*

Somehow she would have to stand between them.

Or if she couldn't, she and Morgan would have to leave.

But maybe the worst was over already. Maybe by tomorrow Miguel would go back to all that really mattered to his wildcat soul. Hunting for oil. If he spent most of his time this summer out on the range prospecting, then maybe she and Morgan could survive him and stay. Get on with her original plans.

The sound of a car door slamming sent Morgan banging out the back door. "He's here! He's back!"

Risa picked up her knife and stabbed a tomato to the heart.

They soon returned, lugging armloads of groceries, blithely dumping them on the table where she was trying to work, chatting a mile a minute. Miguel had seen longhorn antelope—"a herd, *muchacho,* ten or more all bounding along"—on his way back from Durango.

And Morgan had ridden a brown-and-white pony whose name was Guapo, which Mr. Montana said was to be his horse for the summer!

"And *guapo* means good-looking, I hope he told you," added Miguel, lightly punching his shoulder. *"Como tú."*

At last he noticed Risa—or at least, her salad. "Ah, no, you've started cooking! You'll have to stop. I thought I'd make supper tonight, since those were your supplies we ate this morning."

"*No,* thank you," she said determinedly, but Morgan was drowning her out.

"Oh, *yeah!* Supper! What are we having?"

"Hot dogs and hamburgers. I bought a grill. But you'll have to help me set it up. It's still in the Jeep. And we'll have to be careful in lighting it. Once when I was your age, or maybe a bit younger, I burned off my eyebrows lighting a bonfire…"

"We're having spaghetti," Risa insisted, but already they were halfway out the door, making too much racket to hear her. She slammed down her knife. Blast him! She'd forgotten how clever he was, how…how manipulative— easily Ben's match in that.

"And potato chips," she heard him say out in the twilight. "And toasted marshmallows for dessert—do you eat those? We'll have to find some coat hangers."

So today hadn't just been a passing skirmish. This was war.

CHAPTER NINETEEN

WAR, Risa kept reminding herself all through supper.
Though sometimes it was hard to remember that as she sat
back sipping a glass of the excellent zinfandel Miguel had
bought, watching the two of them together.

They might not look like father and son, but there was
an…affinity. They seemed to understand each other instinctively on some level below words—a tilt of Miguel's eyebrows could send her son into convulsions of giggles. Morgan could start a sentence and Miguel could supply the end
of it. Morgan had questions and Miguel had the answers,
whether it was the name of a constellation—they'd eaten
outside at the old picnic table behind the house—or how
to act respectfully around Alaskan polar bears. What the
glaciers of Denali looked like seen from a circling bush
plane.

Oh, this was war all right! Did he think she wouldn't
realize he was playing his Pied Piper song, beguiling her
child away?

But to where? Why? On the face of it, he wanted his
son, but she'd learned that to take Miguel Heydt at face
value was to be burned—scorched to the soul. Why, once
upon a time he'd sworn he wanted her.

And she'd been fool enough to believe him.

But not this time.

Not ever again.

So what was the *real* motivation here? Why was he trying so hard to charm her son?

And what could she do to stop him?

In the loud and lively midst of the Miguel and Morgan show, she found no answers. *Tonight,* Risa promised herself, when she'd have time and peace alone to ponder. But right now she would simply smile aloofly and pretend to go along with Miguel's program.

And be grateful that whatever he was, he wasn't inconsiderate in the petty ways Eric had been.

Eric would never have thought to provide supper if they were eating in. And he certainly wouldn't have hung around for the cleanup. Miguel and Morgan were loading the dishwasher while she put away their leftovers, when the kitchen phone rang.

"Now, who could that be?" Miguel wondered, glancing up. "I thought we were alone in the world, we three."

Ha! She made a face, steeled herself and lifted the receiver. "Hello?"

"You promised me you'd call when you got there. What happened to that?" Eric said with that peculiar playful edge she'd come to dread.

"I...forgot." Miguel had driven him entirely from her mind last night. She'd been coming downstairs to phone, when Miguel had appeared, and after that— "I'm sorry." That they'd stay in close touch was one of the conditions Eric had exacted, in exchange for allowing Morgan to leave Denver.

"I'm sure you are," he agreed, meaning quite the opposite.

Just when had he come to dislike her so? Looking back, she'd never been sure if it was caused by the way they'd started out—her breaking their engagement for Miguel, then changing her mind again, though Eric had sworn when he met her in Vegas that he still adored her. That he'd cherish her always.

Or had she lost his affections when she'd become pregnant so quickly? He hadn't liked it when she lost her figure. Had started his first affair when she was three months along, though she hadn't found out for another year.

"So how's it going?" he added when she didn't speak.

"Just fine," she lied, twisting the phone cord restlessly. She found herself facing Miguel, who leaned against the counter, arms crossed, dark eyes fixed on her. She swung casually the other way. "Same old Suntop." No details, no elaborations. She wasn't about to let Eric insinuate himself into their visit if she could help it; she'd come here seeking refuge from him, maybe permanent relief.

"How's Morgan behaving? He's not running wild yet?" That Morgan stay out of scrapes had been another of Eric's conditions for the visit. And he'd reserved the right to end their trip at any time if he thought that Morgan was getting "out of control." Eric's favorite phrase.

"He's been an angel."

"You'll excuse me if I take that with a grain of salt." Always he accused her of trying to shield Morgan from the consequences of his actions. But what else could she do when Eric's punishments seemed so disproportionate to her son's childish crimes?

"No, really—" She glanced up to see Morgan standing there in the back door like a rabbit frozen in the bushes, hoping the hunter will pass it by. "I mean it. Truly."

"Well, good. I warned him. Maybe he's finally seeing the light. Put him on."

She could lie, say he'd gone to bed. But Eric would keep on calling till he'd had his way. Might as well get it over with. "Daddy wants to talk to you," she said levelly, extending the phone to Morgan.

A wave of disapproval like the shock wave of a dynamite blast almost rocked her on her feet. She flinched, but she didn't look at Miguel.

Morgan shuffled across the kitchen to take the phone. "'Lo…"

Eric's distant voice snapped a phrase or two; she couldn't hear what was said.

Morgan corrected his first attempt. "Um, hello, Daddy."

Risa hugged herself till her ribs hurt and stared down at the flagstones. The conversation wouldn't last long. It never did.

"Yes, sir."

The tiny, hectoring voice, four hundred and thirty-six miles away, yet still determined to dominate, to belittle, spoke again.

"No, sir," Morgan said almost inaudibly—and Miguel lunged off the counter.

Oh, no, that would make things so much worse! Risa turned without lifting her head, seemed to wander straight into his path. "Ooff!" His momentum nearly knocked her off her feet, but he caught her elbow, hooked an arm around her waist. "No!" she said in an urgent undertone, looking up at him, flattening a hand on his chest to steady herself. "Don't. *Please* don't."

Behind them, Morgan's catechism was ending. "Yes, sir…I will, sir. I promise."

Miguel was murmuring words she'd never heard from him before—never seen in any dictionary—but the drift was as clear as his heartbeat, which was slamming under her hand.

Oh, yes, I'm with you! But that's not the way. Let Miguel pick up the phone and blast Eric—and Eric would be here tomorrow to collect his son.

Your son, she realized, staring up at him. And she and Morgan like a couple of bones caught between two dogs.

Her son mumbled, "G'bye," and hung up behind her.

She shoved out of Miguel's grasp. "Why, excuse me."

"Yo no creo," he said with quiet deadliness. *I don't think so.*

Well, she didn't need his pardon. All she needed was to save her son. Risa swung around and found him standing with head lowered, his lovely evening spoiled.

Not for long, baby. I promise you! She went to him and fought down the urge to hug him—he wouldn't take that in front of Miguel, she knew instinctively, not right now. But she could ruffle his corn-silk hair. "Well, sweetie, it's been a long day. Why don't you scoot off to bed and I'll come tuck you in in a minute."

"'Kay." He glanced at Miguel from under lowered eyebrows. "Thanks for supper, Mr. Heydt. I really enjoyed it." Speaking still in the subdued tone that Eric demanded.

Miguel let out a long hissing breath through his teeth. But when he found his smile it was as warm as stirred embers. "It was the best time I've had in years, *muchacho.* Thank you for your most excellent company."

Morgan lifted his head slightly; a smile wavered across his face. "Me, too." He spun and bolted from the room.

"¡Hijo de puta!" Miguel swore in a vicious whisper. He snatched up a glass that had not yet made it to the dishwasher, lifted it high over his head—then glanced toward the front of the house. Set it down again. Picked up a fork—and bent it in half. Dropped it in the sink and spun around. "And you— You allow my son to put up with *that?*"

"I left Eric as soon as I could afford to support us— three years ago, which is about when it started. Before that, I don't think he paid much attention to Morgan. Eric's not very fond of children. But the older Morgan grows, the worse it gets. And *yes,* I'm doing everything I can to stop it. Why do you think I humbled myself and came here?''

"Why?" he asked savagely. *"Dígame,* Risa.''

"Not because I forgave Ben, but to beg for his help. If he meets Morgan and comes to care for him, then I can ask him to buy us a high-powered lawyer. Somebody who can match the ones Eric brings to bear.''

"Ah?" Slowly he nodded. *"Bueno…"* He blew out a breath. Rubbed the back of his neck. Strolled to the door that led to the rest of the house, peered out it and apparently satisfied himself that they were alone. "Well…I can do better than that, now that I know. That was part of the reason I went to Durango today. At the hospital there they can take a blood sample, send it out for testing.''

She'd been bludgeoned by too many emotions today, after a sleepless night. Exhaustion was making her stupid; she didn't follow. "Testing for what?''

"To prove that he is mine.''

But he's not yours—he's mine! And even if she'd felt like sharing, Miguel Heydt was the last man in the world with whom she'd have shared a child. She opened her mouth to tell him so—and it hit her. Why he was really doing this.

"Why, you son of a bitch! Oh, you *sneaky…money-grubbing—*''

"What? *¿Que?* What have I done now?" He caught her wrists as she tried to shove him.

"That's why you want to claim him! Oh, am I *stupid* not to see!''

"See what?''

"Clause two and three of your *filthy* contract! How did it go?" But though she'd read it only once, the terms were etched in acid on her heart. She squinched her eyes for a second, remembering. "You could drill one oil well if you married me. Well, you've earned that already and I hope to God it's dry.

"*But!*" Her eyes shot open as it came to her. "If you got me pregnant within the first year, what did that give you? The rights to drill as many wells as you pleased for twelve years from that date? Am I right?"

He let her go and backed away, wearily rubbed at his temple. "*Sí...* That was how it went. But Risa, you can't think—"

"Can't I? What kind of a fool do you think I am?" She shied back as he reached for her. "No, don't bother to answer that! You fooled me once. Why shouldn't you think you can do it again?"

"And let's see..." She paced away, thinking—whirled back to confront him. "Clause three was the beauty, wasn't it? Ben thought up that one for sure. There he was with three bright, healthy daughters, but would they do to run Suntop? Uh-uh. Ben wanted a boy. And if you gave him one, Miguel—if you got me pregnant and I delivered a healthy son—*well*, the sky was the limit then, wasn't it? Ben would give you the world. He promised you *he'd* finance your wells!"

The tears were flooding her eyes. Tears of rage. Surely she couldn't be weeping for this lost evening of laughter and marshmallows; she wasn't that much of an innocent fool! "And all you have to do to claim the prize, Miguel Heydt, is prove—to Ben—that Morgan is your son, not Eric's."

But he'd learn that proof wasn't easy to come by.

AFTER RISA RAN AWAY upstairs, Miguel took out his frustrations in a walk. He stalked down the road for the main valley, but the downhill route wasn't hard enough. He needed to punish himself, sweat out his guilt. He branched off when he reached the bridle trail that climbed Suntop.

Made it to the summit, gasping and panting, but was rewarded for his pains by the sight of a crescent moon rising above the Trueheart Hills, soaring above the Sweet-water Flats.

Lighting the way to treasure.

He laughed with savage irony and swiped a forearm across his damp brow. *Ay, treasure!* The black gold he'd come for.

But there were other kinds of treasure; he'd never been such a fool to think there were not. Oil wasn't an end in itself—it was the way to buy the things that mattered. Freedom, prosperity, the chance to raise a family and see it thrive.

How could Risa think that oil was all that drove him? That he saw Morgan—his son!—as only a means to achieve the second and third terms of that damnable contract. Was the woman blind?

She'd been half-blinded by tears when she left him in the kitchen. *Risa-Sonrisa, never did I mean to hurt you.*

But apparently he had. Most bitterly. And he hadn't simply wounded her heart and bruised her pride. He'd damaged something infinitely more fragile: her trust. *Only leap,* he'd told her the day he proposed, *and I will catch you.*

To Risa it must seem that she'd leaped into love—and there'd been no one waiting with welcoming arms when she reached the bottom. Her heart had landed on stones.

I should have been honest. I should have told her.

He hadn't. He'd thought to marry her, make her entirely his own, then tell her one night in bed, maybe years later, when it would be no more than a joke between them. One of those jokes that marriages are built upon.

So he hadn't spoken when he should have, and she had been damaged.

But now she had the means to pay him back. She could withhold Morgan.

Unless somehow…someway…he won her trust again?

BY THE TIME Miguel returned to the Big House, the moon was riding high in the sky. No one waited for him down below. And all was quiet above, when he reached the top of the stairs. He glanced longingly toward the room where Risa must be sleeping by now, her hair a sea of rumpled silk on her pillow; he sighed and padded off to the guest wing. *A cold shower for you, hombre, then bed.* Tomorrow, with its hopes and its sorrows, would come soon enough.

In the bathroom he turned on the shower, tested the spray and grimaced. At this end of the house, the hot water took a while to climb the pipes. He left the tap running while he stripped, then brushed his teeth. He turned back to the tub—and blinked.

The shower curtain was swaying, as if a draft had passed through the room.

Or through his adjoining bedroom. Yes, a change in air pressure, such as someone opening a door?

Quietly he reached for a towel, wrapped it around his waist. *Did I lock the back door?* They were so far from civilization and all its uncivil dangers that one tended not to worry. *Yes, I did lock it,* he decided, slipping out the far door, which led to an empty guest room. But he hadn't checked the front entrance.

Passing through the dark room, then into the hallway, Miguel contemplated his door. It stood a few inches open, though he'd left it closed. So indeed he had a visitor.

Friend or foe? He tightened his towel around his waist and edged along the wall.

Peered through the crack.

Risa stood at his bureau. Her slender back and the sleeves of her silky bathrobe hid the actions of her hands. She glanced anxiously toward the bathroom, from whence came the faint drumming of his shower, then she opened the second drawer, reached for something within.

Enough of this! He crossed the room on panther feet, dropped his hands on her slender waist—all day he'd been wanting to do that. "Find something of interest?"

"*Aghh!*" Slippery as a mermaid in her robe of gray-green silk, she leaped, then spun around.

He resettled his grip on those tempting curves and gave her a dangerous smile. It was good to feel himself in the right again. "Scrounging through my things, *corazón?* You had only to ask. *¿Que tienes?*"

One of her hands was hidden behind her. She drew a shivering breath and shook her head. "N—nothing."

Liar. But two could play that game. "Then it must have been me you came looking for. Well...here I am in all my glory." He glanced ironically downward. "And as you see, I'm happy to see you." He swayed her inward so that they brushed, softness to welcoming hardness. Ah, this was precisely what they needed! Let only their bodies speak and the rest of the quarrel could be settled in the morning. Whatever had gone wrong between them, it had never been this.

His thumbs fanned up the silk, then as lazily retraced their arcs, celebrating the delectable curves of her stomach. He dipped his head and inhaled the hot perfume of her skin. She sucked in a breath. *So far, so very good.* Slowly he brushed his lips along her jaw to her ear. "Shall we make it up in bed?" he coaxed in a rough whisper. "*¿Que te quieres? Dígame, cielito.*"

She tipped back her head. "I want you to take your hands *off* me before I..."

The ice in her words left no room for doubt. He sighed, let go her waist—reached behind her and captured her wrist. Pulled it into view.

She held the photograph of Consuela, which she'd taken from his wallet.

Frustrated passion melded with indignation. "And what did you want with this?"

"I wanted to—" She clamped her lips on whatever lie had been about to escape. Cocked her chin in defiance and met his eyes. "I meant to shred it to bits and flush it, if you have to know."

"And what good do you think that would do?"

"I don't want you telling Morgan. But if you do, Miguel, without a picture it won't seem real. It'll only be words. Easier for him to forget later on."

Carefully he extracted the picture from her fingers. Set it gently aside on the bureau. "It's true, this is the only photo I have *al momento*. But I could send for others.

"Or better yet—" Suddenly he wanted to threaten. Make her understand that he was not just a beggar in this. Not helpless. If she pushed too far, he could be a rock. "If seeing is believing, I could take Morgan to meet his grandmother. His aunt. His cousins. All the family, who would welcome him with open arms. More family than you've been able to give him!"

Anger gave way to bittersweetness as he pictured it. Yes, he could do that. And how his mother would smile to see her first grandson—and him with the hair of her own beloved husband. What a gift he could now bring her!

And if I brought a wife, as well? He'd never told her about the wedding. It had been over before it began. And to try to explain afterward how his bride had left him at the altar would have been too humiliating. Like the fish that got away.

"Don't even think it! I'd have you arrested for child snatching before you made it through Trueheart."

"Snatching my own son?"

"Prove it! A resemblance to a photo? Ha! That means nothing! How often has somebody told you that you look familiar—like a friend or a neighbor or some celebrity? Resemblance proves zip! *Nada!*"

"This from a thief of photos. But *bien*. What about the blood test? How will you dispute that?"

"I—don't—have to." Risa recinched her robe, then brushed past him toward the door. Swung back when she'd reached it. "Without my permission you can't have Morgan tested."

"No?" He'd sue her for the right if he had to. But this was madness. *So now it's come to lawyers?* Not an hour before he'd been planning how to win her trust.

"No, never. Not in a thousand years. But meantime, Miguel, I want your promise. That you won't show Morgan that photo. That you won't tell him you're his father."

"If you won't, Risa, then I surely will!"

She paused, eyes glittering with tears. "You do, and that's the last you'll see of him. We'll go straight back to Denver and I'll take out a restraining order."

"You'd take him away from this? His Bravo? And a pony to ride? This ranch where he can run free?" *From me and all that I can teach him?* "You'd take him back to that *monstruo*, that petty tyrant? Did it never cross your mind that Foster knows in his heart Morgan is not his son? That for this reason he wants to crush him?"

"N—n—no." She shook her head. "He couldn't. He doesn't! He's just…Eric." But her teeth found her bottom lip and punished it.

"Are you sure of that, *mamacita?*"

The cry ripped out of her. "If I didn't know, then how could he? I never told him that we—"

The memory hung between them, like an image burned on the air.

When Miguel could see beyond it again, he shrugged. "*Instinto* tells him? Who knows? And maybe it doesn't matter. You'd take your son back to a man who will crush his spirit in the name of love?"

"I *told* you. That's why we're here!"

"Then stay here," he soothed, closing the distance between them. "Don't go back there. Back to that."

"But I *have* to if you— If you insist on—" Her throat closed and convulsed and she burst into tears.

"Then I won't." He caught her shoulders, swayed her to him, brushed his lips across her eyebrows. "I won't. Don't cry, *pasión.*"

"Y—y—you promise? Really? You really won't?"

I promise you that I will find another way, if you won't let me tell him. He kissed the tears from her lashes and tasted salt. *"Te prometo."*

CHAPTER TWENTY

MIGUEL MIGHT HAVE promised to keep his paternity a secret, Risa thought grimly the next morning while she measured oats into the trough in the catch pen beside the barn, but he'd made no promise about leaving her and Morgan alone.

They'd ended up eating breakfast together—how could they not when he'd already brewed the coffee by the time she arrived in the kitchen? He'd handed her a fresh cup, poured Morgan a glass of OJ, then offered to cook scrambled eggs for three.

She'd refused, insisting that she and her son would have cereal and toast. Miguel had accepted her snub with equanimity, then changed his mind about eggs, opting instead to eat cereal alongside them, poured from his own supply. And how could she object to that?

Now he was horning in on their morning ride. She'd driven Morgan down to the ranch yard, but a few minutes later Miguel had followed in his Jeep. Presently he and her son were bringing out the bridles while she captured their mounts.

"There he is, Mr. Heydt! See? That's my horse for the summer," Morgan cried, returning, as the paint pony entered the pen from the home pasture. "Guapo! C'mere, Guapo!"

The pony made a beeline for the trough and plunged his brown-and-white-patched nose into the oats. Risa's assigned mare, a dainty gray half Arab and half quarter horse, accepted the tacit bargain, feed for work, and entered the trap. Risa shooed aside a few four-footed volunteers that they didn't need, then admitted the colt Bravo and his dam through the gate and closed it behind them. *And you, Señor Heydt, may catch your own ride,* she told him silently. No aid for the enemy.

But Miguel didn't look worried as he admired Morgan's Guapo, the loaner Rafe Montana had trailered over from the Ribbon River Dude Ranch, saying that his wife, Dana, highly recommended the pony for beginners. And so far the paint had proven a peach—intelligent, willing and gentle. She'd have to phone this thoughtful Dana and thank her.

"That's Mom's mare, Cinders." Morgan indicated the gray, then frowned. "But who are you going to ride?"

"Bravo's *mamacita,*" Miguel said blandly. "Her name is Columbine. Which means Bravo must come along with me wherever I go."

You are *smart,* Risa thought as she met his smug gaze over the head of her delighted son. And his relentlessness— that was an aspect she'd barely noticed their last time around, though it had apparently shaped her life. Once he'd set his sites on a goal... *You just keep coming and coming.*

Last time she'd been his gullible target. This time his innocent goal was Morgan. But even knowing it, how was she to block him? Especially when the fight was two against one?

A few hours later, sitting on a blanket spread on the bank of the river, she was still pondering that question, still without answers. Entertaining no such concerns, Morgan and Miguel were blithely swimming and splashing. Morgan was clad in the swimsuit she'd packed this morning along with a picnic lunch; Miguel wore his red boxers, to which he'd stripped without a hint of embarrassment.

Their thin cotton did little to hide his endowments. Risa's eyes shot away as Miguel glided in toward her son and stood abruptly in the shallows, water lapping his muscular thighs with their haze of curly dark hair. "*Ay, muchacho,* did you see that?"

"What? Where?" Morgan peered in the direction indicated, across the swimming hole.

Risa's eyes skated stealthily back to Miguel; she couldn't help herself.

"It was very large and very long and rather green and scaly. Do they have *cocodrilos aquí* at Suntop?"

"No-o-o!" Morgan protested on a note of delicious terror. "*Do* they, Mom?"

"Of course not." Her eyes were drawn irresistibly back to Miguel, his lean and beautiful body. Her own throbbed in response. "Sea monsters, maybe. Crocodiles, no." She'd put on her own modest cream-colored maillot in the bushes, but she'd yet to swim. Once she'd realized she'd have to share the river with Miguel, the idea had lost its appeal.

"Then maybe an alligator?" Miguel suggested with doubtful worry. "Are alligators very fast, with lots of *dientes*—teeth—all about as long as my little finger? Look! Over by the cliff, just under water—isn't that him? Let's *get* him!" He launched himself in a flat racing dive. Morgan yelled with delight and thrashed in pursuit.

Crocodile hunters. Men at play. Risa couldn't help herself. She walked over to Cinders, staked out to graze along with the other horses except for the colt, who ran free. Pulling the Nikon from her saddlebag, she returned to the blanket. Framed a picture of Morgan, held aloft by Miguel so he could better search for the elusive prey. Her son's face was radiant, blissful; he balanced himself with one small hand splayed on Miguel's broad shoulder.

Click! A lump was rising in her throat. *Oh, baby, don't be so happy.* Such bliss couldn't last and she was one who should know.

But even knowing, what could she do? How warn him, when such painfully learned wisdom would only diminish his present joy?

Click! She caught him midair as Miguel heaved him into a dive in pursuit of the phantom monster, then surged after. They shot up out of the water under the cliffs, whooping with glee. She refocused her lens and this time there was no way to exclude Miguel from her picture; Morgan was laughing as he gazed up at his companion, his arms thrown wide as he described the lizard that got away, Miguel nodding wholehearted approval.

Click! If she couldn't stop the present joy, or prevent the coming sorrow, at least she could record it. Reduced to a palm-size square, maybe someday this bright and shining moment would be bearable.

When at last the hunters had routed their enemy, they came dripping out of the cool river, Morgan with chattering teeth, Miguel with a look of insufferable satisfaction. They sprawled on the sunny blanket like a couple of big wet dogs, looking hopefully at the foil packages that she'd laid out while they swam.

"Hungry?" she asked, grateful that she'd packed extras of everything. After the pleasure he'd given her son, she would have to feed the man.

"Un poquito," Miguel admitted, accepting a sandwich. *"Gracias, corazón."*

"What's that mean?" Morgan wanted to know.

"He said thank-you," Risa said quickly, poking Miguel's shin with her toes, "so I reply *de nada*. You're welcome."

AFTER THEY'D EATEN, Morgan wandered off to play with Bravo, holding on to his tether but letting the colt lead him where he willed. "Just who is halter-breaking whom?" Risa wondered.

"Mmm." Miguel rolled back to lie full-length on the blanket beside her. "Who cares, as long as there's peace? I never knew before what it took to raise a boy. I seem to remember my little sister sitting quietly once in a while."

"You were only five years older than Morgan when you left home," she remembered. What courage it must have taken to make his way like that.

"*Sí*. But I was in charge of Consuela from the time I was eight until I left, since my mother had to work afternoons and evenings at a café."

She propped herself on one elbow. "Do you ever go back?"

"When I can, of course. I flew back only last year, from Alaska, for my sister's graduation from the University of Guadalajara. She is now a doctor."

"Good for her!" So hard times back home were not so hard as they'd been. His face glowed with pride. "Did you help put her through college?"

He wobbled one spread-fingered hand in that Latin gesture that denotes more or less. "When she needed it. But she won many scholarships."

"That was good of you." She knew men who'd have walked away from hard times and never looked back.

"It's family. How else would one live? Besides—" he gave her a rueful grin "—I tell her that once she's a rich doctor, it'll be my turn. She can invest in my oil wells."

Oh, yes, his wells. While she was admiring, she'd better

remember his ambition and to what lengths he'd gone to
fulfill it.

Miguel rolled over onto his side to study her. "And I
had a question for you, Sonrisa."

"Don't call me that." She sat up abruptly, looked around
for Morgan. Relaxed again as she saw him. The foal had
flopped on his side in the grass, a few feet beyond his dam.
Morgan knelt beside him, adoring.

"It's true you don't smile as much as I remember," Miguel said quietly. "And whatever part I played in that, I
regret with all my heart."

But if he'd really regretted, would he ever have done it?
How easy to act as he pleased first, *then* apologize—if and
when he was caught. She shrugged and looked away. "History." Too late to be changed with pretty words.

"I wanted to ask you," he continued after a moment.
"How was it that you ever learned of the…contract. Who
told you?"

"Tess." She had to smile, remembering her sister, only
two years older than Morgan back then. "You remember
how she was playing detective that week, picking locks?
She broke into Ben's desk."

He swore under his breath in Spanish. "*¡La brujita!* So
that really is why you left—" *Me,* he'd been about to say,
she thought. "Why you ran away. Ended what we'd barely
begun."

"What else could it have been?" she demanded, swinging to face him. *What else would have made me go when
I was crazy for you?* Crazy—period, to accept a proposal
from a sexy stranger!

"I thought—" He sat up abruptly. "Of course we asked
Tess where you'd gone, since she'd been the last to see
you. But all she'd say was that you'd changed your mind.

That you said you'd made a mistake…you didn't want to be married.''

Risa looked down at her hands, twining her fingers. "I suppose Ben was furious."

"That might begin to describe it," Miguel said dryly. "All that expense and fuss, all his friends and neighbors there to witness the fiasco. *Sí*, he was roaring like a volcano. His lady friend, Belle, in hysterics…"

"So poor Tess wasn't about to stand up and admit she'd caused the mess." *I wonder if she even realizes how she changed my life.* They'd never discussed that terrible day; the few times she'd seen her sister over the years, Risa had no wish to relive the pain and humiliation of her first wedding. And Tess also seemed to shy from the subject. They'd had so much else to catch up on.

"No, that would be too much to ask of a twelve-year-old."

Risa looked up from her hands. "So all these years… why *did* you think I ran away?"

"Oh…" Those beautiful, so-masculine lips quirked in a motion that served for a shrug; his dark eyebrows echoed it. "I thought you'd had second thoughts. You were a princess, after all, and I was a *peón*. A wildcatter. A man with plans and ambitions in his wallet, hopes and dreams to offer a woman, but nothing else.

"*Sí*, I'd charmed you for a little while. Piqued your virgin's curiosity. But once I'd satisfied…that—"

Satisfied so much more than my curiosity, and you know it! A wave of heat washed through her as she remembered their day in paradise—*relived* it in every taut muscle and throbbing nerve—Miguel moving inside her like a miracle, his delicious weight bearing her down in the rustling grass…

The rush of liquid heat was followed by a chill—a storm

of goose bumps. She clasped her elbows and rubbed them, looking away.

"Once you'd had your...little adventure," he continued evenly, "you had a week to reconsider. And if on second thought you didn't believe in me, didn't believe I could find oil, then why *not* change your mind? You were used to the good things in life. Why gamble your future on a wandering wildcatter? Why not go back to a sure thing, your rich Yale lawyer, Mr. Mercedes?"

"That wasn't how it was!" she whispered huskily.

"So you say, *rubia*. Maybe you don't even know for sure what made you run."

"Right!" she cried, leaping to her feet. "Blame it on me, Miguel—on my cowardice—if that eases your conscience!" She lowered her voice, glanced toward her child. He was lying beside the foal, his head pillowed on Bravo's red neck, both of them sleeping with the sweet abandon of the young.

Just as well. She needed to cool off before he awoke, let this rage go. Whatever had been done had been done—and as for why? Did it even matter anymore? She splashed through the cool shallows without a backward glance. Launched herself into the olive-green depths and swam from end to end of the pool, letting the current slough away all the sorrows, the betrayals, the foolish desires. Let them all glide off her moving limbs and flow down the river.

That was the unchangeable past; it was the future she needed to find and shape. A happy life for herself and her son. Nothing else—no one else—mattered at all.

After her fourth lap of the pool Risa was winded, her muscles long and loose again, her treacherous emotions back in control. At the upstream end she rolled over to float on her back, sighed deeply and closed her eyes; arms over her head, hair flowing around her like seaweed, she let the current carry her along. She and Lara and Tess used to float like this; see who could drift the farthest before grounding out in the shallows.

Something under the water bumped her shoulder blades, then the back of her thighs. Thinking of crocodiles she caught her breath, opened her eyes—and gazed up into Miguel's somber face. He stood waist-deep in the water beside her, his forearms barely brushing her. "I'm sorry," he murmured, "for what I said back there. I'm sure you do know why you ran. But, Risa—"

"Miguel, it's *over*. Just let it go." *Let me go.* Her body bumped against his forearms just enough to impede her progress. If she broke her float, she would sink into his arms. But if she stayed like this, arching to the sky, laid out as if on a platter of rippling silver for his delectation... She could feel her nipples swelling under his gaze, her hips wanting to rock and rise in instinctive response to his silent call. With just a gentle bump along her back, under her knees, he'd raised the river's temperature from lemonade to lava.

His smile curled into view—whimsical, rueful, hers and hers alone. "I don't know that it is over, *corazón*. I think maybe it's like that windup record player my grandfather had back at the farm. You can lift the arm in the midst of the song and the needle leaves the groove. But when you drop it again—*qué milagro*, a miracle, the music starts once more... Maybe not in the same place, but maybe in a better..."

"Or maybe some clumsy fool scratched the record." He was bending closer, his eyes dark with laughter and longing. Her heartbeat hammered in her ears. Her breath snagged in her throat. *Oh, no, don't do this!*

"He did, and he's so sorry, *mi querida*." Miguel kissed the swell of her breast, just above the line of her swimsuit.

She made a tiny, furry sound of protest deep in her throat—
yes, it was a protest.

"*So* sorry..." Hot and slow, his lips sipped the moisture
from her skin—

And she whimpered with wanting. *Oh, no, I don't need
this!* But her spine was deepening its arc, her breasts rising
to present themselves.

"Ah, Sonrisa!" He sighed—and his mouth found—

"Hey, what are you guys doing?" called an impatient
voice from the shore behind them.

Miguel growled something against her breast, then
straightened with a groan. "I'm rescuing your mother
from a *cocodrilo, muchacho.*" His arms rose beneath her
and flexed—he scooped her dripping out of the water,
turning as he spoke. "Or was that an alligator?" he
added under his breath. "Whichever, this is something a
gentleman must do. When a lady needs rescuing, a man
must oblige."

Morgan snickered.

Risa scowled and kicked her legs. "If you want to oblige
a lady—this one—put me down."

He hauled her closer to his broad chest and waded on.
"Not till you're thoroughly rescued."

"*Down*, Miguel," she insisted in her best tone of com-
mand, which usually worked on Morgan.

"Down? You want down?" he asked with silky astonishment.

"*Yes!*" she hissed between her teeth—then realized her
mistake as she said it. With a wicked grin, he toppled backward; her waving legs traced an arc across the sky as she
shrieked her indignation—the river closed over their heads.

When they surfaced, drenched and sputtering, Morgan

was dancing with delight in the shallows, cackling like a little loon.

And to see her son laugh like that, Risa would have suffered a thousand dunkings.

THAT NIGHT Risa cooked for them on Miguel's propane grill. "I've been wanting one of these," she confessed while she arranged the skewers of steak, mushrooms, onions and peppers above the flames. "So much more convenient than our hibachi, all that messing with charcoal."

"Oh? Why haven't you gotten one, then?" Miguel asked, taking the platter from her hands and replacing it with a drink.

"Not in the budget quite yet." She touched her tongue to the crust of salt along the glass's rim. He'd made margaritas for the adults, a limeade and seltzer for her son.

Miguel cocked his head. "You know, you haven't told me. Do you work outside the house? I suppose I'd assumed..." He shrugged. "Alimony?"

"In your dreams! We made a settlement when we split, but..." She shrugged; why hash over old grievances? Most of their communal savings had seemed to vanish when she left Eric. With more money for lawyers and accountants maybe she could have traced the missing funds, but that reminded her of that old joke; how did it go? *If we had some ham, we could have ham and eggs—that is, if we had some eggs.*

"Anyway, there was enough to make a down payment on a condo." A tiny, one-and-a-half-bedroom condo. "And Eric pays some of Morgan's expenses..." Though each month, sheerly from spite, he held the check till it squeaked. Till she had to call and ask for it—and she'd better ask nicely.

"That stops from here on," Miguel said quietly. "He's my son and I'll support him."

"Oh, hush!" The screen door banged open and Morgan bounced out, clutching a stack of plates to his narrow chest, on which teetered their water glasses, filled with silverware and cloth napkins.

"Such a juggler!" Miguel lauded, relieving him of his load and setting the wooden picnic table. "But I think we'll need the sharp knives tonight, Morgan, if you don't mind?"

"Nope." He grabbed the butter knives and darted cheerfully away.

Eric could have made a meal of such a mistake. Risa bit her lip, remembering some of those times, and glanced gratefully at the man across the table. *I'm so glad he's yours not Eric's.* Whatever Miguel's faults, whether she ever forgave him or not, she couldn't deny that the man had a...a generosity of spirit. An easy, open kindness, whereas Eric and all his family were...pinched. Grasping. Mean in its most basic sense.

She'd always wondered how Morgan could be so perfect. *And now I know. Whatever flaws he inherits, they won't be Foster flaws.* She lifted her glass to the stars and drank to that.

"I mean that," Miguel continued, coming up behind her. "You'll have to tell me how much you need."

She wouldn't. There was no way she could take money from him without acknowledging his paternity. And once she'd done that, she opened herself to all sorts of claims. *What do you want, Miguel? Half my boy?*

And why? *Because he's your son?*

Or because he's your ticket to endless drilling—with Ben financing the gamble?

"What does your mother do for work?" Miguel asked as their son rejoined them. "She won't tell me."

Morgan smirked. "She makes funny movies. Ducks. Hot-dog dogs."

"*¿De veras?*" Miguel turned to include her in the question. "Movies?"

"Documentaries, I guess you'd call them. Very short ones."

"So you made a career of your camera." Miguel saluted her with his glass. "I wondered back then if it was only a hobby."

Morgan looked up from the table, where he was arranging the knives. "You guys knew each other before?"

"*Sí.* We knew each other before you were born. Knew each other...very well...in a very special place." His dark eyes lifted from her child, to taunt her with the memories. *Dare you deny it,* pasión?

She didn't. Couldn't. Not with the evidence looking quizzically from one of them to the other. She whisked her bowl of marinade over to the grill and basted her skewers, letting the firelight hide her blush.

"Oh," said Morgan, apparently satisfied with the explanation. He surveyed the table. "Oh, ketchup!" He loped off to the kitchen.

Miguel came to stand beside her. "Tell me about these documentaries."

"Oh, they're nothing much. Just sequences I put together using a video camera, then edited digitally. They're for children, actually, to make them laugh."

Over supper she told him how she'd created the first one—as an attempt—a very successful attempt, it turned out—to cheer up a friend's child who'd been bedridden for months after being struck by a car. "The poor little thing was so blue, lying there in traction. Anything we could do to make her smile... And she'd always loved feeding the ducks at the park. So I got out my camera and took duck pictures.

"And ducks, well, you can't really look at ducks or hear

them quack or watch them waddle without smiling, you know. So I edited all my shots into a short—parts of it in slow motion, parts in quick time, parts at normal speed. Put it on tape—an endless loop. Whenever Molly was hurting, Susan would play it."

It had worked so well that she made copies for the children's ward at the hospital where Molly was a patient. "And the idea just sort of grew from there. My next film was on dachshunds." She smiled, just thinking of the wiener dogs—clowns every one. "I found that local pediatricians and children's dentists were delighted to buy something that could distract and soothe their patients. Or keep them entertained and cheerful in the waiting room till it was their turn to be seen."

"And then she takes pictures of babies and kids at a portrait studio," Morgan chimed in. "And she's a wedding photographer. And there's her postcards for the tourists. And birthday cards."

Miguel's smile faded. "It sounds as if your mother works very hard. Too hard?" he challenged softly as Morgan got up and went for seconds at the grill.

What was he suggesting? That she was neglecting her son in favor of a career? She hunched her shoulders. "I do what I have to, to get us by." Building up a cash flow they could count on had taken hard work and time. She would have left Eric sooner than she had if she'd had a way to support her child, a way that would satisfy a judge in a custody suit.

"Anyhow..." She brightened intentionally as Morgan plopped down on the bench beside her. "I've been wanting a project, a topic for another happy film, for this summer, and I believe I've got it." She cocked her head at her son. "How 'bout a film starring your Bravo? Every time he bucks or nurses or sleeps or scratches his ear, he makes me smile. The subject doesn't have to be hilarious,'' she informed Miguel. ''Some of my films aim at heartwarming. Just images that make a child feel good.''

''He's perfect!'' Morgan agreed. ''Bravo the movie star—wait'll I tell him!''

''And that brings up something I need to tell you both,'' Miguel said. ''Tomorrow I must begin working. Hunting for oil,'' he explained to Morgan when he frowned. ''Which is what a wildcatter does. I'll be surveying east of Blindman's Canyon, and naturally, I'll have to ride. So Morgan, if you want to continue training your colt—'' his eyes moved to Risa ''—and you want to film him...it seems you'll have to come along with me, since I'm riding Bravo's mother.''

''And everywhere that Mary went,'' Risa growled. Manipulative! How could she ever trust a man who was always three jumps ahead, nudging her down paths she'd yet to see, for purposes that only he knew?

''The lamb was sure to go,'' Miguel agreed, his dark eyes laughing. ''But it won't be so bad. We can pack a picnic, and our bathing suits, be home by sundown each night. And—'' his gaze switched back to Morgan ''—this way, maybe you can help me, too? I'll show you how a wildcatter searches for oil.''

''*Yes!*'' Morgan agreed wholeheartedly. ''I'll help! Both of us will, won't we, Mom?''

Gritting her teeth, Risa nodded; what else could she do?

He shot up from the table with a yell and pranced off into the dark. ''We're going to look for oil! *Yeoow!* And maybe we'll see a grizzly bear? Or a mountain lion!''

''Not if they see us first!'' Miguel called, laughing.

''You have no shame,'' she told him, gathering the plates.

''Ah?'' He reached across the table and caught her wrist.

"Then let me be shameless. Shall I make a fire in the living room while you put our friend to bed? I would like very much to talk with you." He grinned as Morgan made a pass by the picnic table, arms spread—apparently he'd transformed into a jet plane—and zoomed off into the night. "Just one adult to another."

One man to one woman, he meant. All day the sensation had tormented her—his lips on her breast like a new brand on quivering flesh. If he wanted to converse tonight, it wouldn't be with words.

"Thank you, but no, Miguel." She'd been a fool, allowing him to touch her this afternoon. A momentary weakness that wouldn't happen again. "I'm for an early bed."

"Una lástima," he said softly, letting her go.

A pity.

CHAPTER TWENTY-ONE

"TIME FOR ANOTHER BREAK," Risa announced, leaning to touch Miguel's wrist and nod beyond him at the colt.

Trotting on a long lead that was attached to Morgan's saddle horn, the foal traveled between Guapo and his dam, which Miguel rode. Though Bravo was still keeping pace with his older companions, his red ears were no longer pricked but swiveled backward, a sign of irritation or woe, Miguel was learning.

Which made two of them. He'd thought himself so clever, using the foal as a lure for his son. But there was a price to be paid he'd learned over the past three days.

When the colt wasn't a distraction, he slowed them down. This would be the second stop of the morning and they had miles to go to reach the east-west line he was trying to map. "Okay," he growled resignedly, and reined in Columbine.

Bravo swerved immediately to the mare's flank and butted her udder. Risa dismounted, leaving her gray with reins dragging in a ground hitch. Raising the video camera that hung from her neck, she positioned herself to film the nursing baby.

Miguel had swung around in the saddle to untie his folding shovel, and now he paused, watching her from beneath the brim of his hat. She was so intent on her subject, her delectable mouth pursed to a kiss with concentration. Ah, Risa-Sonrisa. Three days since he'd held her at the swim-

ming hole, and each day he wanted her more. But if he
used the colt as a lure, she used her son as a chaperon. Not
once had he been able to get her alone; each night she
retired to her room at the same time as Morgan.

The frustration in him was building, fusing with his
growing worries about his well, how he would choose a
site. Because so far this north central part of the ranch
wasn't rocky enough. It didn't show its bones as did the
canyon land to the west or the gorge of the Sweetwater
Flats. He couldn't look beneath its skin of fertile grassland
to the secrets that lay beneath.

I need seismic readings to be sure what I'm doing.

Tankersly had forbidden him to call in a truck.

And time was fleeting, flying. If he didn't have a rig in
place by August…if he hadn't won Risa before she de-
parted in the fall… If he couldn't find a way to prove his
paternity…

"You going to dig again?" Morgan asked as he unlashed
the shovel.

"*Sí. ¿Quieres ayudarme?* Want to help?"

"*¡Sí, claro!*" Morgan smirked as his *r* rolled out perfectly that time.

"That was said very well," he lauded, glancing at Risa
for confirmation. Masked by her camera, she seemed not
to have heard. Except she was punishing her bottom lip
with her teeth. *Why do you keep fighting it—fighting me?
What will it take to convince you that I mean to be a good
father? The best of fathers to your wonderful son?* "You'll
be talking *español* like a native in no time," he added, to
goad her. She flinched, but simply sank to her knees and
kept on filming.

Choosing a spot fifty feet ahead, where sparser grass suggested thinner soil, Miguel cut into the earth. "The topsoil
doesn't tell us much," he informed his watching son, "but

once we dig beyond it…'' He reached the grittier soil below, then the blade rang against stone. ''You see, here's the bedrock.'' He offered the shovel to Morgan. ''If you'd clear away the dirt so we can see it…?'' He waited, containing his impatience. He could have done it himself in half the time, but how else was a boy to learn except by doing?

When a couple of square feet of rock had been bared, he dropped to his heels beside the hole. ''*Bueno, muchacho,* that's enough. Now look at the color and the texture. What do you think?''

''Can I chip it?''

''Be my guest.'' Miguel handed over his rock hammer. ''I'll have to buy you one of your own,'' he noted, ''next time I go to town.''

The boy glanced up at him, flushing with pleasure. ''Really? A hammer for me?''

''*De veras.*'' *Mi hijo.* If Risa forbade his speaking the precious words outright, he'd find another way to say them loud and clear. ''You have a good eye for rocks.'' As well he should, considering his breeding. Miguel was beginning to see how Ben could have cared so fiercely who contributed to the Tankersly bloodline and who should be excluded. Was beginning to feel honored that the old man had considered him worthy of a donation.

''Um, it's shale again?'' Morgan handed him a gray-green flake. ''Like we found yesterday?''

''*Sí. Muy bueno.* In fact, it's the same layer of shale we found in that outcrop to the west, or I'll eat my hat. But here it lies on higher ground than where we found it yesterday, as you can plainly see.'' He pointed out the ragged little ridge, a mile downslope to the west, where they'd sampled the layers of sediments that erosion revealed. ''Which tells us what?''

"That the beds are still rising...thataway." Morgan pointed east-northeast. "Which means if you're going to find oil, the trap's out there someplace."

"You'll make a wildcatter someday!" Miguel caught the brim of his hat and gave it a congratulatory tug as they beamed at each other. "And now, *dígame,* how does it taste?" They each nibbled with ritual solemnity on the edge of a flake.

Morgan looked uncertain, so Miguel shrugged his eyebrows. "The tiniest hint of hydrocarbons, but no *más que* that. Sometimes when you're drilling, the cuttings from the hole will taste like a mouthful of gasoline."

"Which I don't generally feed him," Risa noted dryly, walking up behind them. "Morgan Harrison Foster, are you chewing rocks again? I told you yesterday—"

"Harrison? That's your middle name?" Miguel laughed with delight. "Truly?"

Morgan squirmed. "Um, yeah."

"An excellent name!" Miguel handed him the shovel. "And we're done here, so why don't you tie this on your saddle."

He waited till the boy had trotted away. Turning, he slid his fingers beneath Risa's shining hair, caught her by the nape—ducked beneath the brim of her hat to kiss her rounding mouth. *"Gracias, corazón.* What a gift!"

"What are you— Wait! Don't—"

But one kiss would never be enough. He laid another on her, short as it was sweet, then released her as her eyes went from round to indignantly narrow. "For Harrison. Harry would be touched that my son carries his name. It makes *me* proud and very, very grateful."

"Miguel..." Fingers at her lips, Risa shook her head helplessly. "I didn't name him for *your* Harry. Eric's mother's maiden name is Harrison, that's all."

"Oh?" But he refused to believe that deep down in her heart she hadn't known who fathered her child. "Still, you accepted that suggestion. Allowed it to become his name." He shrugged and found his earlier cares had blown away on the pine-scented wind. "And whatever the case, Harry would say that you take your blessings where you find them."

"Would he?" she murmured dryly, but she didn't pull away when he dropped a hand on her shoulder and drew her along.

And that in itself was a small triumph, he reminded himself; maybe more telling than a stolen kiss. *So take your blessings as you find them.*

When they reached the horses, he grinned up at his mounted son. "Harrison, that's a very good name. The finest man I ever knew—he was a second father to me—was named Harry."

"Oh," said Morgan on a note of bashful pleasure, then his eyes shifted beyond them. "Hey, look! Somebody's coming!"

As they rode on, a horse and rider converged on them from the northeast, preceded by a large, bounding dog.

Anse Kirby, whom Rafe Montana had designated his right-hand man. They'd met him in and around the yard these past few days. Today the cowboy wasn't wearing his ready smile as he reined in his Appaloosa. "Risa." He touched his Stetson. Nodded to Miguel and Morgan.

The big Airedale that always accompanied him stretched to sniff noses with Guapo, and Morgan laughed delightedly.

"Which way are you all headed?" Kirby inquired after the first pleasantries had been exchanged.

He wasn't a man for idle talk, so Miguel tipped his head in question as he told him. "Due north today, for as long as we have daylight."

Kirby turned to study their route, then nodded approval. "Good. That'll keep you out of the trees."

"And why should we worry about trees?"

The cowboy nodded miles to the northeast, where three or four black dots wheeled in the sky. "See the buzzards? They're marking a lion kill, a foal from the broodmare herd in White Rock pasture. I'm headed back for my rifle. Looks like we're going to have to track the—" his gray eyes shifted to Risa "—the critter down. Or at least hurry him on his way."

This was the first kill on Suntop land, he went on to tell them. The animal had been hunting the McGraw range, ten miles to the northeast, during spring calving season, but apparently Tripp McGraw had made his ranch too hot for comfort. "So now he's onto our stock. A young wandering male, looking to stake out his own territory, we figure. He's still clumsy. Learning the ropes. Stickin' to smaller game." His eyes roved gently over Bravo, moved pointedly to Morgan, then swerved back to Miguel as he raised his eyebrows.

Miguel nodded. *Message taken, and thank you.*

"A mountain lion's not about to mess with groups," the cowboy assured them. "Still and all, next few days if you decide to bushwhack, you might want to invite Woofle along. He's a lady's man," he noted with a grin. The Airedale had reared to brace himself against Risa's boot as he licked her hand. "Belonged to Rafe's daughter Zoe before she went off to college."

"Well, he's welcome anytime," Risa said warmly, leaning down to rub a grizzled ear.

"Wish I had a dog." Morgan watched Woofle lope away at the heels of Kirby's gelding.

"Really?" Miguel considered this as they rode on. He'd never owned a dog himself, but if Morgan wanted one...

Risa leaned close and punched his knee. "Don't you dare," she warned in an undertone. "Our condo's too small and Eric hates pets."

But you're not going back to a condo, he swore to her silently. And most certainly not to Foster. The knowledge hadn't come to him in a lightning strike; more like honey, seeping into an empty cup till it was filled to the rim with the sweetest of glowing gold. *We are a family. Morgan is my son and you,* corazón, *are my woman, my heart,* mi vida.

Now all that remained was to make Risa see it.

FEELING LIKE THAT, he found it hard to control himself when Foster called. In truth, Miguel wished he could reach down the phone line and grab the bastard by the throat.

"No," Risa was saying into the receiver, her face pale, her eyes wide with helpless fury, when he walked into the kitchen the next evening. "No, Eric, that won't do. Ben would never give his permission. No, I don't *have* to ask him—I'm sure of this. You can't! Not at Suntop. Not even one cameraman."

The distant voice snapped a sentence or two and Risa sagged over the counter—hung her head so that a swath of shining hair hid her face from Miguel. "You can do that if you want, I suppose," she said with brittle calm. "It's breaking every promise you made, but I can't stop you."

Oh, but I can.

Or he could, if only Risa hadn't tied his hands. The first step was to prove his paternity beyond a doubt. Then he'd find the lawyer—the very prince of pit bulls of a lawyer—who'd use that ammunition in court to drive Foster right out of their lives. Because what judge would give the man rights once he learned there had been a mistake? That Morgan wasn't Foster's son by blood.

And how much money will a lawsuit like that take?

One good well should pay for it—if he made it in one.

But even if Suntop floated on a Saudi Arabian sea of oil, the first hole drilled—a wildcat well—would be least likely to hit. The following wells, once he had all the data that the first drilling would give him, would be much more likely to succeed.

By the first term of the contract, though, he had only one shot.

And Risa stood between terms two and three. If she continued to refuse to let Morgan be tested...

"Okay," Risa muttered wearily. "All right, Eric. I suppose that's acceptable, if you absolutely insist on doing this. But two days and not a minute more, and that's *it* for the summer. He comes back here and you don't bother him again. Is that our deal? You're quite sure? All right, then. We'll meet you in Durango tomorrow at the train station, twelve sharp. And—*yes*—I'll get his hair cut. G'bye." She slammed down the phone—or tried to. The handset clattered and bumped before she found the cradle.

She blew out a shaking breath.

"What?" Miguel said, coming to stand behind her. "*Dígame.* You're going to Durango, taking my son there? To see that bastard? Why?"

"*Shh!*" she hissed, glancing toward the screen door. "Where is he?"

"Morgan's outside under your car. We're changing your oil, which should have been done months ago, woman—it's nothing but sludge. I came for the paper towels. But tell me, what is this?" He rubbed his knuckles down her spine.

Her hands smoothed along the counter to clutch its edge—and whitened. Her head drooped; her shoulders rose in a sigh. "Eric's fondest dream has come to pass. He's been praying for months that the representative from his district—I mean the congressional rep at the federal level, not the state—wouldn't recover. The man had surgery last winter for prostate cancer, but it was thought—Carson kept telling his party—that he'd be well enough to campaign again for Congress. The election's in November, you know.''

''I try not to know these things,'' Miguel said dryly. He smoothed his knuckles down her spine again, bone by tiny bone, till his fingers bumped her belt. He longed to nudge up against her, mold himself to the lush curve of her hips— knew better than to try at this moment. She was vibrating with tension. ''And so…what? Foster wants to step into this sick man's shoes?''

She nodded tautly. ''He's running for his seat in the House of Representatives.''

''Good. Let him go off to Washington.'' But his hand froze halfway up her spine as he said it. ''And my son? What does Foster think—that he'll take him to D.C? The devil he will!''

She tipped back her head to stare at the ceiling. ''I haven't even thought that far. I don't know. Maybe.''

''He may not do this, Sonrisa.'' He forgot his resolve and moved to cover her, braced his arms outside hers along the counter. His lips at her ear, he whispered huskily, ''*Nunca*. I will not allow it!''

She shuddered, turned her face so that she looked up at him. ''It's not for you to allow or not allow. If it comes to that, I'll ask Ben to help me fight him.''

Trusting even her father before she'd trust him. *Brujita, do you mean to lock me out forever?* But even as he wondered that, her hips rocked inward then back, to bump his zipper in that soft, ancient rhythm of acceptance. Heat exploded from their point of contact and he closed his eyes, fighting the sudden violence of his need to grab her waist, surge against her. *Paciencia.* That way would only lose her.

Instead, he brought his lips within a quarter inch of her arching neck—breathed a lingering path of heat across her skin. "So what of tomorrow? What does Foster want?"

"H—h—he... He has to...land running, now that the party's tapped him to try for Carson's place. His PR people want to update an old campaign film he made two years ago for the state election. He bills himself as a family man, you see. A champion of moms and apple pie and church and all the conservative family values. So they want to film him interacting with his own—with Morgan.

"Eric was hoping for ranch shots here at Suntop, maybe the two of them riding, herding cows. He asked if I could set up a branding. But I said no. No way. Ben would never consent to his exploiting Suntop. As for me, I won't let him come here—I'd sooner shoot him. This is Morgan's sanctuary. There's got to be *one* place in the world where Eric can't touch him."

"Let me prove that I'm his father, and there'll be *no* place that *cabrón* can bother him! Don't you see that, Risa?" He rocked his hips against her, lipped the delicate rim of her ear.

A shudder racked her from toes to chin. "All I see, Miguel, is that once you do that, you win everything you ever wanted at Suntop—oil rights to endless wells... Ben to finance your drilling..."

"You, *pasión,* are a little mule." Yes, he wanted all that. How could he deny it? With a family, he'd need it more than ever. But she was a blind and stubborn mule if she believed that was the sum of his desires. "Al momento, *this* is all I see. All that I want or need." He dipped his head to kiss the corner where graceful neck met velvety shoulder; then, hearing the thump of tennis shoes on the back steps, pushed himself away. Turned in a haze of desire—*what was I seeking in the first place?*

Ah. His eyes fell on the paper towels. He scooped up the roll and lobbed it briskly to Morgan as his son banged through the screen door. "And here they are. I was just coming."

"So..." Risa asked quietly as they drove away from Durango's finest hotel two nights later, "how'd it go, kiddo?"

She could see for herself how it had gone. Morgan had lost his shine. His bounce. His hard-won self-assurance. He looked like a wan little storm-tossed bird, with that close-clipped haircut Eric had insisted on—to give the voters the correct conservative impression—and his drooping mouth. She longed to pull the car over and wrap him in a hug, but letting him decompress, make the difficult transition from Eric's world to hers at his own pace, was wiser. *But I'm waiting, baby. I'm right here.*

"It was...okay," he mumbled, staring out the window.

The producer of Eric's campaign ad had chosen to film on the Silverton railway, a prime Colorado attraction, where a steam engine pulled a train of tourists up a scenic narrow-gauge track to an old silver-mining town high in the San Juans. Photo ops all the way. "I bet the train ride was fun." She'd meant to take Morgan herself sometime this summer. The views were spectacular. But now it was forever spoiled.

"Not really..."

This is the very last time, darling. I swear it! Ben would arrive at Suntop in less than a month. If all went well...if she could only soften his heart...make him see...

"Oh, well," she said, groping for some saving grace. "At least you'll be a movie star like Bravo. I'll have to get a copy of the tape."

"*Don't!* They made me wear makeup, like a stupid girl. And Dad kept t-t-telling me to give him a *real* smile for the cameras, not a— Not a—" He was on the edge of tears.

Oh, baby, oh, kiddo. "Okay, no tape. And it's over now." She dared to stroke his hand. "No more makeup." No more Eric, who would not be satisfied. "Now we can go back to Suntop." She felt a sudden shaft of longing that felt almost like homesickness. "I stayed in town, too." At a motel out on the highway, in case Morgan should need her.

And because, in Morgan's absence, she hadn't dared share the Big House with Miguel.

Given a night to themselves, she knew what would have happened. Her body throbbed in liquid agreement; her lashes drooped for a second. *Oh, Miguel.* Even knowing what he wanted of her—and why he wanted it—she could hardly resist him.

For the past two days, hiding out in her shabby motel fifty miles from Suntop, still she'd felt his pull. Tossing sleepless in her wide, lonely bed, she'd felt like an exhausted swimmer scrabbling desperately at the sand while a riptide sucks her out to sea.

How much longer can I hold him off? Tell him no? When every time he touched her, *yes, oh, yes* was the silent answer that rang in her heart like a tolling bell.

"I missed Bravo," Morgan confided, sliding down in his seat. "And Guapo. And...Mr. Heydt."

Me, too. "And I reckon they missed you, sweetie. Mr. Heydt has a surprise for you, I understand." Anticipating Morgan's present blues, she'd phoned Miguel this morning to propose her idea, and he'd eagerly agreed to arrange it: the best antidote she could imagine to two days of Eric's endless demands and corrosive criticism. Tomorrow they'd

set off on a camping trip on horseback. They'd spend two
nights out under the stars. If that didn't wipe Eric out o*
mind...

Morgan sat up with the first bit of animation he'd shown
"What is it?"

Given that Miguel had done all the preparations, it wa*
only fair that he have the pleasure of telling. "You'll have
to ask him."

CHAPTER TWENTY-TWO

"YOU LOOK LIKE a cat who's been dining on canaries," Risa noted the following afternoon, studying Miguel's face as she rode by his side.

His mood was quite an improvement from the black one of last night. When he'd first welcomed Morgan back to Suntop and noted Eric's effects, Miguel had been silently, savagely outraged. At one point he'd asked her with chilling deliberation if Foster happened to be spending the night in Durango. And she'd been just as happy to report that her ex was not; he and his film crew had flown back to Denver.

But apparently sleep had proven a healer. All this morning Miguel's mood had spiraled higher along with Morgan's, and now as they neared the northern foothills of the ranch, he looked positively smug. "Canaries and Tweety Birds," she decided as his smile widened. During the two days they'd been absent, naturally he'd continued his hunt for oil. "Don't tell me you've found something."

His expression was all innocence—with a whiff of exultation. "Now, what would I find?"

He'd tell her in his own good time. Meanwhile, she needed to check on her wandering boy. Risa lifted the whistle she wore to her lips and blew one long trill.

Her request for a check-in was answered with a silvery blast from just over the hill ahead, then Morgan loped into view. "Elk! We saw three elk!" he yelled, reining in

Guapo. "I was afraid Woofle would chase them, but he didn't."

"He's saving himself for a grizzly bear," Miguel assured him as the dog flopped in the grass with pink tongue waving.

They'd brought the Airedale along more for Morgan's pleasure than fear of any mountain lion. For the past three days, several of the Suntop hands had tracked the big cat relentlessly, guided by a pair of keen-nosed beagle crosses brought in from the Kristopherson ranch.

The tawny predator had never been sighted, but the hunters had followed his scent as far as Blindman's Canyon, then found prints—very large prints, according to Anse Kirby—springing up a side canyon to the western rim—a path that no horseman could follow. At this point the lion was believed to be miles to the northwest, heading up into the high country, where he'd find plenty of calves in the herds on the summer range.

He'd also find the beagles, which had been dispatched along with Kirby to the Suntop line camp. With that pair snuffling at his tail, Risa hoped he'd travel on into the wilderness beyond, and henceforth stick to a diet of deer and rabbits. She was all for coexistence with the magnificent cats.

"You think there's really bears up here?" Morgan scanned the wooded foothills ahead with apprehensive delight.

"If there are, you and Woofle are our scouts. We expect a full and prompt report, *caballero*."

"And we expect you to signal us if there's any danger—blow five times on your whistle, then stop. Five times, then stop," Risa reminded him.

Morgan gave her a jaunty salute. "¡Sí, mamacita—y sí,

señor!'' He wheeled his pony and loped off again, with Woofle in hot pursuit.

"For your information, there hasn't been a grizzly bear sighting in Southwest Colorado in a generation or more," Risa informed her companion.

"Ah, but a man can always hope." They both smiled as Morgan reined in on the crest of the hill, yelled something back at them, then plunged down the far side.

"You see?" Risa said softly. "He's almost as good as new."

Miguel's face darkened. "But why should he endure such treatment in the first place? And he won't from now on if I have anything to say about it."

Which you don't. But she didn't want to quarrel. "I'm just grateful that Eric didn't change his mind entirely. I was afraid he'd insist on taking Morgan back to Denver." Had he done so, she would have had no choice but to follow. And then this... She glanced at Miguel's big brown hand holding his reins; the hard muscular leg that almost brushed hers they were riding so close. Then this would be over, whatever this was, before it had even begun. At the thought, an aching sense of loss spread behind her breastbone, making it hard to draw a full breath.

"Ah, but Foster would never have done that," Miguel said with bitter mockery. "You don't realize what he's up to?"

Warily, she cocked her head. "What d'you mean?"

"Look around you, *pasión.* Suntop land as far as the eye can see. Eleven years ago, when last we were here, this ranch was worth millions—and now, with the way land prices have risen? I'm sure that Foster is nightly down on his knees, praying that you and Ben mend your quarrel.

"Because if Ben should decide to write Morgan back into his will, make him his heir, well, how old is your

father—in his eighties? You don't think Foster can count?
Let Ben die before Morgan reaches manhood, and who will
manage Morgan's interests? Believe me, Risa, it won't be
you."

"You're the one who married me for money, Miguel."

"And Foster did not? You think he married you for your
beautiful golden eyes?"

What was he saying—that no man would want her without a fortune in tow? Was she that unlovable? Tears burned
behind her lashes as she tipped up her chin. "When Eric
married me in Vegas I hadn't a cent to my name—not
enough to pay for a marriage license or—or the parking
meter in front of the wedding chapel."

"*Sí,* Sonrisa, but Foster would have believed you still
had prospects. That after he'd married you, your father
would resign himself to your choice. The real question is—
how long was the *cabrón* faithful to you *after* Ben struck
you from his will?"

Three or four months at best. "So what does that tell
me, Miguel, that all men are grasping, greedy bastards?
Thank you so much, but I'd figured that out already!" She
touched her spurs to Cinders and shot away—or tried to.

But she was the one who'd been stuck leading Bravo
this afternoon. The colt took three or four bounds, then
realized that his dam wasn't running at his side. He dug in
his tiny hooves and would have fallen if she hadn't reined
in. "*Oh,* for Pete's—" She tore at the lead wrapped around
her saddle horn—flung it free. "Here, he's all yours!"

"Risa, wait. ¡*Calmate!*"

"Ha!" Jamming her hat down on her head, half-blinded
by tears, she stormed off over the hill.

A fool's errand, when what she wanted lay behind.

THERE WAS NO WAY, though, to ride alone for long, with
Morgan shuttling anxiously between them like a little nee-

dle, intent on darning the unacknowledged tear. And it wasn't fair to cherish her wounded pride on this day that was meant to cheer him up. So Risa mastered her feelings and rejoined the cavalcade. She flashed Miguel one glance of glowing resentment, then devoted herself to her son entirely.

And when Miguel's horse fell behind, she didn't look back. Let him whistle if he needed them to wait.

A few minutes later he loped up alongside her. Silently he laid a branch of wild honeysuckle across her lap, then reined back to his original position on the far side of their son.

Lifting the blossoms to her nose, she felt as if a weight had rolled off her heart. She tucked one cluster of fragrant white behind her ear, another in her buttonhole, and the next time she felt his dark eyes upon her, she didn't avoid them. He shaped her a silent kiss.

A couple of hours before sundown, they reached his surprise. A low craggy hummock of rock, roughly a mile from north to south, half again as wide. "It's called the Whaleback," she told Miguel when he waved an expansive arm to take it in—as if he'd conjured it out of the ground himself.

"Oh? A better name might be Treasure Rock." He was simmering with suppressed gaiety. "Let me show you something."

They tied the horses near the base of the hill and walked upward through wide-spaced pines that clung tenaciously to the meager soil. A flying buttress of stone had broken away from the slope, and behind it was a cave Risa remembered from childhood explorations.

"Yeow!" Morgan gloated as Miguel flicked on a flashlight. "What d'you think lives in here? Bats? Snakes? *Wolves!*" He pounced on a pile of dry bones.

"Could be," Miguel agreed, "but look at the walls." His light played over layers of stone slanting upward in the colors and textures that Risa was coming to recognize. Beds of shale and limestone and sandstone, like a ruddy layer cake tipped toward the crest of the hill.

"So they're still rising to the east," she said. As they did all the way from Blindman's Canyon, five miles to their west. He'd shown her this phenomenon eleven years ago, below the walls of Paradise.

"Exactly so," Miguel agreed, taking her arm. "And now we move on."

They rode around the north end of the Whaleback, coming to the lovely little meadow she remembered. Ringed by dense aspen and pine forest on three sides and the low cliffs of the formation to the south, it was watered by a creek that burbled along its eastern edge. "This would be a good place to camp," she noted, glancing up at the violet sky. They had less than an hour till sundown.

"The perfect place," Miguel agreed, riding up to the face of the cliffs. "*¡Mira!*"

She remembered the gorgeous curving bands of color from her girlhood, but back then she'd not known their significance. The layers of stone slanted up from the west...were sliced off by erosion along the top of the mound...then reappeared—*diving* into the soil toward the east. Toward the Sweetwater Flats. Curves describing a perfect fold in the stone, a shallow, inverted *u* of many colors.

"You're looking at the sheared-off end of an anticline." Miguel sounded as though he were whispering in church. "An upward fold in the layers of the earth. And of course, the Whaleback is only the tip of the formation. The beds will echo this fold for miles beneath us, and somewhere down there—"

"Is the oil!" Morgan crowed.

"If we're exceedingly lucky," Miguel agreed. Eyes devouring the stone, he absently scratched the palm of one hand, then the other.

After that they had to hurry to set up camp before they lost the daylight. They unsaddled, then staked out the horses along the bank of the creek within reach of both water and grass, leaving the colt to wander free. Risa swatted a mosquito and surveyed the scene. "How about laying the fire here," she suggested, closer to the cliff.

"As you like." Miguel caught Morgan's shoulder. "We *hombres* will gather the wood if you'll think about feeding us."

"Glad to see that *machismo* is alive and well in the twenty-first century," she teased, but she didn't mind. She'd put together a one-pot stew this morning before leaving the house. All she had to do was heat it, add bread and butter, then canned pears for dessert, and they'd think her a magician.

She was in need of a little magic by the time they returned from the forest with armloads of wood. "We've got to move, guys. The bugs are ferocious." The far side of the creek was swampy and the mosquitoes were swarming. "But I've found a trail up the rock."

A game path skirted the creek along the eastern side of the Whaleback, then meandered up its slope. Toting their wood and bedrolls, they found a clearing at the top of the cliffs, overlooking the meadow forty feet below.

"Hey, Guapo!" Morgan called, and the pony lifted his head and snorted.

"Shh! The mosquitoes will hear you!" Miguel cried in mock alarm.

But they didn't. The campsite was perfect, high enough to catch a cool breeze blowing off the distant mountains, with a thick carpet of pine needles to soften the ground and a few wind-sculpted pines to carve the night sky into lacy patches of stars.

They ate with gusto by firelight, while Miguel entertained them with tales of Alaska: drilling on the North Slope. Pipeline leaks and well blowouts. Snowmobiles and bush planes. Muskeg and caribou. Polar bears and the midnight sun.

Then from there, goaded by Morgan's rapt attention and eager questions, he drifted on into tales of his boyhood days in the Texas Oil Patch. "Harry Stories," Risa privately labeled these, with much amusement. From his affectionate telling, Miguel's mentor had been quite the gaudy, bawdy character, with a heart as big as the Texas sky. No wonder Miguel had loved him so.

But at last it was time for bed; Morgan had already drifted off, his head pillowed on the Airedale's grizzled flank.

She'd arranged their foam pads and bedrolls earlier, while the stew heated. A little ways back from the cliff edge, under a sheltering pine. No need for a tent tonight, with that spangled dome of stars overhead.

"Bedtime, my son." Miguel eased an arm beneath Morgan's shoulders. "Up you come, Morgan Harry."

Morgan gave him a drowsy smile. "You said Harry was your...your second father, Mr. Heydt?"

"*Sí, muchacho,* that he was," Miguel agreed, half supporting him as he steered him toward his bed.

"Then...d'you think maybe...would you...could you be my...?" Morgan swayed, looking upward.

"I am already, *mi hijo,*" Miguel told him softly. "But I'm honored that you ask me. So very honored." Tenderly he ruffled his son's cap of corn-silk hair. "And now, if we're to catch those trout for breakfast, we must rise early. Which means..."

"Yeah, yeah, yeah." Morgan yawned so widely he staggered. "Sometimes you sort of think like a dad, you know?"

"*Bueno.* Who knows, with a little practice...?"

Across the clearing, kneeling by her saddlebags, brushing her hair, Risa found the firelight blurring. *Am I crazy to try to stand in the way of this?* And what good was it doing her anyway? She was like a rock standing in the midst of a river. It was simply parting and flowing on both sides around her, finding its own level and course, no matter what she willed. And she was tired of fighting.

Or maybe just tired tonight, deliciously tired. While Miguel shoveled dirt over their campfire, she slithered under her blanket. She'd placed Morgan in the middle bedroll. *Like a sword down the middle of the bed,* she thought dreamily, lying back. If he hadn't been there...not a doubt about it... She stared up at the stars, imagining Miguel's shaggy head blocking out half her sky... Forgiven or not, trusting him or not, she wanted him as she'd never wanted another.

A star shot across the dark, and halfway through making her wish, she fell asleep.

RISA AWOKE to the distant murmur of voices and cool light sifting under her lashes. She stretched luxuriously, rolled over on her side and opened her eyes.

By the blue light of dawn, the men in her life were muttering earnestly as they assembled the sectioned fishing rod that Miguel had brought along. One of the topics last night had been trout: how the stream was bound to be teeming with them, how trout for breakfast were the perfect meal.

Well, that should keep 'em out of mischief. Risa smiled to herself and drifted away.

The next time she awakened, it might have been only minutes later. No sign of sunlight yet, though it felt warmer. She stumbled to her feet, visited the bushes to the south, then returned to brush her teeth with canteen water. *I suppose I should think about making biscuits to go with the hypothetical trout.* Would they be insulted if she cooked bacon just in case?

On the other hand, they might fish for hours. Another fifteen minutes in the sack—could it hurt?

The third time she woke up, it was to the fragrance of coffee. Miguel dropped to his heels beside her. "Sleeping Beauty, would you like a cup?"

"Do bears dance in the woods?"

"Tangos and rumbas, I've heard." He frowned when she propped herself on one elbow. "That won't be *cómodo.*"

"It's perfectly comfortable," she insisted, but he'd already moved behind her.

Lifting her higher, he sat with a long leg to either side of her hips. Miguel Heydt, obliging easy chair. "How is that?" His hand appeared before her face, offering the tin mug again.

"It's…" Heaven. His body was warm, in contrast to the chill mountain air. She leaned back against him, hesitantly at first. "Where's Morgan?"

"To the north of the meadow, such a trout pool we found. I told him I'd start the fire, and that when he's ready to learn how to clean his fish, he's to signal—three blasts on his whistle. We'll do it down by the water so we can wash up afterward."

"Oh. As long as Woofle's guarding him…" She was the one in danger. Miguel smelled deliciously masculine, achingly familiar. Slowly she softened and conformed to his shape, till she could feel his heart beating against her left shoulder blade. Gradually her breathing deepened to match his own. She took a sip of the steaming liquid. "Excellent coffee," she said primly.

She felt anything but prim.

"It's by way of apology," he admitted in a voice gone husky with emotion. "Yesterday, what I said, *pasión,* I don't know what devil made me say it."

"It's forgotten." She sipped again. Heat was sliding down her throat, spreading to her belly and lower. A moist flowing heat, sweet as the syrupy sugar in the bottom of her mug.

"Risa, it's not," he murmured, his lips at her ear. "You've never forgiven me and maybe what I did was not forgivable, but this you should know. *Yes,* your father asked me to take you away from Foster. To marry you if I could. But I'm not the same as Foster—a man with a cash register in place of a heart.

"Believe me, *querida,* not for all the oil in all the world would I have sold myself to a woman I didn't desire. I saw your beautiful golden eyes and I drowned in them." Gently he kissed her temple.

Oh, Miguel. A shiver worked its way up her spine. Nerve endings fired from her toes to her scalp. Her nipples lifted and hardened.

"I saw these lips to drive a man wild..." Slow and warm, his mouth brushed down her cheekbone.

She shuddered again and tipped her head back and around so he could reach the corner of her mouth. Deep in her throat, she purred as the tip of his tongue teased her lips, coaxing entry.

No way to refuse it; she surrendered on a sigh...and parted. He licked the underside of her upper lip. The taste of him sent her reeling back through the years. *Oh, yes, I remember this!* Paradise.

The cup was lifted from her fingers and tossed into the bushes. Hard, hot hands slid under the loose shirt she was wearing to grip her waist. Sucking her bottom lip, he growled wordless, wicked promises. He tore his mouth away to whisper, *"Risa-Sonrisa, Sonrisa—al fin!"*

At last, oh, yes, at last—at last his big hands smoothed higher to cradle her breasts. She arched her neck against his shoulder, moaning a tremulous note of joy, which deepened to an aching groan as his fingertips found the high, hard buds of her desire.

"Mi Risa...querida..." He nuzzled through her tousled hair to kiss her nape, then gently bite her shoulder, and all the while his fingers fondling her, melting her, turning her insides to churning lava.

"Miguel," she panted, eyes closed... "What about...?"

"He's fishing, *cielito,* catching plenty, while his father would settle for one slippery mermaid." He slid a forearm around under her thighs, another behind her shoulders and lifted her, turned her sideways to rest in his lap. *"Ah, este es mejor."*

Much better indeed, she agreed as he lifted her shirt and his lips found her breast, savoring her in fierce, wet, suckling kisses. She mewed, slid her hands up into his shaggy hair and clutched him to her. "We sh—shouldn't—"

"Oh, yes, we should!" he lifted his head to tell her, laughing. "We should have days ago. Years ago!" He kissed the point of her chin, the tip of her nose. "Do not worry, *cielito,* if he whistles, we'll stop. And I'm very fast when I have to be."

Aroused as she was, there was no such thing as too fast. "Wh—what's the Spanish for quickie?"

He told her in a husky, laughing growl as he lifted her

to kneel astride him—ripped her panties off and hurled them aside.

"I must be mad. I'm *definitely* mad," she gasped, taking hold of him—hot velvet over steel.

They both were mad—crazy for each other—and they pressed their mouths together as they joined, muffling their triumphant cries.

At last.

STILL JOINED, she knelt above him, laying tiny, moistly lingering kisses on his lips, the aftershocks of her passion jolting him, making him smile. He cupped her breasts. Her hair enclosed them like a tent of ruddy gold.

"That lacked a certain...finesse," Miguel murmured ruefully between two kisses. "I would not have you think—"

"I think—I know—it was exactly...precisely...absolutely what I wanted." A wild, wanton, passionate celebration; her heart felt as though it were bursting with song.

"And I, *corazón*—how I've been burning for this!" His thumb tips found her nipples, circled with wicked delicacy—a fluttering, subterranean convulsion rocked her hips. "And I can finesse you next time. With a bed and a locked door I could show you such wonders..."

"Oh, modest man." Though she didn't doubt he could. *But will there be a next time? Oh, Miguel, will there?* But that way lay uncertainty and sorrow and she wouldn't have it, not in this glorious now with his hands sliding around her hips, his fingertips deftly delving, inciting her to riot... Good heavens, a next time already?

She smiled and shook her head, caressing his face with her hair. "We're pushing our luck, *amado*. I've been meaning to talk to him about the birds and bees, but show-and-tell?''

''*Sí*, that might bring up more questions than we'd care to try to answer.''

Such as what we are to each other? she wondered. *And what do you really want from me?* Kissing him one last time, she rose slowly to her knees—and they parted. She drew a deep breath, then stood, a woman alone again.

Lonely and frightened already. *Oh, God, if only I trusted you.* But she'd leaped into trust already, thrown her body over the cliff and left her heart and mind to follow willy-nilly, if they only could.

And the hell of it was, the next time he called her, she'd come running.

Running ahead of all her doubts and fears. Was this what it was to be a fool for love?

Stop, she warned herself. *Savor this moment and let the future take care of itself.*

Hastily they dressed, then kissed again. ''Time to go get him?'' Risa suggested, brushing pine needles from his hair.

''*Sí*. But I can't seem to leave you.'' Arms around each other's waists, they strolled to the edge of the cliff to look down on the dew-spangled meadow, not yet lit by the sun.

The horses cropped grass, circling dreamily at the ends of their long tethers. Bravo was a patch of red on the far side of the clearing, wandering beneath the overhanging trees.

''There he is, coming this way.'' Miguel nodded north. Fishing pole over his shoulder, holding a string of silvery trout high in one hand, their smiling child hopped from stone to stone across the brook, while Woofle sloshed chest-deep through the tumbling pool beside him.

Bravo wheeled toward the trees and threw up his head, ears pricked.

He snorted and spun, bolted toward his distant dam—as a tawny shape burst from the forest, to bound with dream-like, feline fluidity after the fleeing colt. The cat launched itself into an arc of rising gold, velvety paws extending, claws reaching—

Risa screamed along with the colt, with his dam. Predator and prey tumbled through the high grass in a welter of spindly legs and snapping teeth and terrified squeals—

And the dog came charging, roaring, a brown bolt breasting the green—with Morgan running behind him, waving his fishing pole and shrieking blue murder.

"*¡Dios mío!*" Miguel dropped one hand to the ground and vaulted over the rim of the cliff.

"*Miguel!*" He'd told her once, "Only leap." Risa fell to her knees and peered over. He was sliding feetfirst down the ragged rock, almost flying, flinging himself from one ledge or handhold to the next. He grabbed, missed, rolled the final twelve feet. "*Miguel!*" He staggered upright, lunged between the stampeding horses.

Lion, dog, colt and boy whirled in a snarling, squealing blur—then the cat broke away in a twelve-foot bound. He cleared twenty feet in a second leap, then spun to face the oncoming Airedale. One slap sent him flying. Woofle rolled, bounced bellowing to his feet; dog and cat shot off through the trees.

Leaving behind a boy sprawled over a fallen colt. And a man staggering to a halt above them, then dropping to his knees. Risa sobbed and spun and raced off down the trail.

CHAPTER TWENTY-THREE

RISA'S JOURNEY down the Whaleback to Morgan was a
tearful blur of snatching bushes and treacherous rocks—a
nightmare, slow-motion dash through knee-deep quicksand
to the breathless chant of "Please—oh, please—oh,
please—oh, please!" that ended as she landed in a wob-
bling heap beside her son, who was sitting up, cradled in
Miguel's arms. "Oh, *baby!* Oh, sweetie! Oh, God! Is he
all *right?*"

"He's fine, Sonrisa. He's fine. He'll live."

"Lemme *up,*" Morgan insisted, squirming in his lap.
"Bravo—"

"You first, *mi hijo,* and then your colt." Gently Miguel
worked his T-shirt over his head and Risa sobbed. "*Calmate, corazón.* It's nothing. He's only scratched."

"*Only!*" Three bloody gouges extended from Morgan's
right shoulder to his elbow. "And—*oh*—there—" The fair,
fine skin of her child's left forearm was punctured front
and back, two ragged holes to a side. "That cat!" She'd
hunt him down herself!

"Looks like a dog bite to me," Miguel said dryly, "from
the width of the punctures."

"We were all sort of confused," Morgan admitted.

Miguel laughed. "I'll say you were! What warriors! That
lion didn't know what hit him."

"And what was he doing here?" Risa fumed. "They
said he'd gone."

"Guess he doubled back." Miguel smoothed Morgan's hair with hands ripped and torn by the rocks. "Kirby was right. He was a young and clumsy hunter, *gracias a Dios*."

"But Bravo," Morgan pleaded. "You've gotta help Bravo." The numbing adrenaline was wearing off; the tears starting to flow.

They had to get him to a doctor before the real pain kicked in. Risa rubbed the back of a trembling hand across her eyes and drew a breath. *Sort it out now. Have your hysterics later, Mom,* she told herself. "All right, how *is* Bravo?" And where were all the horses?

HALF AN HOUR LATER they'd organized the battlefield, triaged the wounded and assessed their remaining resources. Cinders and Guapo were gone. Trailing their tethers and stakes, they must be halfway to the home pasture by now. Risa prayed that one of the hands would intercept them somewhere in their flight, make the logical conclusion, and reinforcements might soon be headed their way.

But that wasn't a hope to count on or wait for while her son seemed to be drifting into shock. His face had gone greeny-pale and he was shivering with reaction. The sooner he reached painkillers and antibiotics, the better.

The only transport they had was Columbine, who'd been fighting to get at the lion, not escape him. The old mare presently stood saddled, trying to reach back and nuzzle her burden. Draped in place of the saddlebags, Bravo lay across her flanks, his front and back legs tied to the saddle skirts. His head drooping pitifully, the colt was as dazed and docile as Morgan. Risa had tied an extra T-shirt over the ragged wounds in his neck and shoulder. Terrible as they looked, she thought the damage might be repairable if he reached a vet in time.

"You're sure you're not afraid?" Miguel fretted as he

knelt and she helped Morgan climb onto his back. "I don't like this separating."

"I'm not scared in the least. That blasted cat is halfway to California by now."

"More likely he's up a tree, with Woofle sitting under it, telling him just what he'll do if he dares to come down."

"Mom, we can't leave him," Morgan roused himself to plead. "What if the cat hurt him?"

Risa met Miguel's eyes and he grimaced. If the Airedale had cornered the lion so that it was fight or die, then Woofle wouldn't be returning. The cat had outweighed him easily three to one.

"That's why you have to hurry back to the ranch," she assured him with a warm smile. "To get rifles and dogs and men to help Woofle catch the cat." Gently she kissed his cheek. "I'll see you very soon, sweetheart, I promise." She kissed Miguel on the mouth and looked into his eyes. "And you. Be…careful." *Don't break your big heart, my love.*

At first Risa had wanted to load Morgan aboard the mare along with one adult and race for home and a doctor. But the struggle to force the mare to leave her foal would have been brutal, maybe not even possible, and Morgan would have rebelled, as well.

Neither could they load up the old mare with a triple burden—Morgan with an adult to hold him, plus the colt. Even if Columbine could have carried that weight, she could not have moved faster than a walk. Bravo was precariously balanced at best, his lungs already compressed; a ten-mile jolting canter would probably kill him.

No, the fastest way to take Morgan to a doctor was piggyback. Miguel insisted he could alternately run and walk the whole way, bettering the mare's pace by hours. Once they reached the ranch yard, he would send someone to help Risa, while he drove Morgan to the hospital in Durango.

It was the only sensible course; still, Risa would have given anything to go along. *I'm trusting you with my most precious possession,* she told Miguel silently as he paused at the edge of the trees to look back. He shaped her a silent kiss. Morgan's fair head rested wearily against his shoulder.

Eyes blurring, Risa blew them both a kiss, then Miguel turned and jogged off to the south. She sighed and glanced at the dark ring of forest. "Let's get out of here, old girl." So they plodded along, dreamily, drearily, and the hollowness expanded behind her breastbone with each hard-won mile: Miguel wasn't just running away from her with her son; he'd also taken her heart.

THE WALK HOME was a nightmare of irrational fears and blistered feet, along with the constant struggle to keep the colt atop his dam. As Bravo came out of his shock-induced numbness, he began to struggle against his ties. If his weight shifted and Columbine started bucking...

But the mare seemed entirely aware of what she carried; she stood patiently each time Risa hurried back to shove the groaning colt this way or that.

The one bright spot in her ordeal was when, trudging along, drawing the mare behind her, Risa felt a warm wet tongue lap her hand. She shrieked and spun—to find Woofle standing there with his stump tail sheepishly wagging.

"Oh, Woofle! *Woofle!*" She dropped to her knees and hugged him, and he yelped. He looked like a prizefighter who'd gone eighteen rounds with a threshing machine, but from the jaunty way he gimped along, clearly the Airedale considered himself the victor on points. After that, the road wasn't half so hard, and Risa smiled wearily most of the way.

Just a mile from the home corrals, she heard the thunder of hooves at last. Three horsemen burst over the ridge, with a fourth saddled horse running beside them.

Two of the cowboys touched their hats and loped straight on past her, rifles swinging from their saddle scabbards. Rafe Montana reined in and swung down from his big bay before it had skidded to a halt.

"How's Morgan?" she cried.

"SIR, IF YOU'LL JUST help us fill out the forms while they start cleaning him up," the pretty emergency-room clerk insisted.

Miguel tore his eyes from the curtained cubicle into which they'd rushed Morgan. "My son—I've got to be with him."

"Of course. But this'll take only a minute," she murmured soothingly. "Your son's name is...?"

"Morgan Heydt," he said without hesitation. Never Morgan Foster again, especially not since... *Dios mío,* was that only this morning that he and Risa—

"Age?"

"Ten."

"And your insurance, sir?"

"Is not local. We're only visiting for the summer." He spun around as a faint whimper sounded beyond the curtain. "Look, here's my Visa card." He ripped it out of his wallet and dropped it on the counter. "That will cover all costs. Call and check my balance, if you like. Now, you'll pardon me, but I must—"

"Ohhhh." She grimaced, looking down at his blood-stained fingers. "We'll need to tend to those, too."

"*Sí,* whatever, but later." He limped off to the cubicle. Nobody was stitching up *his* kid without him there to hold him.

IT WAS LATE AFTERNOON before the repairs were complete. Sometime in all that, while Miguel had sat at Morgan's head, stroking his hair, whispering encouragement and praise while the needle pricked and pulled, himself drifting in and out of a haze of exhaustion, the thought had come to him. When the last stitch had been tied and the surgeon stepped back to let the nurse apply the bandages, Miguel drew him out into the hallway. "There is one thing more while we're here...I would like you to draw blood from us both. For a paternity test."

The doctor's eyebrows shot up. "But surely, sir—" He paused uncomfortably. "I suppose there's some question or you wouldn't be checking. But does it actually matter that much if you've raised him all these years as your son? It's obvious to anyone, seeing you two together, that there's an emotional bond."

Miguel gave him a wolfish smile. *You think I'm trying to disprove our relationship? Wriggle out of my duties?* But it was none of the man's business, and too complicated to explain. "Believe me, it matters."

The doctor gave an irritable shrug. "All right, then. There are two levels of testing. If you want the results to be acceptable in a court of law, then you'll have to make an appointment, bring in your son's birth certificate and a photo ID of yourself."

"I don't have his certificate with me. We came straight down out of the mountains to this hospital..."

"Then all we can do today is the informal paternity test. It would answer your personal questions. Tell you if you care to repeat the test for a court of law. But really, sir..."

Even an informal test would give him leverage. Might be enough to convince Foster that it was no use fighting, that he should back down. "Good enough. If you'd please do it?"

AT THE SOUND of a car parking outside the kitchen, Risa shot to her feet. She banged out the back door and flew across the grass. "Oh, thank *heavens!* They said you'd already left the E.R. when I phoned, so—" There'd been nothing she could do but come home to wait. Another half hour and she'd have gone mad. "Oh, sweetie, how are you?" she cried as Miguel lifted Morgan out of the Jeep.

"I'm okay," he muttered with a wan smile as she kissed him and stroked his cheek. "How's Bravo? And Mom, what about Woofie?"

She told him as Miguel carried him into the house. "Bravo is going to be fine, sweetheart. Mr. Montana called from the vet's a little while ago. He knew you'd be worried. The colt has more stitches than a patchwork quilt, he said, but it was mostly flesh wounds." The vet hoped for a full recovery if infection didn't set in.

"And your brave old Woofie came back!" she assured him as Miguel carried him up the staircase. "He also needed some stitches." One ear would be more raffish than ever, but luckily dogs had no vanity. "Mr. Montana said he gets a hero-size T-bone steak tonight."

"But what about you?" she asked, as they reached the second floor. "They didn't want to keep you overnight?"

"I made a judgment call there," Miguel told her. "They did, but—"

"But I said I wouldn't," Morgan insisted, looking back over Miguel's shoulder. "I wanted to come home to Suntop."

Risa bit her lip, then scurried ahead of Miguel to turn down Morgan's covers and pile his pillows. "What did the doctor think?"

"He thought that as long as his temperature didn't rise in the night or the pain get too much for him—" Miguel deposited their son gently on his bed, then shrugged. "And if it did, to simply bring him back. It's what I would have wanted for myself, *corazón*. I hate hospitals.''

''Me, too.'' Morgan reached up for Miguel's hand.

Hands clasped, they faced her with wary determination, two against one. *Men*. Risa didn't know whether to smile or shake them both. ''What about medicine?''

''We brought bottles and pills and a sling for his arm, all of which are still in the car. And the doctor said he may have a light supper.''

Something at last that she could do. ''In bed,'' she decided. She'd burned off some of her frantic energy cooking this evening. ''Soup and a sandwich on a tray. As for you...'' She turned a critical eye on Miguel. ''A hot bath.'' He was limping badly. That ten-mile run carrying Morgan, plus that headlong plunge down the cliff... ''That way you won't get your bandages wet.'' Someone had taped his hands at the hospital. ''Then supper in bed for you, too.''

''Is she always this bossy?'' Miguel complained, and Morgan nodded gleefully.

''Ha!'' she cried, bustling away.

She kept herself hopping for the next hour, waiting on Morgan, then hurrying to the guest wing to bring Miguel a rum and Coke in his bath—then scrub his back and chest when he pointed out on a note of husky pathos that he was helpless, *pasión*. How was he to soap himself with his hands bandaged *así*?

Then quickly back to Morgan, who was too sleepy to notice all the splashes on her blouse or her kiss-swollen mouth, to coax more soup down him spoon by spoon while they talked of their adventure.

Miguel had assured Morgan that he was going to have some scars to be proud of. ''He says all the girls will go wild when I tell them they're mountain lion scars,'' Morgan said, making a face. ''But who cares about stupid girls?''

Then Miguel arrived, with tousled damp hair, looking very large in his bathrobe, so Risa fed him in a chair pulled up next to Morgan's bed.

Within twenty minutes, they were both nodding. "Lights out," she announced, and nobody protested.

Though out in the hall, Miguel caught her arm. "You mean to check on him during the night?"

"Every few hours," she agreed. Her one fear was some sort of raging infection—animal claws and predator's teeth.

"You'll need help with that, Sonrisa. You're as tired as we are, after your hike and all your worry. We'll alternate checking him, if you have a clock we can set?" He strolled into her bedroom. "Ah, *bueno,* you do." He sank down heavily on the edge of her bed. "Perhaps if you would take the first one…"

"Refresh my memory," Risa said dryly, coming to stand between his knees. "Did I invite you to sleep in here?" She cupped his hard, unshaven cheek, smiling down at him.

"No, but it's such a long way from my room to Morgan's…" His dark eyes were filled with sleepy laughter. "And if I showed you my blisters from running in boots?"

She pressed her hands to his chest and shoved him backward to lie flat on her quilt. "I'd be forever grateful, you big goof. What you did for my boy today…"

"For *our* boy." He reached up to snag her belt and pull her over on top of him—caught her arms as she toppled. "Risa, all day I've been remembering this…"

And she had not?

He kissed the tip of her nose. "But there's something I must tell you… At the hospital, I…"

"What?" she asked as she kissed him back. His lips parted to answer, and she ran the tip of her tongue wickedly along his bottom lip.

"You're not paying attention, woman," he growled,

catching her nape. The kiss deepened, extended through dreamy time like a song with no ending and no beginning, and somewhere in the midst of it, he sighed blissfully—and fell asleep.

Heart full to overflowing, she lay for a while, stroking his soft, thick hair and smiling against his cheek. At last she rose, managed to rouse him just enough to nudge him fully onto the mattress and went off to check her son.

In the end, she did all the bed checks herself, happy to do so, as deeply as Miguel was sleeping. Then after the 3:00 a.m. check, she stopped setting the alarm. Morgan's forehead was cool and he was as serenely asleep as his father.

SHE AWOKE SOMETIME just before dawn, to find they were already entwined and making love.

Slow, dreamy, tender lovemaking, Miguel's delicious weight driving her down into the softness beneath her; her hips rising in answer. A bonfire gradually kindling under the bed—flames wherever his mouth touched...fire following his fingers. Need and urgency building... Yearning emptiness filled and rhythmically filled to overflowing—

Satisfaction like a starburst.

The words tolling like a bell in her heart, *I love you, oh, I do love you!* How could she ever have doubted?

Then, still tangled together from lips to toes...the slow sensual slide down the velvety chute to sleep.

A FEW HOURS LATER, Risa woke up, reaching for him. She frowned and patted the empty space beside her, then opened her eyes.

No Miguel. *Such discretion,* she told herself, brushing off a twinge of loneliness and fear. He'd retreated to his own bed in case Morgan should wake first and find them.

That was one of the things—one of many—she loved about him. In spite of his *machismo,* Miguel was a sensitive man. *Best of both worlds,* she told herself as she looked in on Morgan—fast asleep and forehead still blessedly cool— then showered. She combed out her hair, tightened her robe around her and padded downstairs to make coffee. *Should I bring him a cup in bed? Or let him sleep in?*

She stopped short in the doorway. "You're up!"

"*Ay,* I meant to bring you your coffee in bed," Miguel lamented, turning around from the counter where he was pouring two mugs.

"Lovely thought." She walked into his arms and lifted her face for a kiss—how could anything feel so natural and right? "But now I'm up, I'll take it here."

They sat across from each other, sipping coffee while their bare feet courted and caressed under the table. But halfway through his first cup, Miguel set it aside. "There's something I must tell you, Sonrisa, before our hero interrupts us." He frowned thoughtfully off into the distance, then turned back to lock eyes with her. "Yesterday, at the hospital, I told the doctor to run the test that will prove I'm Morgan's father."

"*What?*" She set down her mug with exquisite care. "But I—"

"You heard me, Risa. We were there. He'd been pricked so many times what was one more, and I decided—"

"*You* decided! Who the hell are *you* to decide?"

"His father! You recall that, perhaps?"

"I recall that I told you I wouldn't permit him to be tested!"

"Ah, you can tell and tell, woman, but that doesn't necessarily mean a man will obey you—not when he knows he's right!"

"You *promised* me you'd—"

"Not tell him and so I have not, but I made no promises concerning the—"

"You conniving, manipulative bastard! *I trusted you! Oh,* you'd think I'd have learned by now! But *no,* one kiss and I forget what you are—

"*One* kiss?" His laugh was incredulous. "Try a thousand or more, honey lips, and while you're counting, don't forget to—*hey!*" He ducked as she threw her mug, winced as it shattered against the black iron front of the stove. "*¡Calmate!*"

"I trusted you—and all the time you were doing it to me all *over* again! Suckering and seducing, turning my head with sweet Spanish nothings, then the *very* first chance you get, you take my son and—"

"*Our* son. Don't forget it again!"

"*My* son—*your* ticket to drill all the wells you want at Suntop! Because that's what this is all about, isn't it, Miguel? Proving to Ben that you've fulfilled all three terms of your crummy contract!"

"You dare to say that? To even think it? You think I don't care for Morgan, when I—" Miguel sputtered out of words and shook his head. "Are you blind, woman, that you'd say that? Do you know so little of love that you could think I made love to you for anything beyond yourself?"

"Like you did last time—with a contract already signed and sealed in my father's desk?" She clenched her hands as that shot hit home and he flinched. "Oh, yes, Miguel, I could believe that about you."

He rose and stood formally, scowling down at her. "Then you don't know me at all."

"*Nor* want to. So get out of my house." She stood to face him, two duelists at five paces. "Get out of my life." She drew a shaking breath. "*And* my son's life."

"Oh, no..." Miguel whispered hoarsely. "If you ask me

to leave you alone I will—you're a blind little fool, Sonrisa, but I will. But Morgan *es mi hijo*. I want half-time custody and I'm willing to fight for it if we can't agree to share.''

''We can't agree on what day of the *week* it is, Miguel Heydt! So get *out*!''

''*Bueno, mi brujita*. Let me pack my bags and I'm gone—and I'll see you in court.''

CHAPTER TWENTY-FOUR

AND NOW WHAT? Miguel raged to himself as he drove around the shoulder of Suntop and down to the ranch yard. He'd thrown his things in his bag, stopped by Morgan's room and found his son still sleeping. *Should I have awakened him? Tried to explain that I don't leave him by choice? Told him I'll be back soon as I can?*

He hadn't. How could one awaken a sick child to confusion and misery? Better that his son sleep, then waken peacefully in his own time.

But to what? What would Risa tell him?

Ay, Risa-Sonrisa. Lips of honey, temper of a rabid coyote, heart like an unforgiving stone. He'd tried to speak to her again on his way out the door, but she'd simply knelt in the kitchen, surrounded by the ruins of her broken cup, and hugged herself, refusing to speak or meet his eyes.

Should I have simply picked you up and kissed you back to sanity?

Torn between pride and frustration and guilt, he hadn't. Because she was doing it to him all over again. He'd opened his heart to her. Laid everything he had and was at her feet. *And what does* la bruja *do? She throws it back in my teeth all over again!* Eleven years ago, she'd flounced out, making a fool of him. This time she was giving *him* the boot, but in the end it was all the same. Ashes and heartbreak.

Enough—*bastante*—a man could only go so far and no farther and stay a man.

"I need a lawyer," he barked, braking the Jeep in the yard alongside Rafe Montana, who'd leaned down with a ready smile from his big bay horse.

The smile faded; the blue eyes narrowed. "A lawyer. What kind of lawyer?"

"Custody matters! Divorce and all its idiot sorrows."

"Hmm." Montana drew a fist across his quirking mouth. "Dana and I've used Jack Kelton on something like that. He's bright and able, but a bit of a cynic."

"Exactly what I need, a cynical man for a senseless world. And where would I find this Kelton?"

HE FOUND HIM where Montana had advised to look first, at the site of the house Kelton was building on the outskirts of Trueheart, since this was a Saturday and he wouldn't be in his Durango office.

Lacking an office, they made do with an old weathered picnic table beneath an apple tree, out back of the bare foundation that would someday be Kelton's house. Miguel laid out his facts then listened in growing incredulity as the man expounded on Colorado law.

"But that is insanity!" he burst out finally.

Kelton cocked a shaggy eyebrow at this eruption. "No, Mr. Heydt, that's the law. Now, Dickens said that 'the law is an ass,' and I find myself frequently agreeing, but it's the ass we must all salute."

"But I'm the blood father," Miguel protested. "This will be proven beyond dispute as soon as the test results come back. Also I have photographs of my sister, who is the living image of my son, her nephew. I could produce Consuela herself in court—place her side by side with—"

But with a rueful smile Kelton was already shaking his

big blond head. "Doesn't mean a thing in the eyes of the law. By state law—by most states in the union, actually—*the man who is married to the woman at the time she gives birth is the—legal—father.*"

"When I can prove that he is not?"

"Even then. You've got to look at it from society's point of view, sir. Society wants that child—every child—to have a father to support him. And to have a long-term, stable, *unassailable* relationship with the nominal father. Because if the law permitted challenges to that fatherhood, what do you think would happen?"

Miguel threw up his hands—it was that or kick the picnic table over and walk out.

"Why, every S.O.B. who decided he'd gotten tired of his wife and wanted out, first thing he'd do is start claiming that her child isn't his offspring, and therefore he shouldn't have to support the brat once he leaves the marriage. See what I mean? So the law forestalls such nonsense by simply stating—you *are* the father. You were holding the bag—your lady wife—at time of birth, so forget it, buddy! You'll support your kid from now on, even if you claim he looks just like the milkman. Even if he *is* the milkman's.

"Because from society's point of view, it's easier to insist that the husband pay than it is to chase the milkman. A bird in the hand, as it were."

"This is madness," Miguel repeated dazedly. "I don't wish to escape child support—I wish to provide it."

"I'm very sorry, Mr. Heydt. That's most commendable. But you can sue and sue and sue, and you'll never win this one. I could make a fortune off you proving I'm right— I've got no problem with going to court and sending you the bills. But you're a friend of Rafe's and Dana's, so…" Kelton shrugged, pulled his hammer out of the dungaree

loop where he'd settled it when Miguel first appeared. A
hint that the consultation was over.

Miguel rubbed his forehead and grimaced as the bandage
on his hand scraped skin. "But...I *could* sue, you're saying. It's just that I wouldn't win."

"Hey, it's America. You can sue just about anybody
over just about any damn thing."

HE WAS GONE.

Somehow Risa hadn't thought Miguel would go far when
she threw him out. Not that she'd been *thinking,* precisely,
in that shattering moment when she'd learned of his treach-
ery.

Still, deep down, her assumption must have been that
he'd retreat to the bunkhouse. Or the foreman's house. Or
possibly he'd slink off to a motel in Durango; the daily
commute back to the ranch would serve him right.

But never once had she conceived of a Suntop without
Miguel Heydt—maddening, deceitful, conniving Miguel—
somewhere in the picture.

Yet he was gone.

If only he'd come back, so she could tell him all over
again, how much she despised him!

And why be surprised that he's gone? she berated herself
for the thousandth time, driving down to Durango two
weeks later. *You know where he's gone—to Ben!*

Because by now surely Miguel had the results of the
paternity test in hand. So of course he'd taken them to her
father to prove that he'd completed terms two and three of
their hateful contract—getting her pregnant within one year
of their marriage. Then that pregnancy resulting in the de-
livery of a healthy boy—*my boy,* she thought with fierce
possession, glancing at Morgan, who sat beside her, staring
out his window.

By now Miguel must have claimed his reward—endless drilling rights, with Ben paying all costs. No doubt he was off finding a rig and crew to drill his first well.

So never you worry, she assured herself. He'd turn up like the bad penny sooner or later, when he was ready to break ground. Any day now she'd see a line of heavy-equipment trucks lumbering into the ranch.

The day I see that, we pack our bags and go.

Beside her, Morgan stirred restlessly and, despite his seat belt, managed to ooze down his seat till more of him was sprawled on the floorboards than the cushions. "Is it gonna hurt?"

Hurts already, she thought, then realized what he meant. They were on their way to the hospital where Morgan had been taken two weeks earlier, to meet with the physician who'd treated him. It was time for the stitches to come out.

"I don't think so, sweetie." She reached to stroke his silky head. "Or only the teeniest, tiniest bit, perhaps."

His lips trembled. "Last time, Mr. Heydt was with me. It wasn't so...scary with him there. He held my hand and said he'd take all the pain if I'd give it to him. So I...did. But this time..." His eyes squinched up, his cheeks went rosy. "*Why* did he go like that? He didn't even tell me goodbye!" As the tears welled, he scrambled up again, to hang his head out the window.

Oh, sweetie, my darling, oh, don't cry. Her own eyes blurring, Risa reached to rub her knuckles down his spine, but he shrugged her off.

Worse even than her own pain was watching Morgan's. Knowing she'd caused it by driving Miguel away. He'd cried this same question from the heart a dozen times or more these past two weeks. "I don't know, sweetie," she lied again now softly. "I guess Mr. Heydt had some urgent business he had to go take care of somewhere."

If guilt could kill, she should be dead by now.

But don't you see, she raged at herself, *that the way Miguel left—his silence since his leaving—proves that I was right?* He hadn't sent Morgan one postcard of explanation or consolation. He hadn't phoned him once to ask how he was feeling.

Because he didn't love Morgan any more than he loved me! We were both pawns to help him reach his goal. No more than that. Once Miguel had obtained the proof he needed, he'd no further use or time for his own son. *I was right to throw him out of our lives before we came to love him even more.*

But how to explain that to an aching ten-year-old?

What was she to tell him—that his father was a wildcatter and a rolling stone and a selfish, conniving bastard? *What do I say—that you should never trust or love or depend on another—because you'll only be hurt if you do?* Was this the lesson she wanted to teach her child?

Was this the lesson she herself had been taught, first by a fickle, self-absorbed mother, then by Ben, who'd manipulated her like a piece on his gameboard—then tossed her out of the game forever when she crossed him?

No, if anybody taught me not to trust, it was the one man in the world I ever loved.

And still she mourned him. Missed him. Miguel had walked off with her heart, leaving nothing in its place but numb despair.

That and a grieving child.

BUT DESPAIRING OR NOT, life had to go on. Morgan's stitches came out with only a twinge or two. The doctor caused more pain by asking after Miguel, then saying obscurely to Risa that he hoped the results of the test had pleased them both.

Delighted one of us, anyway, she told him in silent outrage as she shrugged coolly and walked out of his office. *More than you'll ever know.*

From the hospital they went to a movie matinee—reward for Morgan's bravery—then grocery shopping. Then, driving back through Trueheart, Risa prolonged their off-ranch excursion by stopping at Hansen's for homemade ice cream. Because Suntop was no longer a haven to hurry home to; now it was the bull's-eye of loneliness and longing.

But at least some good came of that last stop. She learned from Sophie Hansen that Jules was now living in Cortez, where she owned a gallery showcasing both her own jewelry designs and those of several Hopi and Navajo artists. Sometime soon, when Risa had found her smile again, she'd have to drive over for a visit.

After Hansen's there were no more excuses to stay away and the groceries needed refrigeration. They drove back to the ranch. Morgan roused himself from his blues as they climbed the hill beyond the river. "Lemme out at the barn, okay?"

Bravo and Columbine were confined to a stall and the barn corral until the colt's wounds had entirely healed. "Fine. Shall I pick you up in an hour?" she asked as she stopped the car.

"Nope. I'll walk up when I'm done."

"Home an hour before sunset, then, okay?"

"Whatever." He slammed the door and slipped away.

He blames me, she thought miserably, biting her lip as she steered on across the yard. *Somehow he knows I drove Miguel out of his life.* Or was that just her own guilt talking?

Her foot came off the gas, allowing the car to coast to a halt. Parked beside the foreman's house was the ancient caramel-colored Lincoln Town Car that she'd last seen sitting up on blocks, in the garage, up at the Big House. Oh, surely not! Ben wasn't due for another two weeks.

But nobody else used that car.

She parked beside it and climbed the steps to the back door and realized she was trembling. *I'm not ready for this.* Probably Rafe or Anse was simply exercising the old dinosaur, making sure it was tuned up for Ben's coming visit.

"There you are," cried Anse Kirby with transparent relief as he answered her knock. "Come join the party."

In the living room, Ben put down his whiskey, set aside a bag of pork rinds and rose, still straight and tall and sharp of eye, but unbelievably frail. "Princess..."

Oh, Daddy! "Hello, Ben." She walked across the room—it felt as wide as the Great Plains—and by the time she'd reached his side of it, her resolution to stiffly shake his hand was gone. She kissed his dry old cheek. "You came early."

"Got t'thinking that two weeks is mighty long at eighty-four. All the time in the world doesn't mean what it used t'mean, so I hired me a plane this morning." His deep-set eyes roved over her deliberately. "You're looking well—looking swell—Risa. More like your mama every day."

"Am I?" And about as lucky in love. Someday she'd have to ask him why he refused to marry Eva, though he legitimized his unions with Lara's and Tess's mothers. Had there been some unlovable something men saw or sensed when they looked at her mother? *Do men see the same thing in me?* Or maybe they'd both wanted love too desperately for it ever to be granted.

Her arrival was the cue for a general exodus. Rafe shook hands with her father, reminded him that Dana would be inviting him and Risa and Morgan to supper in the next few days, then made his exit, taking with him Anse

Kirby, who muttered something about a mare that needing checking.

"Well," said Ben once they were alone. "Drink?"

"No, thank you." She chose the sofa next to his easy chair and watched with wry resignation while he fixed her a weak whiskey anyway. Same old domineering Ben.

"Pork rinds? Lara hides m'bags of these back in San Antone. Have to come to Suntop to eat 'em."

"No, thanks. And save some room for supper, okay? I'm cooking..." She rummaged wildly through the available choices. The tofu-and-chicken stir-fry she'd planned would never do. "Steak and baked potatoes."

"Hmm." He nodded approval, then sat, sipping and contemplating her with eyes inscrutable as an old turtle's. "Been hearing about this mountain lion prowlin' around," he said finally to fill the silence.

"Yes, but he's long gone, Rafe says." Suntop men had hounded the cat back up his escape hatch in Blindman's Canyon. Leaving one cowboy camped there to plug the hole, they'd ridden around to the western rim and pursued him from there, on through the summer range and beyond it into the wilderness. "He must be seventy miles or more away by now, and every time he thinks of Suntop from now on, he'll think barking dogs."

"Shame they didn't nail him," Ben growled. "Sounds like that kid of yours deserves a lion-skin rug."

"Not *your* grandson, Ben—but my kid?" There, she'd thrown down the gauntlet.

The ice tinkled in his glass as he set it on the side table. "Well, that was your choice, wasn't it? You can't say I didn't warn you Risa, what would happen if you didn't back down."

"No-o-o, but *you* didn't ever say to yourself, 'Maybe I shouldn't interfere in my daughter's life. In her choice of a man to marry.'' Forgiveness had flown right out the window. With all her wounds reopened these past few weeks, she no longer wanted reconciliation—she wanted a fight. Needed his confession, remorse, abject apologies, then maybe—just maybe—she could find it in her aching heart to forgive.

"Nope, never thought that once when I was thinking I wanted you to be happy. In the care of a good man.'' Ben fumbled for a pork rind without glancing at his bag. "But say I'd minded my own business and not meddled in yours. Where would you be today? Still married to your snake of a Yalie?''

She flushed and looked down. Yes, he had her there.

He chuckled dryly. "That's what I figured. You had too much horse sense to stay with that knock-kneed, mean-minded weasel for long. But when a filly's in heat, she does the damnedest fool things. I was just tryin' to save you the pain of finding out the hard way what Foster was.''

And you think I didn't feel pain on my wedding day? "So to spare me that,'' she said bitterly, "you wrote out a contract.''

"Mmm.'' He munched pork rinds for a minute, then reached for his drink. "Found out 'bout that, did you? Reckon Heydt told you this time around?''

There was no reason to betray Tess even now. She shrugged. "I found out.''

"A contract to buy you a man we both could live with. A keeper. You want me to say I'm sorry for that, princess? You can't found a good line on scrubs. You're shopping for breeding stock you look for bone and brains and something we breeders call 'heart.' Means a horse that'll run for you till he drops. Who'll face up to any bull you send him after.''

She closed her eyes and saw Miguel vaulting over the cliff, going after a lion with his bare hands.

"And you look for willingness. You want a horse that will, not a horse that won't. And you breed for sweet temper, and Heydt had that, too. I'm 'sposed to apologize for trying to head you off from Foster and pair you with a man like that, instead? But in spite of all my tryin', you stampeded straight to the devil. You always were the stubbornest little cuss."

And you were always a rock-headed old man. If she was holding her breath for an apology, the apology she'd wanted for eleven years, she'd turn blue before she got it. And maybe because she was a parent now, Risa could almost understand, if she couldn't forgive: that terrible urge to smooth out a path through the world for the child you love. To bulldoze anything and everyone out of his way, no matter the cost.

It was an urge that sometimes achieved the reverse of its intention. *Is it possible? Did you act, even partly, through the clumsiest of loves, not just a need to have your own way?*

"'Bout the hardest thing I ever had t'do was cut you out of my will," Ben was saying gruffly. "But once Foster knocked you up, there was no choice. You'd be tied to your kid, and through your kid, forever to Foster. And the kid would be Foster's ticket to get his greedy hands on Suntop if I didn't cut you and your child out of my estate."

Risa sat blinking, glass poised midair. *He doesn't know yet that Miguel is Morgan's father.* Which meant— But if Miguel hadn't run off to Ben to tell him so, then where was he?

"But the land comes first, princess. Before you, before me, before any one Tankersly. Before God himself. Long after we're gone, there'll be a Suntop, and I'll pay any price

I have to, to make it so.'' Embarrassed at his own passion, Ben cleared his throat, dived into his bag and rustled the chips.

If Miguel hadn't gone to San Antonio, where? Back to Alaska? To Mexico? Oh, God, could something have happened to him? That morning he'd driven off enraged—could he have driven into a ditch somewhere? But surely, surely, surely by now he'd have been found!

"Be that as it may," Ben forged on into her silence, "I changed my will again 'bout nine years back. When I die, you've got a pot of money coming. No interest in Suntop, but you'll never go wanting."

Tears flooded her eyes. *Oh, God, what is money without Miguel?* But still, she should be grateful. *You do love me, Daddy, in your own blundering way.* Had she been blind all those years ago not to see it? She stood, leaned forward and dropped a kiss on the top of his grizzled head. "Thank you, Ben, that's mighty sweet."

"Pah…" He looked away, mouth working.

The door in the kitchen creaked as it opened, then Morgan's voice called, "Mom?"

He must have noticed her car. "In here, sweetie. Come meet somebody special."

"Oh." Morgan stopped short in the doorway and frowned, one hand resting on Woofle's curly back. "Um."

Risa stood and reached out an arm. "Come here, Morgan, and meet your grandfather."

The Airedale had already surged into the room, with his stubby tail wagging a welcome. Ben stood, thumped the dog's ribs and tugged on his ear, then rose to his considerable height. "C'mere, son, and let's have a look at you."

Morgan came forward slowly—he'd grown an inch or more this summer, it hit Risa suddenly, and the childish uncertain shuffling of two months ago was gone. He held out his hand. "Pleased to meet you, sir," he said with wary formality, something of Miguel echoing through his words.

They shook and Ben's eyes crinkled. "I hear you and Woofle tackled a lion."

"Yes, sir, he was trying to kill my colt. Bravo."

Ben's eyebrows flew together. "Who gave you a colt?"

"Rafe said he could halter-train him for the summer," Risa translated hastily. Same old Ben, hanging on tight to the keys to the kingdom.

"Hmmph. What you need is a yearling," Ben declared, strolling a slow, critical circle around his grandson, inspecting him from all angles. "You gentle him this summer and you'll be riding him the next. We'll go choose you one of Salud's colts tomorrow, out of the yearling herd."

Salud was the top Suntop stallion, an Arab whose foals were sold for a fortune. So...after all her worrying, could bringing these two together be as easy as that? She'd thought this would take weeks not minutes.

"No, thank you, sir," said Morgan. "If you give me a colt, I want Bravo."

Ben snorted and drew himself up. "You'll take what I give you, boy. That Bravo's going to be worthless after he's had a lion on his back. He'll be shy the rest of his life—scared of a rider."

Morgan tipped up his chin and scowled right back—and Risa almost laughed. She hadn't recognized the resemblance to Ben until now. "Bravo won't be scared of *me*. I can train him."

"*Pah!* You'll find you can't."

Standoff. Man and boy stood with eyes locked, neither swerving an inch. Risa clenched her hands and it was all she could do to stay silent. *Oh, sweetie, find a way! I've tried butting heads with him and it doesn't work.*

Morgan's mouth suddenly quivered then quirked. "Sir? How many horses does a cowboy need?"

"Hmm. Huh. Hah!" A dry chuckle overtook Ben and rattled him to his boots. "So you got the Tankersly brains, at least. A cowhand needs three or more good cow ponies in his string. So you're telling me—"

"I'll take both! Um, I mean, please, sir? A Salud yearling *and* Bravo. If nobody else can ride him, I might as well try."

"Might as well," Ben conceded, trying not to smile. "Now, youngster, I need to talk to your mama. You want to ride with me up to the Big House in a minute? Go look over that old Town Car of mine and I'll be right along."

They stared at the doorway he'd passed through—heard him break into a gallop as he hit the kitchen linoleum. The back door banged shut, then outside, he let out a joyful whoop. "A colt of my own! *Two* colts!"

"Shit," Ben said softly, and turned to glare at her. "Ten years of my life you wasted when I could have been training that boy? Did you do that to pay me back?"

"Ben..." Risa dropped on the sofa and clasped her hands before she was tempted to slug him. "It was you who disinherited us, remember?"

"Because you had Foster's brat—well, I thought you did. But Foster never got that one."

Wonderingly, she shook her head. *If I didn't know—* "How can you be so sure?"

"*Huh.* You're asking an old horse breeder? Foster had girlie thumbs and criminal earlobes and he bounced on his toes—short hamstrings. And he had a way of looking at you said he was counting all the bills in your wallet while he shook your hand. Uh-uh, this one's no Foster—he looks you straight in the eye. Where'd you get him?"

Risa felt her face go pink under her father's stony glare.

"Where do you think, under a cabbage leaf!" She blew out a breath. "He's Miguel's."

Ben blinked, rubbed a big gnarled fist across his slow-spreading grin—threw back his head and laughed. "Scored in one, did he? That night we turned out and searched for you two I reckoned you'd been in the sack, but still, who'd have figured the timing would be perfect?"

Risa rolled her eyes, marched for the door, then sighed and turned back to wait for him.

"And that's the last thing you look for in your stud," Ben told her, still chuckling as he joined her. "That he's lucky."

But she had a small measure of vengeance as they stepped out onto the back stoop and—finally—the implications hit home. *"Shit!"* swore Ben, stopping short. "Heydt. That means I've got t'bankroll the lucky bastard!"

CHAPTER TWENTY-FIVE

HALF AN HOUR BEFORE sunset, Risa climbed the bridle trail up Suntop Mountain. The summer was marching on, the earth tilting on its axis a tiny bit more with each rotation. On this third day of August—for the first time this year— the sun would slide down its slot in the mountains to the west.

She'd forgotten to ask Ben to bring Morgan back in time to show him this particular magic that gave the ranch its name. They'd gone off cruising in Ben's car after lunch, supposedly to inspect the haying crews at the south end of Suntop, though Risa secretly suspected they had other plans. She was fairly certain that Ben was teaching Morgan how to drive, on the ranch's back roads.

She smiled to herself, closed her eyes for a moment and felt the tears burn behind her lashes. *I didn't find you a loving father, Morgan, but you got yourself one heck of a granddad.* Heart's desires weren't always fulfilled, but then, maybe needs were.

And who was she to complain? After all, this was what she'd set out to do in the first place. Ben had already agreed that they'd have to look into a lawyer—the best lawyer money could buy—to restructure Morgan's custody arrangements. There was probably no way to drive Eric entirely out of their lives, but with enough legal muscle, maybe his influence could be contained and minimized.

I think you'd be glad of that, she told Miguel, wherever he was. *I'm doing the best for our boy that I can.*

But it was dangerous to dwell on Miguel for very long; that way lay heartache. Desolation. Instead, Risa lifted the video camera from her neck, set her eye to its viewfinder and scanned the valley below. She'd expanded the scope of her documentary on Bravo. It was now the story of Bravo and how Woofie had saved him—Morgan had insisted he didn't want a part in the film, though he certainly deserved it. How colt and dog had both been hurt by the lion; the stitches and bandages and doctors they'd endured so bravely; how in the end, they'd both come shining through. A tale to hearten any child in a hospital finding his way back from violence or trauma.

She needed a few shots of Suntop itself to site her story, establish its setting, and now Risa scanned to the north, toward the Whaleback, place of treasure and terror and lost love, now just one more dark hummock in the forested foothills. *Oh, Miguel...* The view blurred beyond the frame and she swung the camera. Too far to be useful, anyway.

She aimed the camera down at the ranch yard, with its complex of corrals and barns. Not much action down there at this hour. The haying crew had already parked their tractors and wagons and gone for the day. A few hands lounged on the bunkhouse porch, awaiting the call for supper. A dusty blue pickup bumped through the yard, then turned up the road for the Big House.

Why couldn't it be a Jeep—Miguel's rental Jeep? She couldn't see the driver from this angle, but it must be one of Ben's friends, come calling from a neighboring ranch. She should go down to greet whoever it was, but she was in no mood for company.

Stop moping around, Risa, and get to work. She zoomed

in on the home pasture, a cluster of mares with their colts, and let the camera roll.

Time flowed as she worked; loneliness receded like a tide that would surely return; but for now she was safe, in charge, choosing and refining the images that would make her story.

But the colors were shading from green and tan to blue and ruddy gold, the shadows of horse and barn and fence post lengthening. If she didn't stop now, she'd miss the show she'd come to see. Dropping the camera on its cord, Risa turned.

Bang in the eyes, the rays of the setting sun hit her. A molten ball, dropping down the slot between purple peaks. Lilac shadows swept over the valley, the far-off canyons, the lower hills, leaving the last light of day to kiss this green summit—a stroke of gold like a private benediction, a sizzling splash of fairy dust. She laughed, spread her arms and turned in the light. *Suntop!*

One full turn, and there he was, striding toward her, sil-houetted against the flamingo glow in the west—wide of shoulder, long of leg, shaggy head backlit with a halo of copper. *Miguel.*

"*Cielo,*" he said quietly, stopping before her with his hands in his pockets.

And it surely must be. Heaven was wherever he was. Maybe heartbreak, too, but no pain could compare with the pain of his absence. "That's what you said the first time," she told him, remembering.

"So what has changed?"

Apparently nothing that mattered. Here she was, almost bursting with the need to throw herself into his arms, but Miguel simply stood there looking down at her, his face unreadable in the fading light. *Whatever he's come back for, it isn't me.* She hugged herself hard, grateful for

the twilight that hid her tears. "You've been gone awhile."
I thought you might even be dead.

"*Sí*, I've been very busy." His voice was as casual as
hers, though it sounded hoarse, as if he'd had a cold.

"You didn't go to Ben." *But why? Why?*

"No, I had more important matters to attend to. I've been
in Denver." His big hand drew out a folded envelope from
his shirt pocket. "Dealing with Foster."

"Eric." She accepted the envelope with nerveless fingers. Eric hadn't called in weeks; she'd assumed he was
too busy campaigning to bother. "You didn't—" She
couldn't shape the words.

"Hurt him? No, I didn't have to do that. I simply showed
him and his political handlers how I *could* hurt him where
he'd feel it, in the midst of his run for office. Colorado's
Number One Family Man concluded he didn't want a big
messy lawsuit proving how he wasn't a family man at all.
That he didn't need me giving reporters heart-wrenching
interviews showing how he stood between a loving father
and his only son. That he damn sure didn't want Morgan
standing up for the news cameras, after he'd starred in that
campaign ad, to tell the viewers that if he had to choose
between Foster and me, he'd take me."

You're very sure of yourself. But then, he should be.
Pressed to choose, Morgan would take Miguel in a heartbeat.

"And most of all, Foster decided that if he had to choose
between the pork barrel in Washington and a long shot at
Suntop, which was looking longer by the day, he'd better
put his money on politics."

*So I was wrong about you. You didn't seduce me just for
the contract. You truly wanted your son, as well.* Risa
rubbed the back of a hand across her lashes, tried to find a
smile, no matter how bitter. *But what about me?*

Miguel nodded at her envelope. "So I don't come as a beggar, asking for a share in my son. This time I come as a man. As a father with rights. Foster has renounced all claims in Morgan. He couldn't grant custody to me—that would be too complicated—but he's ceded it entirely to you. So now I only have you to fight, if it comes to that."

"I see," she said shakily. *But I don't want to fight you or keep you two apart—that's the last thing I want!* And she'd lose anyway if she tried. This summer had shown her that. It would be as easy to stop the stars from shining. There was the first one now, twinkling wistfully over his shoulder, waiting for someone to make a wish.

"I see," she said again, swallowing around the growing lump in her throat. "Well, Miguel, what can I say? Congratulations? You've won it all. A son, unlimited oil rights to Suntop and—" She jerked her chin toward the road below, the headlights climbing it, then disappearing around the shoulder of Suntop. "And here comes Ben to finance your wells. You'd better go down and give him the news."

"You think that's all I wanted, Sonrisa?"

"Isn't it?" In the dark, he seemed to loom even larger. Tipping back her head, she tried to read his face, grew dizzy trying—the stars reeled above his head.

"After Denver, Risa, I went on to Texas. Then I flew to Fairbanks, then back here."

"Why?" He was nearer. She could feel the heat of his big body, warming hers. Smell the scent of his skin that would always quicken her heartbeats, as if she raced for the home she'd never known.

"Because it came to me—that I'm my father all over again. I came to Suntop seeking treasure—oil—but I discovered something infinitely more precious. Only a fool would let it go and this man is no fool—well, tries most days not to be one."

His hand lifted—laced into the hair above her ear, to cradle her head. "Ah, Risa, I've realized that you'll never trust my love till I tear up that damnable contract—and so I have. I've been seeking financing for the one well that will be drilled at Suntop. I won't be going to Ben for my money, not even a penny. And I won't be drilling endless wells. I'm staking all on one throw of the dice."

"And did you find it?" Her voice was trembling as she flattened her hands on the hard curves of his chest and leaned into him, tipped up her face for his kiss.

"*Pasión,* that's for you to tell me!"

Their mouths touched...fused; their arms swept around each other and locked tight. They sank slowly to their knees...then down to the wide grassy summit of Suntop. The moon rose over the Trueheart Hills to the sound of whispered exultance—and then laughter.

LATER...much later...when they lay staring up at the moon, her head pillowed on Miguel's broad shoulder, Risa asked again, "Did you find it?"

"Your love, *corazón?* If I didn't, *Dios mío,* what in heaven's name was that?"

She twisted around to punish his earlobe with her teeth. "Financing for your well, I meant, you crazy man."

"Ah. You're thinking like a wildcatter's wife already."

Welcome to Bloom's
where food is love and everybody *loves* food

JUDITH ARNOLD

Love in Bloom's

The Blooms have run the family deli for generations, and
Grandma Ida isn't about to let a culinary mishap change that.
So when her son, the president, meets an untimely demise, the
iron-willed matriarch appoints her granddaughter Julia to the
top seat. Nobody is more surprised than Julia. But no one
says no to Ida. And once Julia's inside the inner sanctum of
Bloom's, family rivalries, outrageous discoveries and piles of
delicious food begin to have their way with her.

Life at Bloom's is a veritable feast.

*Available the first week of June 2002
wherever paperbacks are sold!*

MJA918

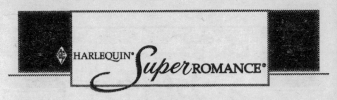

HARLEQUIN *Super*ROMANCE®

One of our most popular story themes ever...

Pregnancy is an important event in a woman's life—
and in a man's. It should be a shared experience,
a time of anticipation and excitement.
But what happens when a woman is
pregnant and on her own?

**Watch for these books in our
9 Months Later series:**

What the Heart Wants by Jean Brashear (July)

Her Baby's Father by Anne Haven (August)

A Baby of Her Own by Brenda Novak
(September)

The Baby Plan by Susan Gable (December)

Wherever Harlequin books are sold.

HARLEQUIN®
Makes any time special ®

Visit us at www.eHarlequin.com

HSRNM

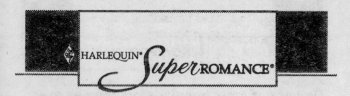

They'd grown up at Serenity House—a group home for teenage girls in trouble. Now Paige, Darcy and Annabelle are coming back for a special reunion, and each has her own story to tell.

SERENITY HOUSE

An exciting new trilogy
by
Kathryn Shay

Practice Makes Perfect—June 2002

A Place to Belong—Winter 2003

Against All Odds—Spring 2003

Available wherever Harlequin books are sold.

Visit us at www.eHarlequin.com

Harlequin invites you to experience the
charm and delight of

COOPER'S CORNER

A brand-new continuity
starting in August 2002

HIS BROTHER'S BRIDE
by *USA Today* bestselling author
Tara Taylor Quinn

Check-in: TV reporter Laurel London and noted travel
writer William Byrd are guests at the new Twin Oaks
Bed and Breakfast in Cooper's Corner.

Checkout: William Byrd suddenly vanishes and while
investigating, Laurel finds herself face-to-face with
policeman Scott Hunter. Scott and Laurel face a painful past.
Can cop and reporter mend their heartbreak and get to the
bottom of William's mysterious disappearance?

HARLEQUIN®
Makes any time special ®

Visit us at www.cooperscorner.com

CC-CNM1R